NONESUCH

Francis Spufford is the author of three novels and five highly praised works of non-fiction, which are most frequently described by reviewers as either 'bizarre' or 'brilliant', and usually as both. His debut work of fiction was the historical novel *Golden Hill*, which won the Costa First Novel Award, the RSL Ondaatje Prize, the Desmond Elliott Prize and was shortlisted for four others. His second novel, *Light Perpetual*, was awarded the Encore Award and longlisted for the Booker Prize. His third novel, the alternative history *Cahokia Jazz*, was recognised by the Science Fiction community when it was awarded the Sidewise Award in 2023. He teaches writing at Goldsmiths College, University of London, and lives in Essex.

by the same author

I MAY BE SOME TIME
THE CHILD THAT BOOKS BUILT
BACKROOM BOYS
RED PLENTY
UNAPOLOGETIC
GOLDEN HILL
TRUE STORIES & OTHER ESSAYS
LIGHT PERPETUAL
CAHOKIA JAZZ

NONESUCH

FRANCIS SPUFFORD

faber

First published in 2026
by Faber & Faber Limited
The Bindery, 51 Hatton Garden
London EC1N 8HN

This export edition first published in 2026

Typeset by Typo•glyphix, Burton-on-Trent, DE14 3HE
Printed and bound by CPI Group (UK) Ltd, Croydon, CR0 4YY

All rights reserved
© Francis Spufford, 2026

Map © Neil Gower Graphic Art, 2026

The right of Francis Spufford to be identified as editor of this work
has been asserted in accordance with Section 77 of the Copyright,
Designs and Patents Act 1988

Quotation from *Look Stranger!* Copyright 1936 by The Estate of W. H.
Auden. Reprinted by permission of Curtis Brown, Ltd. All rights reserved.

*This is a work of fiction. All of the characters, organizations, and events portrayed
in this novel are either products of the author's imagination or are used fictitiously.*

A CIP record for this book
is available from the British Library

ISBN 978–0–571–39717–4

Printed and bound in the UK on FSC® certified paper in line with our continuing
commitment to ethical business practices, sustainability and the environment.
For further information see faber.co.uk/environmental-policy

Our authorised representative in the EU for product safety is
Easy Access System Europe, Mustamäe tee 50, 10621 Tallinn, Estonia
gpsr.requests@easproject.com

Nancy Gwendolen Spufford, 1911–2011
not entirely a good girl

Easily, my dear, you move, easily your head
And easily as through the leaves of a photograph album I'm led
Through the night's delights and the day's impressions,
Past the tall tenements and the trees in the wood;
Though sombre the sixteen skies of Europe
    And the Danube flood.

                    W. H. Auden, *Look, Stranger!* xxi (1936)

PROLOGUE

The time to do it, if she was going to try something so mad at all, was in the gap between the closing of the office and the first checking of the blackout. Mr Seaton, the ARP warden for the Mariner Building, worked in the insurance office on the second floor, and when he put on his tin hat at the end of the day and turned into the voice of authority, he liked to start from the ground and work upwards. There ought to be a few minutes before he got up to the ninth floor. He was somewhere down by the feet of the immense statue of the sea-king that rose from bottom to top of the facade; she was up by its chin.

The other girls were putting on coats and hats and mufflers and leaving one by one. She had already gone through the whole routine of shutting down the teleprinter, but when Mr Cornellis put his head around the door to turn off the light, she ducked down onto the floor behind the desk and pretended to be busy in the supply drawer.

'I'm just changing the ribbon for tomorrow, sir,' she said.

'I thought you'd delegated all the purely clerical stuff,' he said.

'It's a temperamental beast. Sonia hasn't quite got the knack yet.'

'Oh, very well, very well,' he said. 'Lights off quickly, though, please, when you're done.'

'You can do it now, sir. I can see in the light from the window.'

'All right, then. Safe home, everybody.' He tipped his hat, flipped the switch and took his anxious frown away, footsteps receding down the parquet corridor of Cornellis & Blome, brokers. Ordinarily, he would have waited to be the last out, and to lock the door of his kingdom behind him, but the keys were now surrendered to Seaton downstairs, to do his rounds, and to let in the firemen if the worst came to the worst and a German incendiary came spitting and flaring down among the filing cabinets.

In the twilight, the others shuffled out fast. Only Sonia lingered at the door, just sixteen, on her first job and inclined to cling.

'You doing anything tonight, Iris?' she said hopefully. 'You seeing your feller?'

'I should be so lucky. Another night in the Anderson, I expect, reading *Playford on Securities.*'

'D'you want to get the Tube together, then?'

'Sorry, I need to hang on here while I sort this out. It's been playing up all day. You go on. Good night!'

Finally, she went. Iris gave it a few seconds and then shut the door after her. She listened, but the sounds were dwindling ones, retreating ones.

The office was all grey outlines and blue voids, in the last of the daylight. Outside, the blue haze of coal smoke that always hung over the City was dimming, and seeming as it did so to be coagulating back onto the bulk of the buildings, turning them too hazy and indistinct, heavy masses with uncertain edges. The little piece of the river she could see was gunmetal grey, light-absorbent; the dome of St Paul's looked as if it had been cut out of purple paper. By now, there should have been a cheerful glitter of electricity and neon brightening it all, the money that had been made during the day in the veil of smoke shining back out of it in spendthrift promises of food, laughter, pleasure. Instead there was this stillness, this dim abandoned hush, as if the tiny figures departing down there in the gloom were not just getting out of reach of tonight's probable raid – six nights out of the last seven, the bombers had come – but were deserting the Square Mile altogether, fleeing it for good. Or as if this had never been a greedy, wily, striving, noisy, contentious, elbows-out, non-stop temple to human appetites, but had come into being in some silent submarine process. A dark reef, secreted in its marble and brick with no reference to human beings.

She opened the steel-framed window beside her desk. A cold breath of autumn blew in, dusty, riverine, but with a burnt edge from the buildings ruined in last night's raid, and the one before's. She sat down, feeling ridiculous. The words she had insisted Geoffrey write down were on a twist of paper in her bag. She smoothed it out. His precise draughtsman's lettering was still legible in the gloom. She cleared her throat. *If you must do this*, she heard him saying irritably in her head, *you better speak it out, good and clear. It's all in the harmonics, remember. You're setting a hook in the air.*

Meruzababel, read the first line on the paper. 'Me-ru-za-ba-bel,' she said out loud, thinking to herself, *Abracadabra. Hocus-pocus. Honestly, girl, what do you expect to achieve?*

The rest of the – spell, she supposed you would have to call it, made a diminishing triangle.

Eruzababel
Ruzababel
Uzababel
Zababel
Ababel
Babel
Abel
Bel
El
L

She said it all, hesitating over how to sound the last line. 'Luh,' she said. 'Lah? Ell?'

Nothing happened. The letters swam. It was really very dark now. She sighed and rubbed her eyes. When she opened them, it was if anything darker, suddenly darker. And looking to see why, she found that the giant granite head of the Mariner statue that gave the Mariner Building its name had turned, and was blocking the window as it gazed in at her.

It had had only rough stone dimples for eyes. Now, it had opened stone lids, and pupils of black marble as big as coffee saucers regarded her. Black circles, within crystal-blue circles, within eye-whites of marble again. The eyes glistened, but like rainwater on a pavement. That was the awful thing: that the statue had begun to live, yet without turning into flesh, or anything like it. It was still stone, still cold, still hard. Muscles were not making the expression on the huge face, but some mineral stirring. Yet she could read it. A furious, weary contempt.

The mouth of the statue opened with a creak. Behind it a gullet deepened, literally deepened as she watched, a flue burrowing away down into the stone dark, to give the Mariner something it had no need for, except to obey her command. No breathing had ever happened in those depths; no swallowing or digesting. On the inner surface of the mouth, ribbed like a cavern, a pale bloom like frost came and went.

At the far end of the corridor, she heard Mr Seaton turn his key in the door of Cornellis & Blome.

'What,' said the Mariner, and its voice was like a glacier grinding on a cliff, 'Do. You. Want.'

She could feel her pulse in her jaw, a throb under her ear.

'Tell me where all past years are,' she said.

But that was much later.

WILD WOOD
AUGUST 1939

I

She was on the up escalator at Leicester Square Tube station, checking her lipstick in the mirror of her compact. On the other side, tired clerks and shopgirls were being funnelled away downwards, weary at day's end, ready for home and supper, but over here, riding up past the panels of polished wood, past the framed advertisements for face cream and cigarettes, past the bronze torches throwing roundels of electric glow onto the tilted white ceiling above – over here she was in a chattering crowd, being carried up to pleasure on the ever-cycling treads of the magic staircase.

Up ahead was the circular ticket hall, and the hot light of an August evening spilling into it from every exit. Up ahead were shows, dinner, dancing, the teasing and pleasing and tasting and smiling and satisfying of a West End night. A weekday night, true, not the dionysiad of a Friday or a Saturday night – and with the news pressing at it, pinching at the pleasure, trying to extinguish it with worry if you paid attention. But still with anticipation enough in it to quicken the pulse. Still with the hours of promise ahead. The air was warm and getting warmer. She was wearing the silver dress, bias-cut so it flowed over curves and clung there mermaid-close. It was right for the Savoy, but it needed protecting till she got there. Up to August, hem twitched in her free hand to keep it out of the treads. Up to the late-summer glow in the cheeks and the prickle at the hairline; up to city dust and city speed and city noise. Up to the twenty thousand streets! To the babble of the pavements, to the bray of horns and the bells and the shouts of the news boys selling bad news and the snatches of music from opened doors. To the lively air, with all its smells of petrol and beer and perfume and tobacco and cooking food swirled into motion by the busy passage of human bodies. To the foyers of the theatres, where the crowds were in strict evening dress, and the democratic glamour of the cinemas, where people were dressed and dressed up any way they liked. Up to gold and to gilding, to dear and to cheap delight. Up to life, waiting to be seized, moment by moment, every chance not taken lost forever.

But as she stepped out into the evening on the Charing Cross Road, her senses busy, more was happening around her than her eyes could see or her ears hear. Above the billboards and the rooftops where the sunlight was ripening to orange-gold, the air over London quivered, and not just with heat. The August sky was furrowed with vibrations, but such fine ones, such fast and delicate oscillations, such minute needle-point jittering of the fabric of empty space, that she would have needed to be an organism made of something finer than flesh and blood to feel the quick waves moving. Or to turn on a radio. It was humans who had written themselves onto the air, after all, adding the means to carry their own concerns along on the slight accelerations, or the slight deformations, of what was travelling along up there anyway. Twist that dial. Between the bands of crackle were flying voices in all the languages that filled the sixteen skies of Europe, and skimmed more weightlessly than midges over the waters of the Rhine and the Danube and the Thames and the Volga. Fearful voices, complacent voices, threatening voices, triumphant voices, all reporting what Mr Molotov had agreed with Mr Ribbentrop, and repeating Poland, Poland, Poland. And music! Europe danced tonight, frantically, to a babel of rhythms. Congas in Paris, violins in Vienna, kettledrums in Berlin, saxophones in Soho, an impossible orchestra. Last, among the voices and the instruments, a single signal, very recent, carrying pictures. One fuzzy thread of images. Turn the dial to the needle-fine shaking of the sky at 45 million hertz, and what was that? A white pill of light streaked across a grey herringbone soup that was meant to be grass. Len Hutton, 165 not out, was hitting the last ball of the last Test match before war stopped play. A draw against the West Indies. Another fraction of a turn and it was only the thick hiss of static again in the shaking sky.

Charlie Tremlett was waiting for her at the steps of St Martin-in-the-Fields, looking exactly like what he was: a floppy-haired overgrown schoolboy, with a schoolboy's straightforward appreciation and gratitude for what felt good. A pleasantly rangy sportsman's body. Honourable according to his lights; too dumb for complications, in her experience so far. As she approached he was taking a pull from a flask, which he tucked hastily away. It seemed a bit hasty altogether for the very beginning of an evening. She didn't think of him as a drinker, except in the ordinary social sense. But then when she got close she saw there was an expression on his face she was unfamiliar with, and it deepened as he took in the silver dress. Disapproval? No, embarrassment.

'You look ripping, Iris,' he said.

'But?'

'What do you mean?' he said.

'I mean, your next word is obviously going to be "but". You look ripping Iris, but something. But what?'

'Oh, I get you. Well. The thing is, here you are, all dressed up – and the chap we're meeting up with, and the girl he's got along – well, they've rather put the kibosh on the Savoy. They've booked us a table for supper at some frightful little Eyetie place in Soho. And I sort of have to go along because – well – you know how it is . . .'

She did. Because Charlie was a jobber on the Stock Exchange floor, by all accounts a reasonably effective one, he depended for his income on a flow of orders from brokers like tonight's chap, who needed therefore to be cossetted, gone along with, indulged in whatever their idea of an agreeable time might be.

'I'm most frightfully sorry,' Charlie said, sounding as if he were about twelve and on the headmaster's carpet. 'Feel like I dragged you out under false pretences. And you looking so glamorous too.'

'Never mind,' said Iris. 'Not your fault. Come on then, let's go and butter up your broker. We can always double back to the Savoy later, and do a little dancing then. And things. No rule against that, is there?'

'No,' said Charlie, brightening. 'No, there isn't. *Thank* you. You're a wonderful girl.'

'And don't you forget it,' she said, and took his arm, having restored the gleam of anticipation to his eye. Probably to hers too: the advantage of a really expensive hotel, especially if you kept the desk staff well oiled as Charlie took care to, was that they operated by quite different rules of respectability. The beds at the Savoy were wide, firm and comfortable.

'So, who is this chap of yours?' she asked as they were heading north.

'Bit of an odd fish, actually,' said Charlie.

'In what way? You know, apart from his thing for spaghetti.'

'Oh, very good. – Well, he's terribly clever, and apparently he's some kind of *socialist*,' Charlie said, with the air of one naming an obscure disease.

'You don't get many of those in the City.'

'No! But Cleaverings don't mind, it seems, because he *is* so clever. Makes them a packet, even if he disapproves. And he hangs about with all sorts of nobs and intellectuals – tries to teach the Labour front bench the financial ABC, that sort of thing.'

'Charlie . . .' she said uncertainly.

'What? Oh good grief, what a hole.'

They were standing in front of a narrow slot of a restaurant next to an Italian grocer's, sharing with it a strong mingled smell of good olive oil and garlic. It wasn't a hole, though it had none of the Savoy dining room's chromium and chandeliers. It was dim, with candles on the little round tables, but the side wall had a mural on it receding into chiaroscuro that had Serious Art written all over it. She could tell what kind of a place it was, and who its habitués were likely to be, even if Charlie couldn't, and she hesitated on the threshold. But he was already through the door, grinning cheerily.

'Miles, old man!' he cried. She followed.

The odd fish was seated about two-thirds of the way back into the gloom. He had one of those male faces which, even when its owner is still in his twenties, shows what he will be like in confident middle age. Lidded eyes, hair receding from temples gleaming in the candlelight. He stood up.

'Charlie, good evening,' he said. 'May I introduce Eleanor?'

His companion, sprawled in her chair in a tweed skirt and a frayed brown jumper, lifted the hand that was holding a cigarette from table height to head height in salute. She seemed to have a bandage round her wrist.

'Hello!' said Charlie. 'This is Iris. Lovely girl, works at C&B.'

'Good evening,' said Charlie's broker again. 'Miles Ormond.'

'Hallo,' said Iris, 'Iris Hawkins', and heard Watford unmistakably in her own vowels, as if she had whole avenues of prosperous-but-not-posh suburbia tucked away in there. And the Girls' Grammar School. And the future she hadn't wanted, in which a good girl could hope for a nice young man with prospects in the building trade, or a solicitor's office. That world, lost but refusing to be gone, inexorably following her around and speaking out of her mouth.

'I hope you don't mind,' Ormond said, 'I took the liberty of ordering the wine. Montepulciano. Pretty good, I think.' He poured.

'Oh, vino is vino, as far as I'm concerned,' said Charlie. 'In vino veritas, hahaha. Cheers.'

The wine was black with occasional garnet points in the candlelight. Iris looked at Ormond's Eleanor across the table, and saw nothing to contradict her fears and everything to confirm them. Short red curls, darkened like the wine in the gloom. No make-up at all. No nail varnish either; grey stuff under the fingernails instead. Eleanor looked back, something in her face that Iris very much did not want to kindle into amusement.

'What a dress,' she said, blowing smoke, and her voice – oh, of course it did – had the ringing confidence of Oxford women's colleges, and radio announcers, and actresses trained at RADA. 'Very glamorous *indeed*. Almost Hollywood.' Her tone was not hostile. More zoological.

'Isn't it marvellous?' said Charlie. 'Trust Iris for the glad rags! So, what are we eating?'

Ormond passed across the menu. Charlie furrowed his brow at it.

'I thought I was dressing for a different kind of evening,' said Iris quietly. Charlie shot her a look of reproach, evidently taking this as unhelpful criticism of their hosts.

'I can see that,' said Eleanor, kindly. 'Don't worry: you really do look marvellous. I couldn't wear anything like that. I ruin good clothes just by looking at them.'

'Bis-tecca al-la Fi— alla Fi—' Charlie spelled out. 'Is that a steak? I could inhale a steak tonight very happily.'

'What happened to your hand?' Iris asked.

'Chisel slipped,' said Eleanor briefly. 'Occupational hazard. 'Nother one for my collection of cuts and bruises.' She put out the cigarette, and spread her fingers in the candle glow. They were covered in little white lines that Iris realised must be scars.

'Just don't actually chop anything off,' said Ormond mildly. 'I like your hands with all the fingers attached. I'm fond of them.'

'Gosh,' said Charlie. You could almost see, marching across his forehead in illuminated letters like a headline at Piccadilly Circus, the words YOURS IS A RUM ONE, ISN'T SHE? The idiot still hadn't grasped the situation. 'So, sorry, *is* that a steak?'

'Yes,' said Ormond. 'What about you?' he asked Iris. 'I thought I'd fill Eleanor here up with liver and sage, while I had the chance. She could do with the iron. Internally, not externally, for a change.'

He had a way of saying something funny, she saw, while remaining completely straight-faced. It might not have been a test, but ignoring the joke seemed like a short way of demonstrating that she wasn't worth joking with.

'I'm not in a very ferrous mood,' she said, and Ormond tilted his head an appreciative half an inch: probably his equivalent of a hearty guffaw. 'Would you choose for me?' Iris went on. 'I don't really know my way around Italian food.'

'Surely. How hungry are you, if you don't mind my asking?'

'Reasonably.'

'Very well then, one reasonable Italian supper coming up.' Ormond summoned the waiter – summoned him by name – and then ordered, at length and in Italian, for all of them.

'The gift of tongues!' said Charlie. 'My mother spoke French, but somehow it passed me by.' He had downed his glass of wine and he was getting pinker.

'I don't expect you've ever needed it,' said Eleanor.

'That I have not,' agreed Charlie earnestly. 'Always happy to stay with the colonial issues and the Kaffirs, you see. Can't specialise in everything.'

'"Kaffirs"?' said Eleanor, raising an eyebrow.

'South Af—' Iris began, and at the same time Ormond said, 'Mining stocks.' He stopped and waved his hand at her to proceed.

'Shares in South African mines,' said Iris.

'Yes; and talking of that,' said Charlie winningly, 'I had a thought or two you might be interested in.'

'Really?' said Ormond. 'It's hard to believe there's going to be much of a private market for gold, for the next little while at least.'

'You mean because of the news,' said Charlie. 'Come, come, my dear chap: don't people always make a bit of a beeline for gold when there's a crisis? And *I've* heard . . .' Off he went, into a sales pitch for the splendid prospects of a particular mine under development west of Johannesburg. Ormond listened courteously, and went on listening while waiters brought an array of plates and dishes of all sizes. In front of Charlie they placed a steak, sizzling. In front of Iris, two green-and-purple figs, with a tiny cream cheese in the shape of a heart.

'Oh, that's very nice,' said Eleanor. She had been served what looked like a piece of toast, with a smear of tomato on top.

'Would you rather swap?' said Iris.

'No!' said Eleanor, laughing.

Iris cut herself a small wedge of fig and dabbed it cautiously with the cheese. Her only previous acquaintance with figs was with the dried kind, offered as a constipation remedy or the filling of a biscuit, and she was expecting the same slightly fusty, gummy sweetness. Instead the combination was . . . delicious.

'Good, isn't it?'

She took another mouthful. Charlie talked on; Ormond listened on, eating something unidentifiable with a fork, and expressing with the set of his shoulders a sardonic disbelief which Charlie seemed totally unable to read. The two women looked at each other.

'You're a sculptor?' said Iris.

'Yes,' said Eleanor. 'At the Slade.'

'Well, it was either that or a painter, as soon as I saw your nails.'

Eleanor turned the hand that was holding her toast-thing, and regarded them complacently.

'Filthy, aren't they? You *can* get the stone-dust out, but it takes so much scrubbing, and they'll only get like that again tomorrow, so why bother.'

Iris looked down at herself, silver-clad, manicured.

'I suppose you have to, if you work in an office,' Eleanor offered. 'So what do you do?'

'I'm a secretary,' said Iris.

'And is that interesting?'

Iris gave this question the answer it deserved, which was none at all. She pretended instead to be fully occupied by cutting up and eating the figs and cheese, but its deliciousness was of the miniature variety, and all too soon she had to look back up. Eleanor, with a puzzled expression, was trying to catch Ormond's eye. Probably in a moment she would succeed: Charlie's continuing sales pitch for gold stocks was taking on a hectic edge, as Ormond was responding less and less. He had finished whatever-it-was he had been served and was gazing into his wine glass, bored endurance legible on his face. It was seeming less and less likely that the end of the meal could be reached successfully.

'So,' Iris said suddenly, to Ormond. 'What assets *do* you think make sense, if war comes?'

Charlie glared at her. She had never tried to get him out of a conversational jam before, it not having been that kind of a connection, and he did not seem to welcome the idea of being helped. Perhaps he didn't recognise that that was what she was doing.

'When war comes, surely,' said Ormond.

'You think it's as certain as that?' she began to reply, but Charlie talked over her.

'Oh, come on!' he said. 'We don't know, do we? A year ago, war looked like an absolute sure thing, panic in the streets and all that,

I was talking to my old dad about a billet in the East Surreys, ready to do my duty – and then it made a noise like a hoop and rolled away. No war. Everyone calmed down again. My money says: same again. The johnnies in the Foreign Office will do their stuff and this time next month we'll all be laughing about it. Don't you think?'

'I'm afraid not,' said Ormond. 'This time, from everything I hear, we're in for it.'

'Where should the clever money go then, if not gold?' Iris asked him. 'America? Is that far enough away?'

'Interesting,' said Ormond, turning slightly to face her. 'Probably yes, in the sense that, if the world burns, it would take a long time for the flames to reach Wall Street. But not necessarily for British investors.'

'Why?'

'Iris!' said Charlie, between his teeth.

She ignored him, and so did Ormond.

'Because I cannot imagine any way for Britain to fund a war – a big war – without mobilising British holdings abroad. The paperwork is already drawn up to forbid the export of capital. When war comes, and the money runs out, every share that anyone owns over here in Westinghouse or US Steel or Paramount Pictures is going to be requisitioned in short order.'

'The money runs out?' Charlie repeated incredulously. 'The money *runs out*? Poppycock. Sorry, but – really! This is the financial capital of the world, old man.'

The waiter was hovering, trying to take away plates and to put down new ones, but Ormond was ignoring him; he was leaning into the candle flame to light a new cigarette, fully engaged for the first time.

'Take the total of British gold and dollar reserves,' he said. 'Slightly north of five hundred million in sterling. Then estimate the cost of total war – say, four million a week – and divide by it.

The money runs out in two and a half years. And that's if we're winning.'

'Of course we'd *win*,' said Charlie. He poured himself another glass of wine, sloppily.

'I hope so,' said Ormond. 'I really do. But whether we're winning or losing, the emphasis – to answer your question, Iris – is going to be on budgeting for survival, by managing demand and directing resources.'

'You're assuming that Mr Keynes is going to be in the ascendancy at the Treasury?'

'I am, yes,' said Ormond.

'Despite everyone still arguing about the *General Theory*?'

'Oh, you don't have to agree with it to be influenced by it. You don't even have to have read it. He's won; he's won so thoroughly he's become part of common sense.'

'Voices in the air?' said Iris.

'Exactly!' said Ormond, laughing. 'Exactly so. You've read it yourself then, I take it?'

'Yes, I have.'

'And . . . what did you say you do for a living, Miss Hawkins?'

'She says she's a secretary,' put in Eleanor.

'Hmm,' said Ormond.

'Iris!' hissed Charlie. 'You're making a fool of yourself.' He was staring at her as if she'd grown a second head.

She was just as surprised. She had had no clue that anger was anywhere close under Charlie's amiable surface. On the whole she was confident she could spot the angry men and steer clear of them. You had to be able to, if you were of any kind of adventurous disposition.

'One of us is,' said Iris. Eleanor was looking from person to person. There was a sharp burn in Iris's leg. Charlie had tried to kick her under the table, and missed, and got the side of her calf instead, by the feel of it scraping off some skin.

'Now,' said Charlie, with a tight and over-toothed smile, 'that's all very well, but it's a bit airy-fairy for a practical chap like me. Not to mention desperately gloomy! Wine, women and song are more my watchword. Watch*words*, I suppose. Three of them!'

Iris was gazing at her plate, where little pale parcels dribbled with green oil had appeared. She felt a tentative tap on the back of her hand: two of Eleanor's fingers, sandpapery to the touch.

'Would you care to come and powder your nose?' Eleanor asked.

'Yes I would. Thank you.'

'This way, then. We'll leave them to the wine and song, shall we.'

They wove between the tables. Eleanor knew the way, as a regular. The Ladies, at the maximally dark, very back end of the restaurant, was a little cubbyhole with only just enough standing room for two. But it had a light over the mirror bright enough to show, when she pulled up the hem of the dress, that Charlie had torn a hole in her stocking and, yes, in her skin too. A dark-red trickle was running towards her ankle. She breathed through her nose and tried to smile.

'Oh dear,' said Eleanor. 'Would you like a sticking plaster? I never have a lipstick on me, and I rarely have a clean handkerchief, but I do always carry sticking plasters. Peculiar habits of the profession, you see.'

'Yes. Please.'

'Gosh, it's tight in here, isn't it. Tell you what, you roll down the stocking, and I'll get down here and see if I can minister to the affected part. Look,' she went on a moment later, crouched at Iris's feet, 'I think I was rude to you, back in there. *And is that interesting?*' She was mimicking her own voice. 'Just what my mother would say. – Here we go, hold still. – *So* patronising. Do you ever get that? You open your mouth, and your mother's voice comes out?'

'Not really,' said Iris, ignoring the door in her mind, the one with the scorch marks round it, that led to everything mother-related. 'Thank you. You're being very kind.'

'Basic comradeship among females, I assure you. There; how's that?'

'Much better. He's ruined the stocking, though.'

'It won't show, honestly. Not with your hemline down there. It really is a marvellous dress. Give me a hand up? I'm only a trainee contortionist.'

'You all talk such nonsense all the time,' Iris said, heaving at Eleanor. She was surprisingly heavy. Stone-cutting muscles, presumably.

'"You all"?' Eleanor queried. 'Oh, you mean us educated bods. But you don't do so badly at nonsense yourself. "Ferrous" was very funny, I liked that. I suppose,' she went on cautiously, 'that your chap in there isn't quite such an idiot as he seems?'

'He is, though. He's exactly that much of an idiot.'

'Then . . . why . . . ?'

The gap across worlds was just too great. Not so much the class one as the perpetual gulf between bad girls and good. Eleanor no doubt was full of advanced and tolerant ideas about all sorts of things – had queer friends, sunbathed with nothing on her top half, was familiar with the works of Marie Stopes. But if she said to her, *because he's quite good in bed*, there'd be blushing, and awkward silence, and a sudden end to basic comradeship among females.

She settled for: 'Well, he's not exactly my chap. Not in a serious way. He just takes me out, now and again.'

'Oh,' said Eleanor. 'I thought he was . . . Oh.'

'No, he's not. He's just a boyfriend.' The inoffensive word; the one that Iris hoped would stop the downward relegation of the pretty-but-common girl that was going on in Eleanor's mind, before it arrived down in the grim commercial cellar of human arrangements. 'And he *is* an idiot. He's made a complete hash of this evening. He's – *mistaken the nature of the occasion*,' she said, turning her voice into a parody of Eleanor's parody of herself. Eleanor grinned. 'He thought it was going to be a cigars-and-chorus-girls kind of thing. When in fact you're actually Mr Ormond's fiancée, aren't you.'

'We're engaged, yes,' said Eleanor.

'And he still hasn't worked it out. And when he does he's going to be unbearably ashamed, and he's going to be too much of a dolt to hide it. He's going to behave as if he's accidentally brought a tart to meet a duchess. I'm *not* a tart,' she said fiercely.

'I can tell you're not,' said Eleanor. 'I'm not a duchess, for that matter.'

'You're respectable, that's what counts. You belong with the sisters of people he went to school with. He's not a subtle thinker.'

'He's not, is he. He was gawping like a goldfish when you started talking economics with Miles.'

'Well, he's never heard me say anything like that. He looks at me and he sees, you know, bosom and hips.'

'And you don't . . . mind?' asked Eleanor.

'Not till now. Because it's not his brain I'm interested in either. I look at him and – well, anyway. It's been fun, usually. But this is horrible. Sorry.'

'Oh, don't be silly. I see that it is. You're sitting there waiting for him to humiliate you, and when you tried to save him from himself, the stupid swine kicked you.'

'Yes.'

Eleanor considered. 'Do you want a rescue?' she said.

'What do you mean?'

'Well, it would mean ditching your dinner – and losing the rest of whatever you and the swine had planned for the evening – but there's a back way out through the kitchen, I happen to know. We could run away.'

'What about Charlie and—?'

'I can send in a note with the waiter. Miles will cope; Miles always copes, he's very soothing. And he knows where we're going on to. He can meet me there.'

'Are you sure? You lose your supper too.'

'Oh well. Call it my good deed for the day.'

'Charlie will be furious.'

'How tragic . . .'

II

Cambridge Circus was all busy glare from the neon signs in red and green and white and blue. It was dark now, but the night was sealed away somewhere up above, beyond the radiant glow.

'What now?' said Eleanor, when the escape was complete and they were standing on the kerb, getting their breath back.

Already the rush of the laughing run through the alley full of dustbins was fading. Already they were remembering – well, Iris was, and she supposed Eleanor was – that they were two strangers.

'I mean,' said Eleanor, turning the face on her which, now she was seeing it by brighter light, seemed to Iris to have a kind of childishness about it, 'what are you going to do next?' A face left clean and somehow unformed by the refusal to do the labour of being pretty.

'I suppose I'll go home and put on something more sensible. Anyway, thanks—'

'But that sounds a bit dismal. You've lost your evening.'

'Oh well.'

'What *were* you going to do tonight, if you don't mind my asking?'

'He was going to take me dancing at the Savoy,' Iris said, leaving out the part about the beds.

'Yes, well, look: here's a thought. Where we're going there'll be dancing. It's a sort of club, up beyond Fitzroy Street. They're doing abstract film reels tonight, but they're all set to dance music – you know, for the rhythm – and I bet people get up and move their feet. You could come. Why don't you come?'

Iris frowned. 'Why on earth would you want me to? I'm not a stray dog, you know. You don't have to take me home just because you've patted me.'

'Heavens you're prickly, aren't you? I just think it would be fun. It seems like a night for impulses, what with the world threatening to end and all that. Go on! Throw yourself on the mercy of strangers! Even if it's dreadful – even if it turns out *we're* dreadful – it'll still be more fun than retiring defeated to wash your hair.'

Iris looked at the face under the red curls again. Some maddening patronage was in there, yes: but also a kind of innocent recklessness. It was the face of someone who had always found the world safe, the face of someone who had never had to fear consequences. Someone who had never needed guile, or lies, or pretence to ease their path. *Lucky her*, thought Iris, who would have been inclined to hate her a little, on other nights. When Iris ran risks, she knew what the risk was; she calculated risk against reward. But tonight (when the world might be ending) it seemed more enviable to be the kind of person who, having run from a restaurant, wanted to scoop up the stranger you'd done it with and to keep on running while the running was good.

'Dancing intellectuals . . .' she said, cautiously.

'Well, yes,' said Eleanor. And then, defiantly: 'Yes! Oxford bags and peculiar frocks in motion!'

'Wouldn't I stick out like a sore thumb in this?' asked Iris, waving at the silver dress.

'No. They'd think it was ironic, and you were terribly clever for wearing it. And I guarantee, I absolutely guarantee, it won't be the oddest outfit in the room. I said peculiar; I meant peculiar. Last time we went, there was a chap in a suit made of cardboard.'

'Cardboard?'

'Yes! The corrugated kind, cut so the lines all ran north–south and looked like pinstripes. I thought: *my dear fellow, I hope it doesn't rain on the way home, or you're going to turn into a naked surrealist before you reach Highgate.*'

'Pinstripe papier-mâché . . .'

'Exactly! Oh, go on, come with us, do. We've got *different* idiots.'

'You really want me to?'

'I wouldn't ask if I didn't,' said Eleanor, and Iris thought that was probably true. Oh, the hell with it. Time to borrow that sense of immunity, for a little while. Time to follow where impulse led, in the anxious city.

'All right!' she said, and grinned at her own lack of calculation.

'Attagirl!' said Eleanor. 'You won't be sorry. Or maybe you will, but you won't be bored, I promise.'

They walked on northward together, the bright lights of Soho becoming, as they crossed Oxford Street, the dimmer and more bohemian streets of Fitzrovia. A busy evening here too, but more concentrated on pubs, bars, doors into obscurer spaces from which obscurer music leaked.

'What kind of sculpture do you do?' Iris asked, to avoid silence.

'Depends,' Eleanor said.

'On?'

'Whether it's my own stuff or commissions. I've just done a mother-and-baby frieze for a clinic in Islington, and they wanted that, you know, pretty conventional. Smiley white marble. And I'm supposed to come up with something called "The Spirit of Vitamins", heaven help me, for a chemical company. Tosh like that. But when I can please myself I like playing with curves.'

'I see.'

'Do you? It goes wrong more often than it goes right, and I usually can't explain why, even to myself. But what about you?'

'What do you mean?'

'I mean,' said Eleanor, fixing her with the frank and unguarded gaze again, 'what are you? You're not a floozy, we've established that. Though you might be posing as one, for reasons of your own. – *That's* interesting. And you're not a secretary, except in a temporary wage-slave sort of a way. So what are you?'

Iris wondered about saying, *I'm a woman who likes men*, having thought of one more reason why Eleanor might have wanted to carry her off. But she didn't think there was anything unhelpfully romantic going on. The temperature of things between Eleanor and Ormond had been low, but relaxed and affectionate, like a gas ring steadily burning away when its flames were turned down into little blue buds, and she wasn't picking up anything flirtatious now, not that she had much practice at spotting it in girls.

'I don't quite know,' she said. 'But I think . . . that I might be one of whatever your Miles is. If they'd let me.'

'You mean, about money, and the stock market and everything?'

'Yes.'

'Do they let women do that?'

'No,' said Iris. 'Not here. In America women can be stockbrokers, but here they can't be brokers, or jobbers, or even brokers' clerks.'

'So will you go to America, then?'

Iris laughed. 'I don't think anyone's going anywhere for a while, do you?'

'I suppose not,' said Eleanor. 'It's funny, isn't it. You think you've made up your mind to a war coming, but you keep all these ordinary little expectations going as well, and it isn't till something contradicts them, one after the other, that you realise, oh, that's going to go too, isn't it?'

Iris could have said, but didn't, that travelling to America would never have been an 'ordinary little expectation' to her. Instead she nodded. 'We're all imagining it,' she said, 'the war; and the one thing you can be sure of is that we're imagining it wrong.'

'You think it'll be worse?'

'I think it'll be *real*.'

'Miles says he thinks that the stock market and all of that – all the clever money-making – is going to be swept away.'

'Does he? I notice he doesn't mind having enough for nice Italian food. And good wine.'

'And buying pictures,' said Eleanor cheerfully. 'And a house in the country. And a fast car. You know what he says? "I'm a socialist, not St Francis of Assisi." He's got a job at the Treasury ready for him as soon as the balloon goes up. Oh, here we are.'

'Here' was a flight of steel steps leading down to the basement of a newish commercial building, slightly taller than the general three-storey scale of the street. Iris had been seeing an odd multi-coloured flickering coming up from it, ever since they turned the street corner, and now she was looking down the steps she was facing the source of it, a line of basement windows flashing in shockingly bright and pure colours, turquoise and blood-orange and incandescent yellow. Dark human figures were moving against the colours, and they and the colours too were shifting in time to a familiar tune, pumping out at high amplification. It was being played on a weird mixture of instruments, including a violin. But it was, of all things, 'The Lambeth Walk'. Cockney knees-up music. Well, West End Cockney knees-up music.

'Three bob, please,' said a man with a beard at a little table just inside the basement door. Beyond him was coloured chaos. 'I'm afraid we've got to cover the equipment hire tonight.'

'I'll get this!' Eleanor said, raising her voice. 'Welcome to the Kinesis Club!'

Iris stepped past, and the colours engulfed her.

There was a wide white screen on the far wall – maybe just a bedsheet tacked up – and a projector was playing onto it from a metal tower near the man taking the three-bob entry charge. But the room was so low that the dancers were stepping in and out of the beam, so the colours were playing on their bodies as well as on the screen. Not pictures: flying blobs and lines, sometimes splooged in their violet or scarlet as if they had been finger-painted, sometimes in moving motifs as if printed on by a half-potato. She had never seen anything like it. And through the pulsating blizzard of colour, four or five couples, not all couples in which men were paired with women, were performing a meticulous Lambeth Walk, slide steps, arm-in-arm promenades and all. Just as in the show, which she had seen from a good seat in the dress circle with Charlie. Only with the difference that here, instead of stage Cockneys, the dancers were two men in sailors' trousers stripped to the waist, a very tall woman in tweeds with a face like an intelligent horse, an Indian in a turban and a tailcoat, a petite exquisite blonde in what Iris suspected was Schiaparelli evening wear of fabulous price, and a batch of more predictable souls in, indeed, Oxford bags and open shirts (male) or versions of Eleanor's skirt and sweater (female). And all of them were doing the Walk with – not mockery, exactly, but a kind of solemn comic detachment. Bohemian clowning. It *was* very funny, but if you laughed you'd spoil the joke. Iris covered her mouth with her hand.

Eleanor, appearing at her side, said something in her ear.

'What?'

'I *said*, let's *sit down* for a— Oh, here we go.'

The film ended, and with it the dance, on a screen of names that meant nothing to her. Someone turned on the overhead lighting, and in a blink the room was transformed from a cavern of jewel-light to a concrete-floored, bare-walled cellar. Cables ran around the edges, and little tables were arranged in a U around the dance floor.

'They're never very long, these films,' Eleanor said, bagging a table. The dancers settled around them. There was the rasp of many matches being struck. 'They can't be. So you get three minutes of astonishment – three minutes of ecstasy, if you want to be grand about it – and then you have to wait ten minutes while they change the reel and get set back up.'

'I've never—' Iris began, and changed her mind. 'Why can't they be longer?'

'Because the chap from New Zealand who does them paints the film by hand.'

'What, straight onto the celluloid?'

'Yes. So three minutes, at twenty-four frames a second, that must be, what . . .'

'Four thousand three hundred and twenty paintings,' said a boy at the next table, without looking round. He didn't say it as if he meant to butt into the conversation, or as if he was showing off. It seemed reflexive. Someone nearby had asked for a calculation and he had provided it.

'Probably,' said Eleanor.

'No, definitely,' said Iris.

The boy grunted.

'Anyway, it means that making them is incredibly fiddly and labour-intensive. Six months' work for three minutes. I can hardly imagine the patience—'

'Ridiculous, really,' the boy said. 'Looks avant-garde. Actually, handicrafts. Whittling. Crochet. Basket-making, with light.'

'You don't like them?' said Iris. She could only see the back of his head, where a particularly savage crop left a sheen of blond fuzz on long, vulnerable tendons.

'Didn't say that,' said the boy, talking downwards.

'Not modern enough for Geoff,' said one of the other men at the boy's table, comfortably. An older man, forties, with a matinée-roguish face, wearing a dinner jacket that was perhaps not ironic. 'Not electrical enough.'

'Not clever enough for Geoff,' said the Schiaparelli blonde, who was sitting there too. 'Clever Geoff. Stop being clever, Geoff, and give me a light.'

She had a box of matches an inch from her left hand, but instead she folded her fingers together, and leaned over towards the boy with a gold-tipped cylinder inserted in a carmine pout. Iris looked at her, fascinated. She was worth looking at. She must be only about Iris's own age, but if Eleanor was at one extreme of the spectrum in refusing to do any of the performance of beauty, this was a face at the opposite end. It was plucked, powdered, polished, armoured in beauty. The features had, naturally, the delicate uniform smallness towards which everyone else had to struggle by de-emphasising this, exaggerating that and hiding the other. The hair was like white silk. The fatness of the pearls round her neck showed off its slenderness.

The boy struck a match and turned his head to hold it out to her, revealing a flop of hair on his forehead, hollow cheeks and innocently intent eyes; also, on this face, a look of abject adoration. The beauty took the hand holding the match between finger and thumb to steady it. A pinch, not a caress. When she inhaled, a pair of mean little lines appeared, bracketing the rosebud mouth. A small mouth, thought Iris; not a generous mouth.

'Yes?' said the blonde, feeling the gaze. She didn't turn her head Iris's way, but she blew out a thin stream of smoke on Iris's side of her mouth.

'You've got him very well trained,' said Iris.

'Do I know you?' said the blonde, glacially. Her voice had underheated country houses in it. Dogs. Thorn hedges. Icy ditches.

'I doubt it,' said Iris.

'Quite.' One flick of the eyes was bestowed on her, grey and crystalline and contemptuous.

'I say,' broke in Eleanor, speaking to the matinée actor in the dinner jacket rather than to either of them, 'aren't you that chap who does the radio announcements? Michael Frobisher?'

'Was that chap,' said Frobisher, showing off excellent and very large teeth. 'Now the chap doing announcements for the television service. Consequently, seen by nobody. Heard by nobody either. Tragic waste. Three years of pioneering brilliance, and what for? There we sit on the hilltop at Alexandra Palace, pouring charm and intelligence into the ether, where it all floats away unwitnessed – unnoticed – unenjoyed . . .'

He sounded perfectly happy about it. Perhaps because he felt sure that his charm would never run out. There would always be gallons more.

'That's not true!' protested Eleanor.

'You mean you've actually *seen* one of our programmes?' Frobisher enquired.

'Well – no. Not as such,' said Eleanor. 'But a couple of my friends have been in your around-the-galleries thingummy, and *they* say it's very good. Good questions. Serious. The kind of thing with enough to-and-fro really to help build the audience for contemporary art.'

'Does it build ours, that's the question,' said Frobisher. 'But, good; that's very gratifying. Your friends are . . . ?'

'Oliver O'Reilly and Madeleine Levinson.'

'Right, right. Yes. Splendid. I remember them.'

'So do I,' said the blonde. 'The Jewess with the limp, wasn't she?'

'And you're . . . ?' pursued Frobisher.

'Eleanor Armbruster.'

'Heavens, I think I've seen some of your work. The Oriel Gallery?'

'That's right.'

'Well; hallo. I should introduce us. You have in fact got before you a small colony of the BBC. Me, vocal dogsbody. Lall Cunningham, our booker, who persuades visiting stars that for thirty guineas they should taxi up from the West End and do their turn for us, as well—'

'Frightful people, most of them,' said the blonde.

'Lally is *not* in a good mood this evening,' said Frobisher. 'As perhaps you can tell. And Geoffrey here, who is one of our technical wizards, fresh from filming the Test match.'

'What was the score?' said Iris, testing a theory.

'England 366 for three in seventy-six overs, Hutton 165 not out. Hammond, bowled Clarke, 138—'

'Thanks,' said Iris. 'Do you like cricket?'

'No,' said Geoff.

Eleanor and Frobisher went off into a rapid roll-call of all the people they did and didn't know in common, with occasional interventions from Lally the ice cube. Technical Geoff said nothing. Neither did Iris. She had guessed at first that it must be smooth, handsome, middle-aged Frobisher that Lall was really with, with the boy kept on a string for amusement: but that didn't seem quite right now. There was no inclining towards Frobisher, on Lall's side – the spine was ramrod-straight – and no pride of possession on Frobisher's. If anything, a slight disdainful humour at her expense. To which no reaction at all appeared on the alabaster face. Only, the manicured fingers on the hand not holding the cigarette were in motion under the table edge, Iris saw. Plucking minutely at Madame Schiaparelli's fabric on her thigh. Nursing a fold of silk between finger and thumb.

Someone came round with a jug, and poured tumblers of a nasty but powerful fruit punch. Surely it was time for the next film, the next dance? The art-world gossip was not entertaining, if you were on the outside of it, and it wasn't what Iris wanted from an evening of impulses followed, of strangers and bright colours.

The bearded man who'd taken the money was at the projector tower, but pulling at cables unavailingly, and looking frustrated.

'I'm sorry,' he said, raising his voice to the room. 'Could someone who knows more than me take a look at this?'

'Fix it, Geoff,' said Lall.

'Yes, fix it, Geoff,' said Iris.

He was already getting up; he gave her, for the first time, a startled direct glance. His face was all angles – beaky nose, lantern chin – but with a glow of anxiety or self-consciousness on it which counteracted the austere lines. His sharp cheekbones were pink, what with the unexpected experience of being teased by a stranger arriving on top of being commanded by his ice maiden. And as he moved over to the projector tower, she saw that he was gangly. He had long arms and big hands, long legs and big shoes. He crouched to check the connections, knees almost up to the shoulders of his sports jacket, stood on tiptoe to fiddle with the gate of the projector, and then walked the cables back across the floor to the amps under the screen, head down, taking quick weaving steps, a long finger on each hand out and pointing in the air and clearly tracing an electrical pathway. It was deft, even graceful, in an odd sort of way: a body being treated as if it were invisible to everyone else's eyes, a body being used to think with. He adjusted something and came back.

'Try now, Donald,' he said. The projector whirred, the screen lit, a Latin drumbeat came from the speakers, and his face, as he nodded with satisfaction in the moment the overhead lights went off, reminded Iris strongly of something. Something unlikely. Not a person she knew; not even a photograph of a person. Not a real person at all. A drawing: a drawing in a book. The same long face, the same puzzled bright eyes. But with a frame around it. A metal frame. A helmet. Then she got it. It was an old picture-book illustration of Don Quixote she was thinking of. But young, and gazing at technical windmills. Take away the armour, take away forty years, and that was this Geoff. Don Quixote as a boy.

Then the dark filled with vertical lines of colour pulsing and jiggling, swaying to left and right, and everyone surged up from their seats and emulated them, rumba-ing to clarinet and bongos, and to mauve and bottle-green and scarlet printing themselves on moving skin as much as on the screen. Hurricanes of dots swirled and jittered. Eleanor was up dancing with Frobisher, Lall had claimed Geoff as of right, and Iris found herself shaking her hips with one of the two bare-chested sailors. It was a very nice chest, hard and warm and wide and developed, with a satisfactory heat and a satisfactory smell of clean male sweat coming off it. But the hand on her hip as she swung it was light, was entirely proper. And what she felt under her own hand, as it rode on the snaky flexing of the sailor's narrow waist, was all the pleasure of performance, not even slightly the pleasure of female company. Not one for the ladies, this mariner.

Lall went by with Geoff, and Iris saw that detachment ruled over there as well. No touch at all. Geoff, slightly to her surprise, was dancing with enthusiasm, giving himself to the rhythm in bird-like jerks. But Lall, opposite him, was minimal, keeping him focused on her entirely with her face, and reducing her hip movement – not that there was much to her hips anyway – to a set of disdainful twitches. She was perfectly in time, of course, but she moved as if she disliked even the tiny loosening of the space between neck and knees that she was consenting to. Her spine stayed straight. Her pelvis was not being allowed to get any ideas. It astonished Iris that Geoff couldn't see it, but apparently not. The idiot gaze of hope stayed on his face as if plastered there. It was annoying.

When the film ended and the lights went up, she saw that Miles Ormond had arrived, smiling and unflustered. She tried to apologise, but he shook it off.

'I'm used to dealing with wild bores,' he said. 'Think nothing of it.'

She would have liked to pick up the conversation she had started to have with him in Soho, but when she ventured a remark in that direction, he made it politely clear that Charlie had exhausted his entire willingness to talk about the markets. In any case, he too was pulled promptly towards the glamour represented by Frobisher, and very quickly what developed was a three-cornered conversation between Frobisher, Ormond and Eleanor, with occasional contributions by Geoff and Lally, and her sitting at the edge, trying not to feel redundant.

The next film was less danceable. Noodling woodwind accompanied an experiment with human figures in it for once, a silhouetted businessman with an umbrella and a silhouetted tennis player with a racket, who when they moved left a smeared rainbow trail on the air. It was pretty to look at, but it didn't get you out of your chair, and the conversation at their two tables went on regardless.

'The charm of it,' Frobisher was saying, 'is that no one knows exactly what will work on television. It's a new medium. It's *not* cinema, though you can show films on it, and it's not a little theatre in the corner of the room, though we have had some success with squeezing plays onto it.'

'You have to get the close-ups right,' said Geoff.

'You do, you certainly do; and that can be, if you'll pardon my French, a complete pain in the arse, what with the cameras not moving. You have to know at the outset that, at minute forty-three and eleven seconds, you're going to want to fill the screen with the sensitive profile of the younger Gielgud, and your camera has to be lined up ready. And then there's every chance that your actor will miss his mark slightly, since it doesn't matter on the stage, and then what the waiting millions get is a lovely grey-toned study of his ear.'

'"Waiting millions"?' said Ormond, with an eyebrow raised.

'What am I saying? Waiting hundreds. Waiting thousands, maybe.'

'Tens of thousands, now,' put in Geoff. 'I was doing the Radiolympia broadcast last week, and apparently the total number of sets sold is up to twenty thousand or so.'

'Which is not bad going,' said Frobisher, 'for a thing the size of a cocktail cabinet, with a screen no bigger than your hand, that costs ten weeks or more of the average wage.'

'Well, it's not *for* everyone, is it?' said Lall.

'But what I'm trying to say,' said Frobisher, exhibiting his teeth, 'is that it's exciting to be in at the beginning. And there's a kind of freedom in having hardly anyone watching. You can discover what it can do which nothing else can.'

'And what is that?' said Eleanor. 'What are the new tricks in your magic box? What can you do, by painting with electricity?'

'Oh, I like that,' said Frobisher. 'Well: I would say, immediacy.'

'Presence,' said Geoff.

'Enchantment,' said Lall.

'I think you're going to have to explain all of those,' said Ormond.

'Would you, though, if we actually had a, a receiver?' asked Eleanor. 'Art needs explanation sometimes, but does this?'

'No, it doesn't,' said Frobisher. 'That's the thing. If you're actually watching television, it doesn't need explaining at all. It just works on you.'

'A self-evident aesthetic,' said Eleanor, interested.

'But we've never seen it,' said Iris. Lall flicked her a glance, as if to say, *who cares?*

Frobisher extended the broadcast of his charm briefly in the direction of the less important girl, and smiled at her. 'All right. Imagine that the grey little glass circle, in your luxurious cocktail cabinet, warms up to become a sort of magic keyhole. You don't look *at* it, you look *through* it.'

'And what do you see?' said Eleanor.

'Things happening right now. Not grave and considered utterances, but a kind of visual chatter. News, yes; but also tap-dancing feet, movie stars without a script, someone hitting a six, the very moment when a snake-charming lady's python escapes across the studio floor.'

'Nightmare!' said Lall.

'And then somehow it doesn't matter that the keyhole is tiny. You can't look away.'

'That's what I meant about presence,' said Geoff, his ears reddening. 'It makes you feel you're *there*. And not just in one place, either. It's a flow. It's *here*, and then *here*, and then *here*. You're at the zoo, you're watching the Life Guards go by, you're at the races, you're looking at Jasmine Bligh's smile as she answers the phone on *Picture Page*, you're in the world.'

'Montage,' said Eleanor, knowledgeably.

'But not put together by a director. Not someone's deliberate, you know, *selection* of images. That they've thought about and put in order. More a kind of pack shuffled by . . . television itself. Or by life itself – that's how it feels, anyway. And it doesn't need rewinding, or six months' work with a paintbrush. It never stops.'

'Well, not till our daily three hours of broadcast time are over, anyway,' said Frobisher. 'But – yes.'

'Eloquent Geoff,' said Lall, freezing him back into shyness, as she surely intended.

'And enchantment?' enquired Ormond politely.

'Oh, you know,' she said, the carmine lips hardly moving, 'it's a modern spell, isn't it. It makes you look, it keeps you looking. Cinema is for the people. Television is for those who need a private connection to power. A circuit to connect them to what they adore. It's like Signor Mussolini says: man is made to adore and to obey.'

'I . . . think that was Disraeli,' said Ormond, a laugh in his voice that Lall did not like at all.

'Oh?' she said, glacially.

'So you see it growing, do you?' said Eleanor to Frobisher, after a momentary frown. 'Television?'

'In the long run, certainly. When we've ironed out the kinks. When the cameras get better. When the sets get cheaper. I'm sure it's going to be a frivolity that the world will take to, like . . . chewing-gum or nylons. But in the short run,' Frobisher said, losing the smile, 'I'm afraid it's a frivolity the world can't afford. If war comes, they'll switch us off, like that.' He snapped his fingers.

'There'll be no need for that,' Lall said. 'You'll see. Cooler heads will prevail. Sensible people know that Germany has no hostile intentions towards us. Rather the opposite. All we have to do is keep our nose out of European squabbles that don't concern us.'

'You think we should let them gobble up Poland, like they did Czechoslovakia?' said Ormond, all laughter drained out of his voice too.

'I *think*,' said Lall, holding the word with tongs and making it clear she regarded it as a disreputable activity, 'that we should be grateful to the Führer for taking care of Bolshevism, for all our sakes.'

'I'm afraid I have a lingering attachment to democracy,' said Ormond, and turned unmistakably away from her. Eleanor followed suit. Frobisher looked down at the table. Geoff was embarrassed.

Another film began: back to flying red triangles and vibrating dots, to a Cuban beat.

Lall, feeling Iris's fascinated attention still on her as the others seized the excuse to stand up, snapped, 'What are you looking at?'

'A fascist, apparently,' said Iris.

'Well, better that than a suburban slut like you.'

'Oh,' said Iris. 'Oh. Well: come on, Geoffrey. Come and dance with *me*.'

III

Out on the floor, out where the dark shook with colours to the sound of maracas, Geoff started his bird-dance again, evidently expecting Iris to get no closer than Lall had. She put her hand on his shoulder and pulled. When he was up against her, she grabbed his waving right hand and put it on the slippery silver at her hip, where it trembled. Trembled uncertainly, but not indifferently. Then she steered them both back into the rhythm. This one was faster, with skittering horns and then a pounding piano. Across a background like slightly yellowed printer's paper, frantic asterisks rolled and bounced, changing hues every fraction of a second. The two of them sashayed and shook, prestissimo, Geoff startled but willing, a look of concentration on his face. He was pleasingly but not enormously taller than her, despite the gangliness; and despite the look of not having grown all the way into the length of his limbs, what was under the sports jacket and the open white shirt was knotty, not soft. His head, bent forward, was close enough for speech. The dark and the rhythm made a temporary privacy.

'You don't agree with her about that stuff, do you?' she asked.

'God, no,' said Geoff.

'Then why are you so stuck on her?'

'Is it that obvious?'

'Yes!'

'It's just that she's so . . . so . . .'

'Lovely? Yes, she is. But you're not ever going to have her, you know.'

His eyes went wide, and he nearly lost the beat.

'I'm not— You can't— I mean, that's not what I – I—'

'Yes, it is. But you're wasting your time.'

'You don't know her! You don't know *me*. You don't know anything about me.'

'I know she's not interested. If it helps, I don't think it's personal.'

'What do you mean?'

'Lall's not up for passion at all, with anyone. Except maybe the Führer. She doesn't want to feel. She doesn't want to open up. She doesn't want anything getting too close.'

'How can you tell?'

'Because if she wanted you, Geoff, she wouldn't dance with you three feet away. She'd dance with you like *this*.'

Iris put both arms round his neck and came in all the way from conventionally near to skin-mashed-against-skin near, her chest into his chest, pressing up so he'd feel the whole length of her body against the whole length of his. Her shaking hips she brought up hard into him, and added some forward stirring and nuzzling and bumping. The little liquefying flame lit in her; she could feel what she was doing to him. Oh, now the evening had its recklessness back. She bit her lower lip, and stared into his eyes with dumb greed from two inches away.

'Like that,' she said, stopping.

'What – what are you doing?'

'Demonstrating.'

'But – do you . . .'

'You're wondering, is she *just* demonstrating? Or does she mean it? What do you think, Geoff?'

'I don't know,' he said.

The film ended. The music stopped. The lights went on.

'I'll tell you what,' she said quietly, 'call us a taxi, right now, take me somewhere with a bed, and I'll show you whether I mean it or not.'

He stared.

'Come on,' she said. 'The world's ending. So they say.'

'I can't just leave,' he said.

'Yes you can. You can walk me out, right now. Straight past them. Straight to the door.'

He shook his head, but with disbelief not refusal. And past sour-faced beautiful Lall, past laughing Frobisher, past ironic Ormond, past disbelieving Eleanor who was nevertheless patting her hands together in mock-applause – Iris didn't think it was likely she'd ever see her again, but she was glad she enjoyed the spectacle – past all the dancing intellectuals and Donald on the door, she marched him out. Outside on the pavement she kissed him hard, immediately, to seal the bargain, and then ran hand in hand with him in the direction of a cab with its yellow *For Hire* light on.

'Where to, guvnor?' asked the driver.

'Um – Hampstead,' said Geoff.

They scrambled in, the taxi backed and turned, and then they were off, sliding together on the wide, worn, slippery shelf of the back seat while London flowed backwards past them. She had hoped for some mansion block much nearer by, in Marylebone or Bloomsbury, somewhere reachable while the first energy of impulse was still upon them. She didn't want to wait, she didn't want to think. She didn't really want to talk. She kissed Geoff some more – a big mouth with narrow lips, some clashing of teeth as he got keener, a tongue startled to feel her tongue coming exploring – and there it was, the usual feeling of discovery, of difference in sameness, of being permitted to touch and taste the foreign way another body, a male body, did the familiar business of being human. Rougher, bigger, harder: always different, and the same thrill every time. Touch to touch, wet inner lip to wet inner lip, skin to skin. The world getting warmer, and smaller, and all concentrated on this, here, now. She did what she had been wanting to do, and slipped her hand down inside the open neck of his shirt. He was August-bare underneath it, as she had hoped, and she found a long smooth hot hairless boy's chest, skin tight on the ribs. His nipples were small and flat, threepenny bits of creased chamois. She flicked one with a nail, and he made a sound in his throat; she squeezed it hard between finger and thumb, and he gasped into her busy mouth. His own hands, which had hovered uncertainly in his lap, went onto her convulsively, and started to squeeze and grasp, not gently.

'Oi!' said the cabbie sharply. 'That's enough of that. Bit o' decency, please. Get to where you're going and you can grope each other all you like. But this is a licensed conveyance, not a knocking-shop.'

Geoff pulled away, abashed. Turned away, too; looked out of the side window at whatever North London street they were trundling along. In the dark of the cab it was difficult to tell, but she suspected there was another blush colouring his skin. A shameable boy. Not abashed herself, not ashamed, but anxious in case the moment cooled away into doubts and hesitations and second thoughts, she reached for his hand, and held it tight, trying to send into the grip certainty, and assurance, and promise, or all that warm fingers could communicate of those things; enough of those things to win the race against doubt, as the car rose up, and up, and up, on some steepening avenue. She had no idea how much time had passed, or how much further they had to go. Behind, London was starting to gather into a pool of sparkles, diamonds and rhinestones poured together in a black basin.

'All right,' said the driver. 'Where exactly am I taking you two lovebirds, then?'

Geoff cleared his throat. 'Wildwood Terrace, please.'

'Back of bloody beyond.'

Geoff, having looked up to speak to the driver, swallowed and looked at their joined hands, and then at her. The cone of brightness from a street lamp swivelled across his own face, wiping away shadow for a moment. His expression was not one of doubt or of impulse fading away. Not at all. It was the purest look of wonderment Iris had ever seen, let alone provoked on her own account; and seeing it, so palpably not the expression of someone who knew how this game was played, she felt a sensation that was new in quite a different way from the greedy novelty of learning a new body. It was a kind of dismay. She looked at his wonder, and her heart misgave her. She thought of the faces she was used to lovers making. Charlie's schoolboy greed as he spread her wide on Egyptian cotton sheets. Weather-beaten Jack the spirits salesman, looking down at her with cheerful approval, takes-one-to-know-one approval, as she tried something out on him. Sly victorious glances from Lancelot the petroleum futures king, as she sat on his knee in a suite in Brighton, all the while quite confident that the victory was hers. Each face made plain by desire. Nothing mysterious in them, nothing to worry about in them. (Though it was not nice to realise that Charlie's might have been hiding anger without her knowing it.) This was different, this . . . astonished awe. No telling what he understood, or didn't. No telling what such a face might ask of her. Now she was the one looking away, to avoid his eye.

The taxi crested the brow of the hill. Another little street or two, toy-pretty, and then out into a moonlit emptiness of grass and trees. The Heath, presumably. She peered: something was moving there, metallic in the pale white light. Monstrous earthworm segments, rearing and swelling, which suddenly, when she saw the crew labouring at the cables that held one, resolved into barrage balloons being prepared for launch.

'Can I ask you something?' Geoff said, in a near-whisper for privacy's sake.

'Maybe not,' she muttered, looking down.

'It's just . . . I don't know your name.'

It must have never come up, in the conversation at the table.

'Iris,' she said.

'Iris what?'

'Does it matter?'

'Of course it *matters*,' he said, smiling at her as the taxi slowed: and now she was slightly afraid of him and his innocence. But she still wanted him.

The cab dropped them at a leafy little junction, where odd little houses hid behind trees. When the engine noise had died away, there was a countryside hush, loudly silent if your ears were used to London, most peculiar to find *in* London. The nearest street lamp had an apple tree leaning over and around the lantern, so that heavy sprays of russet-and-green fruit dappled the light and shone in it. It was as if, having found a wild space unexpectedly contained within the city, they had now found a village within that; and, going further in and in, might find more and more secrets, ever smaller. It made Iris think of the telescoping children's poem which led you through city, street, house, room, cupboard, drawer and box, until in the inmost chamber of the inmost chamber there was the key that unlocked the whole city. She shivered, and Geoff, thinking she was cold, took off his sports jacket and chivalrously draped it over her shoulders.

'We'll have to be quiet,' he said, leading her away up a lane which after one more street lamp was all green darkness. A garden gate that stuck, and the dimly seen outline of a house, lightless and somehow lopsided.

'Why?' she said – whispered, obediently.

'Because my father will be asleep downstairs.'

'Geoff . . .'

But he had her by the hand, and since she did still want him she followed him across a summer-sappy dimness and dampness where long grass swished, to a door he eased open with a latchkey. Inside, there was no light at all, except stray gleams through the fanlight, but it was paper-smelling, and dust-smelling, and loomingly cluttered. There were silhouettes of unidentifiable tall things along the hall wall, like a collection of many grandfather clocks, and the stairs they crept up were piled high with something-or-other on the left-hand side. It was about the opposite of the setting she had imagined for him – she had thought of ultra-modern bareness, smooth surfaces of glass and steel for technical Geoff, not a chaotic junkyard.

A little landing at the top, with boards that creaked. A door Geoff opened, and beckoned her through.

But she mouthed 'Bathroom?' at him, and he pointed her to the next door along. There was a light switch, but she put in her cap in the dark, not wanting to see what she suspected, lit up, would be the smeared and mouldy fox-den horror of male bad housekeeping. Rings in the bath. Patinated toothpaste spatter on the mirror. Never-dried bathmat growing algae. The darkness could keep it.

In darkness she crept back to Geoff's bedroom, tapped, and went in. Inside, to her relief, order. He had lit a tiny side-lamp, the bulb no bigger than a pea, and the small yellow glow illuminated a rack of identical jackets, a stack of ironed white shirts, shelves on which the books were arranged in strict descending order of size. And an immaculately made-up single bed, with a red coverlet and a clean sheet. There were signs, too, of the child's bedroom this had once been – a model biplane hanging on threads under the eaves, where a dormer window with diamond panes looked out on the overgrowth of the garden, and the last street lamp beyond. But she didn't look at those. She looked at Geoff standing with his head tilted under the low ceiling, and if his eyes were shining disconcertingly, he was also looking at her down and up and down again, in the silver dress, and at the warm lick of his gaze she found that her little flame was still burning. Was growing and spreading, in fact.

He whispered something, but too quietly for her to hear. She stepped closer.

'You said you'd prove me something if I found you a bed,' he said.

She put her hands on his shoulders.

'And that's the bed, is it?'

'Mm-hmm.'

And at this, at the straightforward challenge of it, it became possible to ignore all the strangeness of the place, and the night, and of him, and of her own lurching sense of stepping off the known world's edge and falling – and to get back to the service of her flame. And his. She could kiss him again, and let her hands go exploring again, and feel his on her pressing and moulding and squeezing, with increasing confidence and force. And could tumble him over onto the bed, and join him in his splay of long limbs, and find where the two of them fitted, and where the fulcrum was on his bony hip where you could rub an ache. And feel the world getting smaller and simpler, in the old old way; feel it becoming all one thing that she was confident of, in which she knew she had power. Smaller. Simpler. Hotter.

When they were hot enough, and both breathing hard, an August sheen of damp on both their faces because it was not cool in the little room under the low eaves, she pushed back the flop of blond hair from his forehead and said happily, 'Now take all your clothes off.'

'Are you going to . . . ?' he asked, nodding at the silver dress.

'We'll come to that,' she said. 'But you first.'

He started fumbling at his buttons as he lay there.

'No,' she said. 'Stand up so I can see you. I want to see you.'

She could have turned off the little lamp but she really didn't want to spare his blushes; and indeed, lying on her side watching him like a cat, with a smile and unwavering eyes so he would know how completely he was being seen, it was blushes she saw. They bloomed on him, paleness and fairness and gingery-brownness delicately transformed by slow tides of pink. A better show than any of the dancing asterisks earlier. His knees and elbows were boles of bone, not yet in proportion with narrow legs and arms. Foal boy. Fool boy.

He came back to her naked and she lay on top of him, enjoying the slide of the silver fabric against the stick of his quivering skin. He was really very pale, in the parts the sun did not reach: a stark white that came up instantly in red lines where she scratched him gently. She kissed him some more. He clasped her, and started to heave under her, trying to push up at her where she was pressing down on him, trying to get between her thighs as much as the dress would allow, but she was not quite ready for that. She gave him the bitten-lip look again, this time with a smile in it, and watched him melt into helplessness – and then began to work her way down him, with hands and mouth. A lick and a kiss and a stroke and a scrape and a nip. When she reached his groin, his arms and legs convulsed as if she was sending electric current through him.

'What – what are you doing?' he gasped.

She freed her mouth. 'Something a man taught me. I didn't like him much, but I like doing this. I'll stop if you want. Do you want me to stop?'

'. . . No,' said Geoff, somewhere between a groan and squeak.

The smallest of small worlds now. Closed eyes and a full mouth. If this was the key to the city, there was no cold metal to it. It was a living charm. Warmth in the inmost box of the world. Outside, the night, rumours of war, balloons on steel hawsers rising, Poland, Parliament recalled, Mr Chamberlain to speak on the radio, Stalin and Molotov, Hitler and Ribbentrop. In here, a raw and tender and salty warmth.

When he was ready – when she was ready too – she came back up him, hitched the silver dress up round her waist, and climbed on him. They fitted together well, and now she wanted him to move, using her weight to ease his galvanised upward lurches into smoother riding for both of them. His eyes were wide, and his mouth was wide open too, a silent O of astonishment. She would have welcomed his hands on her but they were clutching at his neat red bedspread. Fast riding. Faster riding, maybe too fast, a canter becoming a gallop—

'I'm going – to . . .' Geoff started saying.

'No you're *not*,' she said, stopping dead. She fixed him sternly with her eyes. 'Tell me the primes, Geoff.'

'What?'

'Prime numbers. Tell me them. One, three, five – go on.'

'Seven!'

'Good.'

'Eleven. Thirteen.'

'Yes?'

'Seventeen. Nineteen. Twenty-three.'

'Good boy. Keep going.'

'Twenty-nine. Thirty-one. Thirty-seven.'

She began moving again, very gently, with extra pressure and attention to what worked for her, because clearly Geoff was going to be just fine the moment she released the numerical leash. A grind against the bone. *There* and *there* and *there*.

'Forty-one, forty-three, forty-seven, fifty-one—'

'Yes—'

'Fifty-three, fifty-seven, fifty-nine—'

'Yes!'

'Sixty-one, sixty-seven—'

'*Yes!*'

She put her hand over his mouth to stop the numbers, and felt him come undone on the instant, pulsing upwards into her as she gripped and shook and blazed around him, drinking the cup of pleasure down and down and down. And down. Then she fell forward onto him, laughing, and lay in a wreck of satisfaction with her face against his ear. Take that, oncoming war. Take that, obstinate world. Take that, Charlie. Take that, posh bitch Lall. Score one for suburban sluts.

It was only when her breathing had slowed that she realised that the faint sound she could hear was not Geoff laughing too. She lifted her head, and found that he was weeping, a trickle of tears running from the corner of each stricken eye.

'Hey,' she said in alarm. None of her other men had cried. 'What is it? Sweet boy, what's the matter?'

'. . . I don't know.'

'Well, hush then. It's all right. Everything's all right, isn't it.'

She twisted round and patted at him awkwardly. She was too unstrung for this. Too dismantled to make an effort of understanding. Or to want to. But then a thought struck her – a simple one.

'That wasn't . . . your first time, was it?'

'. . . Yes.'

'Oh. Well then.' A part of her would have liked to crow. To sing out inwardly, *well, you're going to remember* that *then, Don Quixote!* But the urge was thwarted by the sight of his face. 'Look, it's a bit of a shock for everyone, the first time, that's all. It's a new feeling, isn't it. You think you've been turned inside out, you think you . . . might not be the same person any more.' More memory than she wanted came bubbling up; she pushed it down. 'But then in a little while you find you're still just the same.'

'I don't feel just the same.'

'In a minute, I said. Give it a minute.'

'I thought it would be different from that.'

'You thought it would be with her, right?' His Nazi object of adoration whose thighs were held together with industrial adhesive.

'I thought *it* would be different. I thought it would be . . . less lonely.'

'Lonely!'

'Maybe that's not the right word.'

'I'm just here, you know.'

'I know. You're very kind,' he said politely.

'No,' she said, 'I'm not, particularly. But on the whole people are glad I'm there. On the whole they don't weep and wail if I decide I want to give them what I just gave you.'

'I'm sorry,' he said, his eyes welling anew.

'Oh—' she began, and stopped, anger and compunction hopelessly mixed up inside her. Instead she draped her arms around him in an approximation of comfort. Hell. This was what her misgivings in the taxi had been trying to warn her about. She thought of saying, *don't be so damn innocent*. But he was innocent, wasn't he? She had known that; that was the appeal. And whatever she thought of saying, whatever protest she thought of uttering, it wouldn't restore her animal contentment of a minute ago: the yawning-cat feeling, the well-stroked feeling. All that was tangled now, spoiled now, by knowing that for him what she'd just done had been, of all things, *lonely*. Her mouth, her hands, him inside her: lonely. Her eyes on his skin, her skilful management of his desire: lonely. Lonely! The little bastard. Her draped arms seemed to be settling into a rigid frame. She longed to move them. How much comfort was enough comfort? And her rucked-up dress and her bare bottom half were feeling squalid now instead of pleasantly abandoned. She had imagined that that was going to be Act One of their night together. He was young, he had some go in him. She had been looking forward to getting properly naked herself; showing *her* skin to *his* eyes, and seeing him look. Fat chance of that, clearly.

He made another unexpected sound. A murmur. And looking back at him, from the frustrated place inside her head where she had gone, Iris found that having delivered his spoiling word, having wept, Geoff had gone to sleep. Light snores. The thin, sculpted lips falling open. She was offended, but also relieved. She could get away now. She unlocked her arms and took the hand off his temple, where she had been absently stroking the white-blond hair, and began to lift herself up off him with as much precaution as she could manage, so the weight might come off him in stages too slow to be noticed. No more conversation; please, no more conversation. *When I am standing up*, she told herself, *I will begin to feel normal. And when I find my way out of this hot little trap of a house, located who-knows-where, I will feel more normal. And when I get home, I will be all the way back to normal. I will be my reliable self again. I will.*

She found her knickers on the floor, and her bag, and she turned off the little light by the bed so she shouldn't have to gaze at his fine bones and his closed eyelids as she went. Without it, the room was all shadow, except for the small spill of moonlight and distant street lamp that fell in through the dormer window.

On her silent way out, towards the bathroom and then the stairs, something moved in the bright parallelogram on the floor, catching her eye. Some flaw in the light, some twitch in the shadow. She went closer to the dormer to look, knocking her head on the toy biplane. Something in the movement was odd; wrong. Not in the right repertoire for things seen out of cottage windows.

She squinted, and down under the last street light she saw that a figure was standing. A man in a long coat and a hat, seemingly. Too many clothes to be comfortable on an August night, maybe, but otherwise ordinary enough. Except that this man was slowly bending his head over onto his shoulder. Not just tilting it, or leaning: laying it absolutely flat there, at ninety degrees, in a way that the human neck did not permit. Apart from the hat – why didn't the hat fall off? – it didn't look in silhouette like a head at all, but some flaccid appendage, slackly creasable. She thought of the barrage balloons, half-inflated, swelling and blundering. Then up from the shoulder swung the head, if it was a head, through the vertical and all down onto the other shoulder. A smooth movement, like the swing of a metronome. Or as if he had no bones in him, but were a skin loosely filled with some fluid, like the balloons. She felt the hair standing up on the sweat-damp nape of her neck: back to animal reactions, but fear now, not contentment. A creature's reaction to discovering nearby in the dark a thing that moved as if it lived, but could not be assigned to any of the known categories of safe or dangerous.

And then, as if he felt her eyes on him, the figure turned, and his face was incomprehensible too. Incomprehensibly wrong. He was the distance of a garden and a stretch of pavement away, with the branches of a tree in between and only the uncertain top-down glow of the street lamp to illuminate him. But she should still have been able to make out the familiar pattern of features. A line of shadow for a mouth, dark pits for eyes. There the patches of shadow were, under the hat, but not in the right places for eyes and mouth. Not where eyes and mouth could plausibly be. The face refused to be a face, refused to compose. Yet with this face that was not a face he, or maybe it, seemed to be watching her in return. Its gaze had found her without hesitation, though she should have been completely invisible from the lane, behind glass in a darkened room. Securely out of sight. Instead she had the shocking conviction that neither distance, nor darkness, nor even the walls of the cottage were any obstacle to it at all. In the attention of this thing, walls faded to transparency, were as thin as veils, as spiders' webs. Her damp skin, her beating heart, her clenched hands were no more hidden from it than if it had been standing right in front of her. In the room with her. In the reach of boneless arms—

It moved! It stepped off the pavement, away from the lamplight, into the deeper shadow on the far side of the lane. There she couldn't see it any more, shadow-camouflaged, shadow-consumed. But first she had seen its walk, a *pouring* motion, jointless and inhuman. She stared into the dark, heart pounding. No movement that she could detect. Nothing. No noise either, though she strained her ears to try to catch, over the thump of her own pulse, anything like a footfall. Anything like the rustle of leaves, the swish of grass, disturbed by a boneless tread. Or, worst, the click of the latch of Geoff's garden gate, which would mean that it was coming in, gliding up the overgrown path, preparing to press its way into the cluttered hall. But there was nothing. If she opened the window a crack, she might be able to hear more, to pick up finer stirs or displacements in the hot night air – but she felt an instinctive repulsion at the idea of having any fewer barriers between her and the thing outside, even a thin and useless one like a pane of glass. *Stay in the cave*, said animal wisdom. *Stay very still. If there is any doubt about whether the thing outside in the dark is hunting, you do not want to meet it.* She had shrunk back from the window without making any conscious choice.

But after two minutes, five minutes, some uncountable amount of time had passed, measured by pulse beats, not knowing became an anguish in itself. She had to look. She dropped to her knees and shuffled like that to the floor in front of the dormer. Slowly, slowly, she raised her head, until her eyes were just at the level of the sill. She peered over. There was still no movement at all in the shadows beyond the street lamp. Nothing in the blackness to say for sure that the watcher was standing there, in its wrongness. But nothing to say for sure that it wasn't, either.

She waited till her knees ached. Her heart slowed, and the panic receded, and a thread of a suggestion that she was behaving absurdly entered her mind and thickened there. The longer she saw nothing strange down on the road, the harder it became to be sure that she had ever seen anything at all. For what makes no sense is hard to hold on to. Recognition is what allows us to take hold of a perception, and to hold it fast in memory. Without recognition, a sight scrabbles for attachments in your mind and finds nothing there to fit it, and when the immediate terror is over it fades, dreamlike. Yet very like the residue of a nightmare, though the experience was going, going, almost gone, a sharp ghost of the sensation remained, alive in her body if no longer in her mind: the sensation of being transfixed by inexorable attention through walls turned thin as cobwebs. And she knew with absolute certainty that she was not going outside in the dark herself, to run even the slightest risk of meeting a thing without a face.

But that meant staying here, in the bottled heat of Geoff's room, until dawn. There he still was, naked and sleeping easy, untouched by whatever had just happened. (Or had not.) Already he had begun to seem like yesterday's problem. She was reluctant to get close to him again, but the alternative was an upright chair at his desk, gazing at exactly ranked books it was too dark to read, and which no doubt would be about electrical engineering anyway. She went as silently as she could to the bathroom, to wash; and when she came back she arranged herself next to him on the bed with her back turned.

He breathed, and she couldn't refuse to hear it. A steady push and pull of air, close behind her. *Treat it like wind*, she thought, *or like surf on a beach; some natural noise, soothing if anything.* Between the sound of Geoff and the memory of fear she threaded her way by thinking, her reliable standby, about money. Its complications. Its possibilities. The unsolved problem of where money could safely go, if war was coming. Money reproducing itself at four per cent interest forever, if you had enough of it to start off with. The impossibility of ever growing rich in one lifetime at four per cent interest, if you started off with not very much. The need for risk. The need to find the quicksilver flows of money in quantity, money in abundance, and to divert some of it. Money coming, money going. Money as gold, as paper, as credit. Money breathing in and out of the recesses of the economy like the sound of a man sleeping. Until her thoughts lost all coherence, and she wandered through other bedrooms where boys hung model aeroplanes from the ceiling, but unscathed, unburned, for this was merely a dream visit, light-footed, consequenceless.

Light woke her, brazing its way gold and green through the window. A moment of panic, but her watch showed her that it was only five o'clock, first light of a high-summer dawn. Up and to the window. Anything visible up the lane that shouldn't be? Of course not. The simplest explanation, after all, was that when Geoff had dropped off to sleep so had she, and everything else had been a dream. The bad dream of a night that had gone wrong. Having thought this, she seized on it as the version of things that was going to be the truth from now on. And she gathered her things, and nearly made it out of the room before Geoff woke. He looked at her sleepily. She looked at him and was obliged to agree with her greedy self of the evening before that he was beautiful.

'You're going?' he mumbled. 'How do I find you again?'

'Sweet boy,' she said vaguely, and fled.

There was cool in the air outside, and freshness from the dew. Birdsong louder than traffic. A short walk in the dawn took her to a bus stop, an early bus took her to a Tube station just opening up, and the first southbound train took her home. All in good time for her to shed the silver silk, and bathe and drink a cup of tea and eat a piece of toast; and then to set off once more, a unit in the tide of office workers, reaching the Mariner Building yawning but on time, as if nothing had happened at all.

LEADEN HALL
SEPTEMBER-OCTOBER 1939

1

Iris heard the declaration of war on her landlady's radio, downstairs in Clapham. It was a Sunday afternoon, and the announcement felt more like a confirmation than an event. The world had already changed. For days the buses and the Tubes had been stuffed with children on their way to evacuation trains. Sandbag walls and sentries had appeared outside town halls, railway stations, bridges. Bobbing silver balloons were already normal in the sky. Iris had held the stepladder while Mr Metcalfe from upstairs fixed blackout curtains to all the curtain rails.

But then the world went on changing. After the prime minister's voice had come to an end – not so much defiant as apologetic, Iris thought, like a doctor breaking bad news – and Mrs Tilly had clicked off the radiogram, a sound arose in the distance. A low wail winding downwards and up again, as if an animal had got its tail trapped in a door which was being alternately squeezed tight and loosened. The residents of number three stared at each other.

'Is that . . . ?' said Mrs Tilly.

'Crikey, they didn't waste much time,' said Mr Metcalfe.

'I'll say,' said Miss Grant, who had the room along the landing.

And hesitantly they all made their way out of the back door, to the scar of raw earth where Mr Metcalfe had destroyed Mrs Tilly's raspberry canes to dig in the Anderson shelter. It had rained, and there were a couple of inches of muddy water inside. They sat on the two bits of garden benching Mr Metcalfe had dragged in, and tried to keep their feet up.

'Do we shut the door? I suppose we must do,' said Mrs Tilly.

'Not much use, else,' said Mr Metcalfe, and pulled the corrugated iron across and latched it. 'We should bring in a hurricane lantern or something,' he said after a minute, for it was now very dark, with just a couple of cracks of light showing.

'If we're spared,' said Mrs Tilly.

They waited. The siren stopped, and then there was just the smell of wet earth, and the hush of a South London Sunday afternoon outside. Quieter than usual. Traffic noise dwindled down to almost nothing. All over Clapham, people holding their breath. No one knew what a skyful of bombers would sound like, but there were no candidate noises. Just birdsong. A bumblebee over in the undestroyed herbaceous border.

'I've left the roast in the oven,' said Mrs Tilly.

'I don't think I could eat anything just now,' said Miss Grant, who was a floorwalker at the Bon Marché. 'My stomach's all clenched up.'

'How long d'you think it takes?' said Iris. 'You know, between the warning and them getting here?'

'I think I read five or ten minutes?' said Mr Metcalfe.

'It must be that now,' said Iris.

'Maybe it's a false alarm?' said Miss Grant.

'Steady on,' said Mr Metcalfe. 'We can't know that, can we. We just have to hang on here. But I'll tell you, this is being very educational. I am building up a little list in my head right now of stuff we ought to have in here. And on it is: A, light; B, some duckboards or something to stick on the floor; C, a good book.'

'A pack of cards,' said Miss Grant.

'My knitting,' said Mrs Tilly.

'What about you, Miss Hawkins?' Mr Metcalfe asked Iris, when she didn't contribute. 'What would be your idea for a shelter rekwiseet?'

Some privacy to be afraid in, she didn't say. *A bottle of champagne*, she didn't say. *A good-looking man*, she didn't say. 'Oh, I'm in favour of the book *and* the cards,' she said.

'Or – and here's a thought,' said Mr Metcalfe, 'maybe a song-book? Something we could have a bit of a sing-song to?'

'Oh I *couldn't*,' said Miss Grant.

It was half an hour before the All Clear went. No bombers, no bombs, no rain of destruction. They trooped back indoors, and the Sunday dinner was a little scorched but not ruined.

Then it happened again in the middle of the night. On the stairs she met Mr Metcalfe descending with an electric torch and a mystery novel. Mrs Tilly brought knitting, but Miss Grant turned out not to possess a pack of cards, and as the air raid again failed to materialise she dropped off against Mr Metcalfe's shoulder.

The morning came, and it was Monday morning, so Iris went to work. She caught the Northern Line to London Bridge, as usual. She walked across the bridge to the City, as usual. The Mariner Building was in fact marginally closer to Bank station, the next stop on the Tube line, but she liked to begin the day with the Thames, with the sight of the spires and towers and blocks and alleys of the Square Mile not enclosing her, warren-like, as it did when she was inside it, but for once visibly spread out into a panorama, apparent as a single spectacle.

And there it was above the water, veiled in its perpetual blue mist of coal smoke: a grand higgledy-piggledy ribbon of new marble and sooty old brick, stretching from the dome of St Paul's in the west to the Tower in the east, gradually picking up definition as it drew closer, ramifying out into an endless mismatching crackle-pattern of windows, with the broad roadway of the new bridge pointing into the middle of it like an arrow to the heart. It did not look as if it was doomed, whatever Miles Ormond said. It looked huge, tricky and rich. Not quite what it had been, maybe, before the century's wars began, when the spoils of the whole world flowed to it, but still able to draw in every dawn and push out every nightfall the crowd that now surrounded Iris, to serve wealth or the hope of wealth. Ten thousand men in dark suits and bowler hats walked northward with her, every age from fifteen to seventy. She supposed the younger ones would soon be swapping this uniform for the khaki one. There were fewer women, but still too many to count, dressed slightly less predictably yet still all in dim and sombre colours as she was herself, turned out with appropriate gravity to enter into the presence of money.

Money was experiencing a hiccup this morning, though – this first morning of war. The Stock Exchange, as announced before the weekend, was closed for a week. There were no deals to be done by Cornellis & Blome, no jobbers to be instructed, no constant flow of prices to be monitored. Up on the ninth floor, when she turned on the teleprinter, chattering confirmations came in from each of the dedicated phone lines C&B maintained to those they dealt with most often. *MON 6337*, the machine typed on its roll of paper. *MON 8414. MON 1119. BAN 762. HOL 4745.* But then nothing. Lines open, no traffic.

Instead, Mr Cornellis came into the typing pool after the morning conference, followed by Mr Smythe the chief clerk, and the post boy pushing a trolley stacked high with leather-bound client records.

'Ladies,' said Cornellis. 'Good morning.'

'Good morning, Mr Cornellis,' they chorused: Iris at the teleprinter, Delia and Maude and Sonia and Mrs Sinclair, keeper of the petty cash. *We sound like a school assembly*, thought Iris. Cornellis did not ordinarily deal with the typists direct.

'Hm, hrmph,' said Cornellis, with a pained twitch of his pencil moustache. There were partners in some brokerages, Iris knew, who put on something of a swagger when they came down among their female employees. Cockerel in the henhouse, sultan in the harem. Not Cornellis. Rumour had it that he led a life of great and uxorious propriety up in Hemel Hempstead with Mrs C: Rhoda Cornellis, née Blome.

'Ladies,' he said, 'His Majesty's Government in its wisdom has decided to register all foreign stocks held by British citizens. Any share that is traded on an overseas exchange, or that pays a dividend in any currency outside the sterling area, has to be declared. On one of these: the Bank of England's form S1, which Mr Smythe is holding up. Thank you, Smythe. You will have observed that we have here a gigantic stack of them, freshly emerged from the bowels of Threadneedle Street. I am afraid this is because a form S1, with covering letter, has now to be posted to every one of our private clients who has dealt with us in the past ten years. You will find the addresses in the client books. Each S1 is to be accompanied by a typed copy of this covering letter, which Mr Smythe has drafted. Smythe? Thank you. Our hope is that the whole tedious business can be accomplished before the Exchange reopens. My thanks. My apologies.'

'Sonia?' said Mrs Sinclair as Cornellis led away his embassy of men. 'Be a pet and run down to the post office on Eastcheap and get us . . . five hundred tuppenny stamps. That should start us off.'

'Ain't that Keith's job?' said Sonia. Keith was the post boy, and her enemy.

'Maybe, but Keith'd take forever, and we need to get our skates on. Go on, get along with you.'

Five hundred envelopes, stamped and addressed. Five hundred S1s, folded in thirds to fit the envelope. Five hundred letters beginning *Dear [insert name here], we regret to inform you that pursuant to Treasury Order S.R.&O. 1939 No.950* . . . And that only took them into the Hs in the client books. Five hundred more stamps. And then another five hundred, by which time completed S1s had started to come back, and had to be sorted by the stocks they listed. Canadian Pacific Railway. Crédit Lyonnais. Westinghouse. Svenska Handelsbanken. Dayton Tool & Die. US Steel. Rio de Janeiro Electric. Paramount Pictures. Stacks building up, held together with rubber bands as they grew fatter. It was interesting, in a way, seeing that Miles Ormond had been right. All of these international shares were obviously in line for liquidation, on the block for the war effort and only waiting for the chop. They were no refuge at all for an investor wanting to keep their capital out of the war's reach. But, as a set of tasks, the processing of the S1s was unbelievably monotonous. The same letter to type, over and over again; the same hand movements for folding, licking, sticking, writing. *My career in high finance*, thought Iris. *I might as well be working in a factory*. She could have typed *We regret to inform you* once into the teleprinter, and then set it to print five hundred times onto the output roll – but the teleprinter produced text in jittering, grey, uneven capitals, and the paper was thin stuff with holes at the edges, more like newsprint or even toilet paper than the cream-laid pages Cornellis & Blome thought fit for client correspondence. So on they typed.

When the market reopened, and the teleprinter came back to life, there was a burst of delayed orders to handle, mostly Sells, but not a big one. Volumes were low; the 30-Share Index dropped, but the prices drifted downwards rather than plummeting. Most of the bad news of war in Europe seemed to have been priced in, and as Iris worked out from reading discarded copies of the *Financial Times* on the train home, the new regulations were designed to discourage people from cashing out, unless it was to buy War Loan at three per cent. There was some of that, from the retired-colonel section of the client base, but as a Jewish-owned firm C&B was relatively light on retired colonels. The average client, as Iris now knew from handwriting their names on endless envelopes, was a suburban doctor or lawyer or businessperson, or the widow of one. Volume, anyway, was right down; and this was probably a good thing, given that the S1s went on and on, right through September and into early October. They were busy enough.

Day by day she typed, closed envelopes, opened envelopes, sorted S1s into piles. Day by day she tended the teleprinter, carefully receiving the start-of-day statements from MON 6337 and the rest, carefully delivering the printed-out order confirmations to the brokers' room, at four o'clock carefully sending out the long list of London closing prices to Barracloughs, who as brokers on the Sheffield exchange were the competition, but allowed to pay C&B for information in slight arrears. Day by day, at ten in the morning, she quietly fulfilled her private arrangement with Barracloughs, and sent them the absolutely current prices for the five most highly traded London shares. For this they paid her two guineas a week, mounting up nicely now in an obscure bank account. To begin with, she had betrayed C&B with great caution, waiting till the room was empty or backs were turned, and laboriously deleting the record of the message. Now she didn't bother. No one ever checked on what she was doing with the teleprinter, because no one but her understood how it worked.

The bombers continued not to come. The war, once Poland had been overrun, seemed to be a matter of distant engagements between battleships. The men did start to disappear, gradually at first so you weren't quite sure you were seeing a change, and then unmissably. On the Tube, on London Bridge in the morning rush, in the office, in the streets, the women were the majority now. Keith the post boy went. Sonia moped. Iris took her turn carrying the bales of filled-in S1s over to the booming subterranean hall at the Bank of England where they were tabulated, and all of the converging streams of the things were being brought in by girls in their twenties, with a subfusc coat and gas-mask case at their hip. Under the glazed-tile vaulting of the Bank, the murmur of conversation was higher than it had been before – higher in pitch; and once she'd noticed that there, she noticed it again and again, everywhere, in shops, in queues, at bus stops. The silver dress stayed in the wardrobe in Clapham. It might have been wisdom to erase the memory of Wildwood Terrace by going out and finding some suitable chap, some simple and direct chap, but suitable chaps of all varieties were suddenly in short supply. That was what she told herself, at any rate. The other reason, present as a faint twist of dread rather than an actual thought, was the association between the dress and Geoff's tears. She left it in the wardrobe in case it was still quietly dripping.

The biggest difference was the darkness. Bombers or no bombers, from the very first day of the war the blackout regulations had been enforced, and London after dark was now a dim maze, with the occasional searchlights in the sky the only bright thing, and the ground all the blacker then by contrast. Buildings were coal-black cliffs, pavements were vistas of black on black, grey on black, black on grey, which you squinted along unsure whether the obscure stir of movement you saw was a trick of the eye or another pedestrian about to collide with you head-on. You didn't realise how much artificial light there usually was until it was all taken away. The headlights of cars and taxis had been papered over, leaving a slit through which a mere thread of light came wavering over the tarmac. The papers were full of stories of accidents, of walkers mashed against pillar boxes by drivers unable to see the edge of the roadway. Inside buses, the lamps had all been covered by perforated cowls, so you travelled in a speckled gloom, peering out through a diamond-shaped hole in the middle of the window covering, trying to guess whether you'd reached your stop or not. It wasn't too bad to begin with, getting to and from work. The late-summer light lingered in the September evenings, and Iris could be back in Clapham before the city wrapped on its shroud. But as the autumn days shortened, the blackout enfolded the evening journey home ever more tightly. Despite the announcement that this year British Summer Time would run for an extra month, by the second half of October she was coming out of C&B into dusk, with shadow filling up the deep streets of the City like a rising liquid, and then into unambiguous night.

One evening she was kept late. She had carried a few more S1s over to the Bank at the end of the day – the flow was dwindling at last – and then found, as she walked back into the office to collect her things, that Cornellis needed her to set up a call for him on the teleprinter. He couldn't do it himself, of course. He stood over her while she dialled a number he read aloud from his pocketbook. Not one of the subscriber circuits belonging to the regular counterparties: a number she didn't know at all. The office emptied around them, the last light fading from the sky over St Paul's. Mrs Sinclair hesitated.

'No, no, I'll lock up,' Cornellis said to her. 'This may take a little while.' (The days of the keys being passed to Mr Seaton downstairs were not yet upon them.)

They got their answer, and the line opened.

'Now,' said Cornellis, 'Miss – ah – Miss . . . ?'

'Hawkins,' said Iris. 'Iris Hawkins.'

'Miss Hawkins: this is rather confidential. How do I make sure that I really am talking to the *right* people?'

'You press this button, sir.' She indicated the WHO ARE YOU? key.

'Go on, then, please.'

She pressed it, and the printer obligingly chattered out OXO 8933. Cornellis checked it against his pocketbook.

'Very well,' he said. 'Now, if you wouldn't mind, we'll just change places, and perhaps you'd avert your eyes. – But don't go,' he added hastily as she gathered up her bag. 'I'll need you to make this blasted machine stop again.'

And seating himself at the keyboard, he began to peck out a message with maddening slowness on his two index fingers, hunting for each letter and number individually. After he had typed thirty characters or so, the teletype refused to accept any more. He looked up at her helplessly.

'Carriage return, sir,' she said. 'That button.'

Grey became black outside the window. Then, black with a pallid gleam in it. The moon was coming up.

Cornellis spent ten laborious minutes typing a message that would have taken her about thirty seconds. Iris did keep her eyes averted, but not because she wasn't interested in what this after-hours, boss-only communication could be. Unlike Cornellis, she knew that the last outgoing message sat in the machine's memory until the next one was sent. If she wanted to read it, she could print it out first thing tomorrow morning.

'There,' said Cornellis at last. 'Is there a button for sending it?'

'You have been sending it, sir, every time you finish a line. Just type "END" now, so they know there's no more to come.'

'Carriage return, "END",' muttered Cornellis, slow fingers moving.

The printer began to chatter out a reply, fast. Whoever was on the other end, at OXO-for-Oxford 8933, they either had a secretary they trusted a lot more than Cornellis did Iris, or they could type themselves. The answer appeared to be a list of eight- or nine-digit numbers, one per line. There was no salutation or name attached.

'Hmph,' said Cornellis when the printer stopped. 'And how do I . . . get that off the roll?'

'You tear it like this,' said Iris, leaning in past him. He smelled of a citrussy cologne.

'Very good, very good. Well; thank you for your help, and thank you for your, ah, discretion.'

'I'll turn it off now, shall I, sir?'

'Do. And then I'd better lock up.'

They rode down to the lobby of the Mariner Building in the lift together, a polite smile stuck to Cornellis's face in lieu of anything to say. The little bulb in the lift was the last bit of brightness. The lobby was black; the street outside was a canyon of black, painted with a band of pale moonlight at roof level but still itself shadowed as deep as Hades. There seemed to be nobody around. Everyone had hurried away as fast as may be. The wobbling double thread of a pair of headlights came towards them and Cornellis, spying a taxi, flagged it down. 'Well, good night,' he said, raising his hat to her, and then she was alone.

The Mariner Building stood on a sloping side street. Left and down took you to Upper Thames Street and then to the river, where in the crack between warehouses the shimmer of moon on water could be seen. But all the streets there led under, not to, London Bridge. She turned right, and up. Deep and deeper shade. A rumble and a brief shift in the shadows at the junction up ahead suggested a bus going by, but hers were the only feet on Mariner Lane. There was a walk which she, along with every other Londoner, had perfected for nights when you couldn't see your legs, and didn't know what sudden holes or ridges or obstacles the pavement might be hiding: higher-stepping than usual, with a tentative, probing motion as you put each foot down. It made for slow progress.

The hesitant click, and then click, and then click of her court shoes reached the round postbox at the end of the Mariner Building, into which so many of the outbound S1s had been stuffed, on their way to the lawyers and widows of the suburbs. There was an alley there, no more than a dead-ended slot, where the building's rubbish bins stood in a row. It was lightless as ink now, as an ocean abyss into which sunlight had never penetrated, and never would; and anyone in that darkness looking towards her passing its mouth could only have detected her as the faintest, faintest of moving outlines. An ambiguous swirling of dark on dark. Yet she was suddenly seized by the conviction that she was being *seen*. That an attention as powerful as any searchlight, though invisible to her, was pushing through the darkness – was ignoring the darkness, as no obstruction at all – and gripping her in a remorseless focus, crystal-clear and implacable. It had happened before. It was the same as the feeling in the dormer window at Wildwood Terrace two months ago. Her body recognised it immediately. A flutter of panic ran through her; she could hear her own breath coming stammeringly, in little gasps against her teeth. But her mind was reluctant. It clung stubbornly to the version of the world in which a bad night's adventure had led to a bad dream.

'Hello?' she said, making herself stand still. 'Hello? Is there anyone there?'

She peered into the abyss of ink. Nothing; not a hint of movement except, after a minute of staring, the swimming purple blots and flares created by her own eyes to fill vacancy. No sound at all. Nothing. There was a smell, maybe. Probably the sour rot of rubbish, only perhaps more . . . mildewed.

I will just check, said her defiant reason. It made her fumble in her bag for a box of safety matches. And finding it, fumble one out. And with box in one hand and match in the other, strike it shakily, and hold the flame up in front of her.

And yelp, and drop it. Because what she saw in the flaring light for the instant before the match became a downward bright streak was a shape only four or five feet away from her. The shape of a man in a hat and an overcoat, only more massive than that, bulkier; and with its head lying flat on its shoulder as no head should; and with a face that, from this distance, she could see was made of newspaper. Not covered in newspaper, not masked in newspaper:

made *of* newsprint, old yellowed paper with smeary blocks of black type on it, in an arrangement nobody could mistake for eyes and mouth, only moving, and creasing, and silently swelling and puckering, the skin of something alive within. There was an impression of age about the whole thing. It was old newspaper, it was a battered black hat, it was a thin and ragged old black coat. Worn, dirty stuff, clothes that had been out in the rain and the wind for a long, long time, rotting in place on a body that wasn't a body.

The moment the light was gone – the moment the sight of the thing was withdrawn – she wanted to disbelieve in it again, urgently, passionately. But something – some lingering phosphorescence from the burned-out match, some stray photon from the rising moon bounced to her off looming black walls – alerted her to fast movement. Her retinas informed her instincts. Her instincts ignored her mind and shouted at her body instead. She ducked aside. The newspaper fist that had been coming her way, accelerating on the end of a roughly arm-shaped tube of fluid, hit the pillar box instead. Whatever lived inside the newspaper skin, liquid though it might be, was stronger and heavier than any limb of bone and muscle. It hit the cast-iron wall of the postbox with a resonant clang, and a rending of metal. *Run, prey!* said her instincts.

She ran.

She fled uphill towards the junction, trusting the paving stones to be smooth, the roadway not to trip her, and after her came the thing. Over the sound of her own panting breath she could hear it behind her. Not a sound of breath. A pouring sound, a sloshing sound almost: the noise of whatever the fluid inside it was, denser and heavier than mercury, flowing into the new position for each step.

Was it close? Was it getting closer? Was there an intensifying smell of mildew? She didn't dare to glance back. She bolted round the corner onto Cannon Street with her eyes wide and her arms stretched out in front of her as if grabbing for something, anything safe. Another streetscape carved in coal and capped in moonlight surrounded her. Still no people; no passer-by to seize on for help. But there was a bus coming. She could hear the grumble of its engine getting louder behind her. And something else: as she had come round the corner, she realised, the conviction of being seen, the insect-on-a-microscope-slide sensation, had flicked off. Did this mean it was still in Mariner Lane?

She ran on towards the bus stop, bag and gas-mask case flailing and whacking against her, and now she did risk a backward look. The watery gleams of the bus's headlamps added just enough illumination for her to pick out the dark mouth of the lane – and the blot of moving darkness emerging from it. The ray of the thing's attention locked back on, gripping her like a returning nausea. It was still coming all right. But not, in fact, that fast. The movement of its legs in the dank old coat was jerky, with a tiny pause as it poured itself from one step into the next. It was strong, it was inexorable, but walking did not come naturally to it, let alone running. Its mimicking of a body was partly horrible because it was effortful. Its movements were as wrong as a dining table's would be, if it came to scuttling life, and pursued you caterpillar-style on many wooden legs.

Bus stop, bus stop! Her pursuer was fifty feet behind her when the double-decker overtook her and sighed to a halt. She jumped on the open back platform and yanked fiercely twice on the bell cord to give the start-again signal. The conductor emerged from the gloom to remonstrate, but the driver had obediently taken his foot off the clutch and ground back into gear, and was pulling away from the kerb, with maddening slowness at first, then faster and faster.

'Here!' the conductor was saying. 'Communications with the driver by passengers is strictly prohibited, thank you!'

But all her attention was concentrated on the blob of shadow coming up the pavement, trying to speed up its jerky-fluid stalking.

It was failing, and when it dropped down she thought it was giving up, until she saw that it had rolled itself somehow into a waist-high ball, a mostly black ball with a revolving flicker of newspaper-white in it, and was coming bowling on along the pavement after the bus – across the intersection by the Monument to the Great Fire, and then in a rolling blur up the pedestrian walkway onto the moonlit bridge. She whimpered.

'Miss? Are you all right?' the conductor asked. He shone a dim little torch at her face and, taking in the wild expression, abruptly switched from officious to fatherly. 'Oh, I see. You've had a spot of bother in the blackout, haven't you? It's like a licence for no-goodniks, that's what I tell my own girls. But don't you worry, you're safe now. You come and sit down. You come and sit down, my dear.'

She pointed behind them. The conductor peered, but clearly couldn't see anything.

'You think he's still after you? Love, he can't run faster'n a bus, I promise you. I'll tell you what, though. I'll give Fred up front the special signal – that's for me to do, not you,' he added, with a brief return of officious, 'and he'll put his foot down and we'll miss out the next stop or two. Okey-dokey?'

He gave three dings on the cord, and the double-decker shuddered up to a full thirty miles an hour. Then he put his hand under her elbow and tried to steer her to a seat. But she wouldn't go until she saw the black ball stop rolling, defeated, and unfold again into a man-shape; a stumpy pillar of dark by the railing of the long dim bridge over the silver-strewn river, dwindling, staring after her with its paper face, and at last being left behind in the gloom, its grip on the sight of her fading and dying away too.

II

Next morning, Iris rang in sick. There was a telephone in Mrs Tilly's front hall, but it was reserved for grand emergencies, and it was right next to the parlour where Mrs T sat in the daytime and knitted. She didn't fancy being overheard as she lied. Instead, she dressed as if she were going to work and went out to the phone box where their road bent towards the common. She inserted her pennies, dialled the office, pressed button 'A', and told Mrs Sinclair that she had 'flu.

'Oh, you poor thing . . .'

'I'm sorry,' said Iris, in what she hoped was a convincingly hoarse and feeble voice.

'Straight to bed with a hot drink, that's where you want to go.'

'I will. I'll do exactly that.'

'All right then, dear. I'll let Mr Cornellis know. But do hurry back when you can. That machine of yours is a mystery to me, and Delia'll try her best but to be honest she's a little bit afraid of it.'

And if Delia started pressing buttons, Cornellis's outbound message of the night before would be lost into the ether. Damn.

'As soon as I can,' she promised, and stabbed at button 'B' with her forefinger. But the second penny had already been used up, and no change came back.

She was irritated altogether, in fact. No, more than that: furious. She had woken up in a rage. It was as if the tide of last night's terror had gone out and left a beach of anger behind it. She was raging at having been so frightened, and she was raging at not being able to go in to work, at her life, *her* life, being interfered with. And she raged all the more because, underneath it, she could tell that the fear was not so very far away. The tide might come back in. The day was bright now, with a high grey autumn sky above her as she strode along the edge of the common in her burgundy beret. But night would fall again. The dark would come back, the blackout would engulf the city, and from whatever cranny of darkness it was hiding in – she felt sure, somehow, that it was a creature that required the night to move freely – the thing with the newspaper face could emerge again to hunt. Before that, she had to do something about it. She was not really sure what. But she knew where it came from, didn't she? If last night had been real – and it had been, hideously real – then what she had seen in the lamplight outside Wildwood Terrace had been real too. That was where the thing had seen her, where it had got the scent of her and followed her somehow two months later to Cornellis & Blome. Somehow, somehow, she had picked it up from her night with Geoff. Like a burr stuck to her skirt. Or a nasty rash. Yes: some people, if you made the mistake of sleeping with them, left you with a rash, or regrets. This one apparently left you with a monster. It was his doing – somehow. She couldn't *go* to Wildwood Terrace, any more than she could go to Mariner Lane today. Even in daylight, those were the two places which she knew the thing was definitely haunting. She needed to find Geoff elsewhere. There was only one other possibility she could think of, and that was at his work, at the television studio at Alexandra Palace. Very likely it was all shut up by now, and he called up and long gone. But it was all she could think of, so she was going. She was going to find him, and to confront him, and to demand – to demand – oh, something. That he make it stop. That she be handed her life back. That she be returned to the reasonable world she had inhabited before she bit her lip at him, the one where she only had war, finance and global conflagration to worry about. Something! She didn't know what! Anger, anger, anger: hold on to the anger. She had meant to make sure she never laid eyes on Geoff again, and now look at her.

The old fellow who sold the *Daily Herald* by the Tube station steps, and who had a line or two of creaky banter for her most mornings, saw her face and thought better of it.

There was a strange feeling of truancy about travelling across London against the flow of people going to work. It was already later than she usually went in, what with her having waited till she knew Mrs Sinclair would be in the office to make her call, but for the journey underground from Clapham up to the City there were still lots of people around her, reading and strap-hanging; mostly women, as always now, and men past military age, hemming and hawing at their newspapers. *RAF SCARES BERLIN*, said the front page opposite her. But the train slid on through London Bridge without her getting off; and there, and at Bank, the office-goers all gathered themselves and departed, and beyond King's Cross, travelling north when the crowds were all headed south, she was alone on the hard tartan upholstery, looking at her reflection jiggling blurrily in the curved window opposite, and trying not to think about the tunnels she rattled through, deep in the roots of London where it was always night.

The station for Alexandra Palace was at Wood Green, far to the north of the parts of the city she knew. But when she came up the escalator to the exit, all brand-new white concrete and drum-shaped brickwork, she emerged into a landscape that was a variant, confusingly, of home. Not recent home; not the bedsits and rented rooms in which she'd perched these last few years. Old home. Childhood home. Suburban hills and trees – the net of the city loosening into something which didn't quite arrive into sleepy commuterland, but was recognisably on the way there. Which was nearly Watford. Barrage balloons floated overhead, but she knew these streets of red-brick cottages with neat front gardens, these new semis with a garage for an Austin 7, these scaled-down two-storey department stores, these tea shops named Kardomah and Shangri-La and Mon Repos. The young men were gone, the young women were busy behind tills or in offices, but the mothers were out, pushing prams or holding by the hand the children that had mostly been brought back to the city now that it seemed the bombers weren't coming. She followed a tramline uphill, a busy murmur of family around her in which she felt like an interloper, forced to return where she had no business being.

Up to the low crest of a hill, and by bridge across a cutting where mainline trains sped by snorting smoke, and then she was on the green slopes of a much higher hill, where a skirt of parkland swept up to a long facade of Victorian brick. It might be called a palace, but it was more music-hall than regal, with showy glass roofs and big arches built to beckon in the crowds to a good time – crowds of forty years ago, in long skirts and straw hats. At the near end, it broke out incongruously into a mighty steel radio mast that was not Victorian at all. A flat terrace in front was embellished with endless statues on plinths: nymphs and gods technically, she supposed, but again in fact more like old-style bathing beauties and circus strongmen. Between them she could see a row of grey vans parked. They had *BBC* stencilled on the side, and as she plodded upwards towards them she felt dismally certain that she was going to arrive to find nothing but the last stages of something being dismantled, an empty house just before the removals firm departs.

'Have they all gone, in the television studio?' she asked a man leaning on the bonnet of a van and having a smoke.

'Most of 'em, love,' he said. 'You looking for someone in particular?'

'I was just . . . Where's the way in, then?'

He pointed. 'In there and upstairs. Studio A, left; Studio B, right. Transmission, on through B at the end of the corridor. Cheer up, love,' he added. 'You can always come back and keep *me* company.'

He was a monkey-faced fifty-something. She gave him the Eyebrows of Derision, and he laughed.

Inside, the palace had main passages like the tunnels of a football stadium, and smaller corridors off them that seemed to be mainly arteries for pipes and thick bundles of wiring, marching along the tops of white-painted walls in festoons. She went up a staircase of echoing stone, bare and institutional, and through a glass door into what should have been a diminutive reception area, with a desk and two waiting-room chairs and a months-old copy of the *Radio Times* set out for visitors to leaf through. No one there, though; a staleness and a stillness in the air. She pushed through the swing doors beyond, and was in a passageway with no ceiling. It went on up into dim space above, like the wings of a theatre, and against the walls it was indeed stacked with what looked like tall theatrical flats, only painted entirely in monochrome, white and black and grey; so many of them that the passage was practically choked, and only a narrow alleyway to thread through for walking remained.

'Hello?' she called hopelessly. 'Hello?'

There was, not a reply but at least a sound of human presence, off to the right, so she pushed through that way. The passage opened out, into a rectangular box of a space whose near end was crowded with costume racks. A rubber tangle of cables led across the middle part of the floor to three cumbersome devices like coal scuttles on pedestals that must be cameras – and beyond them there was a tiny parquet dance floor, and a tiny set with in-tilting trompe-l'œil wings, designed to give the effect of a whole ballroom in a space no larger than a reasonably proportioned bathroom. This, presumably, was where the stars of stage and screen that Lall successfully tempted with thirty guineas reproduced their West End acts in miniature, carefully keeping their elbows in. The noise of humans was coming from a slot of a door in the corner.

She put her head round. An even tighter space, metal-walled like a companionway in the bowels of a ship, with a sliding door on the left into a control room, and steps at the far end from which came a faint electric hum. Out of the control room door stepped the handsome, suited presence of Michael Frobisher, head down, marking something on a clipboard with a pencil.

'Hello?' she said.

He looked up and frowned. 'Yes?' he said. 'I'm sorry, who are you? You know, the general public are really not supposed to— Oh. *Oh.* Oh, good grief.' The frown had been replaced by a smile of comfortable, middle-aged lubricity. 'You're – you're . . .' He snapped his fingers, but he had lost her name. 'You're the very decisive dollybird who carried off our Geoffrey that night, aren't you?'

'Guilty as charged,' said Iris, investing a smile of her own in him.

'I suppose you're looking for him, and not me.'

''Fraid so. But I should think he's long gone, isn't he?'

'No, no. They shut us down when war was declared – in the middle of a Mickey Mouse cartoon, in fact – and all the showbiz side of things folded up immediately. I'm only here today to see the props and the flats and so on carried off to storage. But Dallas and his technical boys are still working, at least for another day or two. Apparently the transmitter has to be handed over in good order to— Well, I'd better not go into that. But he's here. Would you like me to find him?'

'Yes, please.'

'Then wait right here.'

Frobisher disappeared up the stairs at the far end with a jaunty flourish. She could hear him calling, 'Geoff! Geoff, old boy! Have I got some good news for *you*!'

But the Geoff who appeared down the steps a couple of minutes later, Frobisher grinning behind him, did not seem so sure her appearance was good news. He was dressed in a brown lab coat, and he seemed to have learned a new expression since she saw him last: wary.

'Hallo,' he said neutrally. 'I thought I wasn't going to see you again.'

There was no point in denying that. Two months of silence told their own story. 'Yes, well,' she said, 'you've kind of made sure I *have* to see you again, haven't you?'

'What do you mean?'

'I mean that I've got a bone to pick with you.'

Geoff frowned, nonplussed, but behind him she could see Frobisher's expression changing, as he jumped to the wrong conclusion about why a girl would seek out a boy she hadn't wanted to meet again, two months after a careless evening.

'Ah!' he said. 'That kind of conversation. Why don't you two, um, young people go and find a more private spot. But Geoffrey, old son – come and talk to me if you're in need of, well, *recommendations*. Yes? Nice to see you again,' he added to Iris, ducking back through the control room door with an inclination of his head, and something pained in the smile lines round his eyes, as if he recognised what was happening – what he thought was happening – all too well.

She'd have bet that the innocent she'd bedded wouldn't have understood what Frobisher meant. But this new and slightly altered Geoff rounded on her, when he'd led her back to the corridor full of sets, and said, 'You're pregnant?'

'What would you do about it if I were?' she said, feeling that a bit of squirming was the least he could offer her, under the circumstances.

'I'd start by finding out the facts. Are you?'

Farewell Don Quixote, apparently. She was annoyed to find herself slightly sorry.

'No.'

'Then what are you doing here? Apart from making more entertainment for the people I work with.'

'Oh, poor Geoffrey. Diddums, did they tease you?'

'Shut up. What are you doing here?'

'Like you don't know.'

'I *don't* know. I don't know anything about you. I don't know your second name, I don't know why you picked me out that night. I don't know why you vanished in the morning. What do you *want*?'

Too much didn't make sense here. Geoff seemed unsure whether he was angry she'd gone, or angry she'd come back. But anger was definitely the mood for him too – it seemed he had a temper – not the sick triumph you might expect, if you'd set some supernatural fishing line and had successfully used terror to reel a reluctant lover back to you. Did that sound like Geoff, in either of the versions of him she'd seen? The naked foal, and this indignant young man with hurt feelings? No. Guilt would have made sense as well, but he wasn't writhing either.

'I want you,' she said, too angry herself to pause and to try to work any of this out, 'to call off that *thing* you sent after me.'

'What?' he said.

'The *thing*. Your monster. Your creature with the newspaper face.'

'With the . . . *what*?'

He was staring. Iris felt a kind of panic at having named the monster, even in this passageway crammed with flimsy makebelieve. To name it, to speak of it aloud, was to take the last step in admitting it to the world. Some small part of her had gone on hoping that, unnamed, the thing might dissolve all by itself back into bad dream. Now she surrendered that hope.

'You know,' she said desperately. 'You must know. The thing that hangs about in the night outside your house in Hampstead. Under the lamp-post? In a rotting old coat? With a body like a horrible gas bag. Only horribly strong. It followed me to Cornellis & Blome. It was waiting for me in the blackout. It chased me. It tried to – to . . .'

She faltered. He was still staring, but his expression now had disdain and a kind of dreadful pity in it.

'Oh God, you're mad,' he said. 'I should have known something was off from the way you jumped on me. Normal people don't behave like that, do they.'

Her mouth had fallen open.

'You—' she said. 'You – you listen to me. I am *not* mad. I fucked you because I fancied you. It may not have been a sensible thing to do – Lord knows I wish I hadn't, now – but it was perfectly sane, thank you very much—'

'And normal girls don't use language like that. Look,' said Geoff, 'I can see you're very upset, but I'm not the person who can help you. I'm sorry, but I've had all the nonsense in my life that I can stand, and I'm not going to listen to any more crazy stuff. I think you'd better go.'

'But what am I going to do?'

'Talk to a doctor? I don't know; but please, don't come back here. There's no point. Just to be clear, I'll be gone. I've had my papers, and I report on Monday. Now—'

He tried to take her arm to walk her out, but she shook him off.

'It lives at your house,' she said, backing. 'It's seven feet tall. It smells of mildew. It flows like it's full of mercury.'

'It's in your head.'

'It rolls along like a ball.'

'It's in your head.'

'It's trying to kill me.'

'It can't kill you. It's just in your head. Goodbye.'

He had got her to the reception area. With a grimace, and a gentle shove, he pushed her through the swing doors and bolted them behind her. Then he turned away.

'Iris *Hawkins*!' she shouted at his back. But he turned the corner and disappeared among the monochrome scenery. And then there was nothing else to do but retrace her steps back down and out, to the terrace at the front of the Alexandra Palace, where grey clouds were hurrying now across the southward view over London, and the bright day was inexorably ticking by. Towards afternoon, towards evening, towards night.

III

She spent that evening in Mrs Tilly's parlour, listening to the wireless and making excuses not to go upstairs so she could cling to the company of the other boarders. They came and went; she stuck fast in the corner of the settee. An episode of *The Four Feathers* with terribly-terribly accents was followed by some wailing Sibelius and then *Songs from the Shows*. Miss Grant brought in mugs of sweet tea on a tin tray, Mr Metcalfe made a joke, the coal fire whined softly in the grate. She held tight to all of it as if it were a shield against the dark outside – though what guarantee had she, she thought, that the creature couldn't find its way to her in Clapham if it had found her in the City? That it would be any protection at all to be surrounded by Mrs Tilly's knitting, Miss Grant's coral nail varnish, Mr Metcalfe's nervous moustache, if with a rolling crash the thing splintered the green front door and groped into their midst? None. Unless of course it *was* all in her head. Perhaps she was going mad. Perhaps it would be better to be mad: safer, anyway. Mr Metcalfe handed round his packet of Player's, and she smoked hers so fiercely that the orange crackle as she inhaled seemed as loud as the fire.

'Are you all right, dear?' said Mrs Tilly. 'You seem a bit peaky. You've not moved from that spot since supper.'

Wild-eyed, with a tendency to shoot glances at the curtains, she thought. She said, 'Oh, just a bit under the weather. You know. There might be a bug going round at work.'

'Will you be taking tomorrow off, then, do you think?'

'No, no. No need.' And she couldn't pull two sick days in a row, not if she wanted to keep a clean nose at C&B. Which she did: it was her future, and she was damned if she was going to lose it. Also, there was a kind of dread in her, probably quite illogical, at waiting day after day – the whole weekend, if she bunked off again, because tomorrow was Friday – before facing the place the terror was. If there's something behind you on the dark road, you want to turn around. You don't want to not know whether it's creeping up on you.

'You should take care of your vitamins, like this doctor fellow says,' Mrs Tilly advised. They were listening in a desultory way to a Talk on Nutrition at this point, though Mrs T was yawning.

'Apparently,' put in Mr Metcalfe, 'if you nibble enough raw carrots, you can see in the dark.'

'And wouldn't that be handy, just now,' said Miss Grant.

'Anyway, beauty sleep is the ticket for all of us,' said Mrs Tilly, pushing herself to her feet. She clicked off the radiogram, and the comforting burble of science died away.

'I'll be so handsome in the morning you won't even recognise me,' joked Mr Metcalfe, and Iris's and Miss Grant's eyes met helplessly for an instant. There was something kind to be said, to stop the implication hanging – to banish the thought that he'd really need a Rip Van Winkle-length slumber to do anything about his weak chin – but it didn't spring to either of their lips. He drooped, and departed, and the women followed him upstairs to their separate doors.

The bedroom was chilly, with the kind of cold on the sheets that your skin can't tell apart from dampness. It was silent too. When she'd turned the bedside light off, she could hear the woodwork of the house creaking and settling, and the occasional rumble from the road outside, making a still space in which to strain her ears, for the heavy thud of newspaper feet, the whisk of box hedge against a rancid old coat. Nothing. Nothing and nothing and nothing. How would she ever sleep? Around the edge of the blackout curtain, enough moonlight leaked through to draw a faint, faint rectangle on the wall. She reached under her nightie to give herself the old comfort of her own fingers – but she heard Geoff's voice in her head saying, *Normal girls don't do that.* In her head, in her head, in her head. She screwed her face into the pillow, and slow tears rolled down each side of her nose. *Now I'm as bad as him*, she thought.

She went to work in the morning like someone facing an execution no one else could see. As if, while you walked towards the axe and the beheading block, people were constantly handing you files, asking about the November estimates, loading you with messages to send and letters to type. She had no plan at all, except to try to get out of the office early, at five on the dot or even sooner than that if she could wangle it, and be on her way back over London Bridge before the dusk had entirely bitten. There was nothing in the alley beside the Mariner Building but dustbins; she had looked. On the other hand, the red postbox at the alley mouth was dimpled inwards, the thick cast iron punched in into a socket of crushed metal, the shape of a fingerless fist. She'd passed a puzzled postman rattling the curved little door of the pillar box to try to get the mail out, and having it to yank it, with a tortured screech. That was real. She didn't know whether she was more relieved or more terrified.

Otherwise the day went on with a dreadful ordinariness. Delia, wrestling with the teletype yesterday, had indeed wiped out the record of Mr Cornellis's mysterious after-hours message, so that was gone. There were Buy and Sell orders to send out to jobbers – not many. There were incoming state-of-the-market reports from C&B's correspondents, to retype on carbon paper and take through to the partners' room, once full of men, now containing only Cornellis himself and Smythe the chief clerk. There was the private little piece of treachery with Barracloughs to carry out. There were confirmations of deals done to paste into the client books, new share certificates arriving by messenger – post girl now, not post boy – to log, and then to post onward to clients, each with a flowery letter to be presented to Cornellis for signature. *With the assurance, as ever, of our closest attention,* he would write across the bottom in gleaming brown ink.

But towards the end of morning, Mrs Sinclair answered the phone, and frowned at it.

'Yes, it is,' she said. 'Yes, she does. But we don't normally— Is there an emergency? Are you . . . family? You're not. Then I really— Oh, very well. One moment.'

She covered the receiver with her hand.

'It's for *you*,' she hissed at Iris. 'You *personally*. Now you know better than this, my dear. You know we don't allow it, so make it clear, please, that this is *never* to happen again. And be quick. The line is for *business*.'

'Who is it?' Iris asked, baffled.

'I don't know. An older gentleman. An older gentleman in a bit of a tizzy.'

She passed over the heavy black bone of Bakelite.

'Hello?' said Iris.

'Hallo hallo,' said an educated, elderly male voice which did indeed have a bleat of urgency in it. 'Good morning! Am I speaking to a, a, a, Miss Hawkins?'

'Yes,' said Iris, 'you are: but I'm really not supposed to take personal calls at work, so—'

'I'm sorry to trouble you, and, and, of course there are excellent reasons not to – the old reasons, you know – and I've been weighing it all morning, and where I come down, you see, is that

I *must* speak with you, you see. Because the moral imperative, as it were, prevails over the claims of secrecy. If you understand what I mean.'

'I'm . . . afraid I don't, sir,' said Iris. 'Who *are* you?'

'Oh! My name is Cyprian Hale. I should really have said that first, shouldn't I? Geoffrey's father.'

'Oh,' said Iris. Mrs Sinclair was looking daggers at her.

'Yes,' said the voice, bleating on. 'You see, Geoffrey spoke to me last night – confided in me, even, which I'm afraid is probably rarer than it should be, but he was *most* upset—'

'I'm sorry to hear that,' said Iris as firmly as she could, 'but—'

'—and he said you had told him a ridiculous story about being persecuted by a being with a face made of old newspaper, which had somehow followed you from our little cottage. And, having no idea what you were talking about, he had decided you were quite mad. I'm afraid he was rather explosive on the subject!'

'Was he,' said Iris grimly.

'Oh yes! He seemed to feel, almost, that you had let him down in some way! I was only, with difficulty, able to calm him!'

'Look . . .' began Iris.

'But that, do you see, was why I decided I must take the, ah, ah, *step* of communicating with you myself, today, despite old, um, oaths. Because I do know what you're talking about.'

'You do?'

'Yes. And I think we had better meet, as quickly as possible. Would you be free for lunch?'

Iris usually lunched at the Lyons' in Eastcheap – soup and a bread roll and a cup of tea for sevenpence – but so did Sonia, Delia and Mrs Sinclair. For privacy's sake, it was in the ABC Tea Room two hundred yards further north, on Leadenhall Street, that she awaited Geoffrey's father.

She had wondered whether she would recognise him, but the figure who came through the door matched the voice on the telephone all too exactly. Cyprian Hale had chosen to descend from Hampstead dressed in a loden cloak and a deerstalker hat, carrying a stick with a silver knob. She raised a hand, and he made his way over through the lunchtime crowd with ceremonious dips and turns. Close up, he had a slightly bedraggled mane of white hair, and a flustered look. Maybe a permanently flustered look. His face was very clearly a pink and aged version of Geoff's – he had been a good-looking young man, once – but these eyes darted about uncertainly, and these lips twitched with little impulses towards many expressions that never quite arrived in full, placating smiles and sulky pouts and ironic compressions. Geoff was definite. This man had somehow managed to reach sixty or so while remaining endlessly provisional. You ought to be able, Iris thought abstractedly, to subtract this face from Geoff's and arrive at a remainder which would be a picture of his mother. She'd be . . . a decided woman, with a still, serious mouth.

'Well!' said Hale senior. 'The old Aerated Bread Company! Do you know, in my younger days I used to spend an enormous amount of time in the branch on Ludgate Hill. Practically haunted the place. Spread out my notebooks, and made a tuppeny cup of tea last and last. And I wasn't the only one! Quite a place it was, you know, for the arts and letters, and those of us of a progressive turn of mind. As if they served the Higher Thought along with the currant buns, ha ha. I looked up one day, and there was, and I promise you this is true, Mr George Bernard Shaw large as life and twice as natural, seated at the next table. Well, I hope I didn't intrude, but I could hardly miss the opportunity, so I took my courage in both hands and went *up* to him, and I said—'

And now I'm having to listen to anecdotes about George Bernard Shaw on the way to the gallows, thought Iris.

'Mr Hale,' she interrupted. 'Or is it Reverend Hale?' There was something in the way he moved and held forth that could easily have been vicarish.

'Oh, no no,' he said, a ripple of dismay passing over him. 'Not for many years. Too narrow a container, you see. Wider pastures were required in the end – a more, ah, adventurous field of enquiry.'

'Mr Hale, then. You said you knew about the thing that's chasing me.'

'It shouldn't be, that's the thing. It shouldn't be chasing you. Or anyone. I was given to understand that the instructions were strictly limited. It was to guard the house, and that was absolutely all. Something has clearly gone awry.'

A double-decker bus was going by outside the plate-glass window, surrounded by the rest of the brown-and-grey bustle of daytime London. A puff of steam rose from the tea urn behind the counter. There were crumbs on the tabletop from a previous diner's scone. The woman sitting behind Iris had a fox-fur on with amber-coloured glass eyes. It was all ordinary, and at the same time it felt as if the ordinary surface of things were just a wrapping, waiting to be ripped away.

'Something is trying to *kill* me, Mr Hale.'

'Oh dear me.'

'So if you know anything about it – please do just tell me. Now?'

'That's what I'm here for,' he said. 'But you have to understand – I have to, ah, balance the responsibilities involved. I swore absolute secrecy, you see. No exceptions. Yet this – your present predicament – was quite plainly not foreseen within the terms of the ah, ah—'

'What *is* it?'

'Ah,' said Cyprian Hale, as if steadied by her ability to keep to the point. He raised a finger. 'It is, in a manner of speaking, an angel.'

'No, it isn't. It really isn't.'

'I believe you are being misled, my dear, by the conventional iconography. The wings, the coloured robe, the sweet and girlish face – Victorian paraphernalia, obscuring a forgotten reality. Our ancestors knew better. If you read in the, ah, Enochian writings, or for that matter in Paracelsus, you glimpse there a more, ah, *feral* truth. In which the *angelidae*, considered as a class, descend through many degrees from the Greater Powers, whom only the greatest of adepts might dare to approach, all the way down to a far more lowly and numerous category of aerial spirits, denizens only of the lowest part of the atmosphere. Crude, limited, yet still immensely powerful in human terms. The, as you might say, proletariat of the angelic species. Your pursuer is one of those.'

'In an old hat and coat. Rolled up in newspaper like fish and chips.'

'He has been bound. Brought into service. Dressed to signify his service.'

'By . . . ?'

Mr Hale, who had been growing comfortable as he lectured, shifted in his seat anxiously and dipped his head.

'Please,' said Iris. She reached over her half-eaten sandwich of cheese and aerated bread and took his hand. 'Please?'

He looked up and blinked at her. His eyes were childish in the uncertain face; a geriatric little boy's. He squeezed her hand, patted it, and took his fingers back.

'I used,' he said, picking his way through the words, 'to be a member of a certain . . . Order, dedicated to esoteric knowledge. I won't name it. And when we, as it were, closed up shop, I agreed to act as the . . . librarian, you might say, or custodian, of our accumulated . . . materials. And for that purpose one of the spirits of the lower air was bound to guard me, and our collection too. A very simple and limited duty, for a simple creature. It was commanded to stand watch, discreetly, outside the house during the hours of darkness. And nothing else – that's the puzzle. I have myself seen it only occasionally, these last, let me see, seventeen years.'

'Does Geoffrey know it's there?'

'No. He has never encountered it. Nor of course would he be at all inclined to believe in the possibility of any such thing. I'm afraid my son is . . . aggressively sceptical.'

I'm not a bit surprised, thought Iris. *I'd be aggressively sceptical of all this rubbish too, if it wasn't coming after me wrapped in the* Daily Chronicle. There was a relief she didn't care to examine in the discovery that all this had nothing to do with Don Quixote: was not some form of punishment being levied for debauching him. But that of course left the main question unanswered.

'Why is it after me, then?'

'. . . I don't know,' said Mr Hale. 'I'm so sorry, my dear. I just don't know. It oughtn't to be.'

'That doesn't really help,' pointed out Iris.

'No. No it does not. But, as to help: I do have one, um, *expedient* to offer. I was provided, when the arrangement for the Watcher was made, with a kind of insurance in case anything should go wrong.'

He felt in the pockets of the cloak, and then with maddening slowness in the pockets of his jacket underneath. Eventually he found what he was looking for: a crumpled envelope, yellowed by age, covered in what looked like Egyptian hieroglyphics, hand-drawn with a fountain pen and faded blue with age. It was still sealed, with a blob of old-fashioned red wax.

'May I borrow your knife?'

She passed over the knife she'd cut the sandwich with. He wiped it and slit the envelope along the top. Then, squeezing the corners to crack the sides open into an oval, he carefully tipped something out onto the crumby table: a small circle of paper, about as big across as a florin, written all over in tiny, indecipherable script. Iris's heart sank, but she reached for it.

'I wouldn't!' warned Mr Hale. 'Not without gloves! I don't know what it does to people!'

She drew her hand back.

'What is it? Does it . . . command the thing to stop?'

'Not exactly. It's supposed to dissolve the binding – to banish it altogether. For emergencies only, you see.'

'I think this is an emergency.'

'So do I. So I want you to have it.'

'What do I do with it? Do I . . . read it aloud?'

'Oh, no no no. Not at all advisable. You wouldn't know exactly who, or what, you were addressing, would you? Anything might be listening.'

Oh, good grief. I'm taking help from a lunatic. But then, this is a lunatic situation.

'How do I use it, then?'

'It must be placed on the Watcher's head, writing-side inward.'

'How do I do that? You've seen it, haven't you? It moves like an express train.'

'Oh. It's always been quite quiescent, in my experience.'

'It isn't any more.'

'Oh dear. I'm so sorry.'

'Better than nothing, I suppose,' she said.

'Yes indeed,' he said. 'Now, let me see . . .' Commandeering a teaspoon, he picked the paper disc up between spoon and knife, and popped it back in the envelope, which he handed to her in both hands with a little bow.

'Thank you,' she said. 'I think. I had better go back to work.'

'Yes indeed. Well; I do hope things work out for the best. I do hope you're not . . .'

'Mashed to a pulp? Me too.'

'I'm so sorry. – But! But, may I just say, before you go, and speaking now as a father, that I am delighted, my dear, that Geoffrey has at last found a pretty young woman with whom to practise the rites of Aphrodite. I have been quite worried about him! I have done my best to unfold to him the, ah, splendour, and, ah, vigour, and, ah, *naturalness* of the sexual impulse, as practised in a spirit of free comradeship between men and women. And yet he has seemed curiously reluctant to claim this fine inheritance of the Life Force!'

Imagine that, thought Iris. *I can't think why, you silly old sod.*

Hale's voice had risen, and he was smiling at her with ghastly sincerity, while other diners according to temperament looked away, or stared at him, grinning. He seized her hand between both of his. 'But now, here you are!'

She fled, with much more of a paternal blessing than she had wanted. There was enough unhappiness in her feelings about her own father, without taking on someone else's.

IV

Despite her best efforts, it was ten past five before she managed to get out of the Mariner Building, and the light was already beginning to fail on the streets. A gloom was upon them, like a thickening of particles in the air; a gloom that would dim into shadow, and then into darkness. There were still people about, issuing out of the bronze doors in ones and twos from the offices on the lower floors. If she hurried, she ought to be able to move in cover with them up to the bus stop, before night fell. She had Mr Hale's hieroglyphic envelope in her bag, for whatever good it might do.

But waiting for her on the opposite pavement was Geoff, and he was furious. He came towards her with the stiff-legged walk of someone just about holding back combustion.

'Oh, lucky me,' said Iris before he could speak. 'I'm getting the whole family today. Will your mum be down shortly too?'

'My mother is dead,' said Geoff.

Iris felt a catch in the rhythm of bad temper, the unexpected extra beat or missing beat that startles you when there's one step more or one step fewer at the bottom of a staircase.

'I'm sorry,' she said. 'I didn't know that. How could I know that?'

'I want you to leave us alone,' hissed Geoff, ignoring this. 'It's bad enough that you come to me with your mad nonsense. But to bring my father into it! Getting him excited about this rubbish! You have no idea, the struggles I've had, getting him to inhabit some, some *minimum* version of the real world. Pyramids and magic rituals and ley-lines and lost continents and bloody *fairies*! He believes all of it! Any old irrational pile of, of . . . *shit and feathers* that someone concocts – there he is, ready to sign up. It's a disease with him. A mental disease. He's ruined his own life over it, and damn near ruined mine too. But at least he's calmed down, the last few years. He's got his museum of claptrap, and he potters about. But now you come to him, with your new claptrap about bloody papier-mâché bogeymen—'

'Hey!' said Iris. 'He came to me, it was his idea, and at least he wanted to help—'

'—and now he's reinfected, all over again. He came home this afternoon talking nineteen to the dozen, with a dreadful light in his eye, and he's covering the kitchen table with books, and if I don't watch out he'll start drawing on the walls again. You've worked him up! You've worked him up! How could you do that?'

The last trickles of people leaving the Mariner Building, seeing that a row was in progress, were politely absenting themselves as quickly as possible. The gloom was thickening.

'Look,' she said, 'I really didn't do anything. I came to your house and since then something I don't understand has been happening to me. Something terrifying. Fine, you don't believe me. I probably wouldn't believe me. But it's still *happening*, so if you'll excuse me, if it's all right with you, I need to go and run for my life.'

She set off uphill at a trot. Geoff came striding after.

'That's right, run away!' he cried.

She stopped, infuriated. 'I'm not running away from you, Sunny Jim,' she said. 'It's the monster in the trenchcoat I'm afraid of, not the pipsqueak in the sports jacket.'

'I've got to go away on Monday,' said Geoff. 'With him in this state. What am I supposed to do? I don't know if he'll even remember to eat. He doesn't sometimes.'

'That . . . is *your* problem. You sort it out. I've got a rather pressing problem of my own. Tell you what: I'll leave you alone, if you leave me alone. All right?'

Onwards up to the junction, Geoff still trailing behind, still remonstrating. She rounded the corner, and saw that a bus was just leaving the stop, with the small crowd she'd wanted to hide among all on board. A groan of gears and it was gone. She quickened her pace. She would just have to get to the bridge on foot, and to try to sprint across. The night aspect of the city was coming on fast. Shade into shadow, shadow into pools of blackness, as if a flood of ink were swirling through the streets, rising and rising, the buildings losing their details and with them the look of human making, becoming instead canyon walls, thick black blocks of forest, through which wound narrow paths. London no longer. The night wood, in which it was natural to be hunted.

Panting, she reached the crossing at the City end of the bridge where five roads met, by day a busy whirl of traffic under the facade of the Friends Provident building, now a lonely clearing. There was more light to the south, up the axis of the bridge, where the remnants of the day hung unshaded in the open space above the Thames. The bridge drew a pale line of promise, leading from her to safety. There were even a few figures visible on it.

'You're really frightened, aren't you?' Geoff said, more hesitantly. He sounded puzzled for the first time.

'Yes!'

'But you don't seem crazy. I don't understand. What is there to be frightened *of?*'

She swung back to face him.

'Have you ever tried listening?'

But he wasn't listening. He was gazing over her shoulder.

'What's that?' he said.

She didn't have to look to know, because she was already feeling the shocking transparency that came with the creature's gaze. But she glanced behind her anyway, to see how far off it was: not on top of them, but not far behind either. It had just stepped out of the shadows of the little cobbled yard around the Monument, fifty yards towards the bridge. It stood there like a detached pillar of night, doing its head-bending thing from shoulder to shoulder.

'That,' she said bitterly, 'is a papier-mâché bogeyman. Run!'

The bridge was closed to her now. There was nothing for it but to pick one of the northward exits from the junction, one of the black crevices leading deeper into the lightless mass of buildings. Her feet chose for her: she swerved right, and was running full tilt in her office shoes up Gracechurch Street, back towards Leadenhall. Breath coming hard, the cranny between the black blocks to left and right swooping and dipping in her vision; Geoff running along next to her, still irritatingly at a foalish canter while she was flat out. If this had been London's first night, back when the forest was literal and there was no city at all, it would have been a wolf at their heels. Now there was a horrid trundling noise, the thing having skipped the jerky-fluid stickiness of its walk and gone straight to rolling.

'This is impossible!' complained Geoff. *Yeah, tell it that*, she thought. *Why don't you stop and reason with it, Geoff?* But she didn't say it aloud: she didn't have enough breath for repartee. Even now he sounded indignant as much as scared. She didn't know why the microscope-slide feeling, the turned-to-glass-and-pierced sensation, didn't undo him the way it did her.

She looked back: it was almost upon them. No time to reach the next junction; no time to try to lose it behind thick-enough brick and stone. The mouth of Leadenhall Market loomed on her right, a high Victorian barn snaking away into blackness on cast-iron pillars, and she veered in with the instinct of any hunted creature to find a hole to hide in. Geoff, not knowing what she was going to do, was late with the turn and she left him behind. But the creature ignored him, and rolled straight on after her. Apparently it was her specifically, and only her, that it was after. She could hear the trundle change sound, as it rolled off the street's mix of tarmac and paving stones and metal drain covers, onto the cobbles of the dark market's floor. It smelled of blood and sawdust in there, from the thousands of plucked geese and chickens and ducks hung up for sale on hooks during the poultry market, but everything was closed, everyone was gone, the place was deserted.

She pelted on into the blackness, and as her eyes adjusted a faint gleaming of light from the glass roof high overhead began to pick out the rough shape of the place: the butchers' booths all locked up tight for the night, the central crossing where the snaking galleries met in a dome and the supporting pillars were as thick as tree trunks. One of those might be thick enough to make her invisible – she couldn't exactly hide behind them, because they were joined to the walls, but she could tuck herself in beyond one. And she did, breathing hard but trying not to make noise, pressed up against ridged iron in the dark, a cold reek of dead chickens all around. With no more protection than a corner the thing could step around. But the searchlight pressure of the gaze was off. Iron three feet across was enough to stop it seeing her.

The trundling sound stopped too. It must be standing up, on its balloon legs, seeking.

'Iris?' called Geoff, from way back at the market's mouth. 'Iris? Are you all right? Where are you?'

It didn't seem sensible to answer, not while iron and silence and dark meant a temporary refuge. She didn't think Geoff had quite got over his disbelief, had quite let himself take in the reality of what was happening. But then she heard a scrape and drag as the thing lurched into motion, and started its way towards her, swiping each pillar with a fingerless fist as it reached it, like a beater methodically flushing out game. The iron rang, huge shuddering resonant discords vibrating in the whole metal skeleton of the market and sending mad echoes reverberating through the blackness.

No more silence. No more refuge, in a matter of seconds: just a brief game of catch to play in the dark before it got her; before inhuman strength mashed flesh and bone. There was the paper disc in her handbag, and she was open to any wild hope, but why ever would it hold still for her to press a piece of paper on it?

'I'm here!' she yelled through the echoing anvil chorus, as much from a wish for company in extremis as because she thought he could do anything. 'In the middle! It's nearly found me!'

'I'm coming!' he shouted, and to do him justice, in he came at once, a smatter of running feet threading under the clangour. He overtook the creature just as it was about to hammer on her pillar, and she darted out into the dim open space under the dome and grabbed at his hand. A moment of stumbling – his eyes not having adapted as much to the dark – and then they were whirling on together, to play the final round of hide-and-seek hand in hand. Geoff pulled her on towards a further gallery, and the creature came after, not quick but inexorable, in stickily fluid strides. Its searchlight gaze had locked back onto her, as if to it she was blazingly outlined, pulsating with unignorable colour. But there had been a sort of . . . flickering in it. An interference. A loss of signal. *After* she'd come out from behind the shield of the iron. When?

When she'd grabbed at Geoff's hand, and they'd stumbled together, swung around by incompatible vectors. She'd been . . . momentarily behind him, from the creature's point of view. Could it be that it could see through non-living matter, up to a certain depth, but not through a person – if the person in question wasn't the one it was hunting? If that were true . . .

'Stop! Stop!' she cried.

'What? No!'

'I've got an idea. I don't think it can see me through you.'

'So?'

'There's something I can do, if I can get close enough to it without it knocking my block off.'

'Or mine!' It sounded as if the fear of the creature had, now, come fully home to Geoff. Its strangeness; its wrongness. The way its movement was unlike the movement of any living thing.

'Please!'

'Very well,' said Geoff. 'Very well . . .'

And rather than scrambling on towards the farther end of the iron gallery, he swung round to face their pursuer, and she tucked herself behind him. Arms crossed in front of her, legs behind his legs. Being merely behind his clothing definitely wouldn't work. If there was anything to her idea, she needed to be in the shadow of his actual body. But stopping running from it when it was coming – that felt deeply dangerous. She was trembling where she stood, and so was Geoff, who was facing the thing. Also, she now couldn't see anything. Two seconds, a second till it reached them, if she was wrong.

A silence fell, which she couldn't interpret.

'Has it stopped?' she said into his back.

'. . . Yes,' he said, out of the corner of his mouth.

'What's it doing?'

'Nothing. I think it's puzzled.'

'Then it's lost me. It's working.'

'So it is,' said Geoff faintly.

Everything was still. The clanging echoes had died away, and there were no footsteps. She leant the tip of her nose between his shoulder blades. Through tweed and cotton, he was warm. Despite everything, news spread through her of contact with the gangly body that had flushed pale to pink when she looked at it. She felt an insane urge just to stay standing there, forever. She shut her eyes for an instant, then made herself open them again.

'Now walk forward,' she said.

'You're kidding.'

'No. I have to be in arm's reach. Go on – very slowly. Left leg, right leg, left leg . . .'

'I thought I wasn't joining the Army till Monday,' he said.

They inched forward, and forward. The smell of mildew intensified. He stopped again.

'Where is it now?' she asked.

'About a foot in front of me,' he said. 'Oh God, Iris. Its face!'

'I know,' she said. 'I do know. Just hold still now for a minute, if you can bear it.'

She felt for the envelope in her bag. She had no gloves, and when she reached through the slit in the paper, when she touched the disc, she did feel something: a sort of pins-and-needles buzz, working its way up her hand towards her wrist. No time to worry about that, and it was reassuring in a way to know that her only weapon at least did *something*. That she wasn't risking the last moments of her life to slap on a luggage label.

'Ready?' she said. 'Stay still when I move. I'm going to do this as quickly as I can.'

She poised the disc on the end of her fingers. She thought of boxers rabbit-punching, cobras striking, express trains coming suddenly out of tunnels, everything that moved at full speed without warning. Then she took a shallow breath and, as fast as she possibly could, came on tiptoe and threw her arm forward at the thing's mask of mouldering black and white, which rose into view horribly close in front of her – right there, almost nose to nose with poor Geoff, except that it had no nose – as big as the moon and crumpling and swelling in its paper skin.

The instant she went at it and therefore came into view, there was movement: its arms up and looping out on each side, lengthening, telescoping out of the rotted black sleeves, to reach easily behind Geoff's head and to close on hers like twin pulverising hammers.

But by some fraction of a second, she got there first. She pushed the disc of paper onto its face – a surface both hard and sluggishly yielding, as if there might be liquid rock inside – and without delay, without any discernible interval, the arms stopped closing in. Not as if they'd been arrested, not as if their momentum had been checked: they hung in the air as if they'd never moved.

There was a glow around the disc, and then a split travelled north and south from it, a crack of intense brilliance. From it, with a sigh, a luminous cloud flowed out, and as it did, as if a long-held breath had been let go, the rotten coat and the ancient hat and the newspaper slipped to the cobbled ground, all emptied, their contents all gone. There was just the white cloud in the air in front of Geoff's face. It made a floating milkiness there, but it glittered. Each white particle in it, if you looked closely, was a scintillation, a tiny point of fizzing purposeful activity. It was alive. More alive than the lumbering monster in the old coat had ever seemed to be.

'Iris . . .' began Geoff, warningly, but before he could say any more the cloud parted neatly, flowed around his head without touching it, and gathered round hers. It filled her whole vision. She couldn't see anything but it, a milky glittering starfield inches away, and all in constant and somehow unmistakably intelligent motion. It was regarding her. It was weaving, ten thousand strong, around her face and hair, and considering the phenomenon of Iris Hawkins. If Cyprian Hale's magicians had thought this thing was crude or stupid, they had misunderstood it. Trapped in the newspaper it had been monstrous; now, it was beautiful. And out of its paper skin it was clear that it was, if anything, stronger. It was an immensely powerful thing moving with maximum gentleness.

The bright particles that made it up began to flow. It wreathed, it spiralled, it wove a dance around her head, closer and closer, until all she could see was flaring, streaking blue-white. And then she could feel it too, a tickling electric stream, whirling across the skin of her cheeks, pinpricking her lips: kissing her, she couldn't help but believe, or blessing her. Thanking her. She was holding her breath, but not from fear. It lingered, scratchy-gentle – and then, with a bound and jump, it flowed away from them both, and poured itself off through the dark air of the covered market, a streamer of effervescent brightness doing loops and rolls of unmistakable joy. Not something banished, something set free. It shot through the black towards the Gracechurch Street entrance, drew a final soda-water knot on the air, jinked upwards and was gone, up and out into the night sky of London.

They stared after it. Iris's vision still flared with green and violet after-images, blooming and fading. Her arm tingled.

'What—?' began Geoff, and stalled. He cleared his throat. 'What *was* that?'

'Your dad said it was an angel. A kind of low-grade, working-class angel.'

'But—'

He gave up. Instead of arguing, he crouched down, fished up a box of matches from his pocket and lit one over the sad little pile of fabric and mushed paper left on the ground. The disc was on top, burned to ash. He stirred at the heap with his finger, spread out one of the bigger fragments of newsprint. 'March the twelfth, 1922,' he read out.

'Well, that fits. Outside your house for seventeen years, just like your father told me.'

Geoff shook his head. The match burnt his finger and he shook the match instead. He got up and walked away from her to the nearest iron pillar, and leant on it, as far as she could make out through the dim fireworks on her retinas. A sound came from him. More tears? No, laughter. A gurgle getting louder, wilder. Fear's aftermath? Hysteria?

'Geoff?' she said. 'What is it?'

'You're not mad,' he said, through ripples of amusement. 'You're not mad!'

'No, I'm not,' she said stiffly. 'And why is that funny?'

'Oh, it's not funny,' he said. 'It's *wonderful*.' He came back from the pillar, and wrapped big hands around her shoulders. 'It means,' he said, 'that you don't have to be mad, to want to go to bed with me.' And then he pulled her against him, and kissed her, hard.

Unlike the angelic kiss, which had been a beatific whisper of a thing, this one was all substance, hot and solid. There was an immediate animal comfort in it, and she kissed him back with equal fury for a minute before she could muster her resolution, and pushed him off.

'No!' she said. 'Stop! I don't want that. You and me . . . are a mistake.'

'Oh,' said Geoff. 'I just thought—'

'No, you didn't!' she said. 'You just *wanted*, which is a different thing. And no guide to anything.' There was a shake in her voice she was having to suppress. 'Look what came of it last time,' she added, trying to fix her alarm to the memory of having a monster in pursuit, when the real trouble was the pit of feeling she felt herself on the brink of, with him.

'That wasn't my fault!' he said.

'No,' she said. 'No, it wasn't. But it was still horrible. And,' she lied, 'when you kiss me, that's what I think of. That's what I'd always think of. So – you and me, that was one night, and now it's over, and you'll just have to accept that. Sorry.'

'You don't sound sorry. You sound frightened again.'

'Well – like I said!'

'Maybe it'll wear off?'

'Geoff!' she said through her teeth. *Please don't be hopeful. Please don't be sweet. Please don't be kind.*

'All right,' he said sadly. 'Now what? Do we just get on separate buses and say goodbye?'

How simple that would be.

'No,' she said. 'I'm afraid not. Now we both go to Hampstead, and find out from your father why on earth that thing' – *monstrous thing, beautiful thing* – 'was following me.'

They went out into the blackout together. And since the night was getting cold, she let herself take his arm. Her left arm in his right arm: her own right one still had faint pins and needles, fading yet also moving upwards past her elbow. And she leant against him, just a bit.

ANGEL PASSAGE
NOVEMBER-DECEMBER 1939

I

'And the moment it came out,' she said, 'it had no interest at all any more in chasing me, or hurting me, or anything. So why was it, in the first place?'

It was the first time she had seen the inside of the house on Wildwood Terrace in full light, and it was if anything even more cluttered than it had seemed when she was tiptoeing about it in the dark. Geoff's father had opened the blacked-out door – 'Thank heavens!' he'd cried, relieved but also, she saw, excited – and the hall behind him blazed from a pair of dusty electric bulbs overhead. There along the right-hand wall was the long row of grandfather clocks. They were crowded in, case against case, leaving only a narrow pathway to squeeze along towards the further doors at the back. Mr Hale had to turn sideways to fit, huffing as he went, his waistcoat buttons dragging on the woodwork. They weren't clocks, though, she discovered as she followed him, but something odder. They didn't tick, and their faces behind smudged glass were oval, pentagonal, hexagonal. They had three hands, four hands, five hands, spidery black or enamelled scarlet, and they pointed not to regular circles of the hours but to pictograms, symbols, miniatures of the planets, hieroglyphs, inset discs of cloudy mirror. All of them had a flimsy, badly finished look, like a magician's cabinets for a trick, or stage-set furniture. There was a certain similarity to the crowded corridor at Alexandra Palace. 'What *are* these?' she whispered to Geoff, following close behind. 'A junkyard of superstition,' he said grimly, not bothering to lower his voice. Through the banisters on her left, every step of the staircase was two-thirds blocked by the shadowy obstructions she had had to pick her way around on the way to Geoff's bedroom, now revealed as mounds of grimy paper; through a door to her right she got a view of a sitting room where only a narrow alley of clear carpet led between high-stacked boxes to an armchair by a fireplace.

'Tea by the fire?' said Cyprian Hale hopefully.

'A lovely idea, Father, which would only require two or three hours of tidying to give us all somewhere to sit down. Come on into the kitchen,' Geoff said to Iris.

The white-painted door at the end of the hall led into a little space of sudden order – the kind of order she was starting to recognise as the signature of Geoff. Scrubbed white china sink, scrubbed white gas stove. Spotless tiles underfoot and on the walls. Gleaming taps, a row of identical white plates in exact order on the dish rack. Identical mugs, identical cups. But the kitchen table, which should obviously have been as calm and bare and plain as the rest of the room, was spread with a slew of volumes, some face down, some face up. *Gems from the Equinox*, Iris read on the spine of one; *Golden Dawn* on the next. On the upward-facing pages, a folio-sized diagram of a pyramid, where all the blocks had something printed on them in tiny type, and a woodcut showing something very unpleasant happening to a winged being strapped to a table. Seeing where she was looking, Cyprian Hale, flustered, covered the picture with his hand.

'Father,' said Geoff, tight-lipped, 'haven't I cleared this rubbish away once already today?'

He tugged at the book with the picture, but his father clung on with sheepish defiance.

'No! No! I need them. And be careful, my dear boy – do be careful – some of these are literally irreplaceable.'

'You have a perfectly good desk in the sitting room.'

'I can't get at it.'

'And whose fault is that?'

'I need to spread out somewhere, for my researches!'

'No one cares about your "researches".'

'I do,' said Iris. '*I* do, if they'll explain what's been happening to me.'

'You see?' said Mr Hale, triumphantly. 'You see? My dear, I am delighted you are all right. I am immensely relieved. Immensely! I have been pacing, simply *pacing* about.'

Geoff rolled his eyes at this sudden and blatant grab for the role of responsible adult. But he let go of the book.

'All right,' he said. 'I will make the tea, and you tell Iris, if you can, why that thing was after her. But first we are going to clear the table. You can do what you like from Monday, but till then we are going to keep one small space in this house free from the chaos.'

Mr Hale consented to stack the books into a heap. He tried to put the stack on top of the white-painted meat safe, but Geoff stared at him, and he took them grumblingly away. When he came back, however, his eagerness was all restored. While Geoff filled the kettle and set it on the hob, he sat down on a bentwood chair on the opposite side of the table from her, and laced his hands together on his stomach in happy anticipation.

'So!' he said. 'What happened? Did the Watcher present itself again?'

'Yes.'

And she told the story of the evening. He listened with wide eyes, and murmurings of dismay, but complacent glances at Geoff, too, once it became clear that his son had seen the Watcher himself, and taken part in the final encounter in the darkened market. Geoff produced three mugs of strong Indian tea and a plate of biscuits, and sat down himself, head bowed and both hands round his mug. Mr Hale took a biscuit and munched it thoughtfully. Crumbs gathered on his waistcoat. He brushed at them, and knocked his spoon onto the floor. It was easy to imagine him as a kind of constant generator of muddles, small and large.

'. . . So why was it after me?' she finished.

'Yes,' said Geoff, 'I'd like to know that too. It was bloody terrifying.'

'Such things are,' said Mr Hale knowingly. 'When one steps beyond a narrowly, ah, empirical understanding of our world, and discovers it for the shadowed temple it truly is, the domain of dark mystery it truly is, one must be prepared for terror and wonder both. One must be prepared for the hair on the head to rise. To *horripilate* – what a marvellous word. How wise were the ancients, to ascribe to the great god Pan the emotion, aha, of panic, and to—'

'Oh God,' said Geoff. 'Just answer her question. Stop crowing, and answer her question.'

'Crowing?' said his father. 'Was I crowing? Why would I be crowing, Geoffrey?' His expression was now a definite smirk.

'Because,' Geoff said, gritting his teeth, 'some minuscule fraction of the rubbish you believe has turned out to be true.'

'Yes. And?'

'And what,' said Geoff. 'That's bad enough.'

'*And* it turned out that *I* had the means to rescue her. Me, and my secret knowledge. Not you, and your . . . valves and wires.'

'Geoff was very brave,' said Iris. But they both ignored her.

'It's my valves and wires that buy your dinner every night,' said Geoff.

'Gentlemen?' said Iris. 'Gentlemen? Shut up, the pair of you.'

Two startled male faces turned towards her. Young Don Quixote and the Magic Sheep.

'Thank you,' she said. 'I nearly died tonight, and I'm not in the mood. If you want my opinion, you two have spent far too much time together. Mr Hale: just tell me why it happened, so I can be sure it won't happen again, and then I'll get out of your hair, and you can bicker to your hearts' content.'

'Oh,' said Mr Hale. 'Are you going? But I thought you two were . . . I thought you were . . .'

'No,' said Geoff grimly. 'We're not. So let's get this over with, and I'll make a start on the supper.'

'Oh. Oh. But . . .'

Mr Hale's face had crumpled, like a small boy's when a promised treat is withdrawn. It seemed clear that he had anticipated a good long period of rubbing Geoff's scientific nose in the mystery of things, with Iris as admiring audience. Also, to do him justice, he had probably been genuinely glad to see some female company for his son appear on the scene. Even if he was inclined to express his enthusiasm in the most embarrassing possible terms, and to talk about 'the rites of Aphrodite'. Iris herself seemed to have arrived at some state beyond embarrassment. The fear, the relief, the awe: it had all been too much for her to be very bothered, now, about the sensibilities of this weird household. She rubbed her elbow. There was no more prickling sensation, but her arm felt indefinably different. Very slightly heavier, perhaps.

'Very well,' said Mr Hale sadly. 'Well; let me see. There are two possibilities. One, it might be that the, um, binding that the Order originally laid on the aerial spirit that became the Watcher had, so to speak, begun to decay. In which case the Watcher's pursuit of you, my dear, might represent a kind of *bleeding through* of the feral nature underneath. There *are* plentiful references to the anger of the spirits, where the ritual of the binding fails. Perhaps it came after you because it had freed itself enough to act upon that inner fury of which we are warned. And you banished it in the nick of time with my little emergency spell.' Faintest emphasis on the word 'my'.

'No,' said Iris. 'That doesn't sound right. It wasn't like banishing it, at all. It was setting it free. And the instant it was free, like I said, it had no interest at all in coming after me. It was like: it had been under orders, and then suddenly it wasn't. I don't believe it was angry with me, before. It was . . . joyful, after. Before, it wasn't anything. Anyway, if it *was* angry, why would it pick me, who'd been here for one night, not you, who'd kept it standing out in the rain in a mangey old coat for seventeen years? No. What's the other option?'

'Or,' Mr Hale said, 'it might be that the terms of the binding had been varied. Altered, d'you see, to send the Watcher on a new mission.'

'There was only one of them, right?' asked Iris. 'It was definitely the one here that went haring off to the City to look for me?'

'Yes. Only one was bound by the Order.'

'So, how would that happen, then?'

'Well, it would all depend on the precise form that had been used in the first place, and what it allowed. You see, when a spirit is summoned down to serve, it is being moved from its natural domain to one less suited to it. It is being *pulled*, so to speak, against the grain of the universe – drawn, and drawn effortfully, from an easier state to a more difficult one.'

'Anti-entropic,' said Geoff, interested despite himself. 'From more probable to less probable. Thermodynamically speaking.'

'I'm afraid I don't know what that means,' said Mr Hale.

'Of course you don't,' said Geoff.

'*I* do,' said Iris, before they could start again. 'It means you'd have to put energy in to make it happen.'

'Why, yes!' said Mr Hale. 'An excellent way of putting it. It requires a mighty working – a great alignment of ritual, of knowledge, of word and action in precise sequence. You must imagine,' he went on, and bass tones entered the foolish voice, and he raised his hands in invocation over the table, 'a circle of the most profound explorers of the Art Magic. A ring of robed figures, gathered around the vessel in which they purpose to draw down the powers of the air. Then, step by irresistible step, word by irresistible word, they form together the incantation that compels, manipulating the angels' own language to seize upon a subject, and then to grasp, to wind in, to subdue, to fix, and at last to command it, taming a being that in its wild state must be far stronger than they. *That* was the path down which the Order drew the Watcher into our service. *That* was the great work we accomplished. Harnessing spirit! Putting a bridle on the very wind! Subjecting Might to Mind!'

The kitchen rang with his voice. It had grown more reverberating as he spoke, and his hand gestures had grown larger, and looking at him it was for the first time possible to imagine, not a silly old man covered in crumbs, but one of the masters of an unearthly power. A necromancer at the tea table. An initiate into secrets. He smiled at them, enjoying their reaction. Then he dropped his hands to pet the bulge of his waistcoat.

'And *since*,' he said, suddenly prosey again, 'the process is thus one of, aha, reduction, tightening (in a sense), the blocking off of all lines of manoeuvre except those desired by the magicians – since that is the case, the binding is necessarily very, very specific. It must lay out in exact detail what the captive spirit must do, how it can and cannot be commanded. Therefore, *who* may command it.'

'Right,' said Iris. 'So what did the Watcher's binding say? Who's on the list who could have sent it after me?'

'Ah,' said Mr Hale apologetically. 'I'm afraid I don't know.'

'What?'

'I . . . don't know, my dear.'

'But weren't you there when the binding was done?'

'Oh no! I was never part of the Inner Circle! I'm afraid I never rose beyond Adeptus Minor.'

Iris revised her picture of Mr Hale's status in his Order abruptly downwards. Not a necromancer, after all. An admirer of necromancers. A fan. A necromancer's librarian. Trusted to store the leftovers of occultism, but not to participate.

'Then how on earth do I find out?'

'I've been thinking about this,' said Cyprian Hale helpfully, 'and I think there's a good chance the papers for the ritual may be in the attic. Almost everything is there, one way or another.'

'Oh God,' said Geoff. 'Abandon hope, all ye who enter here.'

'What? Why?' said Iris.

'You haven't seen the attic. You'll understand when you do.'

'Come now, it's not *that* bad,' said Mr Hale.

'Yes it is.'

'I could help.'

'No you couldn't. You take the rest of your tea and go and sit by the fire. I'll make dinner when we come down.'

'What are we having?' Mr Hale asked with lively interest.

'Sausages.'

'Why can't he help?' Iris asked, following Geoff up the crowded stairs.

'Because he'll get fascinated by the first thing he picks up, talk about it interminably, and turn round and round knocking things over. I'll just get the key from my room. I keep it, so he can't go poking about in there.'

The 'attic', it turned out, wasn't really an attic. It was the other upstairs room, running from front to back of the house on the opposite side of the landing from Geoff's bedroom and the bathroom. Eaves, bare floorboards, a single round window looking out at the front onto the garden and the tree. Except that little of that was evident, at first glance, the room being packed so preposterously full of stuff, a chest-high rampart on both sides of a tiny lane of floor. Geoff turned on the overhead light, exclaimed, and pushed his way side-on up the lane to cover the window with a piece of moth-eaten velvet.

'Haven't had to think about blackout in here,' he said. 'Well, welcome to chaos.'

'Is there a . . . system?'

'What do *you* think?'

'I thought there might be filing cabinets or something.'

'Nope. Just strata of nonsense, on top of each other.'

She looked, and could see what he meant. From the floor upwards, boxes and jars and packing cases and bales of grubby fabric were loaded on top of each other in seams, with something thin and white in between the layers. She reached in and fingered one of these.

'Is this a . . . bedsheet?'

'Indeed it is. When my father took delivery of all this, he laid out the first layer on the floor, put sheets on top, and then started again. And then went on building it up and up, until he couldn't reach any more. There's madness in his method, don't you think?'

She ran her fingers over the nearest objects. A tea-caddy with broken hinges, which, when she forced up the lid, was full of very peculiar chessmen. A collection of ebony frames with no pictures in them. A set of jointed metal rods that might have assembled into something, if the joints hadn't been twisted and broken. A stack of feathered masks, crushed together by the pressure on top. A biscuit tin containing stone eggs of contrasting colour, all wrapped in twists of blue sugar-paper. A wilderness of ruined things.

She looked up. Geoff was observing her, sympathetically rather than mockingly.

'For what it's worth, it gets more paper-y in the middle here,' he said. 'I'll help you dig, if you like?'

'D'you think there's any point?'

He shrugged.

'Oh, let's at least try,' she said.

There was indeed a zone of the room where the geology on

each side seemed to be mainly paper and card, higgledy-piggledy towers of unbound printing, box folders, flat portfolios tied up with perished ribbon, map tubes, lidless suitcases. To get at any of them except the topmost required feats of shuffling and shifting, like playing that wooden nursery game where you had to slide all the pieces of the puzzle laboriously about to move the one little empty space. She lifted things off the pile, looked at them and handed them to Geoff, who found room for them somewhere else. She was very conscious of him nearby, raising dust, collecting black grime on the cuffs of his carefully white shirt.

She began hopefully, because the first stratum she got into turned out to be all composed of typescripts held together by loops of string through eyelet holes, captioned *RITUAL*. But the rituals in question were all for initiating members into what appeared to be infinite numbers of different grades in the Order. Postulant. Novice. Adeptus Minor. Adeptus Major. Hierarch. Grand Hierarch. Apollonian Hierarch. Sub-Master. Master Inferior. On and on it went. *Let the applicant now proceed through the corridor of darkness to the Room of Ordeal, in his/her hand a rod of camphor* . . . Underneath that was a box of receipts from a carpenter for the building of furniture, with diagrams of the furniture in question, looking like the perverse fusion of love seats with confessional boxes. Cancelled chequebooks. A mass of proofs for a series of pamphlets about yoga. Crumpled maps of the lost continent of Atlantis. Crumpled maps of the county of Surrey, with ley-lines marked on in smeared red chalk. Sixty copies of a work entitled *RULES FOR ENOCHIAN CHESS*. A disintegrating old crocodile-skin writing case, to which was stuck a label marked *Directiounes to Ye Pallace of None-Such*. A cardboard folder contained a handwritten denunciation, over many spidery pages, of the 'false and abominable practices' of a rival occult society. An account book showing regular payments to hire the ballroom of the Excelsior Hotel, Russell Square. And so on.

She passed Geoff another armful of papers and their backs bumped.

'Geoff?'

'Mm-hmm,' he said with studied neutrality.

'Geoff?'

'What?'

'How long *have* you and your dad been living here alone, then?'

'Well, my mother died when I was six.'

'Yes, but you must have had someone in to look after you after that, right?'

'Oh, charwomen and people, and one of my aunts came to stay for a while. But none of them could really say no to him, or stop him spreading the mess around. The whole house was like this, for a while. I'd take myself to school in the morning, and when I got back he'd still be in the same chair he was sitting in when I left. He was very dirty. I was very dirty. We were living in the gaps of his obsessions.'

She pictured a filthy little boy, clambering over the mounds of junk. A chimney-sweep lost in the caverns of esoterica.

'That sounds grim.'

'It was . . . hellish. But when I was ten or so I decided it was up to me to make it better, because nobody else was going to.'

'And you've been cooking and cleaning ever since?'

'Yes. And fighting to get this stuff safely penned up in the attic. I mean, I know it's a mess downstairs, books everywhere, but it's *nothing* to the way it used to be. Honestly, the last few years have been fine. I was at Imperial doing my degree, and then the BBC, and he's been much calmer.'

Fine, she thought, *except that when all your scientific friends graduated, they got to go off round the world building power stations and things, and you had to come back here every night.*

'I'd have thought,' she said, passing him another load, 'that you'd be glad to escape. To the Army, I mean.'

'Yes, I suppose. But what'll happen to him here, if I'm gone? You've seen what an idiot he is. He's basically helpless.' Geoff paused. 'I don't suppose,' he said, without much hope, 'that you'd be willing to . . . look in on him now and again, while I'm gone?'

'*No*,' said Iris firmly. 'Absolutely not. I've picked up enough problems already from this house. I don't want to take on your dad as well.'

'Right,' said Geoff. 'Right.' And then, with an effortful change of subject: 'What have you got there? Anything relevant?'

'Only if a diary of a trip to Stonehenge in 1912 is relevant. Or the typescript of a book called *The Druidic Hypothesis Confuted*.'

'Oh, it's all such rubbish!' he cried. 'Such woolly-minded nonsense. So shoddy. – You know, that's what I really mind about him being right, about the, the, *creature* we met. It was so hard getting out of his world. I don't want to go back, not into any of it.'

'Do you have to?'

'What do you mean?'

'I mean, who says this precious Order did get it right, about the thing they captured, and dressed up in a hat and fish-and-chip paper? There's one thing we already know they got wrong, about it being stupid. Or . . . rough. It wasn't, was it, once it was free?'

'No.'

'So maybe they've got the rest wrong too. I'm thinking, here's a bunch of nutters who stumbled on one true thing, by accident.'

He didn't say anything, but when she turned her head to look at him he was grinning.

'Well then, Science Boy,' she said. 'You get to work it out for yourself, don't you. Come on, treat it strictly as a phenomenon. Hypothesis, evidence, conclusion. Apply that brain.'

'You're a peculiar girl, you know that?'

'Like you've known so many. Insufficient sample size, Geoffrey Hale: I'm ashamed of you. Perhaps there are millions of us who say "fuck" and know the word "phenomenon".'

'All the same. – Right, right. The "angel". It was made up of about... ten thousand glowing particles, judging by the cubic volume it occupied. But it was one single organism. It made co-ordinated movements. It exhibited awareness of its surroundings. Which perhaps suggests a cells/body analogy, in the relation of parts to whole. Except that it appeared to have no specialised parts. All the particles were identical, at least to the naked eye: bright, oscillating points, expending energy and station-keeping in relation to one another. Therefore, with its intelligence somehow located not in a centre, but in the communication between the parts. I'd love to have been able to scan the radio frequencies, while it was flying round you. I bet it was using a particular band. Yes, that would be it: all those little scintillations must be signals. It was a mind made out of signals.'

She clapped, unironically. 'You see?' she said. 'Ten seconds of thought from you, and we already know more than the Order managed in ten years. Not bad, Geoff.'

'Not bad for a terrified person. And in fact, you know – here's an idea – if that's right, if it's a kind of . . . *radio intelligence* we're dealing with, then you'd catch it, wouldn't you, with some kind of jamming process. Some sort of calculated counter-signal that over-rode its own, and forced it to move as you chose.'

'Doesn't that sound a bit technological for the Order?'

'Not necessarily! If it was a question of getting the right signals in the right order, and the frequencies were low enough, you could do it with sound waves. Gongs, whistles – the human voice, even. And, like you said, they wouldn't have had to know what they were doing, so long as it worked.'

A plaintive voice came from downstairs. 'Are we having the sausages soon?' it bleated.

'No!' shouted Geoff. Then he sighed. 'You know, none of this is getting us anywhere with working out why it came after *you*. Perhaps I'd better stop and cook him his blasted sausages.'

Iris looked at the next item on the stack beside her. It was a quote from a builder's merchant in 1903 for the supply of marble tiles for a tessellated floor. Underneath were several alternative pen-and-ink designs for the floor, featuring droopy art nouveau ladies. They were held together by a rusty paperclip. She had got about two-thirds of the way to the floor, working down a single stack.

'You're right,' she said. 'I don't think this is helping. I'd better go home.'

'Can I feed you some sausages first? We've got lots.'

She was going to say no, but her stomach reminded her that it had been a very long time since the cheese sandwich in the ABC Tea Room.

'All right,' she said. 'That would be kind.'

They shovelled the displaced papers back into the space they had come out of, turned the light off and locked the attic up behind them.

Once she was no longer standing quite so close to Geoff, and was looking carefully away from him, she said, 'I did wonder to begin with whether the Watcher trying to get me was some kind of punishment. For, you know, debauching the son of the house.'

Out of the corner of her eye she could see him blush, cover one eye with his hand and then push his palm up through the pale flop of his hair. Impossible not to remember what the blush had looked like travelling across the rest of him.

'I shouldn't think so,' he said, gaze also averted. 'I mean, why would they set that up, seventeen years ago? I was only five. Also – they're rather keen on that kind of thing, on the whole.'

'"The rites of Aphrodite".'

'Urgh. Yes. Come on: sausages.'

'Are we having mash with them?' she asked, following him down the stairs.

'Yes.'

'Can I peel the potatoes, if I promise to put the pan back in *exactly* the right place?'

'I'm not sure it's really fair for you to tease me,' he complained.

'I'm not sure I can really help myself,' she said.

Another grin over his shoulder. *Stop it*, she told herself.

'But,' she said with a return of seriousness, once she was standing at the impeccably clean sink with a shining and razor-sharp peeler in her hand, 'it's got to be something to do with what happened when I came to this house, hasn't it?'

'Well, everyone in the Kinesis Club saw you leave with me.'

'But no one who knew you in the club – no one at the BBC – has any idea that the Watcher even exists, do they? Everybody you work with thinks you're an entirely scientific sort of a chap. Technical Geoff. Electrical Geoff. *They* don't know you live in the nooks and crannies of a storehouse of occult bilge, do they?'

'Well, now,' said Mr Hale mildly, as he shuffled into the room, 'that's not— Do you know, I don't think I entirely welcome that sort of, ah, frankly dismissive description of a lifetime's vocation, a lifetime's devotion?'

'Sorry,' said Iris. Geoff smiled, and handed her a spotless saucepan in white enamel. The sausages were hissing on the hob.

'What was I saying, though?' Mr Hale asked.

'I really don't know, Father.'

'Ah yes – that there is *one* person you work with who *does* know about this house. Because she's the Grand Master's goddaughter. I mean little Lalage. Don't you remember how she would come here sometimes with him, when she was only seven or eight? And you always wanted there to be a cake for her, a cake with pink icing – don't you remember?'

'Oh, good grief,' said Iris, laughing. 'It goes back *that* far, your crush on the ice maiden? You were her helpless slave back *then*?' She could just see the anxious boy trying to present the pink fairy-cake to the unimpressed little princess, while the grown-ups talked about Atlantis.

She stopped laughing.

'Wait a minute,' she said, catching up. '*Lall* knows what you've got here? Lall knows about the Watcher?'

'. . . Possibly,' said Mr Hale.

'Then it's her,' said Iris. 'At least, it might be. Wouldn't it be like her? I bet this is her doing. I don't know how, but I bet it is.'

11

They ate the bangers and mash in a state of suddenly renewed awkwardness. Mocking Geoff for his devotion to Lall had stretched the envelope of friendly teasing – his face had gone still and blank – and then blaming Lall for attempted murder seemed to have torn it. She asked where Lall had gone, what she was doing now. He replied, 'Some kind of war work, I don't know what', and retreated into silence. Probably he was remembering that this woman who jabbed at his sore spots had dropped him immediately the last time she left the house, and planned to do it again tonight as soon as the door shut behind her. On her side, Iris was feeling the shock of the shared emergency wearing off. It had lasted all evening, but now she was thinking, *what am I doing here? Why am I in this house, eating with these people?* There was an undeniably pleasant friction to Geoff's company – nice, for once, to keep company with a clever man, even if he was too poor, too young, too vulnerable – but the moment she looked beyond the moment, all the signs said, loud and clear and unambiguous, *Get out now*. A voice at the back of her mind reminded her, *he didn't believe you when you asked for help. He said you were mad. He said you weren't normal*. And now there might be a homicidal blonde with magic powers in the picture. Mr Hale prattled on, but found no takers. Knives and forks scraped on plates.

'I'd better be off,' she said when the plates were empty.

'Yes,' said Geoff. 'I'll see you to— Oh.' He was looking at his watch. 'It's half past eleven. I don't know how it got so late.'

'You were upstairs for ages,' said Mr Hale helpfully.

'I'm sorry,' said Geoff, 'but I think you'll have missed the last Tube.'

'She had better stay,' said Mr Hale.

'Could you bear to?' said Geoff, cautiously. 'It probably makes sense. Look, you can have my room. I'll clear out to the sofa down here.'

'Oh, but—' began Mr Hale.

'Father, just shush. *Please?*'

'No desire to cause offence!' protested the old man, holding up his hands defensively. 'I shall just say good night, shall I, and leave you young people to, ah, sort yourselves out. Yes, yes, that will be best.'

He got up, gave a sort of courtly half-bow to Iris, and took himself off.

Iris and Geoff looked at each other. She tilted back her kitchen chair, and gazed along the crowded hall, past Mr Hale's closing bedroom door, to the blacked-out front door. So near, and yet so far.

'All right,' she said.

And ten minutes later, after brushing her teeth with a borrowed brush, she was alone in Geoff's tidy bedroom, climbing between his clean sheets dressed in a shirt of his. The little lamp beside the bed was the one that had shone on his bare skin, the model aeroplane in the dormer window was the one that had hung overhead when she had cowered in the gaze of the Watcher. She had been greedy in this room, dismayed in this room, terrified in this room, and now there was a strange, calm safety to being here. The ranked books, the organised clothes, the small symbols of triumphant order Geoff had won from the lonely chaos of his childhood: this was his habitat, and she was quietly inside it. Inside his room, inside his sheets, inside his shirt. Which slid, and caught, and clung as she rolled over. Which was very slightly rough, and smelt cleanly of him. Pleasant friction, yes. Her right arm still felt odd, though. Not bad, or painful, or wrong. Just different, in a way she couldn't name. She reached out with it to Geoff's light switch, and clicked off the lamp. The dark slowly and peacefully disclosed streaks of moonlight, coming from the edges of the blackout curtain at the dormer. Dim silver touched the blankets. Outside, nothing frightening waited under the apple tree. She laid her strange hand on top of the bedclothes, and sleep descended on her like further swathes of kindly fabric, soft and heavy.

'Wake up!' said Geoff excitedly. 'I've found something.'

He was in the room, his face not far from hers.

'What? Wait – what?' she said, clutching the blankets to her. He retreated. It seemed to be morning; early morning, judging by the bleary light leaking round the blackout.

'What is it?' she said. 'What time is it?' She had been far away, in a dream involving stairs and flames, losing solidity already like a leaf going to quivering ash in a bonfire.

'Don't know,' he said impatiently. 'Doesn't matter. I had a thought, and it turns out to be right. Get up; come and see.'

'Must I?' she said. '*Must* I?'

'Yes!'

'Oh Lord. Go away then, while I put some clothes on.'

'You don't need to dress.'

'Yes I do.'

When she opened the bedroom door a minute later, yawning but in a skirt, trying to comb her hair with her fingers, she found him practically hopping from foot to foot on the landing.

'What on earth is it?' she said.

'Shhh,' he said. 'We don't want to wake my father. We *particularly* don't want to wake my father. I think I've worked out how you call one of the . . . intelligences.'

'But if it's Lall—'

'I was on the sofa, you see,' said Geoff, ignoring this and clearly in the grip of discovery, 'being a gentleman, drowsing along, with the springs digging into my back, and what I'd said last night floated into my head. About whistles and gongs, and the trap maybe being acoustic. And then I thought: instruments! Musical instruments! We shouldn't have been searching through the papers, we should have been looking at the musical junk in the attic. There is some, you see, and it's very odd. And by then I was thoroughly awake, so I tiptoed up here. And among the tin trumpets with gold paint crumbling off them, and the miniature violins made of ivory, and the phonograph cylinders of wailing, I found this box of tuned things that *has* to be right. It's got instructions in it. A sort of little script that needs two people. Come on! We've got to try it.'

'Is there any chance of a cup of tea first?'

'No! You can have one after.'

He took her by the nearest hand, which was her left, and pulled her laughing and protesting through the attic door.

'Shhh!' he said again.

He had pulled down the velvet from across the round window, and a grey dawn light was coming through the panes. The box of 'things' he had found, he had set up with its lid off, using one of the chest-high ramparts of junk as a platform. Next to it was a dusty old glass cider jar.

'It says we need a container,' Geoff explained. 'Now, look. Here are the instructions' – a page of withered typewriting, headed in brown handwriting *VOCARE SYLPHI AERIS*. 'We put this button-thing in the jar, to be what it calls a focus' – in fact, a flattish brown piece of carved wood about the size of a half-crown, asymmetrical, with a slanted hole bored through it, and curiously unpleasant to look at. Geoff dropped it in with a clink, but she would not have wanted to touch it herself. Although hard, and made of wood, it was somehow slimily organic. The kind of lump of viscera that a very sick animal might cough up. Geoff corked the jar. 'Then, I'll be Caller One, down this side of the page, and you be Caller Two, over there. Let's see, I need this wind-up thing with the handle, and the nose-flute, and the rattle, and the thing like a soft mouth-organ. You get these metal pipes with the numbers on, and this thing that hisses, and at the end here, do you see, you have to give "a high cry", and it specifies a female voice, I suppose because that gets you up above two hundred hertz. Yes?'

He had been dealing out oddities from the box as he spoke. His excitement was infectious enough to stop her yawning. Perhaps it was that the excitement made him look so young: made the boy so apparent in his face. She reached for Caller Two's pile. Everything in it was very evidently a one-off, made for this purpose and this alone. The hissing thing was a cross between a syringe and a curved bicycle pump. The objects he had called pipes were a family of twisted kazoos, machined from a silver on which the light slithered, the biggest as long as her forearm and the smallest a Christmas-cracker novelty of a thing, small enough that she would lose it between her teeth if she wasn't careful.

'I thought it would be words,' she said.

'Maybe they worked those out later,' he said. 'Maybe this is a sort of prototype. – Ready? What do you think, run-through first, or just go at it?'

'Oh, just go at it,' she said.

They leaned together over the page. Caller One and Caller Two had their tasks set out antiphonally, so it was always clear what order they were supposed to happen in.

'I hope there isn't meant to be a special rhythm for this,' she said.

'You'd think they'd say,' said Geoff, frowning. 'No, I'm guessing this is intended to be idiot-proof.'

'Luckily for us.'

He grinned, and picked up 'the wind-up thing', a long box with a crank on the end like the handle of a music box. She nodded, he cranked, and out of it came the tortured sound of a string being plucked. A low, harsh, saw-toothed pulse – more than that, a barbed pulse, that made it feel as if the air was being squeezed. For a device only a foot long, it made an amazingly loud noise, or perhaps an amazingly carrying, amazingly penetrating noise. It dominated the air in the attic. Geoff nodded: she blew into the metal pipe marked *1*. It seemed to have a whirring thing deep inside, or perhaps a whole set of them geared together, tiny zizzing paddlewheels, because what emerged from the metal mouth was not a single note but a complex stridulation, an orchestra of angry grasshoppers. Geoff stopped winding to reach for a thing like a beak to clip to his nose, but the first pulse from the box seemed to linger in the air, and so it went on, with each new instrument seeming not to replace the last one but to add to a building cacophony. A dawn chorus made not of birdsong but of pulses, drones, buzzes, whines, nails-on-blackboard squeals.

Something was happening in the room. The morning light had turned thicker, queasier, with gelatinous currents coiling in it.

I'm not sure about this, thought Iris with the last and smallest of the pipes in her mouth, making a grasshopper sound so high she couldn't hear it except as a stabbing ache in her ears. Geoff's eyes too were glancing about uncertainly over the top of the quivering rubber sac he had clamped to his lips. But when he lifted his hand to cue her in for the last element of the chorus, she spat out the pipe and obediently gave Caller Two's 'high cry', more of a soprano shriek than a sung note, with some real fear behind it.

Then they were both silent, and they panted as if they had lifted something heavy. But though the noise of the chorus died away, its overlapping pulses somehow remained in the air of the attic, as a closing net, a knotted stricture drawing tighter and tighter, and centring as it drew in on the old glass cider jar.

Geoff crouched down to look at it close up, and she followed suit. The dust on the glass made it hard to be sure at first, but soon it was definite: there was a whorl of something white moving in there, a seething of the air growing more energetic. Expanding, pressing against the glass walls in scouring circuits, disclosing as it got bigger that it was composed of rushing white particles all too familiar from the dark market the night before. Was it the same being, or another one of its kind? Iris didn't know how you would tell.

'Self-organised,' breathed Geoff, fascinated, his nose almost touching the glass. 'Self-maintaining. Self-directed. Aware. Hello?' he said experimentally, and tapped the jar. White seething gathered on the inside where his finger touched, frantically energetic, frantically bright, yet not solid white, for every one of its uncountable dots was blinking on and off. A frantic, living mosaic. But it did not look to Iris like a creature trying to communicate. She had understood the joy of the air-spirit the night before when it was released, and she understood the mood of this one now, she felt sure. It was caged, and it was desperate, and it was trying to escape.

'Geoff . . .' she began, and the glass began to vibrate, shaking so hard that the edges of the jar blurred in her vision. A blue-white flame held in by a rind of buzzing transparency. A thin rind. An uncertain rind. Geoff snatched back his finger. They both drew the same conclusion at the same instant, and threw themselves away from the jar, scrambling on hands and knees round the next bend of the junk alley over the bare floorboards.

The jar exploded. It was a high, hollow *bang* that drove glass fragments up and out into the attic ceiling, followed by a shock of air that set off little landslides of paper and mystical detritus all over the room. Looking up from the floor, Iris saw the escaped spirit gathering itself mazily overhead. There were no barrel-rolls of delight this time: it formed itself into a tight cylinder of white, an effervescent battering-ram, and punched its way straight out through the round window, blowing wood splinters and more glass out into the garden.

Iris and Geoff lay there, stunned. A little bit powdered, and strewn with stray gewgaws, yet intact. Iris felt an overwhelming urge to giggle welling up inside her, not just from broken tension but from relief that the horrid ritual was over. She just about had it under control – a jolt or two of laughter shaking her chest – when Geoff said, 'Definitely a prototype', and they both helplessly laughed and laughed.

'I didn't like that,' she said, when she could.

'Me neither.'

'With all due respect to your dad, I'm finding this Order of his less and less appealing.'

'I know what you mean. That was . . . nasty, wasn't it. Oh dear,' he added, staring up.

'What?'

'We've made such a mess of the room . . .'

'Really?' she said. 'How can you tell?' – and that set them both off again, gurgling hysterically and bumping about.

If it could be like this, thought Iris through the laughter, *if we could be like this together, two children exploring an attic, two children off on an adventure – then it would be simple.* And wishing for that simple companionship, she put out a hand – her right hand – and patted him with it as he laughed. An instant later she withdrew it with a yelp.

'What's the matter?' asked Geoff. 'Did you scratch yourself on something?'

No, not a scratch. An appallingly intense and appallingly complete glimpse, all condensed into the sliver of time when her hand made contact, of Geoff's flesh and bones and nerves and blood circulating in a thousand tiny vessels. And alive in all that endless multiplication of detail a Geoff as entirely and thoroughly *there* as her own sovereign self; present Geoff, and past Geoff all the way back to the scrambling and wretched chimney-sweep child, and beyond to the wavering memory of the world warm and his mother smiling; and future Geoff too, all that this recent man might be when the years and the decades settled on him, and the knobbly limbs had rounded out, and his clever mind gained its full power. All that, in a flash. As if she had read a whole novel in a second, and yet had the scrabbling rush of everything in it come to her with total clarity. Or watched a whole film in a second, and taken in the black-white-grey flicker of actors and scenes in it somehow clear and entire. It was too much. It was much, much, much too much. She reeled internally, with Geoff's puzzled gaze on her.

But again, only for a moment, because now something else was happening, and Geoff, distracted, was looking up and past her, and she was turning her head that way as well.

It seemed, to begin with, to be just a change in the light: a rebalancing of the grey wash of dawn through the attic that, for some reason, was shifting the direction of the shadows. A creep, an adjustment, in the outlinings of black behind the piles of mystic junk. But then a source for the change declared itself. A blue glow was brightening in a corner of the roof beside the ruined window; and as it brightened it took on form and movement. Ceaseless movement. Not like the living cloud of white dots she had just seen, which could flow into any shape. This one had more structure. Structure upon structure, structure within structure, an abyss of structure that made you feel that by looking into it you were gazing far down, from the top of some intolerably high precipice into untold depths, even though at the same time the cracked plaster of the wall and the roof beams were faintly visible behind it. And all of that structure moving, metamorphosing, like a kaleidoscope being turned. It looked like a spray of peacock feathers, and then it looked like a fountain of many enfolded blue streams, and then it looked like a sway of overlapping geometric fans, and then it looked like a tree with sapphire eyes for fruit, and then it looked like a many-vaned cobalt whirligig spinning in space: and all these resemblances, before they melted into the next, seemed to be telling you some partial truth about the nature of the thing that shone there. But a truth that dazzled you, and eluded you, and slipped away before you could possibly name it. It was frightening, the creature of light in the corner, but not at all in the same way that the ugliness and discords of the ritual had been frightening. It was frightening because it was majestically incomprehensible. It brought the news that there existed a being of vertiginous complexity which *made sense* – but not to you. Not to a creature with Iris's kind of eyes, or mind. In a funny way, the shock of looking at it, into it, was of all the things that had ever happened to Iris a little bit like the shock of looking inside Geoff just before.

A voice spoke. It did not come from any mouth. It sounded like many wine glasses being rung together. It sounded as if the creature's insides had all momentarily fused into a framework of crystal, being chimed by metal rods. It sounded pure to the point of pain.

It said, 'Pernicious.' It said, 'Pernicious, pernicious, pernicious' – and at every repetition the tuning of the voice improved, and it became less alien, more suited to the ears of human beings, as if the being in the corner were having to rapidly reacquire a skill it had not needed for a long time. 'Pernicious,' it said one last time. And then, the tuning complete, it said in almost human tones, with almost human authority and contempt:

'You pernicious race of odious little vermin!'

'Us?' said Geoff hesitantly. 'Are you talking to . . . us?'

'Who else? Who but you, not five minutes since, was practising foully upon the angels of the lower air?'

'You mean the . . . experiment we were just doing?'

'A clean name for a loathsome thing. I am not surprised you desire to hide its nature from yourself, but a name is no cloak. You cannot hide it, you have not hidden it from the world. All the air hereabouts is roiling with the poison you put into it. Stained with your attempted tyranny.'

'It was just vibrations,' said Geoff.

'*Just* vibrations, when the body of your victim is made from vibrations? I might as well say, *just* chemistry, and feed you a teaspoon of cyanide!'

Another voice was heard, coming from a most definite location. A querulous, anxious, elderly voice issuing from Mr Hale's mouth downstairs. 'Is everything all right up there?' it enquired.

'Fine, Father, it's all fine,' called Geoff.

'I'm just coming up . . .'

'No, don't!'

'Wait a minute,' put in Iris, speaking to the blue being in the corner – it was like addressing a storm, or a mountain, but you could make yourself go on. 'Wait a minute, though. You're saying all these dreadful things about us, but we're the ones who set an . . . angel free last night. You must have felt that, if you felt this. Doesn't that count for something?'

The blue abyss tilted slightly, in her direction in particular.

'If this morning you enslave, what does it matter that last night you liberated? Cease this meddling. Were you mortals not given enough, with the whole of matter and energy to play with, that you must abuse the fabric of creation itself?'

Be ashamed, was the blue creature's message. The blue *angel*'s message, for if she accepted the word for a seething white intelligence trapped in a jar, she had to apply it to this grander being. And she was ashamed. She felt the outrage and the horror radiating out in the crystalline voice, and her own sense of disgust answered it

– rang in response, note resonating with note. They *had* been attempting something vile in the ritual. Trying to take a sick grip on the universe in those ugly sounds, somehow. A rapist's grasp. Taking by force what force should never touch. She had known it at the time, and she knew it now.

But being told off had never been Iris's favourite thing. And even as she shuddered, her old defences against it kicked in. Was the angel not also taking a pompous pleasure in denouncing them? Could she not hear, in the crystal voice, a touch of relish? Wasn't it orating, just a bit? As if it had not got to use language for a while, maybe, and was making the most of the chance. Like a headmaster letting the rhetoric rip as he scolded the boys caught smoking behind the bicycle sheds. Or a headmistress berating the girl caught consorting with the boys smoking behind the bicycle sheds. She was opening her mouth to object when the footsteps they had been hearing, slowly mounting the stairs, reached the top, and the attic door creaked open.

Mr Hale stepped into the room – and cringed back with a cry, his hand over his eyes.

'What is that dreadful *light?*' he said, pain in his voice.

Iris was puzzled. The blue thing was overwhelming, but by virtue of its ungraspable intricacy, its subtlety depth upon depth. It was not especially bright, at least not to her. But Mr Hale was reacting as if there were some scorching, intolerable blaze in the direction where she saw (just now) cogwheels coloured like peacock feathers.

'Can't he see you?' she asked the angel.

'He has deprived himself of the ability,' it said. 'He cannot hear me either. Every warning he has ever had, he has ignored.'

Mr Hale lowered his hand, and you could tell that the room was all glare to him. He set off into it, bumping into the ramparts of junk, with his arms stretched out in front of him. 'Geoffrey?' he said. 'Geoffrey? Where are you? Are you all right?' Muddled, blinded, he reached for his son.

Geoff scrambled to meet him. 'I'm here,' he said. 'I'm here.'

A year later, when Iris had grown wearily familiar with bombs, and learned that the world was divided into those who in the crisis ran towards the bombs to help and those who ran away to hide, she would remember this moment. She would remember its demonstration that, whatever his failings, Mr Hale had been one of those who went towards the explosion when it came to someone he loved.

'I shall leave you,' said the blue angel. 'But you two – you who can still hear me. If you do not desire to be slave-makers or slave-takers, I charge you to stop. Stop now. Desist. Make no more "experiments". Torment the angels of the lower air no further. Leave them alone. Leave all of this alone. Leave this storehouse of folly. Leave the poison in it to moulder undisturbed.' It raised its voice in crystalline clangour, to trumpet strength, to a ringing power that set the walls humming: 'Stop!'

And then it was gone, not gradually but with a suddenness that made Iris's ears pop.

III

Iris walked away from Wildwood Terrace determined again to stay away, but less sure this time that she would really never be back. Resolutions lack conviction the second time around. She had hastily dressed in the rest of her own clothes, and put herself in order for the outside world in the bathroom mirror. She had prevented discussion of the angel by the speed with which she moved. She had wished Geoff good luck in the Army without touching him. She had kissed Mr Hale on the cheek as he sat at the kitchen table having his eyes sponged. She had eluded Geoff's beseeching glances. She had marched to the door and shut it behind her like a person who knew what she wanted. But all the while everything that had happened seethed inside her: fear, and awe, and shame, and guilt, and defiance, and anxiety over what else Lall might do (if it was Lall), and the shocking strangeness of seeing Geoff from the inside, and a sharp regret she couldn't suppress for the warm cotton nest of safety she had found in Geoff's bed. She might look on the outside – she sincerely hoped she did – like a woman in possession of herself. But inside she seemed to be losing her nice, clear hold on her life.

It was a feeling confirmed when she got to Clapham.

'Been staying over with your aunt in Sevenoaks again, I expect, dear?' said Mrs Tilly, intercepting her in the front hall.

'Yes – that's right.'

The imaginary aunt had provided Iris's cover before, for nights at the Savoy and elsewhere, but previously she had always taken care to set the aunt up in advance.

'I thought so when you didn't come in last night,' said the landlady, with a look of almost total scepticism. 'Only I was surprised, with you being so poorly, just yesterday. Fancied a bit of home cooking, I expect?'

'Yes,' said Iris.

'Maybe, though, if this is going to happen a lot, it might make sense to find somewhere a little bit closer to her, mightn't it? Just a suggestion. There's many would be glad of the room, you know.'

'I'm very happy here,' said Iris, and made a mental note to start looking for somewhere else to live on Monday morning.

Her plan had been to live as cheaply as she could, so her savings from her wages and Barracloughs would bulk up fast into an amount worth investing. But when she went in to work at C&B the next week, and was scanning her way with intent through the classifieds in the *Evening News*, she discovered that there had been a fascinating slump in the rented property market. So many prosperous people had fled the city during the initial panic when war broke out that there were apparently furnished flats going begging in the more chichi districts. Although the promised air raids hadn't come, the residents hadn't returned either. Estate agents were chewing their fingernails, landlords were desperately seeking tenants. There was a whole page of advertisements for flats in Chelsea at rents only twice what she was paying at the moment to Mrs Tilly – and here and there the telltale phrase 'any reasonable offer considered' appeared, a signal for cut-throat negotiation if ever there was one. She did sums in her lunch hour. If she could push the price of a flat down to thirty shillings a week, her cash pile would keep growing, although slower than planned. And the more she thought about it, the more the chance of living with no eyes on her, no need for excuses or alibis or imaginary aunts, seemed worth the money. A front door of her own!

So, the Saturday following, she put on her respectable coat and her dullest shoes and a hat with a demure pheasant feather in it, and applied to her mouth the timorous shading of pink that a young wife might dare if she were really not quite sure about the propriety of make-up. The brass curtain ring certain hotels required came out of its matchbox and onto her finger. In Chelsea, she introduced herself as Mrs Saunders, married for only a few months to a young man in the RAF, and as she had hoped, the patriotic note this struck, along with her modest and well-funded demeanour, quite cancelled out the Watford accent for the middle-aged house agent with dandruff-sprinkled shoulders to whom she was speaking. He showed her six flats. She scrutinised them severely, finding fault with plumbing, heating and kitchenettes wherever they went. She scowled especially at the fourth of the six, a lovely thing on the top floor of a mansion block near the Thames. Grey silk wallpaper, golden carpets, sconces of engraved glass that spilled golden light. Neat and sweet and modern.

'I suppose the one in Challoner Court would *do*,' she said sceptically, when they were back in his office and his secretary had brought her a cup of China tea so pale it was virtually hot water. 'It doesn't have a great deal of storage space, does it?'

'Ah, but the advantage of a fully serviced apartment such as this, madam, is the scope it gives for *compact* living. In the contemporary style. Youthful. *Untrammelled*.'

He smiled at his own flight of commercial fancy.

'Exposed to German bombers,' she said. 'And there's no guest bedroom.'

'Plenty of time to think on a larger scale once madam has started a family.'

That, she conveyed with a look of regret, would have to wait until the squadron leader returned from his posting. His very, very remote posting.

'Well,' she said reluctantly, 'considering its disadvantages, if I did take it, I would only be prepared to pay thirty shillings a week.'

'Madam!' he said with a theatrical gasp. 'The price is *three guineas* a week.'

'No,' she said, 'it isn't. The price is whatever people are prepared to give you for it. It looked to me as if it had been empty for at least two months. I'm offering you thirty shillings more than the nothing it is earning at the moment.'

He gave her a sharp, reconsidering glance, as if some different being had suddenly looked out at him from behind the naive maquillage of Mrs Saunders. As, indeed, one had. What kind, though? What sort of opportunist, making the most of the chances of the war? She knew he would not want to let to a tart at any price. That way lay complaints and scandal and the destruction of his business. But she did not look tarty. He inspected her, and she waited. Then he shrugged. Whatever she was, he needed the business, and he knew that she knew it.

'For that sort of price,' he said, dropping the 'madam', 'we'd require a commitment to a year's let. Payable in advance.'

She had thought this might happen. If he was settling for a halved commission, he would at least want to collect it up front.

'Would cash be acceptable?' she asked, opening her handbag and reaching for the sheaf of five-pound notes.

Moving in was easy. Three suitcases full of clothes, and a cardboard box for her few other possessions. So few, she thought, once she had put them all away and the sleek surfaces of the flat still scarcely registered her presence, that perhaps she should get some more. Perhaps she was travelling too light. But how glorious it was to take possession of a domain entirely her own. She walked from room to room of it with her shoes off, squidging her stockinged feet luxuriously in the fitted carpet. *Her* carpet. Her bedroom, with the yellow-gold coverlet on the divan that matched the yellow-gold curtains. Her bathroom, with the glass shelves for creams and perfume bottles and an American shower-bath over the tub. Her sitting room, with the cocktail cabinet in the corner, and the curved metal windows looking out in the late-afternoon glow over the rooftops of Chelsea, towards the river. Hers. This, surely, was where her life could be given back its chosen direction. There was nothing here that was ancient or mysterious. Everything was modern, and material, and comfortable. Here she could banish angels with the chromium swish of a cocktail shaker. She wriggled her toes, and did not think at all about the warmth of Geoff's sheets.

It meant a new route for her commute, though. Up the King's Road to Sloane Square Tube station, and then the District Line to the City. The first couple of mornings, she walked to Sloane Square, but Chelsea had a drawback she had not anticipated: one that perhaps went with the smart modernity of the furniture shops and the clothes shops and the shops selling household items in chrome. On the right, a few hundred yards before the square, there was a big old Victorian Gothic building which looked like a school. But it had been repurposed. Now there were sentries in tight black polo-necks and shiny elasticated belts keeping guard at its pointed brick porch. Above the doorway was a logo of a lightning bolt in a circle. Placards on one side read FASCISM FOR KING AND EMPIRE and on the other FASCISM IS PRACTICAL PATRIOTISM. A loudspeaker van and a limousine were parked in front. As she passed, out of the big black car got an elderly grandee in a wing collar. It was not the prime minister but whoever it was had Mr Chamberlain's look of Edwardian dignity out of its depth, trying to deal with the modern world as if it were merely a new thing like a cocktail shaker. He hurried across her path into the porch and the sentries gave a straight-armed salute. Hail Mosley, presumably, not

Heil Hitler: this was the Black House, headquarters of the British Union of Fascists. It was what the country was supposed to be at war with, theoretically, yet here it was, unembarrassed, confident in its powerful friends. It would have been nice to dismiss it as ridiculous, but the confidence made it horrible instead: a black-beetle eruption into the daylight, a slick of night oozing onto the pavement. The sentries weren't magical – were obviously, as she clocked them out of the corner of her eye, pent-up middle-class bodybuilder types, two editions of Anxious of Tunbridge Wells who had been working on their biceps – and yet they made the same statement to the world as the Watcher had with his newspaper face. Force. Force for the sake of force, force for the thrill of force, force you couldn't reason with or bargain with or pay to look away. Force that only invited you through its door until it had the power to drag you. She had read the reports; she knew what the Nazis did in buildings like this.

The next morning, she put the width of the street between her and the Black House, hoping that was enough, but this time some kind of parade was coming out of a side exit. Two columns of women in black shirts and jodhpurs beat on side drums, followed by a phalanx of men carrying a banner that said *PEACE NOW*. None of the drummers were Lall, but then maybe Lall wasn't a fascist in the signed-up, card-carrying sense. Or maybe she was, and she was something more than a foot soldier. From then on Iris caught the bus up the King's Road, and passed at speed.

The second part of the journey was much better. The District Line went right to Monument station, virtually on the doorstep of the Mariner Building, but there would be something depressing, she decided, about emerging from the stuffy train and two minutes later being inside a stuffy office for the day. She wanted an equivalent to the walk across London Bridge, when the City had rolled itself out before her all at once as a grey-and-brown panorama; as a place that was about to enfold her. She couldn't have that, from this new direction, but she could, she thought, give herself a sense of arrival. She could walk in and let herself feel that she was taking possession of it. So she took the train to Blackfriars, and walked the City west to east to the Mariner Building.

It only took fifteen minutes. To begin with, she went the obvious and direct way, along Queen Victoria Street, past the audibly chugging printing presses of *The Times* and the new deco facade of Faraday House, where a statue of Mercury the messenger god looked down on eight floors of telephone exchange. But it was a diagonal bulldozed through the old streets she was on, she realised, driven through the density so you didn't have to see what was to left and right of you. She wanted to see. She took to jinking north, when she had time, and making the ceremonial entrance to the City up Ludgate Hill. There the grey dome of St Paul's floated huge ahead of her, a half-planet of its own dominating the sky. But all around lay a warren of tiny passages and entryways, crammed with equally tiny and very specialised businesses. Wig-powderers, gold-leaf-appliers, purveyors of the printed forms for obscure licences. Booksellers where dictionaries of ancient Chaldean gathered dust next to this year's *Wisden*. The cobbled alleys had pious medieval names, Amen Corner and Angel Passage, Creed Lane and Sermon Lane. Her heels moved briskly east but her mind wandered, fascinated, in a version of the City with a different romance to it than the ones she knew. This place was mercantile yet slow and crabbed, proudly rooted to its little yards of ground. Its handwriting was copperplate. An inkhorn City. A Dickensian City. The bells for half past eight rang from steeple to steeple as she passed through.

Through the month of November, the 30-Share Index gently recovered. Minuscule volumes, still; but it was as if the stock market was sharing in the general disbelief that this war they were in, which had begun with such alarm and then dwindled into boredom, could really be so very serious. Look: the sky was a-bob with balloons, the blackout was an infernal nuisance, but the genuinely upsetting news about Warsaw besieged and aflame had been replaced by occasional items, usually naval in nature, from far-off spots like Scapa Flow or the River Plate. The enemy planes failed to come, and failed to come, and failed to come. Winston Churchill, back in office as First Lord of the Admiralty, bounced energetically up the steps of the Admiralty in the morning, bounced energetically down them again at nightfall, looking serious, looking resolute, as the car driven by some pretty girl in uniform carried him away. But then – people were starting to say again, now that the initial shock had worn off – Churchill had always been inclined to *exaggerate* the German threat, hadn't he?

Mr Cornellis did not seem to share this view, as far as Iris could judge. He looked strained and anxious in the office. One day his son Harold came in in uniform at the end of the morning to take him out to lunch. Harold was on leave before his battalion of the Bedfordshire and Hertfordshire Regiment left for France. He called his father *Tateh*, but was otherwise an indistinguishable college boy, with a moustache trying for dashing and not quite getting all the way. He smiled uncertainly as his father led him round the ninth floor. The war had come to snatch him from Cambridge and the Territorials before he could begin his inevitable apprenticeship in the family firm, so the staff didn't know him, and he didn't know them. Cornellis senior clapped him on the shoulders when it was time to say goodbye, squeezed his hand and performed warm confidence: but once Harold's back was turned, Iris observed, he watched his boy walk to the lift as if the world were growing more dangerous every moment.

A week or so after that, Mr Cornellis stayed late again to send another solitary message on the teletype. This time, he refused Iris's help, and all she saw as she left the office was him gingerly seating himself at the keyboard in the early-winter dark, and beginning to hunt among the keys. She made sure to come in good and early the next day, riding the Underground straight to Monument and letting the sound of Bow bells take care of itself. No one had touched the machine. Sonia, Delia and Maude weren't in yet. Mrs Sinclair was, but she was off in the little ninth-floor kitchen brewing a pot of tea.

Iris put in the code for Last Message Repeat, and out of the printer came a block of eight-digit numbers. No, not quite numbers. There were letters in there too, here and there:

25B00238
4199QR12
S44330E2
780110DD
5P39731M
823FJ891
H6631756
002711B4

A code? More like a list, but of what? Nothing she had come across in C&B's equity dealings looked quite like this. Bargain numbers varied in format from jobber to jobber; share certificate numbers varied in format from share to share. She tore off the six inches of grey paper carefully, and pocketed it.

Lunchtime was no good for working on it – she was back in the Lyons' eating soup with Mrs S and the girls – but on the Tube home she fetched it out along with a stub of pencil and tried to see what she could deduce. All she came up with was that the numbers ran from 0 to 9, and the alphabet letters were varied enough that they probably ran from A to Z. Also, the letters could apparently be in any position in the row of eight symbols. That meant – well, that *might* mean – that for any position in the row there would be a choice of ten digits plus twenty-six letters, making thirty-six options in total. Giving you how many possible combinations in the row of eight, assuming it mattered what order the symbols appeared? Thirty-six times thirty-six, eight times over. She hadn't finished calculating by Sloane Square, and completed the sum back at the flat, by which time the back of the print-out was covered in pencil. The answer seemed to be 2,821,109,907,456. Two trillion, eight hundred and twenty-one billion, one hundred and nine million, nine hundred and seven thousand, four hundred and fifty-six. What on earth needed that many unique serial numbers? She had no idea.

And did she think of Geoff? Helplessly. She thought of him when she saw the crumpled dent in the postbox every morning, with its reminder that the world contained angels as well as office work; was fierce and fearsome as well as mundane. She thought of him when she passed the ABC Tea Room at Ludgate Circus, still in business, where Mr Hale had had his encounter with George Bernard Shaw all those years ago. She thought of him when she looked at Harold Cornellis in his subaltern's uniform, crisp and pressed with the Sam Browne belt over his shoulder. Geoff would not be an officer. Geoff's narrow neck, with the fuzz over the bones at the base of his skull, would be sticking out of the coarse collar of khaki battledress. He would be sleeping in some long room full of bunks she couldn't quite picture, surrounded by a random collection of louder men who might not be gentle with his oddities. She thought of him when she went to bed herself, under the golden coverlet in the room with the golden curtains, and tried to drown him out with frantic fingerwork in the dark, leaving her sore and still assailed by the memory of blushes moving like cloud-shadows on freckled skin. She thought of him when a postcard from him turned up at C&B – the only address he had, of course.

Mrs Sinclair scolded her, but with a softening of indulgence. Sonia said, 'Is that from your feller?' 'No,' said Iris, and buried it hastily in her handbag. It was a plain buff rectangle, with a military postmark that left her none the wiser about where he was. On the back he had written, *In case you're interested, I'm due a pre-embarkation leave at the end of January*, and had added a return address that was mostly numbers. The script, in black ink, was so tidy that it looked like a printed page, and he had signed it G. D. HALE in little capital letters. She didn't reply.

December saw the weather turn cold. Sharp frosts at morning and evening; an edge like a blade to the winds off the river; the coal smoke coagulating to a blue layer near the ground that moved like a tarry syrup, and tasted like one too. On clear nights, the moon painted swathes of ice-white over the roofscape of the blacked-out city. The stars, far brighter than she had ever seen them in London, glittered and trembled in the black air, and the river wrinkled into minute lines of silver, as if the moon were pressing fingerprints into it. She stood and gazed at her Chelsea window, on the glass side of the blackout curtains and the golden ones. And she shivered. There was a shortage of coke, the only thing one was allowed to burn in the mansion block's small grates. She queued on Saturdays at a coal merchant's on the King's Road, and came home lugging a sack big enough to let her have a scant hour's warmth every second day. If the other flats had been fully occupied, other people's heat might have risen up to her free of charge, but the block was half-empty. She bicycled her feet in her chilly bedsheets. She switched from nylons to lisle stockings, thick and brown.

Rumour had it that fuel would soon be actually rationed, along with almost everything else: food, clothes, cigarettes. With this in mind, and with little idea of how a wartime Christmas was supposed to go, London set out to promise itself a good time, while a good time was still available. Behind the blackout of the butchers' shops, plucked poultry started appearing, ranked in their bony bluish nakedness. Behind the blackout of the pubs and bars, eggnog and punch were on offer. Behind the blackout of the West End, surreptitious Christmas trees twinkled discreetly. Toy trains and dolls for unevacuated middle-class children, one-piece 'shelter suits' in cotton jersey for stylish middle-class mothers. Sugared almonds and sherry. Carol singers grouped in porticoes and archways, safely out of reach of the lightless traffic and, lightless themselves, singing 'God Rest Ye Merry, Gentlemen' from memory, so that on Regent Street you moved from hub to hub of invisible song. Iris took herself out to buy a vase for her mantelpiece, so that there would be something on it to break up the lonely expanse of polished wood; and, rewrapping her muffler, emerged onto Piccadilly to see on the other side the shadows of three well-turned-out women in a uniform of some kind draped around a limousine and laughing. The outer two were turned admiringly inward towards the one in the centre. The one in the centre moved in a way Iris recognised from the dance floor of the Kinesis Club. Elegance with a stick up its arse. This time, it *was* Lall. And Lall not quite alone, but in little enough company to be safely confronted.

She crossed over. Snow was starting to fall: tiny, hard crumbs of flakes, like weightless hail. Thanks to the dark, she got quite close before she was noticed. She had time to take in how fabulous – of course – Lall looked in tailored, wasp-waisted khaki, with a soft cap on her blonde hair and some sort of wheel insignia on her lapels. A chocolate-box girl soldier. No make-up now, but perfect skin and perfect bone structure more than compensated. Iris herself was ordinarily pretty – she knew this about herself – in a slightly softfeatured way that, when she was old, she confidently expected would make her look like a crumpled bun. She relied on careful clothes, and on the communicative properties of a female body that enjoyed being a body. Lall was something of a different order: a maddening freak of nature.

Now they were only feet away. But at the last minute Iris felt herself faltering. That confident braying: who said this wasn't just, for the figure in the middle as well as for the other two, the ordinary braying of ordinary posh girls, ordinarily convinced that the world belonged to them? She had no actual proof that Lall had sent the Watcher, did she. Suddenly the whole thing seemed embarrassingly unlikely, a fairy tale she had cooked up herself to justify a dislike. Or, worse, an envy. She had opened her mouth to make the accusation. It started to drift closed again.

It might have closed the whole way, she might have retreated, if Lall hadn't glanced Iris's way, stared, and then smirked. There was absolutely no ambiguity in it, no puzzlement. No guilt either. Just the surprise of someone who hadn't expected their victim to pop back up. Yes, Lall had sent the Watcher. No, Lall wasn't even slightly sorry about it. The urge to skip the talking and clout her was strong. A roundhouse slap to knock the cap off, and bounce her off the car – oh, yes *please* – but Lall exuded all the imperviousness of her class, and Iris felt certain that seconds after thumping Lall she would find herself in the custody of a Piccadilly policeman only too happy to help an aristocrat fend off an oik.

'Well, well,' said Lall merrily. 'Look who it is. You seem well!'

'No thanks to you,' said Iris. 'That thing you sent very nearly killed me.'

Lall rolled her eyes. 'You poor thing,' she said. 'I think you may be a *trifle* confused.'

The women on either side of her laughed again. Clearly, this was a mad person bothering their beautiful friend.

'I'm surprised to see you helping the war effort,' said Iris. 'I'd have thought with your opinions you'd be in some manor house somewhere, sipping cocktails and waiting for Hitler to win.'

'My dear,' said Lall, 'I don't want Hitler to defeat *us*. Of course not. I just want this ridiculous war to end. Till then, one naturally does one's duty.'

'Lady Lalage is one of our most devoted volunteers,' said the woman on the right.

'Devoted to *what*, is the question,' said Iris.

Lall frowned. 'Excuse me,' she said, with a graceful tilt of the head to each of her worshippers, and led Iris a few steps aside. The little grains of snow blew round them in the dark. Standing next to each other, it turned out that Iris was several inches taller. Lall crooked a finger in a slim leather glove at Iris to get her to lean over, a gesture which all by itself contrived to suggest the extra height was a galumphing deficiency on Iris's part. If Lall was an exquisite miniature, so should all women be. Iris bent towards the fetching cap and the lovely bones.

'Listen, you little bitch—' Iris began.

'If you didn't like what I sent,' said Lall sweetly, talking across her as if she hadn't spoken, 'perhaps that will teach you to keep your grubby paws off what doesn't belong to you.'

'*Teach* me?' said Iris, incredulous. 'It tried to kill me.'

Lall shrugged. 'And yet, here you are. Large as life and twice as annoying.'

'No: listen. It tried to *kill* me.'

'So?'

'Do you not understand how mad that is? I embarrassed you at the Kinesis Club, that's all I did – or maybe "humiliated" would be a better word, d'you think? Yes, I think I like "humiliated". Little Lally was humiliated in public. There are *normal* ways to deal with that.' As Iris said the word, she got an unpleasant flash of Geoff saying it to her, but she pressed on. 'You could have made a catty remark to get all those intellectuals to laugh at me. You could have done it with gossip – told some posh boy you know in a merchant bank to spread it round the City that I'll open my legs for anyone. You could even have competed at the time, if you cared. He wanted you more than he wanted me.' *Not any more*, her mind supplied silently. 'I took Fortress Geoff pretty much by surprise attack, if you know what I mean.'

Apparently Lall didn't know what she meant. Her rosebud mouth had contracted into a dark little knot, and she was staring up at Iris with a kind of disgusted impatience, as if nothing that was being said made sense except that she was being insulted. *Oh God, she's another good girl*, thought Iris.

'Or – I don't know, how are these things done in your circles? You could have . . . sent me a stiffly worded note. Instead you sent me an assassin! As if you think the penalty for offending you should be death. That's . . . *ridiculous*. You must see that?'

'Are you quite finished?' said Lall.

Iris gave up. 'You didn't even want him,' she said.

'Not the point; he was *mine*.'

'He's not a pet, you know. Or a zoo animal. He's—'

Iris broke off.

'Yes?' said Lall. 'What is he?'

'Never mind,' said Iris.

'Oh my,' said Lall with horrible acuteness. 'Has somebody fallen for somebody? How touching. But now look. As to why I did . . . whatever I might have done . . . the answer, my dear, is because I *could*. One uses the power one has. You wouldn't understand, but that's what power is for.'

'It isn't yours, though, is it? The power. It's stolen.'

'Power,' said Lall, 'belongs to whoever is strong enough to wield it. – You *have* been poking your nose in where it doesn't belong.'

'Blame yourself for that,' Iris said. 'You made it my business when you threatened me.'

'And yet you still don't grasp the position you're in. I think you can't be very clever. Let me spell it out for you. I *could* hurt you, and I still *can*. You may roll in the mud with Geoffrey if you absolutely insist – you probably can't help yourself where that sort of thing is concerned – but if you didn't enjoy my messenger last time, and you don't want me to send another one—'

'You can't,' said Iris. 'There was only one Watcher, and he's gone. I set him free. I did. Me. Sorry if that was inconvenient.'

There was a large part of Iris that would have liked to back down, but talking to Lall was like playing tennis. It imposed a rhythm, at least if you were at all competitive yourself. The ball came at you, and so instinctively you whacked it back across the net, harder. She was gripping her hands together on her shopping bag to stop them shaking. Lall, to her satisfaction, was starting to hiss between her pearly little teeth as she breathed. Less pocket Venus, more tea kettle with contents boiling and lid rattling.

'You have no idea what I can and cannot do,' said Lall. 'None. Yet up you march to me, in your cheap clothes, when I'm talking to my friends, and try to remonstrate with me. You! Some common little shop assistant, or whatever it is you are. Stay away from me – that's what I'm saying. If you value your sordid little existence, don't ever let me lay eyes on you again.'

'Suits me, *my dear*,' said Iris. 'You leave me alone, I'll leave you alone.'

Lall hesitated. Evidently she felt that the right note of triumph, or of submission on Iris's part, had not been struck. She grimaced, and appeared to decide on something.

'Happy Christmas!' she said, in kindly Lady Bountiful tones, loud enough for the two women behind her to hear, and she attempted to pat Iris's cheek with a gloved palm, no doubt with enough force to sting. But the rules of a playground fight did not allow a last-minute victory-by-condescension to go unchallenged. Iris dropped her bag, hearing her new vase crack as it hit the pavement, and seized the patting hand before it could make contact. That was with her own left hand, and since her right was free she reached it out for Lall's face with a sudden impulse of curiosity. She hadn't touched anyone else with it since it had given her the dizzy vista inside Geoff. Would it give her a view of Lall from the inside too? What sort of poisonous rose garden would that be? Would she see the godfather Mr Hale had mentioned? Would she see what it had been like to be the Order's perfect little princess?

But Lall intercepted her in turn, holding her off with her other glove wrapped around the reaching hand, and for a moment they were awkwardly grappling with no contact made on either side, an expression on Lall's face that Iris couldn't decipher in the dark. Though light might not have helped either. It was fury mixed with something startled yet also elated. Lall seemed to be made of wire under the tailoring, but Iris was stronger thanks to her height. They pushed and pulled for a confused second, but the other two women were hurrying over and Lall wrenched free, and turned away to be enfolded in their concern.

'Are you blotto or something?' said one disgustedly over her shoulder as they drew Lall away into the dark.

'Hardly!' said Iris, and wished she had a more brilliant comeback on the tip of her tongue. But the conversational battle was over. The snow was thickening, her enemy had withdrawn, and a new flow of passers-by, nothing but black silhouettes, were stepping round her.

She picked up her bag from the ground. Pieces of vase moved gratingly inside it. She put herself in onward motion and immediately she was herself only one more black silhouette, gone into the anonymity of the flow down Piccadilly. Two flows, really. Dark foot traffic below, rushing white gusts above. Now she had better buy herself some glue for Christmas.

IV

By the week before Christmas, London seemed positively Arctic. Iris was picking her way over ice-glazed pavements towards Threadneedle Street to deliver one more packet of S1s when she had the encounter she usually took pains to avoid. Ears aching, skin on her forehead tight with cold, she had her head down in the scouring wind. Little dust-devils of dry snow were whirling between the high dark walls of the street, whispering against the bronze and gold of the doors, moving like currents of icing sugar over plate glass as darkly emerald as frozen ponds. Ahead, buses emerged from swirling whiteness and dissolved into it again. Then suddenly there in front of her was the black bulk of a middle-aged bank messenger in frock coat and top hat, crusted with white on his windward side all the way from his ankles up to the hat. He had a document case chained to his black-gloved hand, and an expression of nervous resolution on his big, gentle face.

'Hello, our Iris,' he said.

'Hello, Dad,' said Iris sadly.

'How are you keeping, then? I do keep an eye out for you, but somehow I don't seem to have run into you for months. I was starting to think you'd got a job somewhere else.'

'No, I'm still at C&B.'

'And doing well?'

'I think so.'

'That's good. I always said, Iris'll do well, with a headpiece on her like that. A real brain for figures, has our Iris.'

They looked at each other helplessly. They had never known quite how to talk to each other, even before there were troubles to complicate the picture. When it came to resemblance, and therefore conflict between two equally quick-tongued beings, the similarity was all with her mother. What she'd got from Henry Hawkins was a family tradition, three generations old, of working in the money mills of the City. Watford existed to get you on the morning train to the Square Mile, where there were always jobs tending the great machinery of finance. Jobs for clerks, jobs for office girls, jobs for solid, reliable men who could be trusted to carry from building to building documents worth ten thousand times the wages the City would pay them in their whole working life. Iris wanted to own what was in the case, not carry it about, but this was an ambition that passed so entirely through the ceiling of what her father thought possible that, to him, it transcended all imagining. His hopes for her were maddeningly small, though not his worries about her, any more; and whenever they met, whenever she didn't manage to see him in the distance and slide away in time up another turning, he would have this hang-dog look. This anxious desire written all over his baby-wide forehead and blue cheeks, to mend what couldn't be mended.

He cleared his throat now. 'I was wondering if there was any chance we might see you over Christmas, love?'

'Oh, Dad,' she said. 'You know Mum wouldn't abide it.'

'But maybe, if you could slip in in the afternoon? On Boxing Day, say. Your uncle and your aunties and all the cousins'll be over. The place'll be full.'

'You know what would happen. It'd happen in front of a nice big audience, that's all. Plum duff and shouting.'

'I just think, there must be a way?'

'There isn't, though, is there.'

'You're my two girls. It ought to be— You ought to be— I mean, at Christmas—'

'She's not going to forgive me, Dad. Not now. It is what it is. I'm sorry,' she said, 'I'm freezing, I've got to go.'

She reached up and kissed his cheek. Against her lips she felt the chill roughness of his stubble. The well-known stubble, once such an object of fascination, such a mighty part of his paternal magnificence, when she sat on the edge of the bath kicking her feet in the air and watching the ceremony of the wet shave. Rasp of the razor. The lather coming off in stripes. The geyser delivering clouds of steam courtesy of good City wages. The wonderful shaving brush with REAL BADGER HAIR printed on its base in a circle of gold letters.

'Bye, Dad.'

'God bless, love. Look after yourself.'

'Bye.'

She was already moving away when she had a thought.

'Dad?'

'Yes, love?' he said, turning back, hope kindling dreadfully in his face.

'Do you happen to know . . .'

'Yes?'

'What comes with an eight-figure serial number, with letters of the alphabet in it?'

It wasn't what he wanted her to ask of him, but Mr Hawkins had by now carried virtually every form of precious paper in his case, bills of exchange and silver certificates and letters of credit and a whole worldful of different kinds of shares and stocks.

'Sounds like it could be— You're not doing anything you shouldn't, are you?'

'No, no. Just something I came across at work, and I'd like to sound like I know what I'm talking about.' Self-improvement he approved of highly.

'Well, now,' he said. 'That could be US Treasuries, couldn't it.

They've got the code with the eight numbers and letters. Dangerous old things, though, those are.'

'Why?'

''Cause they're bearer bonds. Can be cashed by anyone holding them with no questions asked. Lose one of them and you ain't never getting it back.'

'I see.'

'It definitely lent a thrill to the job, carrying them.'

'Why?'

'Well, most of the stuff in here, it's valuable, but only to the party with their name on it. Them, someone could bash me on the head, take this off me with a cold chisel, and they'd be a million American dollars the richer right then and there. Or however much it was. But don't worry,' he said, looking at her face and misinterpreting what he saw there, 'it never happened! And now it never will. All of those kind of things are on the list for con-fis-cation, under the war regs. We won't be seeing them again.'

'Right,' she said.

'You know,' he said, 'we could always have a cuppa tea together one day, you and me, if there were things you wanted to know. I'd like that.'

'So would I,' she said, feeling ever guiltier. 'One day. Yes, we must. But now I better go before, you know, my fingers drop off.'

'All right, then,' he said. And called after her jovially, when she had gone a few steps, 'You should get a warmer hat! Days like these, you know what I do? I stuff the topper with cotton wool, and it's lovely!'

He had shared this secret with her at regular intervals her entire childhood. She lifted a hand without turning, and made it round the nearest corner.

*

She did the rest of the journey to the frigid undercroft of the Bank of England in a kind of self-directed fury, not helped by losing her footing under the eye of the new stone titans and titanesses who marched across the Bank's south facade, and coming down with a wallop on her backside. She scowled at the innocent elderly man who tried to help her up, and who set her the additional problem of not giving him an eyeful as her feet slid opposite ways on the rink-smooth paving. In the end she got herself upright by hauling hand over hand on the rusticated stone blocks of the Bank's front wall. It was no day for heels.

Inside and underground, it was so cold beneath the white-tiled vaults that the air seemed to be made of a thicker, more jellied substance. The staff of the Securities Registration Office were huddled in overcoats and fingerless gloves. Steam rose from their mouths in puffs, and they moved at half-speed as they took the S1s from her. It made the Mariner Building, only intermittently heated as it was by now, look cosy in comparison.

She hurried away – hurried, anyway, as fast as self-preservation allowed. There were particular hazards at junctions, where refrozen slush had hardened into slicks like black glass. The bitter snow blew. Far fewer people were about than usual, and those that were all seemed alone, solitary black blurs being tugged at and buffeted by the winter.

Cutting through one of the lanes south of Cornhill, though, she realised that she recognised the lone figure ahead of her, going the same way on the other side, and weaving slightly. It was Lancelot Eardley, he of the petroleum futures and of the conviction that, if he undid her suspenders, he was winning and she was losing. His overcoat was an enviably rich and heavy calf-length sweep of superfine blue-black wool, like a blanket gone to heaven. He had the collar up and his hat pressed down, so only a glimpse of his black hair and his nose were showing. A handsome hawk's beak of a nose, and a derisive mouth she'd liked, even when the words coming out of it were nonsense. She did not sleep with ugly men.

Driven by a logic she did not care to investigate, but which had something to do with having had two encounters in the street in a row now that she hadn't been able to control, she steered a deliberate course over towards him.

'Hullo, Lancelot,' she said.

He startled; did not recognise her for a minute and, when he did, flickered with dismay and glanced rapidly up and down the street. She was the bit of stuff he had taken to Brighton: not someone one wanted to display to chaps one knew. But she had checked the coast was clear.

'Don't worry,' she said. 'There's nobody but you, me and the blizzard.'

'Hah,' he said. 'But what do you want, my dear? In a bit of a hurry, to be honest . . .'

Close up, he was looking less good than she remembered. The petroleum futures market must be more or less dead, and he had clearly been having a liquid lunch. There was a sag to his cheeks and an unhealthy flush on his handsome cheekbones, as if he had been rubbed blue-red there by a cheese grater. A hawk going to seed. In for a penny, however: it was too late to stop now.

'I was just wondering what your plans were, for Christmas.'

'You know,' he said warily, 'family; that sort of thing. Why?'

'I thought you might like to spend some of it with me.'

'Oh,' he said. 'Oh.' And there it was, on his thin mouth. The slow-dawning smile of concupiscence. She still had her power. 'Can't get enough of it, eh? What a splendid girl you are . . .'

'Iris.'

'Yes, Iris. Well! I might have to be a *little* bit ingenious. But I'm sure something can be arranged . . .'

*

The 'something' proved to be a golf-course hotel near Maidenhead. She travelled there to meet him at lunchtime on Christmas Eve, dressed entirely in silk next to her skin, with heavy eye-shadow and plum-coloured lipstick put on thick. Subtle had never been Lancelot's preference, and she was not feeling very subtle herself. The train was full of chattering people carrying home the last of their Christmas shopping. She folded her hands in her lap and watched them. Children ignored her, women flicked their gazes over her in scorn. Middle-aged men (there were no young ones) either blanked her or lingered, smiling faintly. Outside the carriage windows, winter fields went by, a little bit warmer but not thawed. Still grey-white, grey-white, grey-white, scrawled by hedgerows.

At Maidenhead station, all these travellers scattered: to houses, presumably, decorated with tinsel and paper chains, to the smell of pine needles indoors, and gusts of cooking smells from kitchens. Shops on the High Street were beginning to close. The world was folding itself, packing itself away into the privacies of Christmas. She got in a taxi, as she had been instructed to do, and it carried her less far than she had imagined, through a brief zone of red-brick semis to a piece of snow-covered golf landscape that seemed still implanted in the side of the town. She could see steeples back the way she had come, and hear bells ringing.

The hotel was a new, low, brick-and-glass construction, so taped over with blackout along its wide windows that it seemed to be built from alternating stripes of red and black. Some kind of commercial Christmas party was going on downstairs, a hubbub of many people in identical yellow paper hats, and the porter at the front desk was wearing one too as he winked at her, and waved her upstairs.

Lancelot was waiting for her, already changed into a bathrobe, his black hair wet from the shower-bath, his white ankles seamed with hairs like crushed ants. He had got paunchier than she remembered him being. The room was large, with windows that presumably looked out over the first hole when they weren't blacked out. But scuffed-looking, with worn places in the unpleasant puce carpet.

'Oh my,' he said. 'Look at you. What an amazing little piece you are. I must have been a good boy this year, mustn't I, to get a present like you? What do you say to a quick tumble right now, straight away? Then we can have dinner, take our time, and do it all again at leisure.'

'Steady on,' she said. 'It's freezing out there. I've been freezing for a fortnight. I want to get *warm*, at least, before I get fucked.'

She saw the word do its usual transgressive work: a bad word, a man's word, in a woman's mouth.

'A shower would do the job,' he said eagerly. 'Quick blast of hot water, and you'll be ready for anything.'

'Don't be silly,' she said. 'I'm your Christmas present, aren't I? I've wrapped myself up carefully so you can unwrap me carefully. Piece by piece slithering to the floor, Lancelot. I'm not just going to throw it all off in the bathroom, now, am I?'

'I suppose not,' he said, grinning.

'That's right,' she said, 'so you'll just have to wait. You'll. Just. Have. To. Wait.'

With each word, she tapped the air with a plum-nailed forefinger, getting closer and closer, landing at the last one with her fingertip in the V of the bathrobe. She had forgotten all about the issue of her right hand, until an instant before her finger touched the skin of his chest and it was too late to recall it, or even to brace herself.

And she felt – nothing. Not an unwelcome insight into Lancelot Eardley Esquire as he seemed to himself. Nothing. And not the ordinary nothing of indifference either; not the ho-hum of making contact with another human where desire was weak or absent. Not the faint signal, tending to silence, of touch when you didn't care. This was something different. An utter blanking or suspension of her senses, where he was concerned. It was as if touch had stopped working. She had her fingertip on the grainy whorl of his chest hair, and she could feel pressure from it, but otherwise, numbness, absence. No texture, no temperature, no feeling of there being a body *there*. He was utterly inert. He might as well have been made out of wax, or plaster of Paris – except that even those things had some specific quality to them, a slipperiness or a graininess that would have sent back some small packet of information to her hand.

Her first thought was that this was another piece of magical malevolence by Lall. A sending: one more hollow thing, sent to menace her in the shape of Lancelot, whose inside she could not feel because it possessed none; was just a skin, walking. But there, right in front of her, was Lancelot's incipient second chin and Lancelot's foxy smile, which had not even had time to turn puzzled by her sudden stillness. Terribly particular, somehow; his teeth on one side nipping with anticipation at his own lip as he contemplated the story of himself she was helping him to weave, in which all middle-aged sag vanished, because he was a daring predator and she was the henhouse he was about to raid, with squeaks of protest, flying feathers, and then hot-breathed acquiescence. None of that sounded like Lall, did it? Not the gross heat of his seducer act, when she was so coldly indifferent. Not the exact quality of his Home Counties sleaze. Lall didn't have the curiosity, Lall didn't have the imagination, to send a Lancelot.

But what was happening, then, if this was the real man? She spread all the fingers of her hand onto his bare skin and pressed. Still nothing. A block of absence in human form, under her hand. A void. It was horrible; and all the more horrible because it just made him smile wider. He was feeling a circle of fingernails pinching and probing just fine. The nullity was all on her side. It wasn't something wrong with him, but with her. An incapacity. A dreadful hole ripped in her ability to feel.

Suddenly, staying even an instant longer was impossible. But getting out of this was going to be harder than getting in. Lancelot wasn't one of the out-and-out dangerous men – the sort who, hearing you had ever said yes to any man, thought it meant you owed a yes to them. That, from now on, yes was a formality that could be permanently dispensed with in your case. She wouldn't have gone near him if he had been. But he was almost certainly of the school that believed, if you once turned up in silk underwear talking dirty, your yes was final, and could not be rescinded. And he was stronger than her.

'Champagne,' she said thickly. 'I want champagne.'

'But I'll have to get dressed,' he protested.

'Go on, then.'

'I'm not even sure they'll have it. Wilds of Berkshire, and all that.'

'I'll make it worth your while,' she said.

'Oh God, all right.'

She stood like a post, trying to smile, while he struggled into trousers and a shirt. She watched from the room door while he stumped down the stairs, and the moment he'd vanished into the bar, she grabbed her overnight case and plunged down the stairs herself.

Past the desk – 'That was quick!' said the porter – and out of the door and up the snowy drive at a desperate crunching run, eyes blinded, trees and shrubberies going by in tangled confusion. The taxi was long gone, naturally. At least she was wearing flat shoes. The heels had been waiting in her case, to add some sway to the ensemble as Lancelot did his unwrapping.

Even when she had rounded three bends of the suburban avenue beyond, and it was plain there was going to be no pursuit, she kept up a panting jog-trot, out of a superstitious terror strangely akin to what she had felt when the Watcher's face came clear. She needed to be away, away, from the place where the world had stopped making sense; from the pit of nothingness yawning suddenly before her. Why couldn't the world have stayed solid, why couldn't it have gone on behaving the way it always had? A little bit sleazy, maybe not always to be examined too closely as you took your pleasures in it – but *reliable*. She hadn't asked for magic. She hadn't asked for terror, or for rapture. 'Damn it!' she cried to the rooks startling up from chimneys and aerials, to the elms along the edge of a cricket field, to the lowered shutters and bolted doors of the High Street. Damn it, damn it, damn it. She limped into the station, all the straps and lace chafing that she had worn to serve herself up in.

She had been afraid there might be no more trains back to London, but one came. It was almost empty. In a lavatory, she scrubbed savagely at the warpaint on her face till it was all off. The face underneath was red-eyed, and wretched, and young.

The train came into Paddington in the dark, the unlit roof a great shadowy hollow overhead, feet echoing down below as on the floor of a cavern. But here things were still closing up, not actually closed; London was taking longer to settle into the stillness of Christmas night. There were still parties meeting, parting, hugging, shaking hands. There were still stalls open under shaded lamps. *Above thy deep and dreamless sleep, the silent stars go by*, sang a mufflered choir beside a news stand. Little silver gleams escaped from their covered lantern. Iris felt suddenly, appallingly homesick. Not for the house where her parents lived now – but for the real home, which had been burnt to ashes and was therefore as gone as childhood, as gone as all lost time. She thought of the fine, chilly surfaces that were waiting for her in Chelsea, and of the solitude. But there was one house where she would be welcomed, and she might even be useful.

She made a quick purchase from a poulterer glad to get rid of a last unwanted bird, and another from a fruit stall where little mandarin oranges glowed in pyramids. An hour later she was standing, with loaded bags, in front of the door at Wildwood Terrace. There was a very long pause after she knocked, and while it lasted she thought Mr Hale might have gone away, or expired among the magic trash. But eventually there came a slow scuffling, like an elderly animal making its way to the front of its den, and the door opened to reveal Geoff's father blinking at her, baffled. He looked awful; as awful as Geoff had predicted he would, left alone. His clothes had clearly been worn for many days, and there were food stains all down the front of them. Behind him, the hallway was a trail of litter, and a smell breathed out of the house at her, a rank, sad, stale smell of neglect.

'It's you,' he said, stupefied. 'I was told I shouldn't let you in.'

'By Geoff?' she asked, with a lurch of misgiving.

'Oh no,' he said.

'I've got a turkey here,' said Iris. 'I've come to tidy you up, and to cook us Christmas dinner.'

'You have?' he said, and opened the door wide.

They ate the turkey, eventually, at the kitchen table. She had restored Geoff's bubble of order there, she had found a candle in a drawer and lit it, and the warm wavering light from it fell on Mr Hale in his happy state of grease, the cleanest napkin she had been able to find tucked in his collar. And on another buff military postcard written in handwriting as tidy as print, propped on a shelf by the milk jug. And on her own hands, at rest on the table edge.

'I don't suppose you ever found out,' she said, looking at them, 'what exactly was written on that little round disc that let the Watcher go?'

'Ah! Ah!' said Mr Hale, showing signs of becoming entangled with his napkin. 'As a matter of fact – I did. A most interesting pursuit, and a successful one. The answer was: ideograms, d'you see? Four of them, all qualifying each other and, as it were, enforcing one command. Do we have a . . . Oh, where is a . . . Bother it . . .'

She found him the pencil Geoff used to write shopping lists, and prevented him from writing on the tablecloth with it. On the piece of paper she substituted, he drew four square symbols, like Chinese characters, only spikier.

'And what do those mean?' she asked.

'Essentially, this,' said Mr Hale. And underneath he wrote:

[NOT]   [TO BE USED AS A TOOL]
[STARTING NOW]   [FOREVER]

So a curse then, she thought. Or conceivably a blessing.

'Does that make any sense to you, my dear?' he asked.

'Perfect sense,' said Iris.

THE MINORIES
JANUARY-MAY 1940

1

The cold continued after Christmas and, as if to deepen it, food rationing began a week into January. Only sugar, butter and bacon were included so far, but the little beige-and-red booklet posted out to everybody from the Ministry of Food had pages for meat and for cooking fat too, so it was clear there was more to come.

The tree by the door to Wildwood Terrace was so thick with hoar frost that it had turned a spiky white all over, as if it had quit the vegetable kingdom for a new and crystalline existence. Puffing and stamping, she shoved the door open against the rime of ice that was sealing it shut. Inside the burrow, the air was warm and less dank. All the junk seemed to serve as insulation. But the litter reappeared between her visits, and today she found that the forgotten mail she was standing on on the doormat included Mr Hale's own ration book, shucked out of its envelope and then discarded. It now had a footprint on the back of it from her boot.

'Look,' she said, when he bumbled into the kitchen, summoned by the sound of the kettle, 'this is important. You need to keep this.' She tried to teach him how to use it – the places to write in the name of your grocer and of your butcher, the counterfoils they should fill in when you took the book to them for the first time – but Mr Hale had no idea who Geoff had bought bacon, sugar and butter from. He just looked confused when she showed him the little coupons you were supposed to detach or have cancelled every time you shopped.

It seemed safer to add shopping to the things she did when she came over to Hampstead. As she now appeared to be doing twice a week. It had seemed natural, when she left on Boxing Day, to plan to come back two or three days later just to check that Mr Hale hadn't actually rolled in the leftovers. And then it had seemed natural to go on coming, about that often. That was enough to keep the chaos within bounds, and it was also about the limit of what she thought she could take on. It had not escaped her that the more she did for Mr Hale, the more passive he got. He seemed to take it entirely for granted, after the first couple of times, that this young woman his son knew should keep arriving to look after him. But he was a friendly old thing, in his mad way, and while she moved around him he sat contentedly, and talked, and talked, and talked. She got the rest of the anecdote about George Bernard Shaw, and a labyrinth of other stories besides, about people he had met and people he had known, usually before the Great War, when he had been out and about more, less of a dormouse. Literary types, peculiar clergymen, occultists, theosophists, retired officers with theories about the lost tribes of Israel: a shadowy little world grew from his stories whose inhabitants, she suspected, were probably less nice than Mr Hale had thought they were. Shyly, he brought out a photograph of Geoff's mother, and yes, the powers of decision were all there in that face that were missing in Mr Hale's own, but with more humour than Iris expected. Perhaps you needed a sense of humour to marry Mr Hale. She found she was worrying about him when she wasn't there.

She deduced Geoff's butcher and grocer from paper bags she found in the kitchen drawer, and when she walked down the hill to Hampstead High Street with a wicker basket, trailing cold vapour in the air, they made no difficulties about treating her as the replacement on their books for young Mr Hale. The Hampstead grocer's was different from hers on the King's Road. It wanted to sell her caraway seeds, in case she planned to bake her own bread, whereas the Chelsea one hoped she might be interested in various expensive little tins you could use to make canapés for raffish dinner parties. Canned pâté, canned asparagus, canned olives stuffed with pimentos. The butchers' shops were much the same as each other, staffed by men in stripy aprons quickly becoming conscious of themselves as figures of power, able to dispense significant favours. *Memo to self*, she thought: *always remember to flirt with butchers*. The King's Road butcher's shop had a counter just the right height to lean your chest on while you smiled at the monarchs of meat. She used it.

The question was what on earth to cook, both for the pair of them and for herself singly, over at Challoner Court. She had barely cooked anything on her own, ever. Hangover food, like scrambled eggs, yes, but eggs were already in noticeably short supply. Otherwise, since leaving home, she had relied on landladies for evening meals, and on the bad girl's advantage of being taken out to dinner a lot.

Think about this analytically, she told herself, as the memory of the turkey receded. Protein, fat, carbohydrate, vitamins: that was what they needed. Eight ounces of sugar, two ounces of bacon, two ounces of butter, per person: those were the constraints. No limit on bread or vegetables. Geoff had the cookbook that had come with the gas stove, and judging by the folded-down page corners had made ten things from it over and over again, on rotation. Very rational, but not too well suited to the present situation.

She tried making a bacon-and-potato pie, following a recipe in the evening paper. The pastry came out like cardboard, but they ate it anyway, since it contained a whole week's butter ration. She made an enormous vegetable soup, for Mr Hale to heat up on his own. He forgot about it, with the ring burning underneath the pot. The next time she came she had to scrub a brown-black smoke stain off the kitchen ceiling, and scour out the burnt inside of the pan with wire wool. She continued to feel a dreadful compunction about misusing Geoff's kitchen. His little patch of order must be defended. It was her responsibility, somehow; it had been handed her in trust, despite him not even knowing that she was visiting the house. You'd have thought – she thought – that the same would apply, only more so, to his bed. Shouldn't she be warier still, there? Shouldn't that be the place where the vertigo that went with getting close to him was concentrated, where everything fearsome that the touch of her hand on him had showed her grew close, threateningly close? But instead she was sleeping matter-of-factly under his model aeroplanes every time she stayed the night. And it didn't seem to frighten her, or thrill her either. The comfort remained, and she always hopped under the covers fast because up under the eaves the burrow-warmth of the house drained away and the air was icy. But the charge she had felt from being inside his sheets seemed to have gone. The rub of them didn't bring her out in shivers. The only shivers upstairs were the ones caused by temperature. Perhaps it was because she was bringing over a nightie to sleep in. There was no need to put on one of the white shirts hanging in the neat row on the metal rail. She lay and looked at them in the dark, through a chink in the blankets. There they were. Pale, empty, Geoff-shaped. Eventually, one night, with a sense of stepping deliberately towards danger, she jumped back out of his bed, pulled the nightie off over her head and buttoned on his white cotton in place of her white cotton. The shirt had the same texture it had had before, the same smell, if fainter; it clung the same way, pulled the same way, fretted against her skin the same way. But the feeling would not return to a deliberate summons. It refused to repeat.

Damn you, she told her treacherous right hand, as it cut onions for liver with onion gravy. *This is all your fault. I could be sipping champagne if it weren't for you.* She had wondered about the rules that governed it, given that it had provided her with all too much information about Geoff and (even more frightening) none at all about Lancelot. 'Not to be used as a tool' – what did that mean, exactly? What were its limits? Did it mean that she couldn't use it at all, to get useful insights, or was it only forbidden if the using was too blatant? It would be helpful for business, to say the least, if she could suddenly read people's intentions from a handshake. An experiment had seemed to be called for. When the woman in front of her on her morning bus had dropped a sixpence while paying her fare, she'd swooped helpfully on the coin as it rolled, and made sure to get some skin-to-skin contact when handing it back. A moment later and she had been pulling her hand back as fast as was compatible with ordinary manners. Not a terrifying blank like Lancelot, but not the natural warmth of a stranger's fingers either. There had been a milder, partial deadening. What she had touched had felt like a sluggishly animated clay model of a hand. Quite tightly drawn limits, then, she had thought. Anything where she was treating a person as a means to an end brought on the negative aspect of the spell, on a sliding scale of intensity. *Not* to be used as a tool. A definite command. Though it permitted her to chop any amount of onions, she noticed.

The liver was a success, and after it, as Mr Hale snoozed, she wrote Geoff a letter.

Dear G. D. Hale, she wrote,

Yours of the 15th inst. received as per our invoice. I wonder what the D stands for? It is perishingly cold in London, everything frozen that can be frozen, people on buses going about with a mauve look round the lips, and bright-red ears. I am fairly chilly myself, even bundled up in enough layers of coat and scarves etc to make me nearly circular. But your dad is doing fine. I am popping over every

Tuesday night and Saturday night to look after him, and he is suffering my experiments in cookery with good humour, though I expect he misses your sausages. He is drowsing at the kitchen table just across from me as I write this. The washing-up is done, and all your white mugs are hanging in a tidy row. The kettle is on the stove and the gas makes a steady hiss. So you needn't worry about him. You will be glad to hear that our friend in blue has not turned up again, and I have been leaving the attic strictly alone. However I did run into Lall in the street, all dolled up in a Mechanised Transport Corps uniform like a poisonous fairy. And it _was_ her doing; she made no bones about that. She is a nasty piece of work – not just politically. Many threats and warnings, and there seems to have been some sort of instruction to your father to keep me away from the house, which he has ignored because I bribed him with Christmas dinner. No follow-up so far, though. Take care of yourself, and I'll see you at the end of the month. If you tell me which day exactly you're coming, I'll make sure there's milk and bread and so on in the house.

I remain, with the assurance of our constant attention,
I. S. HAWKINS
PS The 'S' stands for Susan.

She put his own address at the top of it, and dropped it into the pillar box by the bus stop on her way to work the next morning. Whatever it was she was doing, she wasn't ready to let it into the Chelsea flat. That was private.

His reply was on the doormat the next time she went over to the house. Yet another buff postcard, but this one read:

I am so relieved. Thank you, thank you, thank you. Leave looks as if it's going to be two weeks later than I thought, because they're sending me on a course. I should be there on Friday 16th Feb, some time in the evening. Don't you dare tell a soul but the D stands for 'Dionysus'. Guess whose fault that is. At least my mother stopped him making it my first name. Yours truly, Geoffrey not-a-Greek-god Hale.

She snickered at work every time she thought of it. Geoffrey in a dear little laurel wreath. Geoffrey in a wreath holding a bunch of purple grapes. Geoffrey in a wreath and grapes and nothing else. The most awkward person you could imagine to be a god of abandon. And yet—

'Eyes on your work, please, Iris,' said Mrs Sinclair. 'I'm surprised I have to remind *you*.'

The truth was, though, that there was very little to do at Cornellis & Blome that month. As the winter finally loosened its teeth on the city, the 30-Share Index, which had dipped again when rationing began, started to rise once more. It went back to 75, keeping all the gains of the autumn, then up higher still, heading for 80, past where it had been when war broke out, even. But all on such microscopic volumes of shares traded that you couldn't believe in it as a sign of real optimism. It was more like a symptom of delirium – an empty phantasm, a hollow shell, like the war itself. The fascists ran a candidate at the by-election to Parliament in Silvertown in the East End. He stood on an anti-war platform, or rather on the BUF's version of an anti-war platform, in which nothing about the war was Hitler's fault. 'We are fighting for the investments of Jewish financiers,' Mosley told a public meeting, and Blackshirts in the street trying to sell copies of their paper, *Action*, repeated the same message over and over. The fascist candidate only got a handful of votes, but it didn't seem to deter them, or make them any less certain that events were going their way. It wasn't voting that they expected would bring them to power anyway: it was the half-hearted old men in wing collars who rode in limousines, reconciling themselves to the inevitability of a fascist Europe, and to Mosley's lot as the local embodiment of it. Every morning as her bus passed the Black House, the black beetles preened and strutted at the entrance.

Meanwhile, since nothing much seemed to be happening in the war with Germany, the newspapers had more or less given up reporting it. Instead they'd switched to the much more exciting war between Soviet Russia and the plucky Finns, who seemed to be fighting off Comrade Stalin much more successfully than the Poles had been able to do with either Stalin or Hitler. There were concerts for Finland in London; newsreels of Finnish troops swooshing by on skis; knitting drives to send warm mufflers to those troops, though they seemed to be pretty well wrapped up already. In Finland the snow lay deep and crisp and even. In London the thaw had come. Ice softened into slush and then into puddles. Eaves dripped. Gutters spouted. The fluffy skies of snow and the clear skies of frost turned to the low grey skies of rain. She walked up Ludgate Hill to work with a brolly open. Transparent veins of water pulsed from the metal tip of every strut; also, guggled over the cobbles of the little Dickensian alleys, and cascaded off the portico of St Paul's in clear sheets. The world, unlike the stock market, was experiencing great liquidity.

At the end of the month, the backhander from Barracloughs in Sheffield failed to turn up in her bank account. She rang them from a phone box during her lunch hour. 'Sorry,' said Kenneth, the broker who'd been her contact. 'Not worth our while any more.' So that was her stake for the future stalled. She had just under three hundred pounds after subtracting the year's rent for Challoner Court. It wouldn't grow any further while she only had her C&B wages. And she was starting to worry about them as well. A stockbroker's office without commissions coming in was surely a brokerage that would soon be looking to cut costs.

She had still not managed to work out what a clever investment strategy would be for these peculiar times – something she now wanted not just for herself, but so that she could carry it into Mr Cornellis's office and impress him. She chewed the problem over in her mind endlessly, but to no result. You couldn't de-risk by shifting to American shares when access to the New York market was closed. You couldn't make speculative gains from scarcity when the scarce commodities that mattered, like fuel and strategic metals, were rationed and controlled. You couldn't do anything with differing international prices when the currency markets were shut. It was as if someone clever – someone like Miles Ormond, or a committee he worked for – had gone round systematically blocking all the mouseholes from which you could make a private profit out of the war. There remained, she supposed, the out-and-out illegal stuff, the frankly criminal trades that must be possible in refugee property or black-market petrol and sugar and butter. But she didn't want any of those. She had no way in to them, and in any case she wanted money she could keep and enjoy, not money she would have to hide. Or, finally, there was the strategy of true and total pessimism: assuming that the only assets worth anything now were those you could carry on your person, if you needed to run. Gold coins. Jewels sewn into the seams of your coat. A Rembrandt etching rolled up small. Conceivably, an American bearer bond, if you could find one unregistered on a form S1, unknown to the authorities. Or eight of them. She wasn't planning to run. Was Mr Cornellis?

She went in to see him anyway. He was at his desk looking melancholy, with the *Financial Times* open in front of him. He had not turned a page in five minutes, which she took as her cue that he could be disturbed.

'Yes?' he said, not quite as startled as he would have been previously, but still a little surprised to be dealing directly with someone from the typing pool, without Mrs Sinclair or Mr Smythe acting as go-between. 'What can I do for you, my dear?'

She shut the glass door behind her.

'I'd like to be doing more, sir,' she said.

He looked puzzled. 'I'm sorry, I don't follow you.'

'I mean, I'd like to be learning more about how the firm works. On the client side, and on the market side.'

'Well, that's . . . commendable; but—'

'Maybe help out Mr Smythe?'

'Has he asked for your help?' asked Cornellis, with the air of one seizing with relief on a solid point.

'Well, no, sir, but—'

'Better to leave well alone, then, don't you think? And not muddle up the sound lines on which things are organised at present. I'm sure you do an excellent job operating that . . . machine for us. Concentrate on that, my dear, and leave the rest to us.'

She should have come in with something to offer him, she thought, or not come in at all. Asking was inherently weaker than offering. Asking for something, you were at the mercy of the person who could decide whether to give it. Offering, you were starting a negotiation about what you'd get in return. That was why she had always made the first move with men.

'I just think,' she tried, 'that with the market in this funny state, and most of the profitable trades blocked off, we should maybe be looking for all the ideas we can get. Ideas from everyone in the office, I mean.'

'"We"?' said Cornellis, with an eyebrow raised.

'Sir?'

'"We" should be looking for ideas?'

'No, sir. You.'

'Quite.' Cornellis looked down at the pink expanse of the *Financial Times*. He winced, and looked back up. 'Have you *got* an idea?' he asked.

'Not . . . exactly, sir. Everything I think of seems to have been blocked off already, by the war regulations.'

'That being what the regs are for,' said Cornellis wearily.

'But I think I *could* have ideas?'

'Take a piece of advice from an old man,' said Cornellis. 'Ideas you haven't had yet are like castles in the air, and every other kind of daydream. They have to be marked to market at zero. No, my dear: you go and get on with your actual job. Anyway, you'll be quite busy enough soon.'

'Sir?'

'I hear that the first Acquisition of Securities Order is coming in a week or two, to scoop up a good tranche of what was on the S1s. So you ladies will have your hands very full, I assure you, collecting in certificates for American shares and bonds from our clients.'

'It won't be work that earns commission, though, will it?'

Cornellis sighed. 'It's sweet of you to take an interest,' he said. 'But, as I said, you can safely leave all that side of things to me. I promise you, when the next tidal wave of bureaucratic bumf rolls in, you'll soon be sick of the very idea of finance. You'll be longing to . . . go to the talkies at the end of the day, and forget all about it.'

'Will I, sir?' said Iris. 'Will I not want to trouble my pretty head about it any more?'

'I see I've annoyed you,' said Cornellis uncomfortably. 'Though I must confess I— Well, let's say no more about it. Unless there's something else?' he added, seeing that Iris was still standing in front of his desk.

'I was just wondering, sir, whether US Treasury bearer bonds were likely to be in the Acquisition Order?'

'They may well be. I don't know yet. Why?'

Was there any sign of unease in his face? A sharpening of attention? Did he look like a man with a nefarious scheme – a private plan to flee with a fistful of negotiable paper? Not that she could see. He seemed wearily, patronisingly, immovably rooted in place. She would have liked to press him further. To let him know she knew something illegal was going on, and to watch his expression change as the Chelsea house agent's had, and to *make* him take her seriously. But did she know it? Not really. Not for sure.

'It's just my father mentioned them,' she said instead. 'As a type of negotiable we wouldn't be seeing any more of. He's a bank messenger?'

'Oh, I see,' said Mr Cornellis, and this time his face did seem legible. It expressed the mild satisfaction of someone who thought they had solved a mystery of human behaviour – just a small one. Iris was hereditary City, was what he thought he saw. Lowly, only a part of finance's army of clerks, but with a touching tendency to over-identify with the banks and brokerages they served, and consequently to worry their pretty heads (if they were female) about the affairs of their betters. 'Well, he may be right and he may be wrong. We wait upon the judgement of our masters in Whitehall, eh?'

He said no more but he raised both eyebrows expectantly, and Iris retreated. There was a placid hush in the typists' room, and the light filtering through the rain outside wavered silvery on the ceiling. Beyond the metal windows, runnels of wet crept down the grooves between the granite waves of the Mariner statue's hair. Mrs Sinclair had gone to make tea, and Sonia, unsupervised at her silent typewriter, was reading a magazine. She looked up when Iris came in.

'Says here,' she said, 'that frowning gives you lines. Never frown, it says. Always smile, and your skin will thank you for it.'

11

THE NAVY'S HERE! said the headlines on 16 February, as she carried a bagful of groceries up Hampstead hill after work. HMS Something-or-other had just rescued some British merchant sailors from a German ship off the coast of Norway, and the papers had veered back excitedly to Britain's own homegrown war, the one in Finland having suddenly grown much less inspiring and plucky now that the Russians were advancing again.

The bag contained bread and milk and the makings of a dinner. Liver and onions: it had worked last time, and she wasn't taking any chances. She was extremely nervous. It felt as if, when she reached Wildwood Terrace, the pleasant state of suspension she had been living in since Christmas, in which it was possible to flirt with Geoff by mail without anything coming of it, was about to be abolished. In fact, to pop like a balloon. *You've been living in a dream-world,* she told herself. *You don't know what you want, and you've just put off thinking about it.* But she still didn't know what she wanted, and she was still working hard not to think about it. 'Some time in the evening,' he'd written. That could be much later. She would cook, and then she would see. Then she would – she would – she didn't know what she would do. The indecision was not like her, and it made her angry. *I'll probably snarl at him when I do see him,* she thought, stamping up the path to the blacked-out number eight.

But there were raised voices coming from the hall. Not Geoff's voice: Mr Hale's defensive bleat, and another one, an acrid patrician drawl, equally elderly but full of force, cutting through the bleat, talking over it. Berating him.

'But you were told,' the voice was saying. 'You were told *very* clearly. An unambiguous instruction. I simply do not understand how you could then go ahead and ignore it.'

'She seemed such a nice girl—' began Mr Hale.

'You are a custodian. You are a caretaker. Nothing more. Surely you understand that. Surely you remember that the Order permits you to live here on condition that you guard what has been entrusted to you, and keep it safe from prying eyes. You are not required to think. You are not required to question. You are not required – you are not *allowed* – to come to any conclusions of your own about who is permitted to enter here, and to inspect the collection. Your ridiculous son we permit. He is, so to speak, one of the terms of your lease. But nobody else.'

'No, Grand Master. Of course. I see that. I do, do, do see that. Of course. It's just that she has been, um, looking after me. And with Geoffrey gone I've, I must admit, I've struggled, on my own, so I, ah—'

'I suppose it is some idiotic tendresse on your part. Some senile infatuation. Abishag the bed-warmer, is it? I understand from Lalage that she is a very low type. The buxom chambermaid. Dear oh dear, Hale. I would have thought that at your age you were past all that.'

Right, thought Iris, and lifted her fist to hammer on the door. But Mr Hale was bleating on, a sheep on his dignity now.

'No!' he said. 'No! And I must say that I, ah, resent the imputation. I daresay I am old, and perhaps foolish, but I trust that I can still tell the difference between infatuation and kindness. She has been kind to me, and I have been grateful. There is no, ah, question of anything else. She and Geoffrey have a soft spot for each other, perhaps – at least, I *think* they do; it is a point upon which I am puzzled – but I, I,' he said, reaching for a note of confidence, 'am merely grateful. She has looked after me when, I may say, nobody else has. The Order has not. *You* have not, Grand Master. You have not even, ah, enquired how I was managing alone. Let alone been willing to send someone to engage with the mysteries of my ration book! They are very complicated, you know.' *Bless you*, thought Iris. *Good for you.* Then he ruined it rather by adding, 'Of course, I have *enjoyed* looking at her. I am not *blind*, you know. She is delightfully mammalian. And why not!'

She was lifting her fist again when the other voice resumed, contemptuous and amused. It was reminding her of Lall, but also the artfully ugly instruments they had used for the summoning: a device to impose itself on the world by droning, by twisting, by scratching.

'Have you finished, Hale? You have? Good. And you *will* be finished, here, on the instant, if there is any repetition. This is not your house, you old fool. Everything that goes on in it is our business, and we know everything that goes on in it. We see it, we hear it. We have our eyes and ears in here. Did you think we would leave it unmonitored? Did you think we *trusted* you? Last chance, or Kitten here will be bundling you out onto the street right now, in the clothes you stand up in. – They look as if they would stand up by themselves, stiff as they are with effluvium. You disgusting old wretch. Kitten, take his collar.'

'Right-ho,' said a third voice, male and deep and eager and much less cultured. 'Pitch him out the front, boss?'

Mr Hale squeaked. Iris stepped off the path and behind the tree. It was not much cover, but at least it put her out of direct sight of the door, if it opened.

'I don't know,' said the Grand Master. 'That's up to him.'

'No, don't!' said Mr Hale.

'You don't want us to?' enquired the Grand Master, leisurely as a cat with a mouse.

'Please, no,' said Mr Hale, sounding partially throttled. 'I need to be here. I have nowhere else to go. This is my home.'

'Well, well,' said the Grand Master. 'Collapse of stout party, eh? No more defiance, no more brave words, Hale?'

'No!'

'I should think not,' the Grand Master said. 'Gratitude, that's what I want to see from you, you old fool.'

'Yes, Master. Thank you, Master.'

Are all magicians bullies? Iris wondered. Did the urge to dominate that showed up in the magic always show itself as well in mean little displays of power over human beings?

'And obedience,' said the Grand Master silkily. 'I require that as well. Do I have it? Do I finally have it?'

'Yes, Master.'

'No more visits from nosy trollops who ruin workings that should have been good for decades yet?'

'No, Master.'

'You had better hope not. Because Kitten here is moving in; he can help you with your ration book, and perhaps compel you to bathe occasionally – and, if he should see her, if he should so much as glimpse hide or hair of her, he is under instructions to eject both her from the premises and, mere moments later, you too. Isn't that right, Kitten?'

'Yes, guvnor.'

'And he is quite capable of it – a veteran of the Black House, you know. Very skilled on the physical side of things.'

'But . . . Geoffrey is coming home on leave tonight,' said Mr Hale.

'Then all three of you will just have to rub along together, won't you?'

'But—'

'But *nothing*, Hale. That's it. All the appeals, reasoning, plaintive requests, last chances – they're all behind you now. All that lies ahead is either mute submission, or a rapid outward flight over the doormat. Understood?'

'Yes, Grand Master.'

'Very well. Then I shall be leaving . . .'

The Grand Master went on talking, but Iris was extracting herself from the tree, backing as silently as she could up the path, and then retreating at speed up Wildwood Terrace, with the shopping bag banging against her knees. She could not think what else to do.

At the junction with the main road, where the trees grew thick around the street lamps, all blacked out now, she swung around looking for cover. But the road ran along straight and bare in both directions, with no other houses and no driveways, and despite the village-green appearance of the junction, there were fences everywhere, preventing you from slipping into the trees. Left? Right? There was no car parked in either direction, to give a helpful clue which way the Grand Master would turn.

She was going to be seen whichever way she went. Perhaps the important thing was to be seen as a figure walking away, doing something else, something unremarkable and unconnected to the Terrace. And the way the Grand Master had talked about her didn't suggest he had any very precise mental image of her. Probably all he had to go on was a hostile description from Lall. If he was picturing some kind of cartoon barmaid, all cleavage and high heels, he might not associate her with a respectably dressed City worker in an overcoat and beret.

She plunged right, away from the bus stop but the direction with a postbox visible in the distance. Yes, that was it: she was on her way to post a letter. She felt around in her pocket for something letter-shaped, and made herself walk slowly. A person at the end of a tiring office day, doing a little task on the way home. Yes.

But as she made her way down between the black clumps of trees on the almost lightless roadway, only a last grey glimmer in the western sky ahead, she heard a second set of footsteps join her own, brisker and more decided, following along the same way. The footsteps got louder; the upright line of the pillar box with the faint blob of light gleaming on top of it grew closer. He was going to overtake but, damn it, not before she reached the postbox. She did, and carefully dropped into the slot a white paper napkin left over from lunch. Then she had to turn round, and start back: people didn't naturally linger over posting things. The Grand Master approached, mostly shadow, but plain enough to her dark-adapted eyes for her to see that she had been quite wrong to imagine, from his voice, some cadaverously tall aristo with wild eyebrows and an opera cloak. He was actually a plumpish elderly nondescript, dressed in tweeds, with a little metal badge in his lapel and a moustache like a mouse that had died of old age.

'Good evening,' said Iris, with her best Chelsea as opposed to Watford vowels, and the minimal smile appropriate to a stranger passing in the blackout.

'Awfully dark,' he said, raising his trilby and bestowing a similarly small fraction of gentlemanly smirk on her. The badge caught a dim shine from the sky: a lightning flash in a circle, of course.

'Awfully!' she agreed, heart hammering, and moved on past him. On he passed too, footsteps receding behind her. Her ears strained to trace him, over the blood-noise of her own pulse. There he went, without stopping, down the hill into the dark, a brisk clip-clop of brogues on pavement, fading to a thread of sound, and then gone.

She reached the junction again. Extinguished street lamp, blacked-out houses up the Terrace, not a soul in sight in any direction. The baby forest of Hampstead well on its way to becoming the forest of the night, thick and ancient. A wave of nausea rose in her. She stood there, breathing and swallowing, until it sank back. If there had been a man there, she would have begged a cigarette, and nursed herself back to courage on it. But there wasn't. There was nobody, and nothing. Not Geoff, who she had been dreading seeing, and not the house she had been using as a bolthole, blithely ignoring threats and refusing to think about the future. Where *was* Geoff, for that matter, and what was she to do?

She couldn't return to the house, not without endangering Mr Hale. There was a human spy in it now, along with a magical one. She couldn't safely put a note through the door, or send a letter by post. And Geoff, because she had been so wary, so careful, so self-preserving, had no address for her. He knew nothing about her except that she worked at C&B. He had no other way of getting in touch. He needed to be told what was waiting for him – he needed to be warned. But the only way of doing it that she could see was by actually intercepting him now, before he arrived. Which way would he come? He'd be on his way from a railway terminus, presumably. And then the bus?

She set off to the left. More lightless stretches of road, the sky a roof of dim pearl; then the cluster of swathed and shuttered dwellings and the little lightless tobacconist where the buses halted on their journey across the strange mock-countryside of the Heath. She stationed herself by the stop. And waited. And waited. Buses came, and disgorged travellers who went away murmuring in twos, or silent in ones. None of them had the silhouette of a spindly boy in khaki. It got later, though how much later she couldn't tell. It was too dark to read her watch, even when the moon rose and made a silver stain in the clouds. She only knew that the buses were getting emptier, and she was getting chillier and chillier.

She bargained with herself: *I will wait for three more buses*. They came, without Geoff. *And one more*. No. *And one more for luck*. Nothing. A bus came in the other direction, going downhill towards the lip of the Heath, and Hampstead streets, and London, and indoor warmth. Even the golden refrigerator that was the Chelsea flat would be cosier than this. She had her arms wrapped round herself, rocking backwards and forwards. The bus to take her away idled enticingly at the stop on the other side of the road, and suddenly, in a spasm of despair, she snatched up the shopping and ran across the road and jumped on.

As she did so, a taxi went by uphill. It was much too dark to see if there was a skinny blond soldier in the back seat, but it occurred to her that there all too easily might be: Geoff off his late train from Aldershot, or Catterick, or wherever he had been, lavishly blowing a few bob to hurry to a homecoming he didn't know would be with a terrified father and Kitten, rather than with a happy father and a girl who was looking forward to seeing him, no matter how much she snarled. She *had* been looking forward to it. She could see that clearly now it wasn't going to happen.

III

'Does anyone know how long a leave is, before a soldier goes to France?' asked Iris on Monday morning.

'Have you got a feller?' asked Sonia.

'Sort of,' said Iris.

'Embarkation leave?' said Delia. 'I think it's forty-eight hours.'

That meant he was off again today. Iris stood by the window, and looked down at the street over the Mariner's ear. The angle was wrong. She could only see a slice of the pavement, and the doors of the offices opposite. There was coming and going, but no one standing there looking up.

'Ladies?' said Mr Cornellis from the doorway. 'It has come to pass as I was predicting – as I was predicting to *you*, Miss Hawkins. The first Acquisition Order is out. There are sixty American stocks on it – Mr Smythe has the exact list – and I'm afraid another flurry of correspondence now ensues. Any of our clients who declared any of the sixty on their S1s now need to surrender them to us forthwith, so we can in turn deliver them to Threadneedle Street. I will draft you a letter to send to them all, and bring it through shortly.'

'If you dictate it to me, I can type it up right now,' said Iris, butting Sonia away from the nearest typewriter with a hip.

'Oh, very well,' said Mr Cornellis, and stood over her forming phrases, while Mrs Sinclair went to talk to Smythe, Delia fetched out the client registers again and Sonia went to the post office for stamps.

'. . . with the assurance, in these unprecedented times – no, make that *demanding* times – of the firm's unchanging commitment to the highest standards of service, comma, I remain, et cetera et cetera. Got that?'

'Yes, sir. Were there any bonds on the list?'

'Not so far,' said Cornellis.

'And what about compensation arrangements? You've said here "at the prevailing market prices". *Which* market, sir?'

'The New York spot price, today. I should probably say that, shouldn't I? Could you insert it?'

'Of course, sir. Doesn't that imply, though,' she said, winding the paper back, x-ing out the old phrase and putting the new one in half a line above, 'that there's a kind of opportunity for arbitrage in this?'

'How do you mean?' said Cornellis, and though she was gazing at the page in the typewriter and *N-e-w-Y-o-r-k* appearing in fuzzy royal blue, she could hear the raised eyebrows in his voice.

'I mean, our clients are getting a kind of one-off dealing access to New York, courtesy of His Majesty's Government. They get to sell, this once, at un-depressed American prices. Wouldn't this be a good moment for them to rotate their funds into something temporarily cheap, in *our* market?'

'Like what?' said Cornellis. 'It isn't an arbitrage opportunity unless you've got something to arbitrage *into*.'

'I don't know, sir. Yet.'

'Harrumph,' said Cornellis. Then he added, with grim humour, 'What about Polish government bonds? Those are *very* cheap at the moment, what with Warsaw being full of Nazis, and there being no prospect of the things ever being redeemed.'

'I meant something with some value, sir. Obviously.'

'Oh, obviously. Thank you for the typing, Miss Hawkins.'

By the end of the day they had dispatched 112 letters to C&B clients, and there was no sign of Geoff lingering on the pavement outside. She had left a message with the doorman of the Mariner Building when they went off to lunch at Lyons', in case he turned up during the lunch hour, but the note was still there, uncollected, when she and Sonia and Delia returned from their soup and roll. She had a last look around when she came out herself at quarter to six. The days were lengthening noticeably by now, and it was still grey dusk outdoors, with a damp wind blowing off the Thames, and the silvered pillars of the Mariner's main door outlined as if in a kind of faint, monochrome neon. But the grey light inescapably declared his absence. She set off on foot through the City to her Tube home, the lunar weight of St Paul's growing ahead of her, and wondered where he was. In some crowd with kit-bags at Waterloo, she supposed. Milling soldiers at the doors of a troop train. *But I'm getting all this from newsreels*, she thought. It was an image off the peg, not made to measure by actual reality. *I don't even know what he really looks like in uniform.* The blond hair cut to a fuzz, the Adam's apple bobbing, the fragile neck sticking out of the scratchy coarse collar – it was all imagining. Make-believe.

The next morning, though, when Mrs Sinclair was sorting out the office post, she paused on an envelope, and brought it over, frowning, to Iris at the teletype.

'I've told you . . .' she began.

'Yes, yes,' said Iris, reaching for the letter, on which she saw familiar handwriting.

'No, *no*,' said Mrs Sinclair, holding it back. 'Take this seriously, my girl. Private correspondence does *not* come to the office.'

Iris breathed in and out. In several possible futures, she was going to need Mrs S's goodwill. 'I'm sorry,' she said. 'I do know. But that's from the chap I missed seeing on his leave – it was all a mess – and he doesn't know where else to write to. – I know that's wrong,' she added.

'Why ain't you told him where you live, then?' asked Sonia.

'You, young lady, need to mind your own business,' Mrs Sinclair said to her. 'And it's "haven't", if you please.' She turned back to Iris with a married woman's look of worldly understanding. 'Very well, then,' she said. 'But sort this out, dear. You can't go on using the firm as a dead letterbox.'

'No, Mrs Sinclair.'

'Mind, I don't want to see you reading that until your own work is done. This is the firm's time, not yours, remember.'

'Yes, Mrs Sinclair.'

Iris propped the letter from Geoff on the windowsill and pounded the keys. Yesterday's New York prices for the sixty affected stocks had come through on the teletype from the Securities Registration Office in the Bank of England, the Bank being the only place permitted under the war regs to keep open an international phone line to foreign markets. Now they were calculating the compensation payouts to the clients. Two hundred and twelve shares of Paramount Pictures, owned by Mr Ernest Mayhew of 'Greenhithe', The Parade, Great Malvern. $88.10 per share. $4.08 to the pound. Subtract the C&B commission. Type up two copies of the invoice, one for the SRO, one for the client. File a carbon of the client's copy. And repeat. *Zing-chunk, zing-chunk* went the arm of the adding machine, as Delia's arm cranked it.

Finally, in the eleven o'clock break for tea, she was able to take the envelope out into the corridor and tear it open. One sheet of folded paper; words still formed with unearthly neatness, because nothing could ever untidy the mind of Geoffrey Dionysus Hale enough to prevent *that*, but descending at a noticeable slant across the page, which was probably his version of a wild scrawl. *Written in a hurry on Sunday night at the station*, it said.

Iris, I don't know what the hell is going on? I came home expecting you and dinner, and instead I found a thug from the Order camping out in our house without explanation, and my father incoherent even for him. I tried to throw out the thug – an ex-boxer type with Neanderthal eyebrows who just grinned at me, and followed us round the house so we weren't alone for a single minute, and is sleeping in my bed, by the way – but my father wouldn't have it. He just twittered and stammered and said, 'Dear boy, we must make the best of it' and, 'I'm afraid we must regard him as a fixture.' He seems to be terrified but he wouldn't tell me why. All I could gather was that it had something to do with you. And now I've had to leave him with the thug in possession. So perhaps you can explain. Has something happened? Have you <u>done</u> something? I thought when you started looking in on him that you were going to make things better, not worse! Write to me c/o Signals, 5th Infantry Division, BEF. I'm sorry I missed seeing you. I was looking forward to it. Perhaps if you'd trusted me with your address we could have sorted this out in person. GDH

She thought: *that sounds hellish. Poor Geoff, poor Mr Hale.* She thought: *so he doesn't know the Order owns the house.* She also thought: *so suddenly it's my fault that your family is assailed by magical fascist lunatics? I go round, out of the goodness of my heart, to keep your hopeless father fed and clean, and my reward is that I get to take the blame?*

She went back into the office.

'Bad news?' said Sonia, eagerly. 'Here, I'm going dancing at the Palais in Leytonstone on Friday night. Do you wanna come? Might take your mind off it!'

'Oh why not,' said Iris, knowing it was a mistake.

*

And it was, but quite an enjoyable one. Afterwards, sitting with skittering thoughts in the Chelsea flat, looking at Geoff's letter in the ring of light under the ladylike gold-fringed lampshade, she thought she'd better find something else to fill her evenings, before she did anything really stupid.

The scene on the Palais dance floor had started off sedate: girls dancing together and older couples. But about ten o'clock a mass of sailors off a destroyer at Tilbury had turned up, full of sperm and hormones, and taken the place by storm. 'Ooh, the Navy's here,' she'd murmured appreciatively, and for the next hour had been danced far faster, and harder, and closer. 'Guess what,' said Sonia, coming back flushed from a foxtrot with a sailor in tow, 'Jack here wants to take me out for an ice!' 'No he doesn't,' Iris said, looking at him. 'He wants to take you up an alleyway and get your knickers off.' 'Iris!' said Sonia. 'What are you, her big sister?' said Jack. 'She's fifteen,' said Iris. 'Oh,' he said. 'Well, can't blame a bloke for trying. What about you, then, love? You look like you know what's what.' 'No, thank you,' she said, primly. But she had in fact been momentarily tempted. He was as good-looking as he thought he was, and he represented pretty much the opposite of the irritating confusion with Geoff. The opposite of waiting, the opposite of complicated, the opposite of trying to imagine the world through someone else's eyes. But if she'd gone outside with Jack, and let him hitch up her skirt and settle her bum against the brickwork, she'd have had to put her right hand on him, and she didn't want that at all.

She stared at the piece of paper with the slanted handwriting and wondered how to answer it. She didn't feel guilty about weighing Geoff against random sailors, but she was aware she was using the thought of the sailors to fend him off. To distract herself from the reality of him, existing as continuously as her in space and time, somewhere off in France, and presently blaming her, which she supposed maybe had a grain of justice in it, given that she had defiantly ignored all warnings about the Order and the house. But which she did not enjoy at all, and which was scarcely fair to all the cooking she'd done. So he could be bad-tempered and unjust, could he? She had sort of known that already, after the night when he came over to the firm to shout at her, and they'd been chased together by the Watcher. But that had been a one-off. Now the information was settling in. He was acquiring dimensions, her technical boy, her weeping innocent, her debauchable Dionysus: becoming less what she saw (and wanted, and desired) and more a creature in his own right, intricate, shadowy, solid, only half-seen as yet, or less than that. A puzzle she might spend years on and not finish solving. How was she supposed to write to *that*? For that matter, how was she even supposed to explain what had happened with her visits, and the Order, and the Grand Master, in language that would get past a military censor? Strike out 'magic' and 'fascist', for a start. She supposed she might get away with 'lunatic'. Oh, sailors were easy. Square jaw, curly sideburns, tight blue trousers, yes yes yes. And fucking a sailor would be easy. (And stupid.) This was hard. Geoff was right, they should have met and been able to *talk* things through. Her address at Challoner Court was at the top of her reply, but everything below was crossed out.

Evening classes, she thought, skittering off again. That was an idea. And not some commercial thing at Pitman's, not when – she reminded herself – the idea was to move upwards socially, from Watford to the Savoy, not downwards to the Palais. Her mother would have called the scene on the dance floor common, and she'd have been right. She needed some recreation in keeping with the flat. High-minded. Arty.

She managed to get something in the post to Geoff, because he deserved to hear back, but it made her wince to think of it. She had no idea whether it would leave him any the wiser about the Order, it had come out so cautious and encrypted, and all the statements of feeling she had tried to put in had seemed in the end either untrue or unwise, so she had settled for a bland and sisterly goodwill she could hardly even connect to herself. With it gone, she worked; and there was a lot of work to do as February wore on into March, all of it clerical and bureaucratic as Mr Cornellis had promised it would be.

IV

The Finns made peace with the Russians, having been bludgeoned into submission after all. Crocuses came out around the tombstones in the little green spaces around the City churches, and then daffodils. She picked a bunch and put it in her mended vase on the mantelpiece. Geoff didn't write back, and she didn't blame him. In Hampstead, presumably, Kitten the thug watched over Mr Hale. She hoped his thug skills extended to cookery.

She signed up for a class at the City Literary Institute near Drury Lane, and two evenings a week she sat in the dark while a man who pronounced all his Rs as Ws showed slides of modern art. 'Observe,' he said, 'how the *wownded* contours cweated by Moore develop *expwessive* line.' No one else in the class showed any inclination to giggle. They sat there seriously in their practical skirts and sweaters – a uniform very like Eleanor Armbruster's sculpting outfit back in August – and took notes. Iris's office-wear stood out. It was beginning to get loose: three months of rationing meant she no longer had the figure it was tailored for. Perhaps she should switch into sweaters herself, both for practicality and for high-minded camouflage. She laboured over the book the course tutor recommended to them, an essay on Significant Form by Roger Fry, but Keynes's new pamphlet *How to Pay for the War* went down much more easily.

Perhaps she should have anticipated it, but in early April Eleanor herself turned up, to give a talk to the class as 'one of our most pwomising young sculptors'. She was very good: lively, direct, in full possession of her Rs, and she actually made sense, passing around plaster and wooden models of her work, hand-sized, so that you could feel what she was talking about. But Iris skulked at the back of the room, gripped by unexpected embarrassment. Eleanor recognised her, grinned, and was clearly detaching herself from the admiring throng at the end to come over and talk: but Iris slipped out with a grimace of apology, leaving Eleanor's smile turning to bafflement. She didn't feel equal to being, in this setting, among these earnest people, whatever it was that Eleanor would expect, based on the triumphing slut she had last seen in the Kinesis Club. Iris's life had subsided into a minor key, or so it seemed. Subdued, unremarkable, uneventful.

Until suddenly it wasn't.

The collapse of ordinariness that spring happened so fast that later it was hard to disentangle the constituent parts of it, military and financial and political and personal and magical, or to remember what order they had happened in. But something like the starting gun was fired on 9 April, when the Germans invaded Denmark and Norway, and there went from being a dearth of news to an excess. It was hard to tell what was going on, but it clearly wasn't good. Mr Churchill at the Admiralty made excitable noises about amphibious landings and flanking attacks, received with scepticism by journalists who remembered the mess he'd made at the Dardanelles in the Great War, and there began to be a current of suggestion in the press, growing louder and more insistent, that Chamberlain wasn't up to the job of wartime prime minister, and should be replaced. The name that came up again and again was that of Lord Halifax, the foreign secretary. Calm; a realist; a safe pair of hands, the newspapers said. *Old man in a wing collar*, supplied Iris's internal translation service.

Feeling less safe, the stock market lost its fever-dream optimism and began to fall. Slowly at first: 76 on the 30-Share Index. 75. 74.

Then, a few days later, another Acquisition of Securities Order was issued. Iris remembered Miles Ormond's calculation about the cost of the war, and wondered how fast the kitty was emptying. There were ninety-two American shares on the list this time, on top of the previous sixty. Western Union, International Business Machines, Packard. And, this time, bonds. Another wave of stamping and posting and typing and invoicing engulfed the office, and in came the share certificates of C&B clients by return, orange and green and purple and red, swagged and ornamented with all that grand typography and fine rotogravure could do to make paper wealth look solid, but forlorn now, tokens of a melting world.

Iris had expected that she would be walking these over to the Bank in bundles, the way she had with the S1s, but a new security-conscious regime had been imposed. Messengers came to pick them up daily, accompanied by unspecified men in dark suits, with clumping black shoes. These went into Mr Cornellis's office for the handover. There was signing of receipts, cross-checking of numbers and amounts, forms to fill in. Mr Cornellis was looking – not ragged; never that, when he stopped off every morning at the Royal Exchange to have his hair and moustache trimmed, and came in smelling of pomade; but ever so slightly more rattled. Less securely socketed in the world. More wobbly on his feet. He could be seen at his desk turning the pages of the newspapers, and tapping on his forehead with his middle finger as he did so. A slow drumbeat of anxiety.

'Miss Hawkins?' he said, emerging after one of these sessions with the gentlemen in clumping shoes. 'Are you still . . . keen . . . to do more?'

'Yes, of course,' she said.

'Nothing exciting, I'm afraid. I have an errand to offer you, nothing more. Just some papers to pick up tomorrow. I'd go myself, but they're in Oxford, and, as you see, I seem to be needed here for our daily . . . visitation.'

And that's more information than you needed to give me, she thought, her interest sharpening.

'Certainly, sir.'

'Splendid. Draw some money from the petty cash for the ticket.'

'And what's the address in Oxford?'

'Oh, you won't have to go into the town. Or even leave the station. A simple there-and-back-again will suffice. An old friend of mine, Professor Samuels, has offered to walk the papers down from his college. You can just meet him at the ticket barrier, and get straight back on the next London train. As I said, not very exciting.'

Oh, I don't know about that, Iris thought.

Her train to Oxford the next day arrived three-quarters of an hour late, having been diverted into a siding at Didcot while a long, long procession of armoured cars on flat-bed wagons slid past in the other direction. Oxford, where she had never been, was a blur of golden stone through trees, but with a surprising whiff of industrial smoke in the air, tannic, metallic, when she got off the train. She had been afraid that Cornellis's Professor Samuels would have given up on her, and was kicking herself for not demanding the name of his college so she could go and find him – but there he was in the ticket hall, a gnome of a man with a muffler compressing the bottom half of his white beard, patiently reading a book with a large buff envelope tucked under his arm. Really reading it too: when she went up to him he took a moment to surface, and closed it carefully, with a finger keeping his place.

'Ah!' he said. 'You must be the girl of Cornellis, yes? I am to give you this, I think.'

'Thank you, sir,' she said. 'And thank you for waiting.'

'Not a problem,' he said. He, like the tutor of the art class, did not say R as 'R', but in his case it became not a W but a breathy guttural, a 'hhr' from somewhere a long way to the east.

'Have you known Mr Cornellis for long?' she asked.

He looked at her with mild but intelligent eyes. 'Surely an unnecessary question,' he said. 'Goodbye.'

She dug out the pasteboard rectangle for her return journey and had it clipped by the same ticket inspector to whom she had just surrendered her outward ticket. Then she went through to the 'up' platform and waited for the next train back to London. Quite a crowd was travelling in this direction. Her compartment on the way had had only one other person in it; this time the seats were crammed, and there were people standing in the corridor too. The envelope was too big to fit into her bag. She sat with it on her knee, much too surrounded to act on her curiosity, and reread her newspaper as patiently as she could. The 30-Share Index was down to 73. The envelope was a standard-sized envelope for large documents, sealed. It had nothing written on it at all.

At Paddington, under the sooty glass roof where the smoke rolled and the huffing of the engines echoed, she made herself walk sedately to the stationer's booth. She bought another envelope of the same size. Then she walked sedately to the Ladies' lavatories. Only when she was in a stall, with the door safely bolted, sitting on the lowered seat of the loo, did she take a deep breath and rip the envelope open.

A flash of green ink and fine engraving. Oh, good grief. One – two – three – four – five – six – seven – eight Treasury bonds of the United States of America, payable to bearer. She did not have on her the note she had taken of the eight serial numbers that had come in over the teletype, but she would have wagered they were the same as the ones printed here. Wagered how much money? Oh God, this much money. Her fingers shook. Two of the bonds were for five hundred dollars, five were for a thousand dollars, and one was five thousand dollars. Eleven thousand dollars, on her lap. Divide by four dollars for the amount in sterling: nearly three thousand pounds. Unregistered. Negotiable. Her hands made little useless fluttering motions in the air above them, as if she were trying to square the sheaf back up but didn't quite dare make contact with the green ink and the thick banknote paper. She stared.

Well. Here it was. This was her fortune, if she could take it. Dropped literally into her lap. Enough money to work sudden, glorious alchemy on her life. Enough to make the world ignore her sex and her accent. Enough to begin to make things happen; to deal, to *participate*. Nobody ever got rich by being prudent and accepting the terms the world was willing to offer. It was, always, by being bold. By recognising a moment like this, when it came, and seizing it without too many scruples, and diverting some part of the world's grand stream of money so that, rather than accruing at the good girl's patient rate of four per cent interest, the obedient pauper's four per cent, the loyal clerk's four per cent – a drip, a droplet, scarcity forever, your whole life long – rather than that, it poured your way, it rolled your way in riverine abundance, so you got to bathe in it, and to feel its lack of limit, its melting of frustration and work for wages into sheer and liquefied desire. Money wasn't one thing in the world of things. It was everything, abstracted into pure potential. It was the power to grant wishes. She had a genie on her knee, made of ink and paper. It belonged to anyone who was holding it. And she was holding it.

A scheme unrolled in her mind, arriving too fast for words or logic. It was a stack of pictures. Her, emerging from the Ladies and heading, not back to C&B but, right now, without stopping, to Euston station instead. Her buying a ticket for the Irish Mail while the clock ticked and Mr Cornellis began to expect her back. Her at Holyhead, with no luggage, nothing but the coat she stood up in and a large buff envelope, stepping up the gangplank onto the ferry. Her crossing the sea to the Irish Republic, which you did not need a passport to get into, and which was not in the war. Her on the streets of Dublin, walking into an American bank, open for business and free of regulations. Her cashing the smallest of the bonds. A hotel suite. Shopping. Two suitcases and a hatbox. Then a berth on a liner to New York, and her disembarking among the skyscrapers, and vanishing amidst them, untraceable, uncatchable, into the land where women could run brokerage houses. Leaving behind all frustrations, all complications. All of them: magical fascists. Angels with newspaper faces. Geoff. No more of the hazy hopes and uncertainties he inspired in her; back to the main story she wanted to tell about herself, the bright-lit confident one where she won what she wanted by determination and guile.

It was a fantasy. The her in her head was smiling slightly, chin held high, probably wearing a cloud of Jean Patou's Joy, which Iris had never been able to afford. Woman of mystery. The her in the stall in the toilets at Paddington station was scowling. None of it would work. You might not need a passport for Ireland but there was a war on, and there was sure to be some kind of identity card check at least, and someone travelling with no luggage was going to get the customs men immediately curious. Were there any American banks open in Dublin that would cash a bearer bond, no questions asked? Surely not. And surely the committee of clever people who had steadily stopped up the money-mouseholes wouldn't have left this one wide open, would they? One so big and obvious? For that matter, she was not even sure that liners for New York sailed from Ireland. It was just a daydream. But she couldn't think of any other plan. She wrapped a hand round her forehead and squeezed. Two women outside with county voices were having an interminable conversation at the mirror about Coming Up To Town. The seconds of her moment ticked away, and nothing else came to her. If there *was* a way of profiting from the bonds – and there must be one, or Mr Cornellis wouldn't be collecting them on the quiet – it required far subtler arrangements than she had at her disposal. Some very obscure loophole; a network of the necessary people to act on it, probably.

That made the eleven thousand dollars on her knee a cruel joke by the universe. A taunt, to give her what she most wanted and then ensure she couldn't use it. An envelope-full of freedom she couldn't act on. A magic lamp she couldn't rub. She kicked the cubicle door, and the county ladies paused, and then laughed. Iris ground her teeth and stuffed the bonds back into the new envelope she'd bought.

Later, when she understood what Cornellis was doing, and what the bonds were for, she was ashamed that during this whole episode she had not thought once about the consequences of stealing them for anyone except herself. For now she was too busy being furious on her own account. All the way back to the City she told herself to swallow her mood. All the way, on the Tube, she was endeavouring to iron her face into blankness. Nevertheless, when she put the envelope on the table in front of Cornellis, it landed with an audible slap. He blinked.

'Is something wrong?' he asked.

'Not a thing, sir,' she said, and turned away smartly, so she wouldn't have to see him open the safe, and put the treasure trove away out of her reach.

V

The news from Norway went from bad to worse. The Germans advanced. British warships sank German warships in the fjords and then were sunk themselves by dive-bombers. Whatever Mr Churchill's ingenious scheme had been, it clearly wasn't working. Questions were asked in Parliament. Mr Churchill made an awkward statement in defence of the government. It was generally agreed that Chamberlain would be gone as prime minister any day now. Lord Halifax looked calm. The Index went to 72.

And then the downward slope steepened. On 10 May, all the news boys on the King's Road were shouting *Invasion!* as she walked to her bus: the Germans had attacked Belgium and Holland, and the British Expeditionary Force was advancing into Belgium to meet them. She thought of the 5th Infantry Division and its Signals section, and wondered in what lorry full of radio equipment Geoff was on the move, knowing all the while that the picture was a vague concoction, nothing more. Then, at work, Mr Cornellis turned the radio on in his office and opened his door so that the news could be heard by everyone. The War Cabinet had met, Chamberlain had resigned, and a new prime minister was on his way to Buckingham Palace to meet the King – but it wasn't Lord Halifax. It was Churchill. *Well, that's not what we were being encouraged to expect,* Iris thought. Something must have happened behind the scenes to tip the world in a slightly different direction. She wondered if this might throw a spanner into the works for the fascists. The British ones, that is, not the ones invading Belgium. The future that Mosley counted on might be experiencing a local malfunction.

The teletype chattered. The Index had just dropped to 71 on the news. Mr Cornellis's hand was gripping his hair as he listened. Iris went and tapped on his door. She could see the glisten of pomade between his fingers.

'The markets aren't taking it very well, sir, are they?' she said.

'The markets are catching up with reality,' said Cornellis.

'I mean, it being Churchill.'

'At least he'll fight,' Mr Cornellis said grimly.

If reality was what the markets were catching up with, reality was evidently awful. She looked out of the bus window the next morning and saw that the Black House door was closed and the sentries nowhere in sight; then she looked back to the morning paper and found that the Index had gone to 70. More days, more bad news. Another German attack, further south into France. 69. It became clear that the British Army had advanced in the wrong direction, and was now cut off from the French Army. 68. The Dutch surrendered. 67. There were reports of confusion in France, of German tank columns turning up thirty, forty, fifty miles deeper into the country than had been thought possible. Of resistance crumbling, French units cut off without petrol and without orders. 66. Churchill flew to Paris to consult. Churchill promised victory. 65. The papers printed a map with a large arrow showing the BEF making a manly thrust back to the south towards the French. The Belgians surrendered. 64. The large arrow evaporated. 63. It was replaced by smaller arrows falling back on the French coast, within a closing circle of black. 62. The Royal Navy were steaming to the port of Dunkirk to try to evacuate British soldiers. 61.

Nothing in the City felt quite real – or in the rest of London either. Day after day of fine blue spring weather, warm and balmy, the parks and the squares alive with bright fresh green, and all the while a sense when you looked up at the calm and empty sky where the barrage balloons hung still that the focus of events, the core of things, was elsewhere. Iris had only been one when the Great War ended, but she had been told about still days back then meaning that the thunder of gunfire in Flanders sometimes drifted to ears in London. None of that now; whatever was happening was moving too fast and fluidly. It was all happening *there*, and happening out of sight. *Here* there was nothing but waiting. There was a continual, almost palpable tug on the attention; a pull on your eyes or at least on your mind's eyes, away and south, towards smoke and noise you knew you weren't imagining right. Everyone became a voracious consumer of news. The radio in Cornellis's office played every bulletin. She sat at her desk in the Mariner Building and she knew which way France was: behind her, over her right shoulder, through the wall beyond the filing cabinets. 61. 61. 61. Even the 30-Share Index seemed to be waiting.

One good thing happened. On the morning of 24 May, when she gave her traditional wary glance at the Black House, the doorway was a hive of activity again, but this time because there were policemen coming and going through it, leading out little strings of Blackshirts in handcuffs to a waiting police van. A workman on a ladder was taking down the lightning flash. And at the office the radio announced that Mosley himself and several hundred other members of the British Union of Fascists had been arrested, and would be interned 'for the duration'. Perhaps the duration wouldn't be very long, thought Iris, if things went on as badly as they were doing at present. But for now, by the sound of it, the Grand Master and Kitten should have been safely scooped up and locked up. And Lall too. However temporary it was, she *really* liked the idea of Lall being confined in some smelly cell in Holloway Gaol, ideally in an unfetching and badly fitting prison outfit. Some kind of greasy corduroy. As soon as work was over she made for Hampstead, and gingerly approached the house on Wildwood Terrace, going from tree to tree, cover to cover, till she could get a view of the front door.

No sign of life or movement. She crept closer. No sound from inside either. Even if Kitten was gone, she realised, she still couldn't go in, not if there was a magical spy in the place too, an arcane telltale still ready to tattle on Mr Hale and to lose him his home. She considered, and picked up some pebbles from under a box hedge.

The first one hit the door with a polite tap. No response. She threw harder. *Plunk*. Nothing. The rest of the handful, all at once, in a gravel bombardment. Still nothing. She was stooping for more stones when the door creaked open, and a baffled and filthy Mr Hale looked out. She straightened up, finger to lips.

He jumped when he saw her, and a pathetic look of fear crumpled his face. But when she beckoned, and kept beckoning, he looked to left and right, and came up the path, tiptoeing with such elaborate subterfuge that any onlooker could have told he was hiding something.

'What are you doing here? You're not allowed to be here!' he whispered when he had joined her behind the hedge.

'Has Kitten gone?' she whispered back.

'No! He's asleep. How do you even— Never mind. My dear, you must go away, go away! I know it seems unfriendly, and I miss our little chats, but—'

'The police haven't come for him?'

'The *police*? No. Why would they?'

Iris supposed that, come to think of it, officialdom might have no reason to look for stray fascists in Wildwood Terrace.

'I'll explain later,' she said. 'First of all, do you know his real name?'

'As a matter of fact I do,' said Mr Hale. 'It's written on his ration book, you see. Samuel Thibott. With one B and two Ts. He took my ration book away! I was trying to keep it in a safe place, like you told me to, but—'

'Right,' said Iris. 'Look, you go back inside and act normal. And I will be back as soon as I can with a policeman to take him away.'

'I'm not sure that's a, that's a, terribly *safe* idea . . .'

'Nobody will blame you,' said Iris. 'They're rounding them all up.'

'Oh.'

'So you just sit tight, and very soon you can have your house back.'

In fact it took until past ten o'clock that night. Hampstead police station was crowded with shabby and frightened-looking German refugees, many with poor or non-existent English, who it turned out were also being rounded up and interned under the same policy that was hauling in the fascists, despite most of them being Jewish and in flight *from* Hitler. She had to push to the front of a queue to see a harassed and querulous desk sergeant. She had to wait for an hour and more while a list in some back office was checked for THIBOTT, S. Then, when they did find it, she had to win a lengthy argument for them taking action immediately, rather than the next day: an argument in which she gave a harrowing description of a poor old man, and a retired clergyman to boot, being terrorised by a stormtrooper. Then she had to wait again for constables to be available. Two of them eventually drove her back up the hill, not in a very good temper, not with very good grace.

'Comical spot,' remarked one as she led them up the path in the dark. 'Sure about this, are you, miss?'

But when they banged on the door, the shovel-jawed broken-nosed face that appeared behind the jamb made the argument for her. Mr Hale hovered behind, a frightened rodent.

'Thibott, Samuel Roderick?' said the copper at the front. 'Your name having duly appeared on the schedule circulated, I hereby take you into custody under the Defence of the Realm Act.'

'Here,' said the other one. 'Haven't I seen you fight?'
'Could've done,' said Kitten.
'Middleweight bout, Kilburn Empire, couple of years ago?'
'That's me.'
'I had ten bob on you.'
'How'd you do?'
'Came out very nicely, thank you.'
Oh, terrific.
'But then, hang on, wasn't you mixed up somehow with that mob did those burglaries in Gospel Oak?'
'Fuck,' said Kitten concisely, and made a run for it up the path. The constable who'd seen him box kicked him in the balls as he came, the other jumped on his back and floored him, and they had him cuffed and into the car in thirty seconds.
'I take it we leave you here then, do we, miss?'
'Yes,' said Iris. 'Thank you *so* much.'
'You're the tart I was sposed to keep out, aincher?' rasped Kitten from the back seat, scraped and winded.
'Tart?' said the boxing aficionado.
'Oh, leave it,' said the other, and drove away.
Mr Hale tottered cautiously out onto the path, and took in the Kitten-less silence. It was a cloudy night with not much moon, and he was a shadow among shadows, but the smell of spring was in the air. The tentative early tunings of the orchestra of summer insects too.
'There!' said Iris. 'What did I tell you?'
'Oh, not so loud, my dear, not so loud!'
'I don't think you need to whisper. Whatever they've put in the house, it surely can't overhear us out here.'
Come to think of it, she thought, *the Grand Master must have been lying when he said they could see inside the house, because he passed me in the road without recognising me. Who knows how much*

he exaggerated about being able to hear too? But there is something in there.

'How do you know about—' began Mr Hale.

'Magic,' said Iris irritably. 'All right, then, let's walk to the corner.'

'I *suppose* that would be all right.'

'Of course it would. Look, have you heard from Geoffrey?'

'No! I was hoping you had!'

'Not a word. I suppose he didn't want to write you something that Kitten might read, and he and I – well; it's complicated.'

'I believe it always is, with the more, ah, stormy affinities,' said Mr Hale. 'At some point I really must draw up both your horoscopes! But then neither of us knows anything, alas. I suppose we can comfort ourselves with the thought that, because of his speciality, he is likely to be, ah, safely behind the lines.'

Safely behind the lines? 'Have you not seen the news, sir?'

'No; no, I haven't. Why? Has something happened? We have no wireless set, you see, and Kitten wouldn't tell me . . .'

She explained about Dunkirk. Mr Hale's eyes grew wide.

'They are trying to take the whole Army off a *beach*?' he said.

'Yes,' she said, 'while German guns shell it and German planes strafe it.'

'Oh, good heavens,' said Mr Hale weakly. 'Oh, good heavens. I thought it would be like the Great War, you know: horrible, but slow.'

'It sounds like the opposite. Horrible and very fast. So, you see, you and I need to make a compact. If either of us hears anything, they tell the other one immediately.'

'Yes! Yes indeed! But how shall I, er, make contact? I do, you see, have to be dreadfully . . . careful . . .'

'Not as careful as all that, now. You know that *all* the fascists have been rounded up? Not just Kitten but the Grand Master as well, and anyone else in your Order who's that way inclined?'

'Oh!' said Mr Hale. 'Oh.'

'I don't know why you ever got involved with such a bunch of thugs in the first place.'

'Oh,' said Mr Hale, 'I wouldn't precisely say that . . . I wouldn't agree with such a . . . Oh, my dear, I don't know either. Geoffrey's mother was not keen, I must say. But it all looked different once. A *generous* vision. An opening prospect. A sense – you might perhaps put it this way – of avenues for human betterment, if one were brave enough to go down them. To explore without prejudice the, ah—'

'Never mind,' said Iris. She found a scrap of paper and struck a match for light to scribble on it by. 'Look, here's my address and my phone number. And here,' she added, feeling as if she were addressing an addle-pated little boy, 'are two pennies for the call box. If I hear anything, I'll write to you or just come over. You do know how to use a telephone box, don't you?'

'Naturally,' said Mr Hale, drawing himself up with dignity. She was not completely convinced, especially when he then added, 'I don't like to mention it, but I am running *rather* low on groceries. I don't suppose you could see your way to . . . ?'

'Oh God,' said Iris. 'All right. D'you know where Kitten put your ration book? Go back and fetch it, and I'll see what I can do. I've got to go home now, but I'll get you some shopping tomorrow, and leave it by the front door.'

28 May, 29 May, 30 May. The tug of attention away from the city to the unimaginable beach strengthened to an ache, an anxious and continual strain on the mind. No news of Geoffrey; but the radio painted word-pictures of brave little yachts and pleasure-craft bobbing into danger to pick up Our Boys which were supposed to hearten but, Iris thought, did the opposite, implying a chaos that was not touching or comical at all. No news; but

suddenly floods of rescued soldiers, unshaven and hollow-eyed, were pouring through the railway terminuses, being fed doorstep sandwiches and mugs of tea by ladies whose attempts to jolly them along faltered in the face of so much exhaustion. No news. But on the last day of May, a telegram was brought in to Mr Cornellis where he sat at his desk staring at a newspaper. He tore it open, and put back his head and moaned.

The women looked at him through the glass wall. Mr Smythe was off with his bronchial trouble. They turned to Mrs Sinclair. 'I don't know,' she said uncertainly, her hand rising to her throat.

'I'll go,' said Iris.

'Good girl,' said Mrs Sinclair. 'Yes, that's a good idea. You get along with him, don't you. But do be careful. So emotional! He seems so steady, usually, but I suppose . . . His background . . .'

Iris shook this off, and went into Cornellis's office without knocking. He turned on her eyes magnified by the wet of unfallen tears, and then covered his face with his hands.

'What did the telegram say?' Iris asked. He waved a hand, and she picked it up. *We regret to inform you . . . your son Harold Cornellis . . . reported missing . . .*

'Missing, not dead,' she pointed out.

Cornellis lowered his hands and glared at her. 'My brother Nathan has been *missing* since October 1916. I'm not expecting him back. Oh Harry, Harry. Oh, my boy.'

He gripped the lapels of his pinstripe waistcoat and pulled. There was a ripping noise and two of the buttons came off. *Good grief,* thought Iris, *he is rending his garments. I didn't know people actually did that.*

Not knowing what else to do, she came round his side of the desk.

'I'm so sorry—' she began. But when she was in reach, he lurched forward suddenly and banged his head on her chest. Thump, thump.

Oh Lord, what now. 'There,' she said. 'There, there.' *There's going to be pomade all over this blouse.* 'You poor man. Oh, you poor man.' As much to stop the impacts as anything else, she wrapped her arms round his grey head and gathered him against her breasts. He burrowed in and began to sob. Iris glanced back at the secretaries' room and found Delia, Sonia and Mrs Sinclair all gazing through the two layers of glass with open mouths. *Well, what I am I supposed to do?* she wanted to ask. The blouse was clearly a write-off, and he did seem to be taking some comfort from the embrace, so she put her right hand on the back of his neck to hold him there. *Damn!* she just had time to think, as recollection of her hand's new properties arrived too late: and then the torrent of images surged in from Mr Cornellis's mind, tender and wretched. Rhoda Cornellis, triumphant and not at all well after giving birth. Baby Harold, in a basket in the sun. Little Harold, chasing a spaniel round a rockery. Schoolboy Harold at some kind of ceremony, speaking a language she didn't know but with terribly English vowels. Harold at Oxford. Pride and hope and protectiveness and fear arching over all of it. And back to the beginning again. Harold being conceived by two shy and nervous young people on a night of awestruck discovery – *and I really shouldn't be seeing that*, she thought, overtaken not by a simulation of compassion but, helplessly and almost resentfully, by the real thing. 'You poor man,' she said again, meaning it this time, and held his head tight, and rocked him.

When he emerged, sniffing and searching for a handkerchief, they were both embarrassed.

'You should go home, sir,' she said. 'Break the news to your wife.'
'Oh God,' said Mr Cornellis.
'*Be* with your wife.'
'Yes. Yes, you're right. But what about—?'
'We'll hold the fort, sir.'
'Do you . . . know how?'

'*Yes*, sir.'

'I suppose you probably do, at that.'

She found him his hat, and buttoned up his overcoat to cover the torn waistcoat. She walked him to the lift, and as the doors closed he lifted his hat to her.

The eyes in the secretarial room followed her all the way back along the corridor. When she opened the door, Delia and Sonia and Mrs Sinclair looked up at her uncertainly.

'Right, ladies,' she said. 'Let's get this round of cheques out before the last post.'

And Delia, Sonia and Mrs Sinclair moved to obey.

VI

She was the last out of the office that night. It was nearly seven but not even twilight yet. They were getting into the long days of midsummer, and down in the canyon at the foot of the Mariner Building the shade was afternoon shadow, the cool counterpart to the patient blue sky high overhead. It was like the shade behind a cricket pavilion – only with the smell of smashed orange boxes and the fishy grime of the river in it. A tugboat hooted.

There was a soldier leaning on the pillar box the Watcher had punched, a tall soldier with red-rimmed eyes and blond stubble. She almost didn't recognise him.

'Geoff?' she said. He pushed himself off the postbox and came towards her, weaving slightly.

'Hello!' he said. 'I'm home from the wars! If I play my cards right, will you suck me off again?'

'What?' she said.

'Isn't that what it's called? I'm sorry if I got the no— no— nomenclature wrong. I told the fellows what you did with me, and they said that was its name.'

'You're drunk, aren't you?' she said.

'They gave us some beer on the train,' said Geoff. 'And Jim said, I'm going to go home and have a kip in a real bed. And Andy said, I'm going to get my wife's knickers off and give her one, and then I'm going to have a kip in a real bed. And I said, I'm going to go and find good old Iris. And they said, what, Iris with the mouth.

And I said, that's the one. And they said, get in there, my son. And stuff like that.'

She looked at him. The bravado was thin, and wavering, but still desperately unpleasant. Nasty graffiti scrawled over the face of the boy she'd been expecting.

'I think I preferred you when you knew less,' she said, taking a step back.

'Well, I learned it from you.'

'I never taught you to talk like that!'

If you weren't a good girl, if you were borrowing the men's language for desire, you knew that the words that turned you into meat were nearby too. Right next along from the greedy words, the hateful ones. But all the more reason to make the distinction. All the more reason not to want to hear them now.

'Well, how'm I supposed to talk to you? What'm I supposed to say, Iris?'

'I don't know! I don't know! I know how to get what I want out of a man but I don't know how to behave with someone I . . . like.'

A slow, foolish smile curled up the corners of his mouth, and spread and spread till his face was all idiotic happiness.

'You like me?' he said.

'Not very much at this moment.'

'But on average you do? Across the – the distribution of me taken as a whole?'

'Geoff . . .'

'You do. You *like* me.'

'Yes, Geoff. I like you.'

Abruptly the smile upended itself, his face turned whitey-green, and he doubled over and was sick into the gutter. Very sick: jet after jet of thin beer-vomit. He couldn't have had much in his stomach except the beer on the train.

'Sorry,' he said shakily. 'Sorry. Sorry.'

'We'd better get you some coffee,' she said.

'I couldn't . . .'

'Give it a minute.'

He spat, and shivered.

'What a mess,' he said. 'What an awful mess. And what must you think of me. I'm so sorry. I should go; I should go and find my father and let him know I'm all right – except, oh, I can't, can I, because—'

'Kitten's gone,' she said. 'But you can let him know tomorrow. He's only just caught up with the news, and a few more hours of anxiety won't kill him. Come on: coffee, and then some food. It'll all look better after that.'

But Geoff stayed tremulous and ashamed in the taxi to Chelsea, lacing his fingers together in his lap. 'Gosh,' he said uncertainly when she'd got him through her front door at Challoner Court, 'it's very . . . shiny in here.' It was; it seemed extremely so in contrast to a large, dirty, stumbling soldier, dropping his kit-bag on the golden carpet and knocking things with his big hands and (to be honest) smelling sourly of sick. A ludicrously feminine space, with a clumsy male animal in it.

'I'll put the kettle on,' said Iris. 'And make some toast. Why don't you go and brush your teeth?'

'I haven't got a toothbrush.'

'Use mine.'

'But—'

'Go on.'

He went into the bathroom, khaki among the perfume bottles, and shut the door behind him. She heard toothbrushing sounds, spitting, gargling. Then, unexpectedly, the sound of her shower-bath being turned on, and grunts, and clothes dropping to the floor. Well, that wasn't the worst idea in the world. She brewed a whole glass flask of coffee, using up the last of the French roast from the King's Road grocer's. The toast popped up. She buttered it recklessly. The sound of the shower went on. And on. The toast started to go cold, and still there was no sound of movement from the bathroom, just the swish and patter of the water.

She tapped on the door. 'Geoff?' she said. No reply. She tried it, and it wasn't locked. 'Geoff?' Nothing. She hesitated, and then pushed it open.

At first she thought he'd gone to sleep. He was standing with his forehead on the tiles, with the water coursing down his head, and down the rest of him, of which there was more than she remembered. While she had been losing weight on the rations, he had been being built up by Army beef. He wasn't spindly any more. There were ridges of muscle on his back, and he was patched and mottled red-brown where the sun had got at him, day after day in the open, except for his arse, which was lily-white. There was definitely a man in her shower, and not a boy. Then she saw that his eyes were wide, and his mouth was working soundlessly.

'Geoff?' she said. 'What is it?'

'Am,' he said, and swallowed. 'Am I safe?'

'Oh, my dear,' said Iris. She took her own clothes off, quickly and unseductively, and climbed into the shower behind him. She pressed herself against him as hard as she could, so that he could feel her being there, all the way down to his ankles. The water turned her hair to snakes, and she kissed him between the shoulder blades, her face back where it had been when she was hiding behind him from the Watcher; only bare now, with nothing between them but a warm trickling rain and the difficulties they brought with them even when naked. Then she reached her right hand around and placed it firmly on his chest, over his heart. War came up her arm: fearful days, panicked faces, burning vehicles, bodies on the roadside. A terrible randomness. A world without pattern, astrew with pits and horrors and splintered places.

'Yes,' she said. 'You're safe. I've got you.'

*

He ate the cold toast in the end, wrapped in a towel, but he could barely keep his eyes open by then, and the coffee seemed pointless. She led him to her bed, and drew the golden coverlet over him, and he seemed to sink away from her, lying turned away from her on his side, as if he were dropping into a soft well, his profile printed into her pillow. She looked at his yellow lashes while she towelled her own hair dry. *Well*, she thought. And though it was not particularly late, she turned off all the lights and climbed in behind him, not wanting to be anywhere else, or to be doing anything else: and naked him felt better on her skin than any number of his shirts, and the soft depth into which he had fallen pulled her in too.

He surfaced some time not long after dawn, when a silk-soft grey light was easing under the curtains, and rolled towards her, reaching. Instantly the movement woke her; instantly, their mouths went looking for each other, bumping teeth, and things began to happen.

'Wait . . . Wait!' she managed to say, a speck of self-preservation asserting itself. 'I'll just— Wait!'

She fled to the bathroom to put her cap in. Came back suddenly self-conscious, because he was gazing at her naked walk from the doorway as if greedy for every photon's-worth of information in the half-light, every gleam from her moving hips. Every dab of light on her shoulders or her breasts or where she had just applied the spermicide. But utterly serious; a look with no relieving exit into humour possible from it. It was strangely difficult to take the last two steps towards him, and when she got back under the covers she pulled them up to her chin. They stared at each other, intent.

'Now I'm afraid,' she said. It seemed important to trust him with this, since he had trusted her with his fear.

'What of?' asked Geoff across the pillow, inches away, a million miles away.

'Of . . . falling back into the pattern I know. Of taking charge. Of . . . not letting anything new happen.'

'I think it's happening anyway.'

'I'm frightened of that too.'

'You're safe,' said Geoff with the tiniest glimmer of a smile. 'I've got you. But,' he added, 'I've no idea what I'm doing, and if you don't take the lead a bit, we'll just have two confused people in this bed.'

'Maybe that's better,' she said, but her hand was already travelling, exploring the astonishing territory before her.

'Should I—?' he began.

'Shush,' she said, and moved so they were too close for talking.

It stayed frightening, because at every moment uninterrupted news of the reality of Geoff was being communicated to her, and it felt as if the whole of her, unedited, unwieldy, without any prudent privacy, was being laid open to him in return. Their two bodies felt immense. Huge distances had to be crossed with every movement, slow and momentous as a tide coming in, or the weight of continents grinding against each other. She shifted from her back to her side, and she seemed to be in another world by the time she arrived. At the same time, everything flowed; what they were doing seemed to move along of its own accord, without the pauses where you might make a choice, or insert a decision. It was terrifying, and also the best thing she had ever done.

She did not know for sure, after a while, where he ended and she began. It was not just that he was inside her – though he was inside her now, and both of them moving as if some vast ocean swell had them, slow waves as big as mountains – but that there was no *other* there. No dead space that was not-I. One self, and another self, but both equally selves, equally aflow with unfinished lives and histories, and neither a human-shaped parcel of skin and muscle from which you might take something as poor and simple as just pleasure. Iris was different from Geoffrey, and Geoffrey was different from Iris, but the difference was at once too important and too unimportant for the limit of her skin to be a very significant boundary.

They slept again, and this time entangled. Hard parts and soft parts, rough parts and smooth parts, damp parts and dry parts and sopping parts, and no urgency to tell which was whose. What woke Iris was a change of the light. The glow of full morning in Chelsea burning around the curtain edges, yes; Saturday-morning light, with no need to go to work. But also a bluer, cooler radiance growing more intense from the corner of the room. A radiance flickering, cobalt within cerulean, with perpetual movement. Wheels, triangles, impossible geometries. And from the blue light the blue angel said in a voice like chiming glassware, 'With thee conversing, I forget all time . . .'

'Fuck!' said Iris.

HONEY LANE
JUNE–AUGUST 1940

I

She scrabbled for the sheet and wrapped it round herself. This left nothing to cover Geoff, who'd rolled onto his face. The blue glow from the angel painted him all the way down from stubbly lips mouthing the pillow to the long delicate bones of his feet. It was a clinical light, a chill unliving brilliance more appropriate for a body on a slab than for a drowsing, breathing man, sprawled on crumpled cotton.

And fearful to see. It just was. When the blue angel had appeared in the attic, it had been scolding, not threatening; and there had been an elation in seeing the white particles of the captive angels whirl free. But she had met these creatures first in the form of the Watcher, all implacable force, and the terror lingered. She didn't think it would ever quite vanish. Her living body continued to sound the signal for danger at the sight of any of them. However they behaved, they had a power not limited by flesh and blood. They weren't flesh and blood. They were wave and particle. They were irreducibly strange. They were *other*. They could move like a vapour, or like a sledgehammer, or like a swarm of razors. Their choice, not hers. She wanted, this morning, to be admiring the deep groove of Geoff's spine; she wanted to be pressing her hip against the little white hills of his backside. She wanted to be nuzzling close, and sleeping more, and dwelling slowly in the astonishing state of having turned herself inside out with him and survived. Instead she was staring into a blue fluorescence that filled her with the urge to cower. This could not be allowed to stand.

'Excuse me?' said the angel.

She jabbed Geoff in the ribs with three fingers. He woke with a yelp and a groan and a mumble, found her face with a sleepy gaze and began to smile: then took in the blue glow, and rolled away so fast he fell off the far side of the bed with a thud. When he came back up he was draped in the discarded gold coverlet, like a particularly louche Roman emperor. *Hail, Dionysus*, she might have thought at another time, but here and now she was seeing the ease flee his expression, and tension return. *I'd have kept that look off you*, she thought.

'What?' he said. 'What is *that* doing here?'

'I don't know,' said Iris. She turned to the wheels, the cubes, the kaleidoscopic abyss of blue. The expensive chic of the flat had not worked as a charm to keep angels out after all. 'Look, we did what you said. We haven't touched the stuff in the attic.'

'I know,' said the angel, in its voice of inhuman music, of glass tubes ringing and wind-struck chimes. 'I come to you now on another matter. I have terrible news.'

'Do you?' said Geoff. 'Is an army of fascists conquering Europe? Is nobody able to resist? Does it turn out that dive-bombers and machine guns are stronger than principles and good intentions?'

'Worse news than that,' said the angel.

Geoff laughed. 'Have you got a cigarette?' he asked Iris.

'Sorry, no. But I could reheat the coffee. It won't be as nice but we shouldn't waste it.'

'I'll do it,' said Geoff. 'I need a minute before I face whatever this is. If you don't mind me muddling up your kitchen?'

'It's fine,' she said. 'Go on.'

He came round the end of the bed, sidling past the cold blue light at as much distance as he could manage, and slipped out of the door in a slither of gold.

'You really pick your moments, you know,' said Iris to the angel.

'I would not have intruded, were it not so important. I did wait until you were no longer coupling. – The balance of colour tones in your face has changed.'

'I'm blushing!'

'Ah,' said the angel, with a kind of scholarly curiosity. It had no throat to clear, but it gave a preparatory hum, and said, '"Celestial rosy red, Love's proper hue". Milton again. And accurate, I see.'

'Of course I'm bloody blushing. Some things are private.'

'Indeed,' said the angel. 'Thoughts. Those are your own unless you choose to confide them. Actions, not so much, when the walls that surround your bed are, rightly considered, transparent fields of vibration in the void. Will the boy be back soon with your drink? I am eager to begin.'

'Man,' said Iris. 'Geoff?' she called. 'How's it doing?'

'Nearly there,' came the reply. 'I don't want to boil it. It smells like it was good stuff.'

'It was.'

'I anticipate that it will require some time to overcome your disbelief,' said the angel.

'This is going to take a while?'

'How long is, of course, in your hands.'

'Hmm. In that case – do you have any control over the way you appear?'

'Naturally,' said the angel, with a touch of hauteur. 'It is just a matter of wavelengths and frequencies. Why?'

'You're giving me a headache. Something a bit more solid would be nice.'

'What you are seeing at the moment is the most truthful impression of me that your optic nerve is capable of sustaining.'

'I really don't care.'

The impossible gear wheels turned in the blue abyss.

'All right. Well, how about this? This is traditional.'

A burst of fuzz, of rapid simultaneous movement all over that her eye absolutely refused to interpret, and suddenly, where the angel had been floating, there was an immense glory of feathers, filling the whole end of the bedroom. Three pairs of wings, each on a pinion as thick as an oar: one set cinnamon red, one set iridescent green, one set grey-purple like the wings of a celestial pigeon. Vast, rustling arrays of colour, and at the centre of them a throbbing outline of bright white light.

'No,' she said. 'Now you look like an exploding budgie. Something more human, if you please.'

'I wonder what you'd like,' said the angel. 'Ah yes.'

The same blink of untrackable reorganisation, and there was a man standing in front of her: a dark-blue man about seven feet tall, naked, hairless, with extraordinary muscle definition. His skin glistered. His eyes were the pale purple of methylated spirits.

'How's that?' Since the voice now came, resonantly baritone, from the shield-shaped blue chest, it was possible to hear a note in it that might possibly have been smugness. Or teasing. Or both.

She looked down.

'Improbable,' she said. 'How about putting something on?'

'Your ways are strange to me,' he said.

''Course they are,' she said. 'All those years watching us, and you've never noticed we wear clothes.'

The angel sighed, and a knee-length blue tunic appeared, pleated, in a harmoniously contrasting shade. So did Geoff, dressed less glamorously in grubby battledress trousers and a sad vest. He was carrying two cups of coffee.

'Oh my Lord,' he said. 'What now?'

'I was just suggesting some improvements,' said Iris demurely.

'That's an improvement?' Geoff handed her a coffee cup and sat down. 'Go on, then,' he said, taking a sip. 'What's worse than Hitler?'

'A threat,' the angel said, 'to your past. Someone in this city has taken the first step towards the alteration of history. A word has been spoken; an ancient system is awakening in the stones of London.'

'The *past?*' said Iris. 'Why would it be a big deal to alter the *past?*'

'Because a change in the past would alter everything that came after it. The world would be different, and no one would be any the wiser, for nobody would remember the previous state of affairs. Nobody human, at any rate.'

'But it's also impossible,' said Geoff. 'Thermodynamically impossible. Entropy moves in one direction. The present is open and can be changed. The past is closed. It cannot be acted on, by definition.'

'You are correct,' said the angel. 'But only locally correct. It is impossible to alter the past *from here*. But there is a vantage point from which all times are equally present, and intervention in all times is therefore possible. And somebody has begun the journey required to get from *here* to *there*. Which is not impossible. Just very dangerous and very difficult. It requires the building of a bridge through the luminiferous aether.'

'Oh, come *on*,' said Geoff. 'No one has believed in the luminiferous aether since about, what, 1870! It doesn't exist!'

'Ah,' said the angel. 'I see that I have used terms you find anachronistic. Would you prefer it if I said that quantum tunnelling was involved? No; that hasn't been discovered yet, has it. These conversations were much easier when I could simply refer to black magic. Suffice it to say that we know the thing is possible because it has already been done.'

'No it hasn't!'

'Yes it has. Your history was pushed out of its first shape into a new one, by the original contrivers of the system to which I referred. The fact that you don't remember it only demonstrates the power of the change. We spirits of the air remember, because the thing was achieved through the abuse of us. Yes?'

Iris had raised a finger. 'It still seems pretty . . . abstract, as a danger, compared to the Nazis.'

'That is because you have not thought it through. Think now, I beseech you. Think of the extremity of what might be wrought by one with the power to edit the past. Think how you might blight human freedoms while they were still in the bud. How you might prevent knowledge, if you were able to remove certain minds. How you could arrest the rise of human intelligence altogether, if you reached far enough back. Think how you two might without warning have woken here this morning, and found bed, house, city all gone, and yourselves languageless mammals in a forest of unending peace. Peace without reason, without change, without guilt, without hope. A perpetual present tense. An animal eternity, in which what had been lost would never be missed, because it had never arisen. You could crouch under the trees when it rained, and couple in the open without blushing when the sun shone. You would die without fear, having no comprehension of what was happening to you, and when you did, your children would not trouble to bury your bones. Would you like that?'

'No,' said Iris, staring at the angel. 'Is that what you think is happening?'

'No,' said the angel. It was uncanny how little the blue face moved. 'I am only trying to induce a wholesome terror in you.'

'Thank you very much!'

'You are welcome. But no: I think this new threat to you in time is closely related to the present threat to you in space. It will be the recent past that is the candidate for change. Consider: the wolves are at your gate. But at least the gate is locked. Your enemy can be resisted. Therefore you have hope. But what if the gate were opened to them? What if someone were to go back and arrange for it to be *already* open to the wolves? It seems suggestive, does it not, that the word to awaken the old magic was spoken only hours after the Cabinet meeting at Downing Street, where Mr Churchill won an argument with Lord Halifax over a German peace overture. Halifax wanted to accept that the war was lost, and to talk. Churchill, as prime minister, was able to prevail. It was a very close thing.'

'You can't know that!' said Geoff.

'I *can*,' said the angel. 'What is human speech but vibration? Nothing travelling in the air is hidden from us. Not speech; not the chatter of a hundred nations on the radio waves; not those pictures that started to turn up recently.'

'Wait a minute,' said Geoff. 'You *watched television?*'

'Yes.' The angel closed his mouth and opened it again, and for a few seconds what came out was not a voice but a scrambled burst of broadcast sounds, unknown to Iris but all as familiar as the back of his hand to Geoff, judging by the way *his* mouth dropped open. A bugler; a sonorously pronounced line of Shakespeare; tap shoes dancing. '*And over here to the north of Manchuria—*' The angel shut the blue lips and the garble shut off as completely as if a switch had been thrown.

'That was . . . That last bit was *News Map*! With J. F. Horrabin presenting! But without a receiver – *how* . . . ?'

The angel shrugged the blue shoulders. 'I don't know. It was there; the air was full of it; I saw it. I couldn't help seeing it. Can you explain exactly how your liver works?'

'Well . . .' Geoff began.

'Nazis,' reminded Iris. 'Churchill. Halifax. War. Peace.'

'Yes,' said the angel. 'If somebody wanted you *not* to fight the Germans, would it not appeal to them to go back into the past and make sure Churchill never became prime minister?'

Iris thought of Mr Cornellis saying, *At least he'll fight*, and then of Harold Cornellis lying dead in some French ditch, and then of what

Geoff had seen and what she had glimpsed too, when it came up her arm. There seemed to be a lot of war visiting her bed this morning.

'So you're saying,' said Geoff, 'that someone came out of this Cabinet meeting and—'

'No,' said the angel. 'Knowledge of the means to do this thing is rare now. Most likely, somebody leaving that meeting told somebody else who in turn told somebody else, until the news reached the correct ear. But not a very long chain of persons, because of the timing.'

'And can it be stopped?' asked Geoff.

'It can,' said the angel, 'for the journey to Nonesuch is perilous by nature, as the beginning of the price it exacts, and the way opens only occasionally.'

'The journey to where?' Geoff said: but when Iris heard the word 'Nonesuch' a half-memory came half into reach in her mind, like the orange fin of a fish twisting into view in the green water of a pond, then slipping under again. She groped for it.

'That is what the first devisers called the destination from which they meant to lay violent hands upon time,' the angel explained. 'A kind of witticism, you see. There was in those days a real place named Nonesuch, a palace of the king's, so called because *no other such* building of a like beauty or grandeur existed. Yet a name capable also of bearing the meaning that *no such place* existed at all. A paradoxical name. Therefore seeming to the alchemist Hieronymus Dawe and his collaborators to furnish a fitting cypher for that place from which all times are present. Also I believe they called it "Nonesuch" in fear, to stop themselves from considering too far the true nature of what they proposed. They were not ill-intentioned men—'

'Wait,' said Iris. She had caught her fish. 'There's a slightly bigger issue to deal with first, isn't there. Such as, why you're telling *us* about this at all. Can we address that, please – Bluey?'

II

'"Bluey",' said the angel. '"Bluey". Is awe extinct among humanity?'

'Nope,' said Iris, 'but neither is the ability to tell when we're being diddled, fleeced in a bunko game, worked like suckers.'

'I do not know what those terms mean,' said the angel, lifting his mighty blue chin, 'but I assure you that every word I have spoken to you is true.'

'Yeah, no doubt,' she said, feeling better by the minute, 'but you didn't come along and stick your large blue proboscis in this morning because we're noble souls ideally suited to saving civilisation, did you? Or as a reward for keeping our mitts off the secrets in the attic for six whole months. Did you.'

'No,' said the angel.

'No,' said Iris, 'it's because there's a crocodile-skin writing case in that very attic which says on it, in olde-worlde, *Directions to Nonesuch*. Or words to that effect. Isn't there. Buried in with all the rubbish up there. This is all to do with the bloody Order again, isn't it?'

The angel looked at her. Or rather, the purple eyes of the image she was being shown turned her way. Behind, or beneath, or beyond, she felt the far stranger attention of the real being.

'It is,' he said. 'The Order, alone among humans, relearned the secret of enslaving my kind. And it is through a web of captive spirits that Dawe and his companions prised open the gate to – let's say, to Nonesuch.'

'But they're all in prison! Rounded up with the other fascists!'

'Are they?' said the angel. He nodded to Geoff. 'Your father is not.'

'Yes,' said Iris, 'but that's because he's a non-magical non-fascist librarian.'

'Where there is one member at liberty, there may be others.'

'And, what, you want us to go and look for them? Why can't you do it? Why can't you, I don't know, go and glow menacingly at them?'

'I hoped to appeal to your self-interest – to your desire not to wake up one morning and find Lord Halifax showing Hitler around London in an open-topped car, while swastika flags unroll on public buildings. On a more practical note: I cannot. Do you remember that Cyprian Hale could not see anything when I appeared at the house, except a painful blaze of light? Despite being, as you say, not magical and not a fascist, he had still sufficiently corrupted his understanding to the point that he was unable to perceive me. And anyone who is trying to make the journey to Nonesuch, in order to deform your time into a dark age, will be much further gone. So far as they could detect my presence at all, it would be only as another potential slave.'

'You'd be in danger from them?'

'We have to obey our own rules. That was the loophole that Dawe and his followers exploited. If we are addressed in something that sufficiently resembles the Voice that created us – even if it is a malignant parody of that Voice – we must respond. So you see, my choice of allies is limited. I come to you, yes, because you are already concerned in the affairs of the Order. But also because you two are among those few who can hear me. One of you, because he is too committed to science to deny the evidence of what is in front of him; the other, because she is an impertinent baggage who refuses to be intimidated by what is more powerful than her.'

'Steady on,' said Geoff.

'No, no,' said Iris, grinning, 'that seems . . . fair. In fact I think that may have been a compliment. Was that a compliment?'

'I shall now tell you about Hieronymus Dawe.'

'Is there any more coffee?' asked Geoff.

'Could make some tea, if you like,' said Iris.

'I shall now—'

'Yes, yes. Go on, Bluey.'

'I am not a budgerigar,' said the angel. 'My name is—' And it produced a blast of harmonious overlapping chords too complex for the human ear, like the result of someone with at least six hands playing a cathedral organ. 'You cannot say that. You may use my old title, if you wish: Raphael, Prince of the Air.'

'Go on, then.'

'Well. Dawe hatched his scheme in the year 1612 as a magical solution to a crisis. Prince Henry, the heir to the throne, had died suddenly of typhoid, and there was no other inheritor. Such a vacancy in the state was thought to portend calamity. Anarchy; civil war; general immiseration. Therefore, when Dawe brought to the court a seeming way out, he was welcomed, encouraged, funded. He represented his plan as a collaboration *with* angels, rather than a gross atrocity against them. Thus, holy.

'We spirits are all connected to the place beyond time; it is our home, our native land. In the structure of our being there is, as it were, an umbilical, impalpable but never severed, joining us to it through space and time. It was Dawe's discovery that this connection could be compelled to act as a pathway on which others might walk to the same destination. Not one spirit's filament of connection would be sufficient to accomplish this, but many. A number he determined on in secrecy, each braided together in sequence, one after another, to thicken the path. A procedure as disgusting for the spirits in question, I may say, as it would be for you if some small creature should walk down your throat, and those spirits, to be held in place for the operation, would themselves have to be literally petrified. Encased in stone; fixed. Trapped. Dawe's circle set to work to call down into new-made statues upon the rooftops of London enough spirits to act as the gagging, horrified, living stones of their bridge.

'The possibility of this could not be absolutely prevented, it following as I said from the constitution of my kind. But it could be made dangerous, and difficult. Of the party who at last set off over the aetheric bridge, only Dawe himself reached Nonesuch alive, where it was explained to him that any change to past time exacts a cost on the changer beyond that of personal peril. He proceeded nonetheless. He opened a door – to the deathbed of Prince Henry in 1612? No; for he had no more idea than any other man of his time how to cure typhoid. He reached instead back to the moment in 1610 when Henry's younger brother Prince Charles had died, crushed between barges in the Thames while leaning out to view an actor orating on the back of a wooden dolphin. This was during his brother's pageant of triumph upon the river, *London's Love to Prince Henry*. Grabbing a toppling boy was within Dawe's power. So he did it; and the little prince lived; and when Dawe returned from Nonesuch to the London of his own time, he found himself in a changed world, where Charles had succeeded as heir to dead Henry. (And would later become the most disastrous of kings, stirring up civil war, at last decapitated on a London street.) Dawe expected golden gratitude, a great reward, but he was turned away as a madman, for of course, having changed the history in which the death of Henry caused a great crisis, he had also abolished the version of time in which he had been commissioned to save the day. He died in obscurity soon after.

'But his network of slave-statues remained. Immortal spirits, they retained the memory and purpose of their imprisonment.

When their statues were destroyed, they might go free; but most unfortunately Dawe had, to keep secret his arcane art, represented to the sculptors trapping the angels for the great project that the words he gave them to say were in the nature of a good-luck charm, agreeable mumbo-jumbo. And so the ritual continued as a craft superstition. Continued, after the world changed, from some deep impress on human memory. Continues still to this day. So though the original spirits of Dawe's design were almost all delivered from bondage by the Great Fire that burned the city, the webwork was unwittingly renewed, changing shape, persisting higgledy-piggledy on new rooftops, ever more dangerous to negotiate, but preserving onwards through the centuries the malign chance of forcing the way to Nonesuch and revising the order of time according to the greed or ambition or desperation of human will.'

There was a silence.

'You're telling us,' said Iris, when the stunning effects of the angel's prose had had a chance to wear off, 'that there's a sort of accidental time machine made of statues on the rooftops of London?'

'Yes. *Old* London. Effectively, the City.'

'And that someone is starting it up?'

'Yes. Or trying to. Someone has given the first word of command to the ancient engine. They have awoken one captive. The newest, in fact: the statue of Mercury on the roof of Faraday House.'

Iris remembered it – the hundred-foot fortress of cream stone near St Paul's containing the international telephone exchange. She saw the glint from the tip of Mercury's silver art deco wings as she did her morning walk up Ludgate Hill.

'And you want the two of us to do – what?'

'Find out who it is, and stop them. So that you and your city at least have a chance against the wolves, and do not forfeit life, hope and freedom because someone has snatched out your time from under your feet.'

'You know—' Iris began, but Geoff interrupted.

'It wouldn't be the two of us,' he said.

'What?' said Iris.

'I've got to report back on Monday morning; I was going to say. I'd help, when I'm home. But I'll be who-knows-where most of the time. It's you he's asking really.'

'It is you that I am asking, really,' confirmed the angel.

'Oh, terrific,' said Iris. It was amazing what a difference it made, Geoff pulling away from the *us* to whom the angel was speaking. And how her heart sank. All through this strange conversation she had had someone to exchange glances with, raise an eyebrow with, collaborate with in yanking back the angel's call to arms into the category of things you could be funny about. Now, apparently, she didn't. 'You know,' she said, 'I had my hands full *already* when I woke up this morning. Things to do. Plans. Ordinary-sized fears about the war. And – whatever it is we just began, the two of us, except that apparently there already is no *us*.'

'I didn't mean—'

'Didn't you? I made myself trust you last night. Despite the vile thing you said to me. And that was more than I was sure I could deal with. And now you're buggering off, and I'm supposed to do this as well? Just me? It's like a punishment,' she said, getting angrier as she went, or discovering she was angry as she went. 'Dare one hard thing, and your reward is you immediately have to do something else hard too.'

'That's right,' said the angel, and as he did so his voice changed back from a giant's baritone to the unearthly hollowness of a desert wind blowing through glass. And the exaggerated and delectable male body dissolved too, into a tight whorl of blue light, shrinking in on itself. 'But it's not a punishment. It's the pain of hope.' The last word was almost lost in a sizzle of moving air. Then the angel was gone.

'Iris—' Geoff began.

'Leave me alone. Just leave me alone. That is what you're planning, after all.'

'Fine,' he said stiffly. 'I'll go and put the kettle on. You can stay here and feel sorry for yourself about the awful things you have to make yourself do with me. "Like a punishment", is it?'

He stalked away. She heard the kitchen door pulled shut behind him. A click, not a slam, but one of the most slam-like clicks the door was capable of. Iris scowled at the floor. The difference between this and the tenderness she'd woken up feeling was infuriating. There was a lot to be said for being able to edit the past. She'd delete Raphael Prince-of-the-Air from the morning for a start. And wind back to an unawakened, unoffended Geoff, and show him— 'Damn, damn, damn,' she said to the floor. From the kitchen came the hiss of the kettle, but not loud enough to drown out the loud male silence also coming from that direction.

She hitched the sheet and went to find him. He turned his back when she came in, and busied himself with teacups.

'Sorry,' she said.

Rattle, rattle, clink. 'You know,' he said, 'it's not that easy being with you either. It takes a certain amount of daring on my part. One minute you're being kind, the next you're a complete bitch. I never know when you're going to mock me.'

An unhelpful part of Iris immediately wanted to confirm Geoff's accusation by saying, *ah, diddums*. She suppressed it.

'I'll tell you what,' she said. 'If you forgive me for "like a punishment", I'll forgive you for "Iris with the mouth".'

'I only said that because I wanted – because—'

'I know why you said it. You told them about it because you wanted to have something to swap for their dirty stories. It was still horrible to hear.'

'You're not going to forget it, are you?'

'No. And you're probably not going to forget me letting slip that I have to make myself be kind, with you. I have to make myself do, and not do, a lot of things. It's hard work. We've only just begun, and it's already hard work. I'd quite like to stop. When you told me you had to go back on Monday just now? I hated it. But a bit of me also thought, *oh, thank God, what a relief, only two more nights to get through*. But only a bit. Because I've just found you. And I want this . . . thing, whatever it is. However scary and exhausting it is. If you do.'

Geoff turned round. 'I do,' he said. 'Of course I do. But do you think you could stop telling me it's "scary and exhausting"? You flirt with bloody angels, for heaven's sake. Why not me?'

Because you're real, thought Iris. *Because I may be your first girl, but you're not my first man. You may want the gloss and the shine. I want what's under it.* But what she said was, 'Are you . . . jealous?'

'No.'

'You *are*,' she said.

'I am not jealous of your conversations with a large blue force field, no.'

'What about my conversations with an exquisitely beautiful blue man with an enormous—'

'Nope. Nope, nope, nope.'

She put her head on one side, and smiled up at him.

'Yes you are.'

'Am not,' he said, reluctantly beginning to grin.

'Are too.'

'Am *not*. And you're very annoying.'

'Am not.'

'Are *too*.'

She stuck her tongue out at him. And Geoff, who could clearly move very quickly when he wanted to, gently seized the wet tip of it between finger and thumb, and held it. She lost all desire to move: to do anything but melt entirely, then and there.

'Ood bedder ed me o,' she said with an effort, eyes fixed on his.

She felt the ground beneath her crumbling away, and herself floating out on a honey tide, into a honey ocean, sweetness below sweetness, a depth with no bottom, no safe footing at all. *I shall drown, I shall drown*, she thought. The sheet fell to the kitchen floor.

III

They reached Wildwood Terrace at lunchtime in the end. Mr Hale opened the door, and for a moment there was straightforward joy on the faces of father and son. Then Mr Hale's look of anxiety came back, and he flapped at his ears. *Magical spy!* he meant.

Geoff rolled his eyes and put his finger to his lips. He disappeared upstairs, leaving them silent in the hall. Rummaging sounds, and in a minute or two he came back, lips pursed in disgust, carrying what looked like pieces of an old crystal set, connected by trailing wires to a bike dynamo. He handed Iris the dynamo and made twirling movements with his finger: *Wind it!* She wound, and the radio came to life in a thin scritter of noise. *Hisscracklewheepthruhh-funkenmitkkhrr.* Geoff turned a dial and the signal settled into a pure fuzz of static. Then he walked slowly along the hall, followed by Iris faithfully winding, and held the set near each in turn of the cabinets that weren't grandfather clocks. Apparently he was listening, but what for, Iris had no idea. They got almost all the way to the kitchen, and then in front of the next-to-last not-clock – a thing zebra-striped in black and white with a green face the shape of a teardrop – there was a tiny glitch in the static. A catch; a minuscule alteration in the note. He went past, and it stopped; he came back, and there it was. Geoff opened the front of the cabinet and felt about. His hand emerged holding a very non-magical contrivance of wires and valves. He took it to the front step and stamped on it with his Army boot.

'There,' he said. 'Gone.'

They gazed at him.

'What?' he said. 'A simple application of resonance. We're working on the principle that the Order only knows how to do one magical thing, aren't we? So this had to be eavesdropping by microphone. Find it; deal with it; done. Right. – Oh God, look at the state of this house.'

He pushed past them both, exclaiming. Mr Hale mumbled after, to protect the books he'd strewn across the kitchen table. Iris sighed, and followed them.

'Your dad has been worried sick about you,' she told Geoff. 'Geoff is happy to be home,' she told Mr Hale, 'and more relieved than he can say to see you in one piece.'

The two men looked at each other, embarrassed. Mr Hale cleared his throat. 'That's very kind of you, my dear,' he said, 'but—'

'We know that,' said Geoff.

'Oh, you do,' she said. 'Fine.'

'You don't have to interpret us to each other.'

They both smiled at her and she, embarrassed in turn, left them to bicker, and went and sat on the front step with the door open. On the way from Chelsea she and Geoff had bought a packet of cigarettes along with a bag of groceries, and she scratched a match into flame and lit up, admiring the grainy plume of smoke she blew into the warm air from her pursed lips, and then the finer, oilier blue curl that rose from the cigarette by itself. It was the first day of June, and just on the line where the fresh sun of spring tips over into the saturated blaze of summer, tentative yellow into hot orange. The tree on the doorstep that had been a jagged ice sculpture was a mass of glossy green leaves, trembling very slightly in the moving air; the overgrown hedge was a tumbling froth of new shoots and thorn flowers; on the other side of the lane, elms rose up in canopies of sappy brilliance, raftered with grey, shadowed in deeper greens beneath. Near birds and far birds across Hampstead's toy countryside sang to each other. Behind her, she could hear Geoff searching for the cheese. Her body ached. Geoff had no finesse as a lover at all, and for that matter neither did she when she was with him. They went somewhere where finesse, or anything deliberate, was beside the point. They blundered together like dodgem cars at a fair, like thunderclouds colliding in the sky. Geoff had a nasty line of bruises coming on his back, from falling onto the corner of her bed with her on top of him. He had groaned, and she had meant to be sympathetic, but they hadn't stopped. Now she felt almost painfully alive in her skin – as if some filter had been removed, and everything, not just making love but birdsong, early-summer heat, the acrid richness of smoke in her mouth, was coming to her much more strongly than usual. Burningly, fiercely present. *Do I like this?* she thought. *Do I want this? Can I stand this?*

'Soup!' called Geoff.

He had contrived something with pearl barley and carrots that would never have occurred to her. It was soft and mild, and they were shy and ceremonious with each other as they ate it – passing the salt, catching each other's eyes and then looking away, while Mr Hale chattered happily. They hadn't told him that Geoff had in fact returned to London the previous night, and there didn't seem much point now. Everyone was making for neutral ground, it seemed. Mr Hale told Geoff things about how it had been without him that emphasised the kindness of Iris and hardly mentioned Kitten at all; Geoff told his father a little about France and the wait on the beach for evacuation in terms which set it quietly in order, and held back almost all of the chaos and terror she had felt; she praised the soup, and felt no urge to raise the issue of angels, or to start making sure that Geoff understood about the Order owning the house. She stole surreptitious glances at Geoff. Tall man who still hadn't shaved, therefore with a yellow softening on his long chin to match the yellow fuzz on his head. Quiet man, affable man, at home. Listening to his father with crinkled eyes, reserved amusement, relief. Little sign of the being who, with her very active participation, had been trying to dig himself so deeply between her thighs that they seemed to be climbing inside each other, trying to occupy the same space. Interpenetrating. She had been afraid that this morning – angels apart – she would be feeling she had given herself away, lost her edges and her control of herself, and he would be behaving like someone who had taken those things from her, be swollen with them, be moving with a new insufferable masculine swagger. None of that was visible at all. Now she was worrying instead that he seemed to be receding, backing away somewhere imperturbable, leaving her to deal with being ragged, opened up, raw. A new anxiety round every corner. Hadn't he felt it too? (Yes, he had.) Why was he so far away? (Two feet to her right, at the end of the kitchen table.) How was she supposed to reconcile the lover and the soup-maker?

'Would you like some more?' asked Geoffrey.

'Yes, please.'

She spooned up the soft mouthfuls of the second helping. As she scraped the bowl clean, an enormous yawn swelled inside her and pushed out of her mouth. She was suddenly very sleepy.

'Could I lie down?' she said.

Geoff looked down at his bowl. 'Actually . . . I was going to suggest – I was going to ask if you wouldn't mind – going home.'

'You don't want me here?' she said, and to her horror found that tears were pricking her eyes.

Mr Hale discovered an urgent need to look for a pencil in another room.

'No!' said Geoff. 'No, of course I do.' He reached across the whole two feet between them and took her hand. It was her right hand, so with his touch came news. An exhaustion like her own; a nervous but steady friendliness. He held tight.

'Then . . . why . . . ?'

'Will you come upstairs while I change? So I can talk more . . .' He nodded in the direction of Mr Hale's humming.

'All right then.'

She followed him up the book-loaded stairs. They seemed mountainously high; and the thought of having to trudge back down them again, and then endure a whole journey across London, was so intimidating that her mind slid right off it. Geoff opened his bedroom door, and revealed the mess Kitten had left: the congealed bedclothes, the tin lid on the bedside table full of dog-ends, the alien smell. He threw open the dormer window – the one she'd seen the Watcher through – and in rolled a soft front of summer air, sounding of birds, scented with cut grass and blossom, to begin cleaning the place. The bed looked terribly tempting, even in its squalid state, but since she had not been invited she stood where she was, near the door, and watched Geoff reuniting himself with his refuge, moving things back into their places, feeling critically among the clothes on the hangers. He picked out some flannels and a white shirt – who knows, perhaps the very one she had put on, to see if it conjured him – and matter-of-factly stripped off his uniform in front of her. The Army had taught him shamelessness. Or maybe it was her. His body re-emerged. It was getting to be familiar, but she saw now in the green-and-gold light from the window that it was looking rather mauled, battered by love as well as by war. The bruises blooming on his back. Scratches. His cock blotched and abraded-looking. She was sore too. He saw her watching him, and stopped stepping into the clean clothes; held them away from him, so there was nothing blocking her view.

'Do you remember,' he said, 'when we were . . . first here together? That first night, last summer, when I said it didn't feel the way I hoped it would? And I hurt your feelings?'

'You were right, though. I don't know what that was, but it's not the same as this.'

'I'll say! – What I'm trying to say is, that I don't want to hurt your feelings again, but now I'm feeling it so much that I think I need to stop and let it . . . settle down for a bit? Be private for a little while. And kind of – see that I'm all still there. Could we say goodbye now, and then meet again tomorrow? I know there's a lot to talk about. But I'm just . . .' He waved his hand beside his head to indicate a distracted tangle.

You couldn't fault someone for feeling the same thing as you. Not logically, anyway. She was used to thinking of men as creatures of permanent appetite, where your problem was always how much you wanted to give them of what they were sure to want, and want, and want. It would be a different problem altogether, a man who had your own hesitations – who wanted both to greedily push forward and to anxiously draw back. To check *his* soul was still his own.

'Of course we could,' she said, assailed by mysteries and responsibilities. He put his trousers on, having apparently felt that he ought to remain naked until he had her agreement. If there was something to worry about in that, she was too tired to face it just now.

He pulled on his shirt, and started doing up the buttons methodically, from the bottom. She crossed his bedroom floor and did the top ones for him, working down. They met in the middle. She leant her head on his collarbone, he leant his head on the top of hers, and they supported each other like two weary drunks.

'I'm just really sleepy,' she said into his shirt.

'Oh, me too,' he said into her hair.

'Do you suppose I ought to ask your father if he's got a membership list of the Order before I go?'

'Surely it could wait till tomorrow.'

'But what if we wake up to swastikas tomorrow, and it's all our fault?'

'Well, we wouldn't *know* it was, if I understood correctly. Everything would have already changed, and we wouldn't even know we were supposed to try.'

'That's a comfort,' she said vaguely.

'Iris,' he said. 'Iris? You're not going to sleep now, are you?'

'No . . .' she said. 'No! Right. Off I go. Soonest begun, soonest done, and words to that effect. I'll tell you what, though, let's get the crocodile-skin thingummy from the attic, and I can take it with me to look at.'

'Right.'

On the landing they discovered that Kitten had fitted a large new steel padlock to the attic door. Geoff groaned, but at the technical incompetence on display. 'Ridiculous!' he said. 'Look, the screws for the hasp are just sitting there on this side.' He fetched a neat selection of screwdrivers from his room, picked the right one, and twenty seconds later was through the door. Summer light only leaked round the patch over the broken window in the attic, and the mouldering mounds of the Order's archives still lowered gloomily. But it was easy to find the column of papers they had disturbed, and to pick out from it the case in scaly old leather. Geoff solicitously found her a hessian shopping bag to carry it in, from an intensely orderly drawer in his kitchen.

Then she kissed him on the lips and Mr Hale on the cheek, and made herself set off, mazed and slow, into the June sunshine. She tottered down the hill. Bus and Tube and bus again; a very long journey, or so it seemed, until she could drag herself into the lift at Challoner Court, and ride upwards propped on the chrome wall. The flat was empty of both men and angels. She opened all the windows as far as they would go, to let in the air and the birdsong, the first more riverine and briny in Chelsea and the second less loud, but both still feeling as if they served the cause of freshness. The bed looked as wrecked as you would expect it to, after an attack of violent abandon: but although it was only four o'clock, rather than make it she kicked off her shoes, pulled the covers over her head, and was gone.

IV

She woke up sometime in the small hours, not suddenly but as if she was rising to consciousness as to the roof of a building, in some sideless colourless container that was a dream counterpart to a lift. She opened her eyes to dark. The big world was in her bedroom, let in through the wide-open steel windows and the unclosed curtains, a deep hoot juddering in from a tugboat on the river, a buffeting night-wind that was crossing the room from corner to corner, stirring fabrics, pushing against her hair. Beyond her feet, tangled in the bedding, she could see out into a street reduced to plane behind plane of black silhouettes, and beyond again to the slow-creeping grey flood of the Thames. Too much world, too much disorder for a frowsty body still twisted up in yesterday's clothes. She wanted back her neat little golden box. She extricated herself from the mess of the bed and went round restoring it, shutting out the wind, pulling across the blackout curtains and then the delicate inner drapes. Changed into a dressing gown. Stripped the bed in the dark, redressed its bareness in squared-off silk that had ceased to be a depraved toga, and put the sheets in the laundry along with the reprobate's outfit she'd slept in. Then she turned on a cautious light in the little kitchen. More disorder: a pile-up of dirty plates and toast crumbs. Stained pan, unrinsed coffee pot, marmalade jar with its lid off, trailing stickiness. She washed up and put away, chewing at her bottom lip.

Then the bathroom. A ring of sand and dirt that had washed off Geoff. She scrubbed the bath, before stepping under the shower-rose herself. Cold cold cold, but she shampooed the clagginess out of her hair and soaped herself till she smelled of nobody else – of nothing but herself and lemons.

That was better. She padded back with a towel as turban and turned on more lights. There was her domain, restored. The pleasant nubbliness of the clean carpet under her toes, the yellow silk tassels hanging from the shades of the side-lamps, the clean circles of light under them, showing slender-legged dressing table, polished style moderne chrome-framed chairs, smooth-sliding closet doors. A lady's apartment. The fruits of her labours. A little bit bare, perhaps, a little bit under-provided with signs of her individual presence, but comforting in its enclosed, deliberate luxury. *Be private for a little while*, she heard Geoff saying in her head. Yes. Her wristwatch, located in a bedside drawer, said that it was half past three in the morning. Not dawn yet, but not long till dawn at this time of year.

Only, there on the dressing table where she had flung it rested an anomalous object: the old leather case from the attic, bulging, lopsided, furred with dust. She went and equipped herself to face it with a cup of tea and a dampened rag.

Wiped, it came up in a saw-toothed waveform of yellow-and-black scales, a pattern that had once slithered through undergrowth. Not crocodile, and thinking about it, she supposed they probably weren't importing skins from the Nile to bind things in, back as far as when this was made. Snake. Good old English adder, containing obligations she hoped weren't going to bite her. Brown ink on the pasted label still read *Directiounes to Ye Pallace of None-Such*. No zip, of course, to keep it closed, but a complicated assemblage of horn buttons. The leather had shrunk and hardened round them. Getting them open required force, and shed brittle crumbs and worm-casts of snakeskin – and when she had the front of the thing lifted and bent back she was dismayed to see inside not a sheaf of organised pages, but a brown mouse's-nest of crumbling paper slips, written on in ink of a deeper brown. On top there was a more modern rectangle of card, hardly time-stained at all compared to the tea-coloured mess underneath. It said, in blue-grey handwriting from a fountain pen, *Epitomised and summarised by me, E. H., Grand Master, November 1911.* Which was at least legible: all the rest of the script on the slips below was a riot of sepia incomprehensibility, every word – so far as you could tell where one ended and another began – a thick abstract squiggle of loops and pot-hooks.

'Oh God,' said Iris.

But it didn't do to give up. She went and fetched a notebook and pencil, and squinted hard. The tall letters, she knew, must be Ss, not Fs. *Evisegplid*, she wrote. *Troffe. Vargansplew. Visgargool. After.* After! Well, at least it wasn't in code. But that meant all of the rest of it was – presumably – in plain English too. Just concealed from her by very un-plain handwriting. If these were the secrets of Hieronymus Dawe's wicked bridge to Nonesuch, constructed from the bodies of captive angels, she needed someone else to read it for her. All that she could learn from the contents of the case was that the Grand Master had been there first, and that at least one copy of Dawe's *Directiounes*, or a summary anyway, was out there in the world. Which fitted with what Raphael had said. Presumably it was in the hands of whoever had woken the first statue in the chain, the Mercury on top of the telephone exchange near St Paul's. If she needed a set of her own in order to stop this leftover remnant of the Order, she had better get these transcribed by someone who could read them. She could think of precisely one candidate. And Mr Hale would probably enjoy the task, if he could be induced to concentrate on it. The question was, was it safe to ask him? He was the Order's librarian. The Order had scared him, treated him with contempt, but Iris thought he still exhibited a little-boyish fascination for them and their works.

She closed the case with a rubber band, unwilling to wrestle with the buttons again. Then, instead of thinking about magical fascists and how to resist them, she wrote a list of everything the firm needed to take care of on Monday morning, assuming that Mr Cornellis didn't come in. Now the pencil flew. All the regular stuff: the statements and invoices and cheques to send out, the collection of the securities surrendered under the ASO, the upkeep of the books. But also the relationships with the stock jobbers to maintain – and she wouldn't mind making herself a known face to them, someone from whom C&B business might plausibly come. The next edition of Mr Cornellis's round-robin letter to investors was due soon. Other brokerages needed to know C&B wasn't rudderless, couldn't have clients poached opportunistically. The same firms, considered as fellows rather than rivals, lunched together, sat on committees together, represented 'the City view' or more precisely the stock market view to the Bank of England and the Treasury. She needed to get a sight of Cornellis's diary for the next week. She needed to read through the wartime finance regulations properly and in detail. She needed . . . At the bottom of all the notes she wrote *STRATEGY?* in capitals and drew a square box around it.

There was birdsong outside again. She turned out the lights and lifted a corner of the blackout cautiously. Day had come, the early light of almost-midsummer, picking out the tiled rooftops of Chelsea in stripes of rose-gold and black like some giant geometric puzzle. The tugboats hooted on, as they never stopped doing. The river had silver points on it. The buffeting wind of the night had dropped to a teasing dawn breeze. The sky was eggshell blue, cool for now with the potential for heat later. It seemed to be five o'clock.

Iris shivered pleasurably. She felt like herself again, she realised. Collected, determined, clear about what she wanted and able to plot a path to get there. But – if that was her, who was the woman drowned in honey? Who was the friend holding the weeping man in the bathtub? Who was the lover who, with slow awe, had moved like geology? Who was the creature who had panted and thrashed about with no thought at all? If Geoff too had a magic hand, maybe he could tell her how what was inside her fitted together. But he didn't. Luckily.

Clothes. Clothes that made her feel like herself. Clothes that let her enjoy being a body in the sunshine. Clothes she could wear respectably to the office tomorrow, on the assumption that she wouldn't be back in between. Something at the intersection of those. Forest-green gaberdine skirt and blazer. Grey silk blouse. Green hat. Bare legs and tennis shoes. She could put court shoes and stockings for tomorrow in her bag. She did her hair, gathered herself up, and went out.

It was too early for traffic. The cool breath of the day filled the street from side to side, chill where the sun had not reached the shadows, stirring with bright motes where the light slanted in. Chelsea was in a prettily grand or grandly pretty mood, this Sunday dawn in June. Elsewhere doom might be coming, the last soldiers were being snatched off the sand dunes, the Wehrmacht was advancing towards Paris: but here, the stucco was clean and white, the bricks of the old houses were a soft apricot, creepers and flowering trees decorated a place that might once have been bohemian like Hampstead but now was sweetly, comfortably rich. Artistic like a society portrait. Artistic with a gold frame around it. She turned towards the river. Not a decision; her legs carried her that way, cool air on her skin, drawn by the pull of the moving water. Letting herself be tidal. Down Danvers Street onto Cheyne Walk, Chelsea at its Chelsea-est, where the elegant eighteenth-century facades, perfect and poised, as carefully stacked as jewel boxes, faced out over the sudden width of the river. She ran her fingers covetously along the bonnet of a parked Lagonda and crossed the road to the pavement on the river side.

The tide was low but rising, the tugs working the centre channel and silver-flecked wavelets creeping to cover slick grey mudbanks at each shore. The breeze stirred a tiny bit more strongly here, bringing the ancient perfume of the Thames to her from downstream. Tar, fish, oil, spices, rotting rope. An atomiser's-worth: Old Mud, for the woman of the world. The cast-iron furbelows of Battersea Bridge were to her right, the birdcage cables of the Albert Bridge on the left, and opposite, the burly green trees of Battersea Park with the silver blobs of the barrage balloons above them seeming as visually inevitable now as punctuation in a sentence. Naturally part of the scene; part of London. She leant on her elbows and gazed. Boats passed. The very first walkers with dogs appeared under the trees across the river. A tram clanged across the water towards Battersea. An elderly gent of military appearance emerged from one of the beautiful doors of the beautiful houses in singlet and shorts, did knee bends till he turned the colour of the brickwork, and then huffed past at a trot, admiring her rear view as he went. 'Good morning!' she called brightly, deploying her most cut-glass vowels. A thin scrim of cloud floated in high up from the east, considered blocking the blue, and instead dissolved in the warming face of it, sapphired to death. Lazily, slowly, her city was waking up.

She turned downriver towards the city's heart and began to walk to see more of it, again without any conscious decision. She walked along the Chelsea Embankment until the prettiness gave way, in the noisy blackness under the railway bridge, to the rookeries of Pimlico, once-grand blocks gone to crumbling plaster, snot-nosed kids appearing, sent out to play by parents wanting their Sunday lie-in. Then on again, Pimlico crumble giving way in turn to the beginning of official and corporate Westminster, grand new blocks for ministries and oil companies rising eight, ten, twelve storeys high on her left, in soot-rimmed white marble. Vans and cars beginning to pass. But always on her right, the swelling, filling river; always above her, the wide dome of blue, the sky so bare and open except for the bobbing balloons. She walked and walked. She bought a currant bun and a tin mug of bright-orange tea from a cab shelter. She studied the headlines on the Sunday papers at a kiosk just opening by Westminster Bridge. Heroic Dunkirk; disaster, disaster, disaster. It was coming; it was coming *here*. What she had felt from Geoff, the burning vehicles and the shattered buildings, the panic and the bodies in the street, was on its way. Would happen in these streets next.

Yet all around her the stirring city went on with its Sunday-morning routines. Big Ben struck seven. The kiosk owner slit the string on another bale of newsprint. The red buses came and went. A yawning naval officer sitting under the plane trees on the Victoria Embankment threw crumbs to the pigeons. A miserable child in respectable clothes was led somewhere respectable by a respectable lady. It was all either oblivious or defiant, depending on how you looked at it.

But looking at it had given her walk a destination, she discovered; and since she knew now where she was going, she was no longer content to mooch and wander. She walked up from the river to the Strand, ignored the siren call of the giant Lyons' Corner House there, open twenty-four hours a day and sure to sell something more substantial than the bun, and went underground, down where the machinery of the Tube blew hot air on her knees instead of cool breezes. It was the last part of her ordinary daily commute she was doing, only with no one on the trains and an eerie Sabbath hush when she came back above ground at Blackfriars. She had never seen the City like this, still and almost empty, like a stopped clock. Occasional denizens of the little Dickensian shops were creeping about, outside their nests of paper and sealing wax, but there was no *flow*, no grand rivers of foot traffic swirling along to do business. Without them the streets looked naked, and wider than usual. The bells of St Paul's were ringing out for an early service, and the belfries of other City churches were answering in lopsided silver peals, for once the loudest sound in the place. *Oranges and lemons* . . .

But she was going up Queen Victoria Street today, not Ludgate Hill. Faraday House, she saw, had changed since she last came this way. The statue of Mercury now presided over something like a literal fortress, down at ground level, not just a metaphorical one. As well as a wall of sandbags taller and more methodical-looking than the usual ones ringing public buildings, it was plastered with red keep-off signs. NO PUBLIC SHELTER, they said, and OFFICIAL BUSINESS ONLY, and ENTRY BY AUTHORISED PERSONNEL ONLY. There were two profoundly bored soldiers with tin hats and rifles with fixed bayonets guarding the revolving main door. They were sharing a quiet roll-up, but when Iris came up the steps towards them in her tennis shoes they sprang back into position, one on each side of the door.

'Yes, miss?' said the one on the left.

'What's going on here, then? Are you two guarding the telephones or what?'

'Can't say, miss. Orders.'

'Definite case of: *or what*,' added the one on the right, taking a last drag on the roll-up and crushing the stub under his boot. Seeing he was the wag of the pair, Iris moved over that side and smiled at him.

'Top-secret, is it?' she said.

'You won't get a word out of me, Mata Hari. My lips are sealed.'

'Very likely,' said the sentry on the left.

'Here, though: what you doing out and about at this time of day? Sunday morning – should be getting your beauty sleep. Not that—'

'Couldn't sleep,' said Iris. 'Fancied a walk. So, what, you've got some kind of government thing going on in there now?'

'That's about the size of it. And it all relies on me and Sidney here to keep off the Nazi hordes.' He said it *Nah-zee*, like Churchill on the radio.

'Well done,' said Iris. 'Keep up the good work.'

'Oh, it's nothing, really. Not for a pair of heroes like us.'

'Bravely checking passes . . .'

'Eck cetra.'

'Miss?' said Sidney-on-the-left. 'You should be moving on. Really.'

Iris considered. If Faraday House had been taken over for the duration by some kind of official operation, it was hard to see how anyone was getting up to the roof to 'awaken' Mercury unless they were in government themselves. That would be very bad news; it would mean there was a magical-fascist worm right in the core of things. But looking at this doorway, imagining it on a weekday with military types and civil service types thronging it, she had another suspicion, she saw another possibility. A plausible person in uniform might be able to get through, on a plausible errand and aided by the kind of voice people tended not to question.

'On my way,' said Iris. 'I can see you're . . . busy. I was just wondering whether you two'd come across someone I know? I think she's been in and out of here. Driver. Mechanised Transport Corps. *Very* pretty girl.'

'Oh, well, you know,' said the wag, 'pretty girls, ten a penny round here. (No offence.) What with all the telephonists. Overwhelmed with feminine whatchamacallit, me and Sidney. Can't help you there.'

'You'd remember this one,' said Iris. 'Not ordinary-pretty: beautiful. Beautiful like a film star. Little and perfect and blonde and very posh. Not known to smile.'

'Goldilocks!' said Sidney-on-the-left.

'Little Miss Frostypants,' agreed the wag. 'Oh yes, we've seen *her*. Friend of yours, is she?'

'Definite case of: *or what*,' said Iris.

V

'It can't be a coincidence,' said Iris at the kitchen table in Hampstead later. 'It's her at work – again. I just don't see *how*. Surely she's supposed to be in chokey with the rest of the British Union of Fascists.'

They had just eaten a highly competent shepherd's pie, eked out with pieces of swede. One of Geoff's ten recipes, adapted for rationing. The house was noticeably tidier. Whatever the two Hales had or hadn't said to each other out loud, they had regained their equilibrium, brought things back to their familiar order. Mr Hale impractical, Geoff exasperated; him caring, Mr Hale cared for. There was a comfort in it for both of them, she saw. But Geoff made room for her. He was holding her hand under the table. They were being cautious with each other, but not the kind of caution that comes from uncertainty. More the caution you'd feel when picnicking together on the slopes of a volcano.

'You don't know when exactly she was there,' Geoff pointed out.

'I couldn't ask. But it can't be that long ago. The angel said it had just happened, and that was yesterday morning.'

'Rounding up the fascists has only just happened too. Lall could easily have gone to Faraday House and then been arrested. Mind you,' said Geoff, frowning, 'you shouldn't underestimate how confused official things can be: really, I mean, and not on paper. That's what the Army's like. Everything pretends to be terribly tidy and organised, and then when it actually comes to it, it's all running and shouting. And frantically coming up with a tidy story about it afterwards.'

'You think they may just have left her out by mistake?'

'I wouldn't rule it out.'

'I must say,' put in Mr Hale, 'it does seem rather *drastic*, don't you think, to *imprison* a whole group of people, just in *case* they make trouble? Not that I'm not, ah, *relieved* to be rid of the, ah, *particular* encumbrance of Kitten.'

'They're our enemies, Father,' said Geoff. 'And the Order is your enemy.'

'Oh, but—'

'They threatened you!'

'That's true, yes, but—'

'They said they'd throw you into the street.'

'Yes, they did,' admitted Mr Hale.

'You know,' said Iris, who had been thinking about how she might simplify things for Mr Hale, 'you could be loyal to the books, sir, without being loyal to the Order. You could be loyal to what you thought the Order represented, even if it turned out not to.' To her mind, the Order from the moment of its foundation had represented tosh with a vein of poison. But for Mr Hale, she could see, the mountain of esoteric nonsense packed into the house was a life's work. He couldn't reject it without rejecting a huge proportion of himself.

'That's a thought,' said Mr Hale. 'You know, that *is* a thought. What a helpful idea, my dear. I could think of myself, could I not, as the custodian of the *better traditions* of the Order. Yes indeed!'

Geoff squeezed her hand under the table.

'I suppose,' said Iris, 'that there isn't anyone, maybe not *in* the Order but somehow near to it, who might be able to tell you if Lall was arrested? 'Cause if she has been, it's all solved and I don't have to do anything.'

'Oh no,' said Mr Hale. 'It was a secret society, you see. Only the Grand Master knew who was in it, and I only knew the other members through him.'

'There must be some of them still on the loose, though.'

'I wouldn't know, I'm afraid. It's such a long time since we met.'

'Really? When was the last time you did?'

'Oh . . . twenty-two, twenty-three, maybe? It would have been . . . around the time the Watcher was put in place? The Order was shutting up shop, so to speak, and packing everything away – here, upstairs, I mean. All the old things we'd done; all the things *I'd* been interested in, really. The group around the Grand Master had some new enthusiasms I didn't really *cotton on to*, if you know what I mean. Things I didn't really . . . like. So it was a relief when the decision was made that we were stopping. I didn't mind much, honestly, that there were no more Friday-night gatherings to go to.'

Iris looked across at Geoff. It was occurring to her that the Order might be less quiescent than Mr Hale thought it was. Seeing that he wasn't keen on the Grand Master's new direction, they might simply have retired *him*, their naive librarian, and let him think the whole shebang had shut down. But Geoff was pursuing a different thought.

'What about the other way round?' he said. 'Get a look at the list of BUF members interned, and see if she's on it?'

'They don't publish that sort of thing,' Iris said.

'No; but do you know anyone in government you could ask?'

On the point of saying no, Iris realised that possibly she did, at least at one remove. Miles Ormond at the Treasury, if she could reach him through Eleanor.

'I might know someone who knows someone.'

'Now then,' said Mr Hale, rubbing his hands, 'let's have a look at this unreadable document of yours.'

'When I've wiped the table,' said Geoff. 'Wait – wait – all right.'

Iris slipped the rubber band off the snakeskin, and Mr Hale gazed at the brown mess of papers.

'Secretary hand!' he said brightly. 'Rather *wild* secretary hand but by no means indecipherable. By no means at all. Let us see: this one says, "Effigie of a Greene Manne, eponymically elevated uponne taverne at confluence of Honeye Lane and Milke Streete." And this one says, "Mr Jones, his groupe of Nine Muses, Terpsichore the vessel of spirite, entablatured in frieze, west portico, Stringe-Chandlers' Halle, Cockspurre Streete."'

'It's the original list of Hieronymus Dawe's enchanted statues,' said Iris. 'All of them on buildings burned down in the Great Fire, by the sound of it. There certainly isn't a string-chandlers' hall in Cockspur Street any more. What else? There must be more, or Lall can't be using it at Faraday House.'

Mr Hale stirred with his finger.

'There is more,' he said. 'But interspersed, and it looks to me as if the, ah, narrative of the alchemist's doings has been deliberately cut up into tiny fragments, to make it more difficult of reassembly. Here, for example, we read, starting absolutely in mid-sentence, "unwarie hee, strayinge to too close a proximitie to the spirite as yette not wholesomely bound to the purpose, he vanished with sounde of suctioune and grate shriekinge, and—" Oh my goodness. Oh dear.'

'What?'

'It is rather disgusting, I'm afraid.'

'Go on,' said Iris.

'Ahem. "—and was retourned to us, a mere instante elappsinge, reducted to a perfect cube of flesshe, there beyinge visible uponne the upper playne of this bloodye solidde, Mr Joyner's flattened hatte, and one staringe—" There it breaks off again.' Mr Hale looked earnestly at Iris. 'My dear,' he said, 'are you sure this is something you should be involving yourself with? Frankly, it sounds dangerous. I mean, far be it from me to counsel against, ah, spiritual experiment. Of the boldest kind! The fearless path of the mature child of the universe! But, but, but,' he said, running out of grandiosities, 'I wouldn't want anything to happen to you.'

'I'm not keen either,' said Iris. 'But it sounds as if something may happen to all of us if I don't.'

'For that,' said Mr Hale, 'I must point out that you have only the word of this, ah, blue creature who you say visited you. Are you sure of its intentions? Of its benevolence? I am, as you know, unpractised myself in the, ah, *direct* arts of summoning. But all the texts agree that *angelidae* and *demonidae* – angels and demons, that is – are notoriously hard to distinguish. May this creature not perhaps be leading you astray out of (to use an old-fashioned word) devilry?'

'No, it's good,' said Geoff.

'Annoying, but good,' agreed Iris. 'So, could you please be a sweetheart, be a doll, and transcribe all that for me, and maybe see if you can put it into order?'

'I do of course have other work on hand . . .'

'Father,' said Geoff.

'. . . and it will take a little while, but if it's you asking, my dear,' said Mr Hale, making quotation marks in the air with his fingers, 'I could be that "sweetheart". I will be that "doll".'

Upstairs, at the end of the evening. Lights off in Geoff's room, summer moonlight coming through the dormer window. Everything silver and black. Skin a mystery. Her clothes arranged on Geoff's hangers. The two of them lying naked on their sides facing each other, still, looking. Eyes dilated in the dark as wide as owls'. This too, apparently, a possible mood of the thing. Not volcanic at all, but infinitely patient. Geoff's finger slowly, slowly tracing her, as if she were a windowpane clouded by breath, and his touch cleared the obscurity in shining lines, left trails of pure transparency behind.

He did not have a magic hand, but it felt almost as if he could see all that was inside her after all.

They rode the Tube together to Euston, where Geoff had to get his train. He hesitated, then kissed her goodbye, and was abruptly away in the crowd, a familiar back and then nothing at all; and Iris experienced a sensation completely new to her, of being reduced, of contemplating her ordinary two arms and two legs and being startled that that was all there was to her. Surely she had been bigger just now? Geoff was not gone like a person she missed, he was gone like a piece of herself that had been suddenly amputated. Reduced, she was carried onward into the City.

The composition of the people in the carriage had changed. Any time these last few months, it would have been the now-familiar mixture of women and men too old for the services, with the women in the majority. Now, looking along the crowded aisle, she found she had soldiers around her, a shattered-looking crew like Geoff had been, presumably fresh from Dunkirk too, or at least from the ships and the south coast and the train journey and the doorstep sandwiches. And the ones who weren't completely vacant with exhaustion or actually asleep where they stood were looking, looking, looking at the selection of office girls the world had provided them with, on an Underground train beneath London at eight thirty in the morning. The pressure of eyes was back. She hadn't noticed it disappearing since last autumn, at least not consciously. Now that it had returned, now that her legs waist breasts neck hair lips were back in the massed gaze, she realised its absence had been nice. The Canadian swaying right in front of her was staring at her with a feral lack of disguise. She fished out her notebook and studied it as if she couldn't see anything else.

Mr Cornellis *had* come in to work. He was haunted, and distracted, and he hadn't made his usual call at the barber in the Royal

Exchange, but he was there. It occurred to Iris that he might be fleeing whatever scene of misery he had left behind with Mrs Cornellis in Hemel Hempstead. Unwilling to lose the ground she had gained, she launched into his office all the same.

'Here is the print-out of the opening prices, sir,' she said, laying the page from the teleprinter in front of him. Usually, it would have gone to Mr Smythe as clerk, but bronchitis had fortunately kept him at least at home. 'All the cheques have gone out. Here are this morning's client orders' – a meagre handful – 'and if you'll make out your orders to the jobbers, I'll pass them on. You also need to be making a start, I'm afraid, on June's client letter; I can have a draft ready for you by lunchtime, if that would be a help. And may I please see your diary, so we can lay out some plans for the week?'

'What a whirlwind you are, Miss Hawkins,' said Cornellis, obediently passing over the book. 'But I'm not sure there's really much point.'

'What do you mean, sir?'

He waved at the morning paper he had brought in. 'The Dutch have surrendered, the Belgians have surrendered, the French and the Norwegians surely will surrender.'

'The Index is still at sixty-one.'

'Not for long, I'll be bound. Collapse everywhere. The news will eventually percolate through even the thickest head on the Exchange.'

'Come on, sir. You've had bad times before. You saw the firm through the great crash ten years ago. You're still here.'

'Yes, but . . . that was different, Miss Hawkins. That was an event *in* the market, affecting the world. It could be navigated with the usual tools, if you held your nerve. This is the other way around. It's an event in the world that makes the market almost irrelevant. When Britain collapses too, who will care about the stock market?'

'That's no way to talk. I will make you,' said Iris menacingly, 'a nice cup of tea. And when I get back, I want to see all those orders to the jobbers filled out.'

Mr Cornellis laughed. It was not a happy sound. But he unscrewed the cap of his fountain pen.

'He's doing as well as can be expected, poor soul,' Iris reported to the women, 'but he's going to need us to keep things going for now. Mrs S, can you get today's requisitions ready for when the gents from the Bank come by? Sonia, tea for Mr Cornellis. Delia, can you call the jobbers and ask them to ring back at ten for the day's orders? I'll take the call in Mr Smythe's office.'

'Yes, Iris.'

And so it went on all that week: Cornellis in a state of despairing passivity, inclined to treat the office as a refuge rather than a place of work, requiring to be jollied along or bullied along through the days. There were, it turned out, sharp limits to what Iris was able to do, speaking on his behalf to C&B's various counterparties. Everything was questioned, treated as provisional, if it came in her voice. She really needed a male front man or glove puppet if she was going to run the firm without Cornellis. Or for him to revive enough to collaborate properly with her, trickier though that would be to achieve. Remembering what the loss of Harold had felt like, when it flowed to her through her hand, she made sure to sit in with him for half an hour or so every day, asking no finance questions, making no demands, but allowing him to talk. Mrs Cornellis, she learned, had reacted to the news by refusing to eat. He was going home every night to try to gentle her into feeling more hope than he could manage himself – enough hope for mouthfuls of bread, spoonfuls of soup.

Meanwhile, Iris resumed her old routine of nights at Wildwood Terrace twice a week, feeding Mr Hale, who never needed any encouragement to eat. He claimed to be making progress with a transcription of the contents of the snakeskin case, but would not show her any of it. She cut recipes out of the evening paper. She slept in Geoff's bed, she slept in her own bed. In both of them she missed him to an alarming degree, not assuageable by wearing his shirts or by any amount of solitary fingerwork. After a couple of days, he wrote. He was in a camp in Something-shire, the name obliterated by the censor, and the Signals section of the regiment was being reorganised; there was a chance he would be posted back nearer London, or even to London, soon.

In the daytimes she was so busy trying to keep C&B on the road that it was difficult to find the time to go in search of Eleanor Armbruster. She'd given up the evening class, which already seemed to belong to a previous era, but she remembered Eleanor saying she worked at the Slade art school, which a little investigation proved to be part of University College, in Bloomsbury. It wasn't until lunchtime on Saturday that she was able to make it over there, hoping that artists didn't keep to a regular working week.

It was a zone of the city she didn't know well, high-minded like Hampstead but respectable, with long grave runs of matching houses in austere black. She found the college, but the Slade proved to have been evacuated to Oxford, leaving a vacant quadrangle baking in the sun: one of those contained spaces of hush in which the city-dweller notices the traffic noise beyond the walls all the louder but continues to perceive silence, on the inside of an urban seashell. Annoyed and also relieved, she was turning away when she realised that she wasn't quite alone. There was a figure sitting on a dried-up fountain in one corner, eating an apple and reading a book. It was Eleanor, dressed in overalls and a kerchief, and blasted with white stone-dust to the extent that her red hair had gone a pallid ginger, like sugared fruit.

Iris hesitated. Harder to make yourself conquer a hesitation when you've just believed you were let off.

'Hello,' she said.

'Good grief,' said Eleanor, looking up, 'it's the runaway. What are you doing here?'

'Looking for you,' said Iris, 'but I thought you'd be in Oxford.'

'Oh, because the school—? No no no. I don't work here, I only *work* here. I have a studio, I mean; I don't teach. So I'm still here. But why are you? The last time I smiled at you, you more or less sprinted into the distance.'

She said this with a certain amount of reserve, but as if she were curious, not offended.

'Well, I wanted something – to ask a favour . . .'

'Of course you did,' said Eleanor. 'The infallible requirement to get one over a sticky threshold.'

'. . . but I also wanted to, well, to make up for vanishing last time. If I did find you. It was rude. And you were really kind when I met you last summer.'

'Never mind all that,' Eleanor said, with the handwave of someone who had always been able to afford large amounts of kindness. 'But put me out of my suspense. Why *did* you disappear? I couldn't work it out.'

'You'd met me when I was behaving like . . . one kind of person, and then there I was at the City Lit trying to be another kind. I was embarrassed.'

'Really? I didn't think you were the easily embarrassed type. That night at the Kinesis Club, when you wiped the floor with that horrible Mosleyite blonde – you were *glorious*. I wanted to cheer.'

'I can be embarrassed,' said Iris stiffly. She saw that Eleanor had forgotten the uncertain first half of the evening they'd met, and simplified her into the being who snatched Geoff from Lall. She found she didn't want to exist in Eleanor's mind with a legend of simple shamelessness attached, the bad girl providing vicarious thrills for a good girl. 'That evening was – it was—'

'You don't have to tell me anything,' said Eleanor. 'We don't really know one other.'

'But I'd *like* to know you!'

'Would you? Well, for that matter, I'd rather like to know you. I think you're interesting. Look – at a wild venture – you haven't had much practice at female friendships, have you?'

'Not much, no.'

'Mm-hmm. Man's woman and all that. The thing is, I *have*. All too much, in some ways. Boarding school and then Somerville: years and years of confidences, tears, break-ups, and long *long* sessions of excruciating emotional analysis. The result is, I rather like my own company – and I like people who can't spout devastating eloquence about their own moods at the drop of a hat. Frankness and silence: both highly to be recommended, to my mind. My Miles is very restful on both counts. So go on. Just tell me, if you want to.'

'All right. Do you – remember the boy at the Kinesis Club? The one I – I—'

'Flung over your saddle-bow and galloped off with? Oh yes.'

'Well, as it turned out, that was a really terrible night, and it began some quite frightening things, and I'm not proud of it. But now he and I are . . . together.'

'Oh,' said Eleanor. 'Oh.'

'He's my— I don't know what he is. "Boyfriend" I used up on my previous chaps, and he's not like them. He's my something. He's definitely my something. I'm in a new world of . . . something. And I'm not very good at it.'

There was a mad pleasure in saying this out loud to someone.

'Oh, my dear,' said Eleanor, 'who *is*? Now I see. The more serious it is in the present, the more a sort of retrospective writhing applies to the way it began, am I right? And of course here's me making it much worse by talking about it as if it were a notch on your bedpost. Sorry!'

'I don't think you've got anything to be sorry for.'

'Then,' said Eleanor cheerfully, 'I'll just be sorry on general principles. Look here: I should get back to work, but do you want to come and see what I'm doing? The lump of stone I'm presently ruining? Then you can ask me what you came here to ask me.'

'I'd like that,' said Iris. 'I did enjoy your talk at the City Lit. It made sense.'

'Unlike some of the other blether you were treated to in the class, you mean? Poor old Cedric. Here,' said Eleanor, leading the way, 'I'm up these stairs in the corner.'

Iris followed the filthy overalls, sharply aware of the difference between them and her own careful summer turn-out, and that Eleanor's bedraggled indifference followed a far grander and more confident code. The art school stairwell, with its bare stone steps and battered metal railings and pockmarked walls, was quite like the corridors of Alexandra Palace. Obviously a backstage area, where the deliberate and beautiful things under construction were stored, toted about, occasionally bashed into the plasterwork. There were multi-coloured paint spatters on the banisters. But it was all deserted: four storeys of echoing empty space, hot under a stained skylight.

'What were you doing there?' Eleanor asked, climbing. 'In that night class, I mean. The rest of them – all highly recognisable arty types. Teachers in girls' high schools, assistants in galleries . . . Not you, though.'

I was practising how to be posher, Iris couldn't say. 'Killing time, I suppose. Trying to give myself something to think about that wasn't just waiting for the war to start properly.'

'And oh, how happy we all are now that it has!' said Eleanor.

'Yes,' said Iris, laughing, 'except, have you noticed, we actually are? I mean, not those of us who have already been hit by it. But the rest. Suddenly everything is simpler; horribly serious but sort of light-hearted, because we *know* we're in for it?'

'Interesting . . .' said Eleanor. 'In here.'

Her studio was a long room under the eaves of the building, with high metal windows on one side, all open so the air could move, letting in city light on a massive hunk of blackish stone supported in a metal cradle. Rock-dust everywhere. Iris had dimly expected hammers and chisels, and there were tools of that kind over on a table, but Eleanor was presently at work with a compressor and a pneumatic drill of the kind road-menders used, only smaller. A coil of wires and rubber hoses ringed the floor around the object in the cradle.

'Well,' said Eleanor, 'what do you think?'

Iris might not know much about Significant Form, but she could recognise perfectly well in Eleanor's voice both a slight helping of real anxiety, the stage nerves of the artist showing an unfinished thing, and also a kind of test. What sort of friend do you have it in you to be? Will I make sense to you? Will you understand me?

She walked around it. Eleanor stood by the wall, hands behind her back, waiting. There was a smooth hole a foot wide bored through the middle of the rock, connecting its two faces, but they were very different. On one side, it had been left raw and irregular, covered with many rough gouges, fiercely dug in to make the black stone look as if it had been pecked, or plucked. On the other, the central hole opened out into a shallow dish almost the breadth of the whole stone. Eleanor had not got very far with this, but it was clear that she was meaning to smooth or even to polish the rock on this side, to a shining black gloss.

'It's . . . an eye, isn't it?' Iris said. 'Gathering in the world, taking in what's here and now, passing it through.' She thought of the way she had felt the distant pull of Dunkirk, the blue sky over the city making a lens of air across which the planes were now moving. 'A focus.'

'Yes!' said Eleanor, clapping her hands together. 'Also, maybe like a giant hagstone – you know, those pebbles with a hole through you can find on a beach, which are supposed to be lucky. But it's all about the seeing. If I don't mess it up.'

'You won't. What rock is it?'

'Basalt. And I might; I often do. You know, you really do remind me of Miles. If I ask him about something I'm stuck on, he'll apply his mind to it, and since he's fearfully clever he usually comes up with something fearfully clever too. He gets the point. But it's always from scratch, it's always some piece of reasoning from first principles – it's not that he knows about art, or that he's comparing mine to anything that anyone else is doing. And then, since my stuff is very much not his intellectual centre of gravity, after about five useful minutes of intense concentration, he drifts back to thinking about fiscal stabilisers, or the equity risk premium, or something.'

'And . . . do you mind? Is that – enough?' It sounded like another world from the tender, unreasoning thing that seemed to have her and Geoff in its grip.

'Do you know, I think it is, for us? For one thing, I can actually count on the five minutes of concentration, when I need them; that's pretty decent intellectual companionship, and I'm not sure he gets that from me, when it comes to *his* stuff. Even five minutes on the fiscal hoo-ha is beyond me. So that's a reason for gratitude. But the main thing, honestly – the thing that makes him The Man For Me, as they say in the women's magazines – is that he doesn't want me to stop. He's happy to have a wife who's an artist; he doesn't want a full-time hostess, nursemaid or financier's helpmeet. That's *unbelievably* rare. What about your chap? How is he with your plans for tycoonhood?'

'We . . . haven't really talked about that yet. At all.' They hadn't. Everything between her and Geoff had been either extremely present tense or, she realised with renewed resentment, focused on magical fascists.

'Ah. Well – if I may be allowed to strike a sisterly attitude for a moment here – I'd really recommend a conversation. You know, if you and he are . . . serious. It's not a nice feeling when you suddenly discover that you've been making completely different assumptions from someone else. Carpet pulled out. Sudden impact of nose on floor. That sort of thing.'

Iris wondered if Miles Ormond was perhaps not Eleanor's first fiancé. But she didn't know what to say. Eleanor might well be right, and Geoff might harbour all sorts of expectations about turning her into a television engineer's little wifey in the suburbs, and she probably ought to find out. But just now, all futures seemed rather remote and unlikely, thanks to the war, and the present tense was quite challenging enough without adding in a future one too.

She said, 'In fact, it was about Miles that I wanted to ask you the favour.'

'I thought it probably was,' said Eleanor. 'Go on, then: what do you need?'

VI

Eleanor agreed to pass on a request for Miles to find out if Lady Lalage Cunningham was on the list of interned fascists, and to make contact with her at C&B when he knew. 'Tell him I'll lunch with him in the City,' Iris said. She thought: *that'll be more expensive than soup and a roll at Lyons'* – *where does one take a socialist banker?* For every step she took into the world of moneymen, there was a hinterland of knowledge she needed to acquire. She paid close attention, but the gaps were very obvious to her. 'Right-ho,' said Eleanor.

And that seemed to be all Iris could achieve, on the Lall front. It was difficult to go on worrying very actively about the angel's warning. It wasn't that she disbelieved it. There had been quite enough confirmation of the abysses of strangeness the world contained. Nor was it just that she tended, she knew, to keep anxieties confined to separate boxes in her mind. (The family box, for example, a mere touch of which, the mere mention of the existence of which, caused the contents to writhe and swell and try to spill her mother screaming and her father's helplessness and flames flames flames, till she forced the lid back on good and hard.) It was more that the threat to history had to take its chances, in her head, among so many others. When the order of things already felt as if it had slid off a cliff, when the world already seemed to be dissolving into madness in broad daylight, when an army of fascists *was* conquering Europe, it was hard to feel uniquely panicked by one more danger, even if it was a magical one. June rolled on, in both green-and-gold glory and catastrophe. Norway did surrender to the Germans. Then fascist Italy, giving up its pretensions to act as go-between with the Germans, joined the winning side instead and declared war on Britain too. Then, shockingly, France surrendered. Suddenly, there were no more allies. All the world was darkened, it felt like, except this one waiting island, this one waiting city full of blossom and fresh leaves. And of course, as Mr Cornellis had predicted, the Index plunged. 60, 59, 58, 55 – faster and faster, individual shares making new lows for the century every day. And then another. And another. The strange thing was that, as the Index fell, people's spirits did indeed continue to rise, as she had pointed out to Eleanor. The hesitancy was going; the situation was becoming simple. Disastrous, but simple. Comings and goings in the sky overhead noticeably intensified: white trails high up like scratches on the blue dome of the sky, nearer planes like black dots, or flies, or occasionally roaring low enough over rooftops to shake the glass in windows. All the Royal Air Force so far – friendly flies – but a German plane had dropped the first bombs on the city's edge, down in Croydon. Mangled architecture, no one hurt. The papers reported quantities of people arriving on bicycles to spectate the next day, and standing around staring excitedly at the holes in the ground.

A week, and a week, and another week. On Sunday in Hampstead without Geoff, after a careful reconstruction of Geoff's pearl barley soup, she made an effort and got Mr Hale to spread out the contents of the snakeskin case on the cleared kitchen table, and report his progress. 'It isn't so much the *individual* difficulty of reading the slips,' he said, 'as the *cumulative* problem of ordering them. They've been cut into such small pieces, you see, that there are endless ways of putting them together. And I do wish to be able to present you with a *coherent* narrative, my dear.' There was something comfortable in the way he said this which suggested that he might not be hurrying with the task quite as much as he absolutely could. She scolded him, but with frustrated gentleness. A trial of being fiercer had revealed that, beyond a certain very limited point, pressure on Mr Hale was counterproductive. It didn't make him work faster, it made him go all to flustered pieces.

She walked on Hampstead Heath in the sun, and what worked on her, what made her anxious, was the practical concern about when the bombers would come. (There had been a raid on Cambridge, of all places, but still nothing significant in London.) She looked at the canopy of leaves over the path, and tried to recall the chill she had felt when Raphael had tried to inspire – what had he said? – 'a wholesome terror', with the story of history being altered so that they all woke one morning in a forest without mind. In a state of animal innocence where the sight of green leaves produced no thoughts, where there were no wants any more for the human-shaped animals they had become but eating, fucking, fighting, dying. The leaves waved over her head, and she still had her thoughts. Though she would not mind a little more to eat, and a wild and self-forgetting fuck too, if Geoff would just come home.

But there was an exception. She could sense the danger represented by Nonesuch much more at night. Then, the dreamlike quality of the angel's warning gained dreamlike strength. It infused into the uncertainties of darkness a nightmarish sense, impossible to pin down but therefore impossible to banish, that under all the tangible threats there was now, also, a deep shivering undependability. An instability. A slipperiness. As if the ordinary ground might melt to quicksand; as if events, ordinary, prosaic, sufficiently troubling events, might take on nightmare's potential for sudden horrible transformation. A face become liable to hinge open and to reveal horrifying strangeness behind. A room become replaceable by flame-roofed inferno. A kind touch turn into a slither of cold scales. What would it be like, if the Nonesuch machine were activated, and a wave of change passed through the world, altering its present and its past as well, making it not just a different place but a place that had always been different? Would you know it for a moment, when the change came? Would you know what you were losing, at all, or would it be lost too fast for sensation, for regret, for fear?

Then, she lay in Geoff's bed in the moonlit dark, looking at the gleam on the spars of the model biplane hanging in the window. Then, she felt it. Then, she thought that any kind of update on the progress Lall was making – if it was Lall – would be a relief. 'Raphael?' she asked the dark experimentally. 'Prince of the Air? Bluey?' Nothing. She thought of his seven feet of naked blue magnificence. She thought of Geoff's more real, more solid nakedness. The thickened boles of his joints. The new width of his back. The muscle that had covered his collarbones, so they no longer looked like a bone torc he was wearing just under his skin. His still-delicate chamois nipples. The column of his throat, when his head was bent back. She cuddled up to the thought of these things. She wished she had the actual presence of them and not the thought. She slept.

On the Tube to work the next morning, reading the City pages of the morning paper, she suddenly saw the solution to the problem she'd been chewing at for months. An investment strategy for a world reeling to disaster. It was very simple. The key was what Mr Cornellis had said to her, despairingly: if Hitler invaded, who would care about the stock market? You just had to turn that thought around. Yes, if the Nazis came, there was in one sense infinite downside, immeasurable downside, so much downside that losing money would be the last thing you'd worry about. But that meant, in effect, that there was no downside at all, of the conventional kind: no reason for prudence, no reason for caution, if the loss would be absolute. It was all upside, looked at rightly. Not so much *heads I win, tails you lose* as *heads I win, tails I lose and die and don't care any more.* It would be a wild gamble to invest now, but only the wild gamble on survival that the country was taking anyway. Looked at like that, the entire market was a screaming Buy. The point was not to fix on some individual clever stock choice that would be miraculously exempt from the situation. It was to take advantage of the situation; to make a lopsided bet on the lopsided nature of the times. *Any* basket of British blue-chip stocks would do, because the market had mispriced them all. It had mispriced them at: shockingly cheap, when their actual value was either zero or (in the long term, with the war won) their usual peacetime price.

The trick would be to get in fast enough, before the world caught up. She bounded up the steps of the Mariner Building, thinking of a circular to post out under Cornellis's name to the clients today, this morning, right now. But when she came out of the lift on the ninth floor she found that the man himself was already there: a transformed Mr Cornellis, newly kempt, trimmed and cologned in the Royal Exchange, with a fresh orchid in his buttonhole.

'Something has happened,' she said, stepping into his office. 'Sir? What's happened?'

'Prisoner of war, Miss Hawkins,' said Cornellis, as if each word were a delight to utter. 'Harold is alive, and a prisoner of war. We had a telegram from the Red Cross on Saturday. I know,' he said more soberly, 'that this makes him a Jew in German hands, and that the protection of being a British officer may perhaps be uncertain. But he is alive! Hope therefore returns. And so do I – with apologies for the vagaries of the last weeks, and a determination to get back in the saddle. Now: where is Mr Smythe?'

'He's still off sick, sir, with his bronchitis. He has been, for the last three weeks.'

'Three *weeks*! Good grief, who's been running the firm while I maundered, then?'

'. . . I have, sir.'

'What?'

'I have. I can give you a full report on the position.'

'I think you'd better! Good heavens, my girl, what were you thinking of?'

She opened his office door to show him out, and he headed automatically for the typing pool.

'No, sir,' she said. 'I've set up a centre of operations in Mr Smythe's room.'

Cornellis followed with raised eyebrows. She settled him behind Smythe's desk, and then, for an extremely anxious half-hour, she passed ledgers and statements and carbons of dealing orders before him, leaning forward to provide annotations by voice. The eyebrows descended. Instead, he chewed his lip, and stroked his moustache with a forefinger, left, right, left, right. When she finished, there was a silence.

'Well,' he said eventually. 'You took a lot on yourself. An outrageous amount, frankly. But this is not the mare's nest I feared. In fact, you appear to have been . . . highly competent. I'm not surprised you couldn't get Tomlinsons to take your order flow; they don't react well to change at the best of times. Which this emphatically is not. Well; we have survived the experiment of your regime. But I'll have my firm back now, if you don't mind.'

'Of course, sir. But sir: I have an investment strategy for us.'

'Oh you do, do you,' said Cornellis. His voice was sceptical, but he stayed put at Smythe's desk and listened. Perhaps he felt he owed her that much, or that her display of competence had earned that much. She explained, trying not to emphasise the element of gambling. It was that he picked up on, all the same.

'Bold,' he said. 'Very bold. But I don't think I could in conscience recommend it. Our clients are, on the whole, risk-averse. Elderly. Dedicated to preserving capital rather than placing it all, as it were, on red, and letting the roulette wheel spin.'

'I'm not recommending speculative stocks, sir. I'm saying, get them into Imperial Chemical Industries, and Midland Bank, and Morris Motors, while the market is mispricing them.'

'And if the invasion comes, they'll be ruined.'

'If the invasion comes, they'll be ruined anyway. You said it yourself, sir: stock prices will be the least of our worries.'

The finger was back on the moustache. Left, right; left, right.

'. . . No,' he said. 'I'm sorry, you may be right, but it's not in the character of—'

'I'm prepared to stake my own capital on it.'

'What?'

'I'll put my money where my mouth is. I wish to open a client account with C&B. Now; today.'

'My dear, I can't let you gamble some little nest-egg on this . . . this *scheme*—'

'It isn't a nest-egg, it isn't an inheritance. It's my own savings, built up so that when the opportunity is there, I can act. And now it is. I want to put three hundred pounds in the market, as soon as possible. Are you refusing my business, sir?'

Instead of answering he looked at her. It was a surprised look – a recalculating look, as on the face of the estate agent in Chelsea – but there was some intrigue in it, and even a kind of amusement, as if he was quite entertained by what he saw peering back from behind the mask of the-girl-who-does-my-typing. Also, he was wearing the orchid of hope in his buttonhole.

'You're serious?'

'Yes,' she said.

'ICI, Midland Bank and Morris. Are you wedded to those three in particular, or would you be willing to take advice from . . . your broker?'

'Very willing,' she said.

Mr Cornellis shot his cuffs theatrically. 'Well, madam—' he began.

In the end they settled on ICI, Thorn Electrical and the De Havilland Aircraft Company, Cornellis having pointed out that she might as well pick companies guaranteed to have full order books for war work. There'd be urgent need for chemicals, radios and planes. She wrote him a cheque that emptied her account. He uncapped his fountain pen and made out the dealing order. Then, ceremoniously, he rang the jobbers and put it through. The Index, according to the teletype, stood at 51.

'There you go,' he said. 'Welcome to the anxious world of backing your own judgement.'

'If it goes down again tomorrow . . .'

'It will, unless you're extraordinarily lucky. It'll go down again, and you, my dear, will have to manifest some Sitzfleisch. Literally, well, never mind that, but metaphorically, perseverance.'

They looked at each other.

'In any case,' he said, 'we need it to go down a little further, if we're to have time to shepherd the clients in. Don't we, Miss Hawkins? I'd better draw up a circular.'

'Would you like me to draft it, sir?'

'No, I think I'll do it myself. I feel confident that I can make it sound . . . less wild and impulsive than it would coming from you. But do write me a list of all the biggest clients, who have had most US shares requisitioned for cash, and we'll work through it on the telephone this afternoon.' He got up. 'You might as well stay in here for now, I think.'

'And when Mr Smythe comes back?'

'Steady the Buffs,' he said. 'We'll talk about that then.'

VII

Progress at work made her irritated by the lack of progress on the issue of Lall. It really shouldn't be impossible to quash the night-time fears with some solid facts. She was still waiting for Miles Ormond to get back to her with news of who had, and hadn't, been scooped up among the fascists. Her thoughts veered back towards the other end of the problem, and the Order. *Did* it still exist, unbeknownst to Mr Hale? Wasn't there something – anything – she could do to find out?

The next time she was in Hampstead, she took a deep breath and re-entered the grand junkpile of the attic. There had been, she remembered, some kind of record of payments for hiring a meeting place in a hotel. Yes: after some heaving and digging in the zone of the mausoleum she and Geoff had disturbed to find the snakeskin case, she found it, an old red account book. For years and years, the Order had rented the ballroom of the Excelsior Hotel, Russell Square, every Friday night. The last entry was for April 1922. It was a long time ago. The Excelsior Hotel might not even be standing. But, barring any other lead, she might as well have a nose around in Russell Square. Apart from anything else, it would give her the relief of activity.

The Excelsior did still stand, she discovered after work that Friday. *But only just*, she thought, looking up at its four storeys of semi-derelict grime, its fading sign, the rotting windows and pigeon spatter. Yet another lovely June evening tried and failed to renovate its facade. There was a limit to what sweet golden light could do; and it reached it here, where what had once been Edwardian glamour had darkened to a mask of soot and decay. It was not quite *in* Russell Square, whatever the address said, but on a side street where London did one of its quick changes, and high-minded Bloomsbury gave way to taxidermists whose windows hadn't been washed in a decade, obscure organisations behind brass plates worn to unreadability, and surgical-supplies emporia which looked the opposite of hygienic. The feeling here was threadbare rather than austere, crankish rather than intellectual. If the Excelsior had been a person, it would have muttered to itself, and lurched from side to side on the pavement. But, having no better plan, Iris went in.

It might be bright evening outside, but in the lobby it felt like the small hours. The Excelsior appeared to save effort by keeping its blackout up permanently, and she advanced to the reception desk through a cavern lit only by dim electric bulbs in dusty glass sconces. Stalagmites of dust-covered furniture rising from the echoing tile floor. Stalactites of shrouded chandeliers in the gloom overhead. There was a lift – with an OUT OF ORDER sign on its bronze door – and a once-grand staircase twisting up into darkness on both sides of it. The carpet had a powdery feel underfoot. There was a brass spittoon in the shape of a baobab tree, with a crust of dried residue inside it. Generally, the effect was of a rotted 1910. It was impossible to associate any of it with Lall's immaculate tailoring.

'Yes?' said the relict of 1910 behind the desk, without putting down her knitting.

'I was wondering—'

'No vacancies, dear. All rooms is let to long-term residents.'

'No, no, I have a friend who's . . . looking for somewhere economical to hold her wedding reception. Do you have a ballroom?'

'No.'

'Oh, really? I thought I heard of a, a, scholarly . . . *society* that met in it.'

The relict's gaze sharpened.

'We don't discuss other clients' bookings. And we don't have a ballroom – haven't had for the better part of twenty years. So get along with you, miss.'

'But—'

'Goodbye.'

Iris retreated, relieved in a way she could not possibly have defended rationally to find that the gold of seven o'clock in June was still waiting out on the pavement, and the cavern had not, as in a fairy tale, clapped its mouth shut to trap her inside the magic mountain. The very shoddy magic mountain.

She crossed the road at relieved speed, and was rounding the corner when the oddity of the relict's phrasing struck home. Not, *Never heard of anything like that*, but: *We don't discuss other clients' bookings.* Present tense. She groaned inwardly, and arrested her feet.

There was a pub on the corner, not quite as down-at-heel as the Excelsior, whose saloon bar gave a view of the hotel's front steps. Though it was Friday night, most of the noise stayed in the public bar, and she only had to fend off two drunks and a Czech squadron leader while she nursed a whisky and watched. Nothing happened for a long time, except the gradual fall in the angle of the golden light. Long enough for her to decide five times over that she was on a fool's errand, and to stay anyway from cussedness. And then, at half past eight, a car drew up outside the Excelsior, so out of place in the scene that it was an alarm signal in itself. It was a grand old shooting brake: front end Rolls-Royce black, back end a sort of mobile half-timbered cottage. Except the windows were tinted blue, obscuring the inside completely. The engine idled and stopped. Iris pressed her forehead against the pub window. Out of the back climbed two arthritic old men, neither so far as she could see the Grand Master, struggling to carry what looked like instrument cases and a wicker basket that rocked as if it had an animal inside it; and after them, gymnastically smooth in her movements compared to the codgers, a familiar slender figure in white linen, who looked up at the crumbling facade of the hotel with a wince of sulky distaste. Lall. Lall, not in Holloway Gaol, not re-dressed in greasy corduroy by His Majesty's Government.

The old men creaked their way into the Excelsior and Lall followed, making no move to help with the luggage.

Now what? She had done what she set out to do, Iris told herself. She could go now. But there on the other side of the road, somewhere in the dismal recesses of the hotel, the nightmare threat to the solidity of things was presumably underway. The remnant of the Order was meeting with Lall *for* something – to *do* something. How could she walk away whistling from that? There was a precious chance here to know more. But there was the dragon on the desk to get past. And the problem, if she did get past, and get upstairs, of eavesdropping on a conversation that would certainly be taking place behind closed doors. She needed, to rob a magic mountain, the kind of fairy-tale equipment a magic mountain called for. She needed a cloak of invisibility.

A tired-looking woman about Iris's height and age and build came out of the Excelsior in a maid's black uniform, and lit a cigarette at the bottom of the steps.

'Oh God,' said Iris, and flew out to intercept her.

'Let me get this straight,' said the maid, in the saloon bar a couple of minutes later and furnished with a port-and-lemon. 'You'll pay me ten bob to change clothes with me—'

'Yes, here in the pub loos—'

'And then I wait here in your clothes—'

'And have another drink if you want—'

'And you swear you'll come back within the hour.'

'Yes. And you'll have my clothes as a hostage, to prove I will.'

'What's your game, then? Here, you're not going to nick anything, are you?'

Only information. 'No, no, nothing like that. I just want to have a look around in the hotel without anyone paying attention. And people's eyes tend to, well, slide over you, if you're in . . .' Iris waved her hand at the black dress and the white cap.

'You got that right,' said the maid. 'Ah, I see it. I know what you're up to.'

'Do you?'

'You're one of them private enquiry agents, incher? I thought they was all blokes: but yeah, that'll be it.'

'How clever of you,' said Iris.

'I'm amazed any of them lot in the Excelsior can still get up to hanky-panky, mind,' said the maid. 'Hovering at death's door, most of 'em.'

'You'd be surprised.'

'Ten bob, then? And my name won't come into it.'

'Ten bob. And it absolutely won't.'

The dress was sour and sweat-heavy from the shift that had just been worked in it, and Iris wasn't sure that the cap was pinned on securely. But when she entered the lobby, the dress's black merged with the dark, making her feel she was halfway to camouflaged already, her face a pale vagueness gliding through the gloom; and, as she'd hoped, when she passed the desk, social magic did the rest.

'Forgotten something?' asked the relict without looking up.

'Mm,' said Iris, and took herself out of sight round the left-hand curve of the stairs. There was so little lighting that she was feeling her way by foot primarily, on worn and slippery carpet that must surely be a death-trap for elderly residents. The corkscrew turns passed as a dim suggestion of cracking woodwork and dusty plaster.

At the first landing, she poked her head out nervously. Then reminded herself: cloak of invisibility. Maids vanish by looking as if they know what they're doing. They become more visible if they skulk. So she strode along the first-floor corridor from end to end. A slightly brighter space, with most of the light bulbs working, the burgundy carpet swept – but the impression of order undercut by a persistent smell of mixed disinfectant and urine. And all the doors had room numbers on them. Iris wasn't quite sure what she was looking for, but this wasn't it.

Up another storey. Another corridor, identical. No guests in sight. Were they ambulant? Were they present? Were they even alive? Did each door have behind it some pupating mass into which a cash-strapped retired major or penniless maiden aunt had deliquesced, organs gone, sticky threads filling the room? A sort of hive of the genteel dead . . . She was giving herself the horrors, and hurried up another flight.

Ah, this was more like it. A different layout: doors to guest rooms only on the near side of the corridor, and on the other, one bigger door with a once-fancy pediment and a helpful faded sign in gold reading *BALLROOM*. Two smaller doors, one each side of it, of the broom cupboard or service door variety. She tiptoed to the big door – not being heard was a factor now – and put her ear against its chill panelling.

Definite sounds of human presence. Stertorous breathing, as of old men who had carried burdens up three flights of stairs without assistance. Footsteps. Some echo: there was a bigger space in there. A querulous old voice speaking, a sharp younger one replying – but too indistinctly to make out the words. She was not close enough. She tried the handle of the door, as silently as she could, but it refused to turn; refused to turn at all, in a way which suggested not recent locking but a doorway locked and bolted for years, and probably rusted shut as a result. Lall and the old men hadn't got in this way.

The left-hand smaller door was a literal broom cupboard, containing a dank mop in a bucket positively reeking of the piss-and-carbolic combination. No. She tried the right one. *It'll be locked, it'll be locked,* she thought. But it wasn't. It opened – *don't squeak, please don't squeak* – onto a kind of crowded anteroom, not lit except by a thin ray of the evening light, shockingly bright and natural, coming in through a further door left very slightly ajar. She eased shut the door behind her by anxious fractions, then stood motionless waiting for her eyes to adjust. The lumpy opposite wall resolved into a coat rack, on which were hung not just coats but, on hangers, two complete sets of elderly male garments in rusty black, and one white linen summer suit for the perfect-of-figure. *Oh, Lall, what* are *you doing?*

She stole to the inner door and put her eye to the crack, having to conquer an irrational conviction that, if she blocked the ray, the trio in the room beyond would somehow know it. Dazzle. They must have taken down the blackout from some quite large window in there. Dazzle; and then the resolving into visual order of the big space beyond. The Excelsior really didn't have a ballroom any more, in the sense that the ballroom they had once had was now a maze of junk, stage-set junk, hermetic junk very reminiscent of the plywood not-clocks in the hall at Wildwood Terrace. Curling cardboard archways painted with zodiac signs. Pentagram hangings the moths had got at, dangling off their curtain rings. A frieze of tangled flesh, where the flesh tones had all faded to the dirty yellow of old varnish.

The voices were much louder, but the speakers weren't in sight. She tilted her head sideways, and they came into view, standing together at a little table in a cleared space of parquet. They were not, thankfully, naked. The old men were in stagily monkish black robes, and Lall, between them, was wearing a white shift. You could see through it, but the effect was antiseptic rather than carnal. She looked like one of those photographs of young women in the Third Reich sunbathing naked in sand dunes in August, skin on display not for anyone's pleasure, least of all their own, but as if to be certificated by a health inspector. She was holding a candle, the flame almost transparent in the evening gold. There was a curl of contempt on her lips. A mewing was coming from somewhere down near her feet.

'I don't see,' she was saying, 'why you can't just give me the bloody document and let me go to work.'

Her pretty fair head came up no higher than their shoulders.

'Read the words on the card. Read the *words* on the *card*, girl. There must be a ritual.'

'Why must there? I am as competent at summoning and binding as either of you. Probably more so.'

'You are not an *initiate*. You must be commissioned, you must be purified before you can serve as an emissary of the Order.'

'I can get into the building; I've proved that. I've woken the first servant. I am ready to begin.'

'You are not ready until we say you are.'

'My godfather would disagree, Mr Weevil.'

'*Wyeville*. My name is Wyeville! And your godfather, you insolent child, is not here. Neither is your father. Neither are any other of the men who have so unwisely indulged you. *We* are the Order now.'

'Weevil and Beetle.'

'*Wyeville* and *Beecham*! Hold your tongue!'

'It is up to us,' said the other old man, 'to decide whether you are worthy to be the Order's emissary. It is us whom you must . . . satisfy.'

A trace of antique smirk passed between the men.

'Tell me you have at least brought the Dawes transcript,' said Lall. 'Neither of you seems to have the faintest sense of urgency.'

'Oh, it's here,' said the first old man, whom Iris was now helplessly thinking of as Weevil. 'You shall have it once we are satisfied.'

'Fully satisfied,' said Beetle. 'Read the words on the card.'

'Oh, for heaven's sake. Very well. *I come as a seeker after wisdom, a postulant in great humility. I, in search of the light, submit myself to the darkness of seeking. I, in search of the bliss of knowledge, submit myself to the pains of ignorance. I, in search of purity, submit myself to the filth of its discovery.* What does—'

'Is all prepared, brother?' intoned Weevil.

'Brother, it is,' replied Beetle. 'The rods of oak, the rods of ash, the rods of birch. The tools of purgation are at hand.'

'What on earth are you talking about?' said Lall.

'A necessary scourging is the price of wisdom, my dear. Before enlightenment, the ordeal. We have both been through it, and you must pass through it too. It will not be pleasant: not for you, at any rate. For us, I expect the experience to have a certain . . . zest. Don't you think, brother?'

'Absolutely, brother,' said Beetle. 'We shall lay on with a will, in proportion to all your impertinences, until a wholesome submission is achieved. I myself have never thrashed a girl. I expect it to be most stimulating.'

'You pair of old perverts,' said Lall, with a calm Iris didn't understand. 'You won't be doing any of that to me.'

'Too late, my dear,' said Weevil. 'You asked for Hieronymus Dawe's document. You brought this upon yourself. And I don't think, now you're here, that we can permit you to back out. To be honest, I wouldn't miss this for the world. You have put yourself in our hands; you must run the whole course of the initiation.'

'Through the gate of earthly pain,' said Beetle, 'and then through the gate of earthly desire.'

'The way we do that,' said Weevil, 'is really intended for boys, but I'm sure it will work perfectly well for you too.'

'Do you think we are still capable?' asked Beetle.

'I expect Lady Lalage to inspire us to *great* feats,' said Weevil. 'Only then will you be ready for the sacrifice of the beast, and the sharing of the blood that makes you one with us.'

'Is that what the little knife and the cup are for?' asked Lall, looking ever smaller between the two of them. *Run, you fool,* thought Iris. *Don't you have any sense at all? Don't you recognise the sound of men working themselves up?*

'The blade and the chalice,' corrected Weevil. 'All in good time. First things first. Put down the candle, postulant, and take hold of her, brother. I am senior; I get first crack at her.'

'Disgusting,' said Lall. Again, though, she said it without agitation, even with a kind of anticipation.

'Bend her,' said Weevil, and the black robes converged on the white shift.

Basic comradeship among females, declared Eleanor's voice in Iris's head. Oh God, she was going to have to go in and try and rescue her, wasn't she? But while she was still thinking this, a sort of convulsion went through the struggling group she was seeing through the chink in the door. At the same time there was a series of rapid, sharp thuds. The sound, maybe, of a small hard heel being kicked into the side of an elderly knee with enough force to crack the joint, followed by the sound of the same heel stamping on the delicate bones of an elderly foot. Weevil and Beetle fell away from the slot-shaped view Iris had of the proceedings, making noises of pain and distress. Up rose Lall, breathing hard but grinning. *Good for you, you little horror!* Iris thought. *Now run!* But Lall opened the penknife on the table and stood there, waiting for Weevil to waver back up into sight, face twisted with pain.

'Let's skip straight to the blood, shall we?' she said, and with hands moving very fast stuck him in the forearm with the silver blade and twisted it there. He screamed.

'And we catch it in the cup, do we?' she said happily. 'Hold your arm up, then. Higher, higher! Higher, you vile old pervert!'

'Augh! Ah! Beecham, for God's sake, take it away from her!'

'No,' said Lall.

There was a wet sizzle and another scream. As Beecham clambered up on the other side, she had stuck the candle in his eye. He crumpled back to the floor clutching his head, and fell out of Iris's view. A minute earlier Iris had been on the verge of running in to the rescue; now she was shrinking from the sight of a predator in action, and fighting an urge to run away herself. *You don't have to be particularly strong to hurt people*, she realised. *You just have to be willing.*

'Is that enough, do you think?' Lall enquired brightly. 'Perhaps a little bit more. I do want to do this *properly*.'

'Stop, stop,' said Weevil. 'I beg of you.'

'Oh, don't make such a fuss, you big baby. Heavens, it comes out in squirts, doesn't it. *So* difficult to catch. – Stay down, you.'

There was another crisp noise of impact. She had heel-kicked the back of Beetle's head.

'There. And I drink it, do I?'

Scarlet lines ran down from the corners of Lall's mouth when she lowered the cup, and dripped from her chin onto the white shift. Weevil staggered, clutching the gashed arm. Then he seized the table edge, gasping.

'Oh now what, fusspot?' said Lall.

'My chest – angina – I need my nitroglycerin tablets – please – in my bag—'

'I'll fetch them for you, shall I?'

Iris had a sudden head-on view of Lall coming towards her, mouth wide, cleaning her red teeth with her tongue. A blood-boltered little goblin. She sprang behind the door, as the only place to hide in the anteroom, and flattened herself against the wall. The door flew open and crashed against her. Lall might have noticed the more cushioned impact of the wood on a body, but she was moving, for once, as if she enjoyed being in her skin, and all her attention was on a Gladstone bag under the clothes rack. She crouched and fished about inside, coming out with a yellowed typescript held together by a rusty paperclip, and a brown glass medicine bottle.

'Got it!' she said, and went back into the ballroom. But this time she pulled the door all the way closed behind her, leaving Iris in the pitch dark. Iris began to feel her way towards the door out into the corridor, but it was hard not to make noise. Her heart was thumping; she could feel her pulse in her fingers as she palpated surfaces she couldn't see: cold wood, tangling fabric, piled cardboard.

From the ballroom came the sound of the body on the floor being kicked a second time.

'Stay where I put you, you disgusting creature, unless you want me to attend to your other eye. Now, let's see. "Dose: one, as needed." There you are. Nothing to take them with, I'm afraid. Swallow. Have another one. No, don't close your mouth. I'll poke them down your throat if I have to. Now shut it. Swallow!'

'Not safe . . . Heart . . .'

'Safe? *Safe?* For that, have another.'

Gagging noises.

'Swallow!'

A scrabble, a slither, a slide, a slump, as a second elderly body toppled.

Pause. A creaking sound from the ballroom, which Iris only interpreted as a strap being loosened on a basket once it was followed by the louder, unmuffled mew of a released cat.

'Poor kitty,' said Lall. 'Poor pussums. As if I would ever let them hurt *you*.'

Iris's fingers found the door-crack, a lock plate, the knob.

'Do you think they understood, pussums?' said Lall. 'I think they did. Oh, I think they do. *I* am the Order now.'

Purring. Iris pulled open the door and fled.

'No, she's not on the list,' said Miles Ormond. Iris arranged her face to express a civilised surprise. It was not difficult to do civilised manners here; they were meeting over steak and a glass of burgundy at a chophouse that Mr Cornellis had recommended as suitable for lunching a contact at the Treasury. The steak was considerably smaller than it would have been before the war, but restaurant meals were still off-ration, and there was more meat on Iris's plate than she had eaten at once for months. The mix of fat and juice in her mouth was as heady as the wine. She had considered dressing in more Eleanor-like clothes, come up against the needs of dressing for the office, and settled for the most plain and severe of her work outfits, accessorised with a slightly avant-garde necklace of wooden beads and amber beads that she'd spotted in a Hampstead junk shop.

'Sir Perceval Cunningham, yes,' said Ormond. 'The Honourable Clive Cunningham, yes. But not Lady Lalage Cunningham. Fascist father and fascist son, presumably – but not fascist daughter. Would you mind telling me what's going on? Eleanor vouches for you; I turned over in my mind whether it was safe to oblige you and couldn't see any harm in it, but it took a little asking, this, and I did have to extend myself.'

He was wearing Treasury pinstripe. He looked thinner, and wearier, and a little balder than he had done last August: but in good spirits. A man who was being allowed to apply his mind to serious things, she imagined. She had thought about the question he was asking now – the inevitable question – and decided that, as with Eleanor, all talk of magic and angels had to be kept out of it, if she was to be taken seriously at all. She had come up with a non-magical explanation that she was, in fact, rather pleased with.

'Well,' she said, 'I've had a couple of encounters with her since meeting her that first time. And they've confirmed that she's at least as fanatical as the rest of her family. But what concerned me was finding out that she's on the Mechanised Transport Corps rota of girls who are trusted to drive senior politicians around. Cabinet ministers, generals and what-have-you. She's been in and out of Faraday House, I know, and that's . . .'

'Quite,' said Ormond.

'On the strength of, you know, her accent. Of being a gel of good family. When in fact she's a gel of good family with a portrait of Hitler on her dressing table. I thought there might be . . . security implications.'

'You think they're underestimating her because she *is*, as you say, a girl, and not a fascist brute of the male variety.'

'Yes.'

'Well, I certainly don't like the idea of a car with Winston in the back and a BUF fanatic of either sex at the wheel. Not a safe picture, is it; not a safe picture at all. I'll have a word, and we'll get her taken off the MTC drivers' list, and kept out of Faraday House. Would that set your mind at rest?'

'Yes. Thank you.'

'I suspect we should be thanking you. So,' he said, cutting off a piece of steak and adding a flourish of watercress, 'how are things in the City?'

'Tricky,' she said. 'You lot have sealed off almost every speculative possibility.'

'Good!' he said, twinkling.

'And how are things in the Treasury? Are we still going bust?'

'Oh yes, if anything rather faster than predicted. We're burning down the house to keep ourselves warm. And quite right too.'

'Was it . . . a close thing, when Chamberlain stepped down? Which way we went?'

He looked at her sharply.

'I can't say much,' he said. 'And I'd urge you not to pursue this line of thought in other company. But . . . essentially, yes. If we'd cared a little more about the empire than about fascism, it might have gone the other way. But that's where Winston is so useful. I hate to give credit to any kind of Great Man theory of history, but in this case . . . He carries a whole swathe of the country with him, because he really doesn't understand that there's a choice between fighting fascism and keeping the empire. Not a clue, economically; just not interested. But with him in charge, we'll do the right thing. Or try to, anyway, unless they kill us all. May I top you up?'

He poured.

'You know,' he said, 'I have given some thought to the question you were asking that night last summer. About what a broker should be recommending, given the war regs. And my best idea, I'm afraid, is just blue-chip domestic industrials. As a bet on eventual victory. Why are you giving me that shark-like grin, Miss Hawkins?'

'Because we sent out a general Buy recommendation last week. For blue-chip domestic industrials.'

'*Did* you. Well, good for you. And good timing too. I suspect that, with Hitler parading through Paris, we must be somewhere near the market bottom.'

'Unless . . .'

'Indeed. Unless. Well, here it comes.'

'Here it comes,' agreed Iris.

They touched glasses.

'I think,' said Iris triumphantly to Mr Hale, 'that I've stymied her. I've put a spoke in her wheel by completely non-supernatural means. She shouldn't be able to get inside Faraday House again, so whatever dear little Lall had planned up on the roof will be out of reach for good now. Done and solved!'

And it means I won't have to go near that maniac ever again.

'Oh,' said Mr Hale. 'Does this mean, my dear, that you don't need me to finish my transcription? I'm almost there.'

By now, Iris had grown expert in picking the tones of actual feeling from the general dishevelment of Mr Hale's demeanour. These were the tones of disappointment.

'No, no, you go on,' she said kindly. 'You can show it to us both when Geoffrey comes home next weekend.'

VIII

Scenes from a summer.

Churchill on the radio called London 'a city of refuge'. He said the 'vast mass of it could easily devour an entire hostile army'. He said, 'We would rather see London laid in ruins and ashes than that it should be tamely and abjectly enslaved.' But there were no ruins yet, not in London; the war was all in the air overhead. Radiant day followed radiant day, scorchingly blue, and across the blue, fighter planes drew white lines, scrawled tangled circles, formed hieroglyphs on the sky that you knew, from the ground, were only a flat view of desperate three-dimensional pursuits, ending in insignificant-looking puffs of smoke, downward streaks of dirty grey. Mrs Sinclair turned the radio in the office on hourly for the news, and the BBC reported the running scores, so many Germans downed for so many British planes, the figures changing hour by hour, as if covering some deadly Test match. Indeed, Iris saw a placard chalked up by a news boy that said *Biggest raid ever! Score 78–26 – England still batting!* When the planes came low, the air hummed and shook as if it were being sawed apart. Iris, over in the deserted courtyard of the Slade to eat a sandwich lunch with Eleanor, lay back beside her on an old rug dragged out on the flagstones, and gazed up at a slice of the battle held within the square of the buildings as if in a grey stone frame. Eleanor offered binoculars, but she didn't want to see detail as boys the age of Geoff killed each other in the sky.

*

Geoff, alive, came home, not just for one weekend leave but every other weekend through July and August. He had not been transferred to London, but to an outfit he couldn't talk about, somewhere in the West Country. Though he was still in uniform, it was, he said, more of a research set-up than a military unit, and if he didn't mind the long, slow, often-delayed train journey, he was free to make his way periodically back to Hampstead. Or back to Chelsea. They had also promoted him. He was no longer Private Hale, he was now Second Lieutenant Hale. 'Apparently it makes them feel better if the research types are officers,' he said. She liked the way the new brown jacket and khaki tie looked on him. Far better than shapeless battledress.

The Index dropped to 48 and a half, and then rebounded. 53, 56, 57, 60. 60, 61, 60, 60, 60. The C&B clients who'd followed the Buy recommendation were sitting on a twenty per cent gain, as was Iris; sixty pounds up on her three-hundred-pound stake, and every penny of it as brittle and subject to reverse as the battle in the blue sky.

Geoff went with her to *Pinocchio* at a cinema in Leicester Square. Geoff went boating with her on the Serpentine. Geoff went with her to the fair on Hampstead Heath, and they rode in a swing-boat and ate ice cream. They had never done the outdoor part of being together, and there was a proud, unpractised awkwardness on his part as he squired her about which sometimes maddened her and sometimes brought her near tears. A Free French officer in a uniform ten times more dashing even than Geoff's new one winked at her while they queued for *Pinocchio*, and Geoff looked at him, and then looked at her, as if to ask what he was supposed to do about it. She sighed, and kissed him demonstratively.

*

Bed remained astonishing. If it was not quite the earthquake it had been at first – the bliss near to terror – it was still, every time, a journey into parts unknown. Fiercely or gently, patiently or impatiently, they laid down his shyness and her knowledge along with their clothes, and blundered away together, intensely curious.

One night, as they lay in a heap afterwards, he said, 'You know that . . . thing you did, the first night we met? The thing I shouldn't have talked about the way I did?' It took her a minute to return enough from the floating place she was in to work out what he meant. 'Yes?' she said warily, when she had. 'I was just . . . wondering. Do you know . . . anything else?' Was he getting greedy? Had he swung to judgement, to thinking despite everything in terms of Iris-with-the-mouth, while she was wandering in another world, thinking he was with her but actually alone? She studied his face, pulling back to get him into focus. No, not greedy, as far as she could see; and what her right hand reported, when she laid it on his cheek, was just more innocent curiosity. He was still with her, naked as her, unashamed as her. Perhaps he didn't have the experience to know the difference between a skill at making love and what they had been feeling. 'I know what you mean,' she said carefully, 'but I think that would be like . . . a recipe for feeling less. And I don't want to feel less, with you.' She wasn't sure how to put it, out loud. It was something about not forcing a pattern on desire, a deliberate and exciting pattern, and then ending up having the pattern instead of the desire itself. She looked at him some more. He nodded, but he didn't seem quite ready to let the subject go. 'Hmm,' she said. 'You're a little bit excited by the idea of me being an expert, aren't you?' 'Maybe?' he said. 'The thing is,' she said, 'I'm not a . . . not a . . .' '. . . an odalisque.' 'What the hell is an odalisque?' 'I'm not absolutely sure,' said Geoff, 'but I think she's a lady who hangs about with nothing on in a Turkish bath, waiting for the sultan to crook his little finger at her.' 'Well, I'm not one of those. Or anything like that. I'm just Iris, who loves you.'

The instant she said this, a spasm of panic ran through her: that she might have trapped herself, said something irretrievable, after which she would no longer be her own. Followed by an equally acute confusion. *Was* this what people meant, when they talked about being 'in love'? No hearts, no flowers, no moonlight serenade; this awkward, clumsy, sticky, exposed, unbearable, unleavable thing? But Geoff smiled at her, and gathered her up and rolled her over on top of him, so that instead of crumpled sheets in the summer heat, she was lying on Geoff, Geoff, and more Geoff. Outside, somewhere far off south of the river, there was a thudding and a droning, and the world got on with possibly ending. She thought: *is it wrong to be so happy?*

But there came a morning in August when she descended from the bed of astonishment in Hampstead to find Geoff at the kitchen table frowning at his father's transcript of Hieronymus Dawe. They had begun a grand reading of the reassembled document a few weeks earlier, but page after page of it was a roll-call of City statues that no longer existed, and it was hard to care very much what else might be in it when they had the assurance that Lall was, in any case, locked out of the mysterious rooftop time machine. When, halfway through, Mr Hale had grown distracted and gone off to investigate an etymology that had caught his eye, they didn't bother to call him back. They'd shuffled the pages back together, put them on a shelf and gone upstairs.

'Iris?' said Geoff.

'What?' she said, milk bottle for tea in her hand, bare legs pressed against the cool plaster of the kitchen wall. It was early, but the day was already beginning its rise to baking heat. Outside, there was already a whine of engines overhead. The air battles were going on with ever-greater intensity. The August sky was a blue hard as enamel, day after day, and the elms were getting to look a little ragged in the heat. Fresh green had become high summer's old green, veteran green, tired green.

'Listen to this. It says here, "Greate the debatynge amonge the savants of oure companye, what the geometrie revealed at last of the aerialle roade to Nonesuch might be, some sayinge a convex figure of regular proportioune, polygonall-Platonique, as being thereby most perfect; otheres holding most probable, the patterne of a Quincunx, as precedented in antiquitie, in the mysticall history of Cyrus &c. Others againe, an arrowe, a letter in Hebrewe, an emblem of old Aegypt. Yet—"'

'D'you want some tea?'

'*Listen.* "Yet in the proofe of it, failed all these for very elaborateness. It transpiring, that mere sequence sufficed. Eight arches to the bridge, eight steps along the roade, achieved the portals of the pallace (and those eight perilous already in alle conscience). This, indifferent to directioune by the compasse, and beginning at any point of the webbe. It mighte be entered uponne anywhere, and yet serve to supplie the transit all compleat."'

'Oh hell,' said Iris.

'*Yes*, oh hell. Iris, I think that means you haven't blocked her off from the machine at all by keeping her out of Faraday House. She can get into the "web" wherever she can find another statue with a trapped angel inside it. She could be up there on the roofs already.'

PATERNOSTER ROW
AUGUST-OCTOBER 1940

I

Instead of an invasion, the bombers came. The bombers might be a prelude to German soldiers on the streets, the chaos that haunted Geoff spilling out here into gunmen firing from ruined houses, shot children, elderly men trying to stop tanks with milk bottles of petrol. But the bombers brought such sufficient chaos of their own that the other prospect receded. It was a worry that would have to take care of itself, when every day was consumed by a cycle of fear and relief.

The first bombs fell on central London on the night of 24 August. The sirens had been sounding in the outer boroughs for a couple of weeks already, but that night they sounded in Chelsea. Iris trooped downstairs at Challoner Court, to sit on a bench in the half-dark among other tenants of the building who had been virtually invisible till now: the man with the reeking pipe who had rubber interests in Malaya, the woman with the high, maddening laugh like a whinnying horse, the woman in pearls whose nervousness manifested as a continuous need to speak. No sounds from outside reached through the concrete walls of the cellar, but occasionally the ground shook. It was hard on the backside, and also on the vowels. *Sitzfleisch*, she thought. Just before midnight the All Clear sounded and up they all ascended, politely silent once more, Iris wondering what had been hit and how badly, but with no means of finding out.

In the morning she picked her way cautiously east from Blackfriars into the City, unsure whether she would find the Mariner Building still standing. It was; but there was a new smell in the air, a scorched gunpowdery smell with a hint of drains. And partway up Cannon Street, a Victorian building no different from the other red-brick four-storey affairs in a row with it, picked out from them by no principle except pure randomness, had been riven from the top down, destroyed in a descending V by something from the sky. There was a little bit more left of each floor, going down. Nothing but air where the roof had been, and then a narrowing path of ripping and shattering, with paintwork and wallpaper and dangling furniture and the building's hidden inner surfaces all exposed, turned inside out, put on violent view. Strangely horrible to see. Like being left for dead with your knickers showing. The pavement crunched under her feet with broken glass; a middle-aged man with a wheelbarrow moved her out of the way so he could start shovelling up the spill of broken bricks. And on she went to work.

That next night – it was proudly announced in all the papers – the RAF raided Berlin; and then, as if this had been the last straw for Hitler, as if he had been goaded into a lethal tantrum by this on top of the British refusal to be sensible and make peace, the German planes began to return nightly, this time it seemed bombing to punish, to annihilate.

Every morning there were more gaps in the streets where buildings had been, randomly selected from above to be poured out across the roadway in a slew of rubble and plaster and tangled wires. Sometimes there were still fires burning, black smoke eddying over the rooftops. Yet the Mariner Building still stood, randomly saved from the random danger. And the city still stood, despite the new holes punched nightly in its fabric. Almost more surprising, it still worked. With delays and pauses and strange reroutings, the Underground trains still ran, water was restored to the taps each time the mains in the ground were blown up, the middle-aged men with shovels pushed the rubble back off the roads into neat heaps, buses ran their familiar routes down streets altered like a mouth in which teeth were being broken one by one. And through the damaged streets every morning came the women to open their offices at 9 a.m. sharp, if they still had an office to open. Iris was much less eccentric now in finishing her commute on foot. Thousands were doing it; a quiet female flood coming in good shoes over the broken glass. Sonia from the basement of the Co-op in Walthamstow, where she and her mother were fighting a vicious turf war for sleeping space; Delia from a church crypt in New Cross; Mrs Sinclair from an Anderson in Penge. Somehow, there they always were, looking better than they smelled. It was easier to preserve a set of clothes for work than it was to find a time and a place to wash.

In Hampstead, Geoff had spent a Sunday afternoon digging an Anderson into the overgrown little meadow of a back garden behind Wildwood Terrace. Iris brought him out a glass of lemonade, having found a withered lemon for sale and mixed the juice with a precious spoonful of sugar. He drained it, leaning on his spade, and then went back to work, sweat sheening the groove of his bare back, his shoulder blades flexing like wings.

'A bit of help would be nice,' he said when she went on standing there, watching.

'I am helping,' she said.

'Really? What are you contributing, exactly?'

'Admiration,' said Iris.

But it was harder to tease him into a smile when he was so guilty about leaving the city by slow train of a Sunday night for the safety of the country; leaving her and his father to take their nightly chances. Mr Hale, to make matters worse, complained that the finished Anderson was stuffy, and looked for excuses not to use it.

'Could you please, please keep him in there?' Geoff implored

Iris. He quoted at his father figures he'd seen which proved that even a remarkably close explosion, a bomb only a few feet away, was survivable under the buried iron roof of an Anderson. But Mr Hale was not a man easily motivated by statistics. She tried her best, on the week-nights she was at Wildwood Terrace, leading him out there when the raid warning sounded, keeping him distracted with cocoa and questions. But he fidgeted terribly. He was a little elderly ball of twitches, sitting opposite her in the dark, and jumping at the drones and whistles and crashes they could hear, nearer, nearer, nearer, then safely past and receding. The Anderson was far less soundproof than the deep concrete in Chelsea. One night she had dropped off, and woken with a start to find him missing in the dark, and the shelter door open to the night. Fumbling her way after him, she had found him waist-deep in the long grasses outside, mesmerised by the red glare on the southern horizon, the clangour of the AA guns on the Heath, the drifting bright lights of incendiaries floating down. It was the first time she had been outdoors in a raid, and the red light staining the meadow grasses seemed to her like the colour scheme of a nightmare.

'Come in! Come back in!' she shouted in his ear.

'But it's beautiful,' he protested.

'It's *dangerous*!'

'I know, but don't you want to see? Instead of hiding from it in the dark?'

Iris looked at him, with his disarranged white hair and the shine of apocalypse in his eyes; then at the horizon; and thought that, fire-besotted old gnome that he was, he had a point.

'One minute more!' she bawled. 'Then we're going back in! Think about *shrapnel*! Geoff would never forgive me.'

'Oh, very well.'

They gazed together at the spectacle of destruction.

'The floating lights,' said Mr Hale. 'Would you call that colour cerise, do you think?'

'More like coral,' said Iris, matching it to lipsticks. 'It has some orange in it.'

'So it does.'

'Yes.'

'What a thing to see . . .'

'Yes. Right! Time's up, and in we go, and I don't want to hear any more argument.'

She didn't tell Geoff about that.

He was worried enough already. Because the other thing that was stopping him smiling was the argument they were having over what to do about Lall.

They'd read carefully through to the end of the Dawe transcript together, that morning at the kitchen table when Geoff discovered the bad news. (Already, looking back at that moment only a few weeks later, a haze of unreal bliss surrounded the memory. It was a scene from a lost paradise. Not because of desire, not because from time to time she'd been licking Geoff's bare shoulder as they read, but because when she'd come downstairs to him she'd just had *a whole night* of uninterrupted sleep.)

Eight statues to be awakened, to build the bridge to Nonesuch, that much was clear, and it didn't matter where you started.

'But what are we supposed to do?' she said. 'All the statues in here are gone. How are we supposed to know which modern statues have angels in them, so we can stop her getting at them?'

'Hmm,' said Geoff, thinking about it. 'How is *Lall* supposed to know, for that matter? She can't just wander the City in the blackout, chanting at random and hoping that something hears her.'

'She knew about Mercury.'

'That statue must be very new. It's on top of a *telephone exchange*:

it can only be ten years old at most. What if she, or maybe the Grand Master, happened to know the sculptor, or something? It's their kind of thing. Fascist kitsch, frankly. Shiny, powerful. With muscles.'

'You've got muscles too, thanks to the Army. D'you think she might be interested now?'

Geoff gave her a look.

'Sorry,' said Iris.

'I thought you were working on being kind?'

'It's an uphill struggle.'

'Anyway – what if she only knew about that one way in to the machine? What if she's as stumped as we are?'

'What if she isn't? Or – what if she is, but she's out every night systematically searching?'

'But she can't, though. Try it every night, I mean. Look here, look at this bit. "Narrowe the gate, and impossible of discoverie save at the darknesse of the moone." That's . . . once a month. Lunar minimum. And at other times, by the sound of it, the whole set-up doesn't work at all.'

Geoff went and rummaged out an astrological chart from the clutter on Mr Hale's desk, and they looked at the phases of the moon for autumn 1940. Where the disc was black, or nearly black except for a last sliver of old moon or a first sliver of a new one, they read off the dates. 1 September. 30 September. 30 October. 28 November. 29 December.

'So those are her only chances?' said Iris.

'Yes.'

'We still have no idea *where* we're supposed to intercept her. There could be hundreds of bloody statues. Why didn't our blue friend brief us better?'

'Perhaps you distracted it by flirting. No, I am not jealous. No, I am *not* jealous, stop tickling me. – You haven't had any luck calling it back?'

'None! Not for want of trying. *Bluey, Bluey, Bluey. Raphael, Raphael, Raphael.* Till the cows come home. – Oh.'

'What?'

'Come upstairs, I've just thought of something.'

She drew him up the crowded stairs to the door of the attic.

'What's the one way we've ever successfully summoned him?'

'No no no no no. I am not making that horrible noise again.'

'The whole thing, God no. But maybe if I just blow an evil kazoo and you bang on an evil triangle, it'll irritate him into turning up.'

'. . . All right.'

A horrible drone and a warped jangling later, a blue light pulsed reluctantly into existence in the corner of the attic. It did not expand all the way, either into the fractured abyss of lines and wheels or into the beautiful blue giant. It just hung there, a whirl of blue no wider than a porthole.

'Why are you two making that racket?' said the voice like a desert wind in a glass tube.

'To get your attention,' said Iris.

'A simple message in a scrying glass would do.'

'In a what?'

'Oh,' said the angel. 'The anachronism problem. Very well. What do you want?'

'We need to know what statues apart from the Mercury on Faraday House have angels in them, and whether Lall has found them yet.'

'There are at present,' said the angel, and then there was a pause, not as if it were thinking but like someone sending out a query and waiting for an answer, '. . . eleven other such captives. And no, she has not. But she is actively working on it. She made a telephone call to the widow of the sculptor Sylvester Sills, who made the Mercury and habitually used the binding spell in his work, believing that it represented "archaic energy". The widow has promised to post her a list of other statues of his in the City.'

'Then we're not too late! So, tell us which the eleven statues are.'

'. . . No,' said Raphael.

'What do you mean, "no"?'

'I mean, I am not permitted to. Your intentions may be good but, once released into the world, such knowledge becomes available in the future to those of any intention, good or bad. I may not hand it to you, as I may not hand you a venomous poison.'

'Hey, you were the one who started us on this wild goose chase in the first place,' said Geoff, exasperated. 'What's the point, if you're going to refuse to help?'

Silence from the whirl of blue.

'No, wait,' said Iris. 'You're telling us that there is a prohibition on directly giving us that specific item of information?'

'Yes.'

'And is it your judgement that, despite this, you have given us enough indirect information for us to be able to . . . take action?'

'Yes.'

'All right; thank you. Is there,' she added carefully, 'anything else useful that you would be permitted to tell us?'

'Yes,' said the angel. 'I may point out to you that any span of the bridge to Nonesuch created by you becomes unavailable to another bridge-builder. Is that all?'

'Yes it is,' said Iris.

'Goodbye,' said the angel, and the blue porthole shrank to a point and abolished itself.

Geoff tossed the twisted metal hoop he had been beating back into the cardboard box of instruments, and she dropped the droning thing in after it, feeling the urge to wipe her hands on something. Instead she laid them on Geoff's chest. Her left hand reported his heart beating, a steady thump in her fingertips; her right hand, a puzzlement beginning to curdle into anxiety.

'Well,' she said, 'looks like I'm going to be clambering about on some rooftops.' She thought it might help if she put it lightly. Help with her own fears too. 'Time to buy an all-black outfit, probably.'

'What?' said Geoff. 'What do you mean?'

She looked up at him. 'Come on, technical boy,' she said gently. 'Keep up.'

'I don't know what you mean.'

'Yes, you do. What did we just learn from that?'

'That if we find some other statues by this Sylvester Sills bloke in the City, we'll know where Lall is going to look for a way in. And then you can stop her.'

'Really?' said Iris. 'How? Suppose I do find her, on one of those nights, trying to work necromantic hocus-pocus – what do I do? Sit on her? Perform a citizen's arrest for unlicensed black magic? Knock her on the head, and bring her back to Chelsea to spend the rest of the war chained to a radiator? – I quite like that one, but it's not very practical, is it. No. No, the way I *stop* her is all in the other titbit Bluey let fall. Which is the information that this is a logic game. As you understood perfectly well. Come on, Geoffrey Dionysus Hale. Explain the logic game to me. Eight links to make the bridge to Nonesuch, only twelve statues in total, including the one on Faraday House that Lall can't get at. And any link, or arch, or step, whatever you want to call it, that *I* claim denies that one to Lall for her collection of eight. So . . . ?'

'So a bridge of four arches would be enough to stop her building a bridge of eight.'

'Yes. Because then there wouldn't be enough statues left for her. Hence clambering about on roofs. Hence black outfit. World saved. Three cheers for brave Iris.'

Geoff bent his head and buried his nose in her hair.

'No,' he said. 'Zero cheers for insane Iris. It's bad enough having to leave the pair of you to the mercies of the Luftwaffe every week. I want you to be safe. I need you to be safe. I've only just found you.'

'I know,' said Iris. 'But I'm not safe, am I, anyway? I'm taking my chances, like everyone else. And as for this – you can't do it. It has to be me.'

'Didn't you notice Hieronymus Dawe going on and on about danger? Mortal peril? Getting . . . squashed into a . . . cube of meat with a bloody *eyeball* on top? No, Iris. You're not doing this. I won't let you.'

She pulled back and stared at him. He looked upset, but not like a man aware that he had just crossed a line. She thought of Eleanor's advice, which she had not followed. She had started no conversations with him about what he expected. Too stupidly happy.

'I beg your pardon?' she said.

'I won't let you,' he repeated stubbornly.

'Ah,' she said. 'Here it is at last. The claim of ownership.'

'That's not—'

'Yes it is. If you start talking about what you'll *let* me do. You don't have the right.'

'Don't I? Doesn't loving you give me the right?'

It was the first time he had said it.

'No,' she said sadly. 'It doesn't.'

11

And that – as much as the arrival of the nightly raids, and the exhaustion that came with them – was the end of something. The era of rapture, when every question could wait. When no question had any power in comparison to the melting sweetness of touch. Now, there a question was, unmeltable, indissoluble. There was a splinter in the honey. It wasn't that she thought Geoff actually could tell her what to do. She proposed to ignore him if he tried. She was going to ignore him about waking a statue, if they could find another Sills she could get at. It was that, if he thought he had the right to allow or to forbid in the name of love, a moment was surely coming, not yet but someday, when he would demand she give up something she seriously wanted. She wouldn't *do* it, obviously, but then she would have to choose between him and it. There was a shadow on the future where there had been none before.

Yet futures of any kind seemed remote. Night after night drowsing uncomfortably upright, in the Chelsea cellar or the Hampstead Anderson with Mr Hale, hearing or not hearing the bombers overhead, aware that there was no protection against a truly direct hit. For everyone in London, whether you lived through the night was therefore a matter of luck. The odds were long – only one in twenty thousand chances of being hit, said the papers – but still every bomb landed somewhere. Every night, for some people, the dice roll was going wrong. Instead of the whistle and crash rising to a peak of noise and then receding as the next bomb fell safely past you, there'd be a descending whistle that only grew louder, and then some unimaginable instant of violence and light and pain and dissolution. Each bomb might be that one; you couldn't know it wasn't till it hadn't fallen on you.

And then, when you had survived another night of that, you tidied yourself up, put on your work clothes and stepped out. The hot bright summer had become a hot bright Indian summer: shorter days and cooler nights, but still a blaze of clear blue overhead. She walked up the King's Road to the Tube, past ruins still smouldering and holes in the ground where repair crews were already at work on mangled pipes, and she felt the light revving up the engine of her organism. Beat, heart; breathe, lungs; hunger, stomach. Now, now, now, said her body. There was only a faint ache in her eyes, looking at the bright and damaged world. An ache so permanent that after a while she started to think of it as the world itself aching faintly, all the time.

She joggled eastward on the Tube, she joggled westward going home again. And she thought: *he is motherless, I have to remember that. He is frightened of the people he loves disappearing. That's natural. I promised him safety, though I can't give it to him, and the safety is me; it's my skin next to his, warm in the bed. Whole. And now I've said I'm going to put myself at risk. At more risk. Of course he minds.* She thought: *but he said he wouldn't* let *me. He went off to war, and did I complain? No, because at that point I was treating him as an embarrassing roll in the hay. Now the very idea of what might have happened to him on that French beach makes me feel sick.* She thought: *I have to be fair to him. But that means treating him the way I'd treat myself. Will he do that?* Shut up, shut up, shut *up, Iris,* she thought. *Oh God, I'm so tired.*

Yet none of it spoiled the times when they did manage to meet. The long, sweet, astonishing nights were gone, when the whole world had been nothing but shuddering continents meeting. But from time to time they would coincide for a while. They would fit themselves together, weary and grimy, too weary for desire. She would be asleep in his bed in Wildwood Terrace, seizing an hour or two before the sirens went. Distantly, she would hear him coming in, off a late train from the country, having walked all the way from Paddington through the blackout. There'd be, distantly, the sound of buttons being undone, and clothes being tugged off. And then him climbing in behind her, smelling of smoke and train cushions and far-off cut grass and underneath it all his plain male self. He murmured incomprehensibly in her ear, she grunted incoherently back, the bond of skin to skin was remade and then they were gone again, slipping beneath the precious surface of sleep together. And whatever the complications, whatever the future held, it felt profoundly right.

'Sylvester Sills?' said Eleanor with a grimace. 'What d'you want to know about *him* for?'

'What was wrong with him?' asked Iris. She only had a part of Eleanor's attention. They were in the studio, with a couple of art-loving Polish soldiers Eleanor had rounded up, and Eleanor was trying to work out how to get the finished eye sculpture safely downstairs with the cargo lift not working. A bomb had hit the quadrangle of the Slade, and she'd been told the building was no longer structurally sound. Miles was fixing up some alternative working space out in Sussex.

'Oh, just very commercial. Always in the fashion; nothing individual or unexpected about him. But always wanting deference as a capital-A Artist all the same. And a grabber! At anything female in reach. *Not* a man to be alone with. – Maybe on its side? Przewracać, boys! Over, please!'

'I need to find out what there is by him in the Square Mile.'

'Curiouser and curiouser. Steadily less as the bombs fall, I should think. *There's* an encouraging thought for you. Come, friendly bombs, and fall on Sills.'

'Eleanor . . .'

'Sorry. Yes. Look, I really don't know. But if it's important I can probably find out through my gallery. Scribble your address down for me. Chelsea? Very chichi. Now, boys: jeden, dwa, trzy, lift!'

She had missed the dark of the moon on 1 September, and so presumably had Lall, given that the world and its history appeared to be in the same dire shape as ever the next morning. No better, but also no worse. However, on the nineteenth of the month, a postcard turned up from Eleanor.

Mathoms Court, Drakeling, Sussex

Iris – have pursued your inscrutable request, and apparently there are three Sills master-works in or around the City. One is the ghastly silver statue of Mercury on top of the telephone exchange in Q. Victoria St, one is a mock-Epstein-type head on the facade of the Chronicle offices in Fleet St, and the last one, from much longer ago, is some sort of giant art nouveau-ish thing near London Bridge. 'The Mariner Building' – isn't that near where you work? Try not to get blown to smithereens, please. The bombers go over us in waves, but the warning doesn't sound, out here, and we sleep the sleep of the unjust. Spare bed if you need it. Eleanor x

Her own building. She went and stood beside the teletype machine, where she no longer worked except when she was training Sonia, and considered the granite head of the Mariner. A familiar sight, a comfortable sight, so long as it remained part of an outdoors being seen through steel windows and safety glass. Considered as any kind of platform you might step out on, it became a slippery dome no wider than a coffee table, nine floors of empty air above the cobbles of the lane. Nine floors of empty air through which to fall flailing and screaming before smashing your skull. An invitation to vertigo. Her stomach twisted. At least it would probably be more dangerous still for Lall, who must be planning on entry via the stone head on the *Chronicle* building. No doubt, as a daily that had flirted with the Blackshirts, it had a night porter willing to let her in. But she'd have to have feet as sticky as a fly's, once she got up high and climbed out of a window. Every carved decoration Iris had ever seen, looking up on Fleet Street, had been a mere flattish face in relief, with little to cling on to. Perhaps Lall'd fall off unmagically, all by herself.

'Bad news?' said Mr Cornellis, as Iris headed back to the chief clerk's office.

'No, sir. Just brooding on the new Securities Order.' It forbade dealing in the bonds of all the rest of the neutral countries, as well as of the United States. Not a flicker from Cornellis but then she was used to that, by now; the Treasury bonds remained in the office safe, as far as she knew, serving their mysterious purpose by doing nothing at all.

'Canadian stocks next for the chop, I hear,' said Cornellis. 'But that won't trouble us, will it?'

He was maintaining a state of slightly brittle good humour at the moment. The Index was at 63. The clients were in profit, and other brokers had displayed flattering envy at C&B's success in calling the market bottom. Harold had been sent a muffler and a fruitcake via the Red Cross – 'oddly like sending him things at boarding school,' said Mr Cornellis – and all the dealing books and client files had been photographed so that, if a bomb wiped out the Mariner Building, C&B's business could be reconstituted from Hemel Hempstead. If Hitler landed at Dover, all this would be useless; but till Hitler did, it was to be understood that all was well with the world.

'No, sir,' said Iris, yawning. Mr C retained the healthy pinkness of a man still getting some nights' unbroken sleep at home. The London staff, on the other hand, were developing a greyish-yellow tinge. She went into her office and shut the door. Mr Smythe had retired, his daughter having insisted on taking him away into Essex, but Iris was not, officially, chief clerk, that being a job closed to women. She was merely doing the chief clerk's job, without receiving the chief clerk's wages. 'Let's not pick a fight we can't win,' Cornellis had said. 'Tragically, the post remains unfilled.'

'Can I talk you out of it?' asked Geoff.

'You know you can't,' said Iris.

It was five o'clock on the Sunday before the Monday on which 30 September fell, and she was walking him down to the bus stop so he could catch his train and be out of the city before the raids began. The city below them, as they crested the brow of the Heath, looked like ridges of torn paper, one behind another. Though summer warmth lingered, summer's length of days was over. It wouldn't be actually dark until sometime between six and seven, but the light was dwindling to a hazy teatime blue-grey. The days were shrinking, the nights were growing, and with them the bombers' time: the share of the hours when the life of the city had to stop, and they all became troglodytes, tucked away from the dangerous dark as deep underground as they could get. Geoff was smoking, in short, tense drags; Iris was smoking too, more calmly. Everyone was, at the moment, all the time. Cigarettes to wake you up, cigarettes to soothe you down, cigarettes as comfort. A nicotine teat to suck on. Her forefingers were turning yellow.

'What if it's all nonsense?' he said. 'Statues. Time machines. Lall trying to change history. What if none of it's real?'

'It is, though,' said Iris. 'And is it really any madder or harder to believe than the rest of this?' She waved at the ripped-paper city, dimming in the early evening light. 'Look at it,' she said. 'Another couple of hours and we'll all be hiding in holes. And then boys from Hamburg and Munich – nice boys, probably, on the whole, who love their mothers – will fly overhead trying to kill us. It's a crazy world.'

'But—' said Geoff, and stopped. 'I don't know what to say to you.'

'How about: *be careful?*'

'Well, yes.'

'Sweet man,' she said, stamping her fag-end out and putting her arms round his neck. 'You can't protect me, and I can't protect you. This is the awful truth.'

She mashed her lips hard against his, smoky mouth to smoky mouth, and turned away quickly, so that he shouldn't see that she was afraid.

And alone in the office at dusk the next day, with Mr Seaton on his ARP round audible on the floor below, she recited the words Geoff had copied out for her. *Meruzababel.* Darkness at the window. From it, stone eyes the size of plates gazing in at her.

III

'*Tell me where all past years are,*' she said to the Mariner.

Moving in his dark stone like a cold lava flow, like a reluctant puppet weighing many granite tons, the sea-king raised one arm from his body – till now only a grooved section of a single piece of stone, and not an arm at all – and creakingly lifted a stone hand four or five feet across until it was level with his chin, palm up. His mouth, which was not really a mouth, stayed open; and his breath, which was not really breath, blew its bloom of frost onto the edge of the palm, advancing and retreating there, a slow wavelet of white. Then, from the fingertips of the hand, something extended, raying forward into the distance straight ahead.

Iris had hoped, when the Dawe manuscript talked of building bridges, that something was going to appear with a solid surface, and ideally parapets on each side. But this was like a spar of glass, a sort of transparent girder. You could tell something was there, because it deformed the light. There was a thickening, a slowness. The drop into the depths of Mariner Lane was still visible but refracted through a substance that glistened slightly. And around and above the glassy pathway the air, too, had thickened, as if a passageway had formed with soap-bubble walls, through which the unlit reefs of the City's blocks appeared twisted, stretched, compressed to ribbons, distorted into impossible geometries. A glass floor, soap-bubble walls, a purplish tunnel. At the far end, indistinct, a small lumpish shape impossible to make out, like dough seen in twilight through the wrong end of the telescope. Perhaps the next statue.

It was a terrifying vista, and everything sensible and self-preserving in Iris told her to leave the window closed. But Mr Seaton was turning his key in the door of Cornellis & Blome. It was now or never; and pride made her undo the steel latch, and climb, stooped, up onto the radiator, horribly near to the unalive stare of the statue, regarding her with its blue mineral pupils. Pride, and the thought that Lall must be daring something even worse. *Sane people don't climb out of windows on the ninth floor!* her mind screamed, unavailingly. She gripped the edges of the steel frame, and put a cautious foot out onto the stone hand, half convinced that it was illusion, that it would melt away like smoke.

But no: it took weight. She could feel under her shoe the ridges of real stone, chipped by Sylvester Sills's chisel. She stamped, keeping her weight back in the frame of the window. No movement. Solid as a . . . rock. She suppressed a demented urge to giggle.

The next bit could not be done cautiously. It committed her; it had to be done whole-heartedly or not at all. *Not at all!* voted Iris the chief clerk, Iris the careful calculator of odds, Iris the prudent investor. *All in, all at once, and fuck it,* voted the bad girl, and the lover, and the risk-taker, and the suburban slut not willing to be defeated by some whey-faced bitch of a fascist. And they had the majority, it seemed. She lurched forward onto the hand, supported by nothing but the dubious powers of enchantment, and gasped there on all fours.

One of her feet was close to the statue's mouth. She felt the Arctic cold of the not-breath on her ankle, and then a strange suction, faint at first but mounting instantly to a real yanking pull. She looked back, and wrenched her foot away, not a moment too soon: the Mariner's jaws had widened beyond the point where the stonework was representing anything human, and in the flue of its throat a jittering twist of colour had appeared, like a miniature of Raphael's body at its most headache-inducing. It was from this that the suction came, and Iris had no doubt that flesh and blood pulled in there would be mangled through the dimensions on the instant. It seemed the enslaved angels were allowed to try to bite their tormentors. Part, no doubt, of making the way to Nonesuch as close to impossible as it could be.

'Nope,' she said to herself, 'no you don't', and scrambled to her feet, teeteringly, with fear behind and fear ahead.

To step off the hand and onto the glassy spar laid across the air took another moment of mad resolution. She stood with one foot on the fingers and tested ahead with the other. Firm, despite appearances; a surface as smooth as glass, and probably as slippery. *Walk*, she told herself. *And look ahead, not down.*

She went heel to toe, not knowing how wide the pathway was, with gaze fixed ahead, and breath coming raggedly, and arms stretched out for balance. At either side her fingers trailed on, or rather in, the soap-bubble walls. There was some substance there, but nothing thick enough to lean on, or catch her if she fell, and where her fingers touched the stretched and slivered images of the City rippled in the corner of her eye. Heel to toe, heel to toe. She tried not to look sideways, for fear of dizziness, but even in her peripheral vision she could tell there was more in the jumble of images than just the things you could see from above the literal rooftops of Mariner Lane. There was the long glass roof of Cannon Street station, but upside down; there were the spires of City churches, bent towards each other to touch at their tips like a star; there were streets and streets and streets, tilted every which way. Wherever she was going, it wasn't just across Mariner Lane.

Heel to toe, heel to toe. The darkness was growing around her, but there was no wind, that was a mercy. And slowly the object at the far end was getting bigger. *Come on*, she thought. *I can do this. Steady does it. Slow and steady wins the race.* It was some kind of ornamental vase, with a golden pineapple on top. No, not a pineapple: a spiked golden ball. No, not a spiked ball: a ball in flames. And as it grew closer it continued to expand. It was very big indeed. The vase part was twice as tall as she was, and the flaming golden ball, on the level of which she was arriving, was her height by itself, and bigger around than she would be able to stretch her arms. But what was it? Here it came, a bulging golden surface filling her vision, with flames of gold-painted stone like curving handles, just the right size to grasp.

She did. And the instant her hands touched the stone, glass surface beneath her feet and bubble-tunnel through the air vanished as if they had never been. Wind returned, a roar and a bluster in her ears; she dropped, hanging by her hands; and with a horrible lurch of clarity she found herself clinging on, barely, to the very top of the Monument to the Great Fire, a good hundred feet higher than the top floor of the Mariner Building, although there had been no upward ascent as she walked across the glass bridge. She was alone in the sky with her feet kicking in empty space. London swung about her, unmagical and far below, a maze of brick and stone waiting for her to fall into it. She screamed. Her grip was failing. The stone flamelets were smooth and curved, and her hands were beginning to slide, to slide, to—

'*Tell me where all past years are!*'

Silence, restored. A purplish chamber of the bubble-stuff around the top of the Monument, and – something under her feet. A rim of the glassy substance, not wide. But enough to stand on, to creep around the rim of the golden ball upon, going hand to shaking hand on the flames.

On the far side, a new glass spar stretching away: the next arch of the bridge. All right; yes. She had begun to manoeuvre herself to turn, and to step outwards with the same caution, heel to toe, heel to toe, yes – when she realised that her hands, far from slipping now on the flames she presently held, slick though they were with her nervous sweat, were experiencing something like the opposite. They were being held in place. Gripped. And this far face of the golden ball was crumpling inwards, turning concave, forming a mouth – a sucking mouth with a flitter of impossible geometry in its depths—

She screamed again, and wrenched at her hands. It was as if a force had glued them there. The stone bent in, pulling her forward. The flitter grew. An open door to a mangling furnace. She yanked and she twisted – some movement now; pain, and then, with a rip that felt as if it was taking off skin, her hands were free, and she was twisting away and leaping with no caution at all onto the next glassy span, feet slipping and skidding but pelting along it full tilt, arms out, carried by the momentum of terror.

No resolutions this time about where she looked. Images on the bubbled walls streamed past her in kaleidoscope glimpses. Images, crazed and splintered, of London, but not all now of the London she knew, built of brick and powered by coal. A cathedral standing where St Paul's should, but with a black and ramshackle tower instead of a dome; a structure all in glass like an impossibly tall spearhead with a broken tip; men with iron collars chained together digging in a ditch. And among the babel of pictures as she ran with hair flying and mouth open and outstretched arms, one that loomed at her of a small fair woman in neat black who seemed to be trying to use a mountaineer's axe to fight off a hungry eight-foot statue of a woman waving a stone sheaf of corn. The vision was clearly mutual. Their eyes met. Lall saw her, running and screaming; she saw Lall, snarling and struggling. Then the image flew away in shreds and ribbons, and Iris reached the end of the glass and crashed into her own next statue, thinking: *not too high, oh please not too high.*

It was not. Or at least, it was located on a square plinth, and when Iris fell off it she dropped only a few feet, into a triangle of roof behind a sooty stone balustrade next to some kind of pillared thing. Roof, glorious firm everyday roof. Lovely stone balustrade to stop you falling off glorious roof. She peered cautiously over the edge, and found she was only one floor up, looking down on the very familiar roadway of Lower Thames Street, deserted and almost dark. Then this was – she rolled round, wincing, to gaze up – the Coal Exchange building, of all places, where futures in thermal coal, coking coal and coal for gas were traded. And the statue on the plinth was, of all things, one of the cast-iron City of London heraldic dragons, metal wings curled back and the City's coat of arms held on an iron shield in front of it. Seriously?

She levered herself to her feet. Her palms were raw and her shins were bruised. She felt a deep disinclination to endure anything else magical and terrifying. But she had only crossed two spans. Lall *was* out tonight, and plainly well beyond the stone face on Fleet Street. Two more spans needed to be crossed before she was safely thwarted.

Iris waved a finger at the iron dragon. 'Listen, you,' she said, 'no funny business. *Tell me*— No, wait a minute.' She moved until she was out of reach of its mouth. 'Right. *Tell me where all past years are.*'

The air gelled, the narrow bridge of light appeared, projecting out from between the dragon's feet, across the black alleyway on whose corner with Lower Thames Street the Exchange stood, and into a distance that had not previously existed – into the brick wall on the other side of the alley, by all ordinary calculation a flat and impenetrable surface on which there was just enough light still to read SAMUELS, ALL STYLES OF FANCY HAT. Now, through it, the purple tunnel ran.

But while Iris was staring, the hem of her skirt was being delicately mouthed, seized, and then sucked inwards by an orifice that had appeared, not between the dragon's jaws, but in its cast-iron side.

'Dammit,' said Iris. 'Get *off*. Get— No—'

It had fabric in its grip, not flesh, but the pull was fierce. Iris tugged back. It was like a contest of strength with an iron dog. *Bad boy!* she felt like saying. *Leave it!* But the struggle would stop being ridiculous if it managed to winch any of her in, along with the skirt. In theory, she supposed she could take it off . . . *I am not undressing on Lower Thames Street*, she vowed, and leaned back against the dragon's pull so her weight was added on her side of the tug-of-war. There was a ripping sound, and the hem tore free. She stumbled back, cursing and panting – and with a rising wail all the sirens of the City sounded the warning of an incoming raid, the path to Nonesuch blinked out of existence, and the dragon was only dull iron again.

A window opened behind the pillars, and a middle-aged fire-watcher in a stiff old-fashioned collar looked out at her aghast.

'Miss!' he said. 'What on earth are you doing there? The warning's gone!'

The descent through the blacked-out interior of the Coal Exchange, limping after the bobbing bulb of the fire-watcher's torch, was almost as dreamlike as anything she had experienced up above. She had never been in the building before, and the black space inside was all hollow, a vast dome sitting on tiers and tiers of balconies, round which they passed with the dim gleams of the torch flitting over tiles marked black on black, like a real coal seam, with the fossils of leaves, and the bones of ancient creatures. It was a fossil forest, a coal mountain hollowed out into a carbon jewel.

But all the way the watcher fussed, troubled by her inexplicable appearance on a roof that was his responsibility, and by her scratched and battered looks. Probably, if it had not been for the war and the increasing familiarity it was giving respectable London with scratched and battered people, it would have been worse; but it was bad enough.

Had she fallen there? Sort of. Did she need him to get out his first-aid box? No, thank you. Should he call the Metropolitan

Police? No! Was it, he asked eventually, rummaging through some dusty Edwardian archive of explanations for the bizarre behaviour of young people, perhaps *a rag that had gone wrong*? Yes, she agreed gratefully. That was it exactly. A rag that had gone wrong. And no doubt the young gentlemen who had put her up there had run away when the warning sounded? Indeed they had. It was not very responsible of them, was it, considering that there was a war on. No, it wasn't. Naughty boys that they were.

That seemed to do it, so long as it didn't occur to him that all of the naughty young gentlemen who might boost a secretary onto a rooftop for an amusing jape were presently dressed in khaki and likely to be away with their regiments somewhere. But he wouldn't let her out of the Coal Exchange, not with the raid underway. The planes could be heard in the sky, droning closer, almost overhead, coming westward from the docks explosion by explosion. Red light through the panels of the dome briefly stained the dark well of the Exchange. He hurried her down stone steps into the building's cellar, and left her there while he rushed back upstairs to be ready for firebombs with a bucket of sand and a broom. The cellar door clicked suspiciously behind him, and to her outrage she found that he had locked her in.

She spent the night lying alone on a bench among steam pipes in the Exchange basement, listening to descending whistles of bombs, feeling the building shake, waiting for it to do more than shake. Waiting, too, for whatever it would be like if Lall reached Nonesuch and changed the past. She would have no memory of it if the world changed, the angel had said: but from moment to moment the world did not change, and the raid went on. One set of droning engines would recede, and it would seem to be over, and then another procession of them would come out of the east, and the crashes and the rumbles in the ground would resume. It occurred to her that if the Coal Exchange was hit dead-on and fell to ruins, taking Mr Wing Collar on the roof with it, no one would know that she was in the cellar, or have any particular reason to excavate the rubble of what they thought was an empty building.

But just before 5 a.m. the All Clear sounded at last, and shortly afterwards the fire-watcher came and let her out. There was soot on his wing collar, a pattern of holes burned into the sleeve of his jacket and a light of modest triumph in his eye: the triumph of one who, with bucket and broom, had personally defeated Hitler's aerial armada of death.

'A stiffish night,' he said. 'Two incendiaries – but both of them dealt with.'

'Gosh,' said Iris, recognising her responsibility as the young woman on the spot to be impressed.

'Now you'd better get home, hadn't you? And tell those silly friends of yours to be a little more sensible in future, hey?'

'I certainly will,' said Iris.

Dawn was on the way. It was too early for the Tube. The gates of Bank station were locked, and behind them there would be blast doors locked as well, protecting the hundreds presently sheltering down there on the platforms. The stiffish night had left the City still aflame in places. Up Bishopsgate, she could see a four- or five-storey building solidly ablaze, a black skeleton holding a kind of orange barn of flames, with in front of it the black silhouette of a fire engine, ladders extended, playing hoses on the fire. But past it matter-of-factly came a bus. She flagged it down and got on. There was just time to go home to Chelsea, wash her face, change her clothes, shake her head over the ruined skirt and head back to C&B.

Lall, she decided, must have failed too. Stymied at some junction in the sky. Dropped from a height. Inhaled by a stone mouth. Beaten senseless by a carving of a wheatsheaf. Clipped by a spray of hot shrapnel if she had been still out and dangling in an exposed place when her friends in the Luftwaffe arrived. One of the above.

IV

'You're alive,' said Geoff from a call box in some Somerset village, when she answered the phone in the Chelsea flat that evening.

'I am alive,' she confirmed. They had arranged that he would ring, but she was finding it hard to summon any energy at all for the call. There had now been a day of stockbroking on top of last night, and she was so tired that her reactions to absolutely everything were muffled, as if they had been packed in cotton wool. The sirens would go again in a couple of hours, and all she wanted to do before that was to fall over and close her eyes.

'And did it . . . work? Something real happened?' His voice seemed to be coming from very far away. The West Country night. Soothing birdsong instead of sirens, no doubt.

'Oh yes.'

'That's . . . good?'

'Yes. I suppose.'

'What was it like?'

What *was* it like? She thought about the terror of the bridge to Nonesuch. The vertigo, the knowledge of gulfs of danger only one misplaced foot away, the familiar streets she worked in turned into precipices she had teetered on the lip of. The sense, too, at the same time and all mixed up with the danger, of being on the brink of wonders. Of having a forbidden door opened into the secret heights and depths of her city. Of travelling, one perilous step at a time, away from London and yet into London. Of—

'Iris? Iris? Are you there?'

'Sorry. Yes; yes, I'm here. I got two spans along and nearly fell off the top of the Monument.' That was how a heroine in a film would say it – only brighter, and more brittle. And she wouldn't say 'off', not if it was a British film. She'd say 'orf'. *I nearly fell orf the top of the Monument.*

'What? Why?'

'Because that's where the bridge led. And it turned out that all the statues I met wanted to eat me.'

'Iris! Are you all right?'

'Yes, yes, I'm fine. Sore hands but no harm done.' There was something irritating about his concern. A pressure. Unfair, but there it was: anger was the one emotion that could penetrate this degree of tiredness. A smouldering from below. A red glow in the smoke cloud of your being. People snapped at each other in the office now; strangers on the Tube, all the time. The insouciant stuff, the London-can-take-it stuff, flattened into bad temper by thirty-plus nights of continuous raids and counting. She was going to snap at Geoff now if she wasn't careful. She wanted to.

'I spent last night picturing all the ways you might be dead,' said Geoff.

'Did you?'

'Yes. And I thought how much rather I wanted to be there too. Doing what you were doing. Seeing what you were seeing. Like in Leadenhall Market.'

'That's . . .' Sweet? Irrelevant? A kind of intrusion? The word failed to present itself. She said instead, 'I thought you just wanted me not to do it. So you didn't worry.'

'You know, when someone worries about you, they're not *doing* something to you.'

'Aren't they?'

'No. And I'm worried anyway. I might worry less if I were with you.'

'I might worry more. If I had to think about you too.'

'"Had to".'

'Oh, Geoff, please. Not now. I've got to do it again next month. Lall was out there last night; I saw her. Something must have gone wrong for her – or, you know – but she'll try again, if she isn't dead. So I have to too. But now I'm going to go to sleep. If that's all right.'

'Of course it is. I'll see you on Friday.'

'See you on Friday. I'll tell you properly then, I promise. Geoff?'

'Yes?'

She remembered feeling things other than weary irritation. Effortfully, she lowered an internal bucket into the place the other feelings had been located, and winched up the contents.

'I'm still your girl,' she said.

'I *know* that.'

'Do you?'

'Yes. Go to bed.'

And somewhere in Somerset, by the edge of some slumbering common where the trees shed their autumn leaves in their own good time, without any help from high explosive, Geoff put the phone down.

'It was strange, though,' she said on Friday night, finishing giving a rather fuller description over the emptied plates at the kitchen table in Hampstead. She was back from that outer limit of exhaustion into the more normal, permanent, gritty-eyed version of the state; tiredness constantly present, but with at least a little something in reserve for rising to emergencies.

'What?' said Geoff, pushing her a cigarette. Flare of match, instant hit of artificial wakefulness.

'The Monument is two hundred yards *behind* the Mariner Building, and then the Coal Exchange is behind again. East from the Monument, like the Monument is east from Mariner Lane. But

I got there by going *west*, out of the window. And it all seemed to be in a straight line. I didn't turn.'

'Everything you've said suggests non-Euclidean geometry,' said Geoff. 'You found yourself high up without ascending, low and near the ground without descending. Turning without turning is no odder. But . . . I wonder. Hang on a minute.'

He left the kitchen, tapping his teeth thoughtfully. Mr Hale watched him go. Iris cleared the table. There were sounds of rummaging overhead, and Geoff came back with four shaving mirrors.

'There should be some putty somewhere but I can't find it,' he said. 'We'll make do by propping them. Pass me a couple of mugs, and the salt and the pepper. You see,' he said, his hands busy, 'your bridges seem to me to be behaving rather like light rays—'

'Ah, the rainbow bridge to Asgard,' said Mr Hale happily.

'Certainly not very solid,' said Iris.

'—and *like* light rays, they may bend predictably when they hit, as it were, a reflective surface. Periscope principle. Squat down there, and tell me what you see.'

Iris got onto the floor as indicated, with her eyes just above the tabletop, and looked into the first little mirror, angled against the side of the salt cellar. Instead of her own face, she found she was looking from angled mirror to angled mirror in an apparently straight line, though the mirrors were really placed in a zigzag. A tiny mirrored corridor led towards something fluffy.

'What do you see?'

'Your father's moustache.'

Geoff sighed. 'Father, lean back, do.'

The grey fluff withdrew, and there was a chessman instead, looking indeed very like the Monument had done at the end of the first arch. She shivered.

'What is it?' asked Geoff, noticing.

She got up. 'The thing I can't describe – the thing I don't know how to tell you – is that it wasn't just frightening because of the height or the danger. Though those things were quite frightening enough. It was frightening because it *was* strange, and getting stranger the further I went. As if it was showing me things I didn't know how to see. Maybe, things not jumbled in themselves but which *I* could only see all tangled up and distorted.'

'Like looking at Raphael.'

'Like gazing at dear old Bluey, yes. The first arch twisted space around, and the second one started twisting time too. I think I saw some Romans, and a pointed tower that must be from the future. What do you think the third arch will be like? And the fourth? And the rest?'

'You sound excited,' said Geoff.

'I suppose I am, in a terrified kind of way.'

'I wish I could see it.'

She squeezed his hand. 'The next dark-of-the-moon nights are all on weekdays,' she said. 'You'd have to be back in London.'

'We are coming back,' Geoff said, 'but I don't know when.'

'Well, maybe you'll be with me at the end of October, then. Or the end of November. – This thing with the mirrors. Does it mean anything useful for dealing with the statues?'

'I think it may mean that the captive angels in the statues could be thought of as polygonal reflectors bending the bridge into progressively higher dimensions.'

'So . . . ?'

'So, since they *are* trying to grab you and eat you, I'd wear tighter clothes with less to grab at. And probably gloves.'

'Thank you, Dr Einstein.'

*

She acquired a black sweater and a black pair of slacks, which she took in around the ankles so there was less grabbable material there. Both of these were in smaller sizes than she was used to buying for herself, not that she had any practice anyway at buying trousers. Iris disapproved of them, not for women in general but for herself, on grounds of allure. If you showed off your shape unambiguously, once and for all, there was no room left for suggestion. You became a forked, practical creature, like a man with slightly redistributed bulges. She stood in front of the floor-length mirror in the hall in Chelsea, and considered herself. She looked like Eleanor, she thought, or the women at the City Lit class. She had put on highbrow social camouflage, as well as dressing for the rooftops. That, at least, might be useful.

'I like the way you look in those,' said Geoff, sprawled on her bed and gazing through the bedroom door at her. 'Specially from behind.'

'Shut up,' she said. She turned round and craned at herself over her shoulder. 'Really?'

The other essential preparation that she made was to volunteer for the fire-watch. It had occurred to her that by the time 30 October came around, with the next dark of the moon, dusk would be arriving nearly an hour earlier, and with it the Luftwaffe. She would not be able to creep out onto the Mariner's palm as the office closed. It would be night already, night with fire and bombs. The staff of C&B would have scattered towards home and relative safety. If she wanted to be still in the building then, she needed a reason: and she thought of the wing-collared defender of the Coal Exchange, licensed to climb about on its dome. Mr Seaton, the ARP warden for the Mariner, seemed like the sensible first port of call, and when she went looking for him at start of business in the Home Counties Provident office on the second floor and explained her intentions, he was delighted.

'Excellent idea,' he said. 'Excellent. Grateful to you, Miss . . . ?'

'Hawkins.'

'Yes; seen you in the lift, of course. Difficult finding cover for these City buildings, when everyone wants to get home to their families – understandably, understandably. My money says, change in the regs sometime soon, make it a *duty*, so everyone takes a turn. Now though, strictly voluntary. And I and old Brown from the sixth floor – widower like me, you see, nobody to rush home to – have been stretched pretty thin, I don't mind saying.'

He did look thinned out, with a particularly wan and waxy edition of the universal Blitz face.

'So, another warm body for the rota – tremendous, and much appreciated. Let's see, when can you do? I'll look out the list.'

She agreed to four weekday nights in October, the last to be the thirtieth, the first to be a night shared with Seaton himself – 'so I can show you the ropes. Not that there's much to it. Common sense, you know, mostly.'

She had been worried that she might find herself landed with some uncontrollably gigantic commitment, to deal with on top of the office and the nights babysitting Mr Hale. But Mr Seaton, though he had got used to the idea of women putting themselves in harm's way on the fire-watch, had preserved some gentlemanly views on how often they should be asked to do it. It seemed appropriate to him that she should take on a smaller, ladylike portion of standing up on the slates in a tin hat while shrapnel and debris rained down. Iris did not feel inclined to point out the illogic.

She did her first and supervised night of watching on a Monday – they were all Chelsea nights she was giving up to it, not Hampstead ones – and Mr Seaton walked her through the whole building from the basement up, rattling the bunch of keys he had collected which let him through all the doors of all the businesses on all nine floors.

'Whole building's in your custody, d'you see,' he said. 'I do a tour first thing of an evening, 'nother at dawn, and one more in the middle of the night, if it isn't too hot up top to leave. (You'll see what I mean.) Just . . . keep an eye out for anything odd, d'you see? I mean, the job is ninety-nine per cent dealing with our friends in the Luftwaffe, and the little surprise packages they drop. But . . . they do say that quite a bit of, well, *robbery* is happening during the raids. Some of the boys in Rescue are rather light-fingered. Fact, the rumour *is*, there's one Rescue team working the City who travel with gelignite. They dig out the people all right, but then they find the safe and blow it and make off with the contents. One kind of bang hiding the other, d'you see? Now, up we go.'

They had reached the final staircase, leading up round the top end of the lift shaft, past the steel cage full of winding gear, to a short passage and then a door out into a little leaded valley with further steps at the end up to the wide expanse of the roof.

'How's your head for heights?' asked Seaton.

'Not bad,' said Iris.

'Good, good. Tin hat on – pick either of them from the peg, one size fits all I'm afraid, and they fasten— Oh, you've got it. Now, this is what Brown and I call "Base Camp". Flask for tea and the biscuit tin just there, as you see, and a couple of camping stools for comfort. Then here we've got the water tank and the sand buckets. Any we use up during the night we refill in the morning from those sacks I showed you in the basement. Bit of a nuisance, but it'll be safe to use the lift again by then, and it does mean you're leaving things shipshape for the next fellow, doesn't it. And these are the brooms. Now, the Ministry claims these are fireproof, but I beg leave to doubt it; I think it's much the safest to give them a good wetting in the tank every time you've used them. All clear so far?'

'I think so,' said Iris. 'Tell me, how often do you have to . . . use the brooms and the sand?'

'It all depends on the night! Talking of which,' said Mr Seaton, 'come on up, and let's see what we've got.'

She was eager to see. Except for the brief minute with Mr Hale, looking out over doom descending with fire on the darkling plain of London, she had never *seen* a raid, only heard them, or not heard them, from hiding, from down in the roots of the city. There was something elating, if frightening, about regaining a view of what was happening, up in the free air.

The roof was a big square of lead panels the size of two tennis courts next to each other, with a slight ridge in the middle to encourage rainwater to run off through the gaps in the parapet round the edge. The only interruption was the Mariner's thick brick stack of chimneys. Otherwise, nothing to see but the dim grey of the leads underfoot. But Iris was looking out and beyond. For there in the night was the whole darkened perspective of the city laid out below them: the lightless reefs of all the commercial blocks westward towards the silhouetted dome of St Paul's, the silent silver of the river to the south, the lightless spires in the north, and east the fatal column of the Monument, pale in the dark, with beyond it the Tower of London faintly printing its castle-shape and then the far black muddle of river bends and the docks' spidery industrial clutter, all under a clear but moonless sky of dark, dark blue. From out of the east there was a droning, like a far-off hive of bees.

'Well,' said Mr Seaton, 'no moon, that's a plus, but no cloud, that's a minus. And no wind.'

'What difference does the wind make?' asked Iris.

'Means incendiaries drop straight down, more or less; makes it easier to guess where they're going. Here they come. Sirens any minute. Ah yes.'

The howl rose around them, and instead of making for subterranean shelter, Iris and Seaton only descended into the gully by the door where the brooms and buckets were.

'Here's the drill,' said Seaton. 'HE we can't do anything about, obviously—'

'HE?'

'High explosive; that falls where it falls. If it seems to be getting very close, you *do* have the option of making for the basement, but considering you can't use the lift, I always think best to ride it out up here and take your chances. Incendiaries, though – those are our bailiwick. Idea is—'

The sirens ceased, or possibly were drowned by a monstrous crashing, bass thuds and splitting cracks that rolled round the sky. At the same time, searchlights flicked on to the east, and roved backwards and forwards, trembling stalks of light.

'Don't worry!' bawled Mr Seaton hoarsely. 'Ours! AA guns – Blackheath, Isle of Dogs, Hampstead – there goes Regent's Park – comforting, really. Where was I. Yes: idea is, put out – or brush off – anything that falls on our roof before it can burn through. Nothing has, glad to say. If it does – go downstairs – note location – call fire brigade *first* – then do your best with extinguishers, so on – but not at peril of life and limb. Or too much peril, anyway!'

The searchlights had found something. In the crossover of two trembling beams, a flight of little black specks had appeared. They were no bigger than midges, but from them, through the redoubling crashes of the anti-aircraft fire, the drone came, louder and more saw-toothed, as if someone were cutting wood, gratingly, in the sky. Then a new sound: descending whistles. And to the east, gouts of fire appeared among the dockland cranes, only for a second rising as orange fountains, but leaving spots of dull crimson behind them. A little delayed, tinny sounds of shattering and slow crunches like a wave stirring pebbles on a beach arrived to join the cacophony.

'Looks like it's mostly the poor old docks,' cried Mr Seaton, who Iris guessed had never got to narrate a raid before, and was now delivering the monologue in his head out loud for her benefit. His face was tilted back, and under the helmet the flashes and pulses of orange light were reflecting in his horn-rimmed spectacles. 'No – no – some coming our way, I think – heads down—'

They crouched, and the sawing sounds grew splinteringly loud and passed overhead. Whistles fell from them, each terminating in a shock of sound so loud and blunt that it hit the ear as more shock *than* sound, a blow of silence that momentarily stopped the world. The air flickered, the ground shook. The burning-dust smell she'd been catching the remnant of in the mornings reached her nose with full force: a gunpowder stink.

'*Rather* close,' shouted Seaton in her ear as the last shock faded. 'But we're all right! Now it's our turn! Bucket and broom, my dear, bucket and broom!'

She followed him up onto the open leads with bucket in one hand and broom in the other. Pink stars were falling slowly out of the sky. It was the scene she and Mr Hale had seen, only close to; and even close to, it had a strange stately beauty, like a firework display in slow motion, the pink stars casting enough glow to swirl dancing shadows over the stone and the brick, the steeples and domes down below.

'Keep an eye on them, these sparkly chaps – you get the hang of it – those are going in the river – those are too far off – that one's going behind us – but *that* one – let's see – possibly, possibly – yes! North-west corner. Off we go!'

And Mr Seaton scampered gaily towards the thing settling onto the Mariner's roof. But as it came nearer yet it had ceased to be a stately star and become a spitting, crackling, chemical fireball suspended from a small parachute. Iris meant to follow, but all of a sudden her legs refused to move. Somehow, she had managed to sign up for fire-watching without paying attention to the 'fire' part of the contract. She had offered, her legs were telling her now, late and loud, to put herself within fire's reach; and not fire in theory, fire in the abstract, but the skin-blistering, flesh-charring thing itself, the thing that spread in running licking serpents' tongues. The demon. The devourer of houses.

'Come on!' cried Seaton, finding her not behind him. 'Best to get to it before it can take hold!'

He looked very small outlined against the flare of it. A midget with a bucket. It occurred to her that the rooftops all around must be scattered with Seatons. The city was being defended by hundreds of gallant midgets with buckets. She lumbered forward, something between a giggle and a sob stuck in her throat.

The incendiary was certainly a nasty device up close, quite hot enough to melt the roof and drop through to torch the building if allowed; hot enough too for her to feel the scorch of it on her face, the frizzle of the ends of her hair. But Mr Seaton was all practicality.

'Don't be afraid of it,' he said. 'The trick is to get close enough for a good aim.' He leaned in close and delivered the sand in his bucket with a solid, well-aimed *flump*. 'There, like that. Now you.'

Her aim was less exact, but between them they had the firebomb under a decent mound of sand: which, nevertheless, still hissed and glowed between the grains.

'As you can see, it doesn't quite extinguish them,' said Seaton. 'But this is where the brooms come in. I'll go this side, you go that side – nice to have two of us – and now we work it to the edge of the roof. Slowly, so that it stays under its sand.'

Between them, they eased the incendiary to the parapet. It left a trail of shine behind it where the top of the lead had melted.

'This is like hockey at school,' said Iris, trying to strike the right note. 'Only with a smouldering ball.'

'Is it?' said Seaton. 'Splendid. We did cricket, of course. Now give it a shove – luckily, those pillar-things are far enough apart – and: there she goes!'

They craned over the edge, and watched the incendiary drop ten storeys, past the granite Mariner, into the lightless slot of Mariner Lane. A burst of sparks when it hit the ground, but no conflagration.

Die, you blob of evil, thought Iris shakily. *Die. Die. Die.*

'Done for you, you little bugger!' crowed Seaton out loud. 'Oh. Oh, I am sorry. Do excuse me.'

'It's fine,' said Iris. 'If you're not allowed to swear at a moment like this, when are you?'

'Ha!' said Mr Seaton. 'Quite; quite. Not a point I could ever really get my Matilda to accept. – Now, I can't guarantee it, but there's usually a little bit of a pause before the next wave.'

They trailed back to the gully, where he insisted they dunk their brooms in the tank. The hammer-and-crash of the guns continued unabated, but Iris had got used to it by now; it had become the baseline of the night, unremarkable in itself.

Mr Seaton set up the camp stools and poured two mugs of milky tea from the flask.

'Jolly well done for a first time,' he said. 'Keeping calm, that's the ticket.'

He levered off the lid of the biscuit tin.

'Ginger snap?' he said.

V

'I have a suggestion,' said Geoff.

'Do you?' said Iris, a note in her voice she recognised but did not seem to be able to help. A note of scepticism, withdrawal, return by stages to the person she had been before a magic hand and a desperate tenderness for a skinny boy remade her. What had been hopeful and new between them seemed to be fading away in the doggedness and sullenness of the endless air raid nights. She was beginning to be able to imagine a story she might tell later, of a summer romance with someone who ultimately wasn't her type. It made her miserable, but she didn't know what to do about it. Didn't have the energy either.

'Yes,' said Geoff. 'You're looking awful . . .'

'Oh, thank you very much.'

'Awfully tired, I mean; which broken sleep over and over again will do to a person. How many nights in a row of raids is it now?'

'Forty-two.'

'Well then. And you're doing your job, and you're calling in on my father, and now you're fire-watching as well—'

'It mostly isn't very dramatic. Last time it was almost quiet. They were going for the stations, nothing came down near the river, and I just sat and snoozed.'

'All the same. I don't think you notice how much it's taken out of you, because it's been so continuous. I do, because I leave London and come back. I walk out of Paddington station and everything is moving at half-speed. All of the people – you're all . . . haggard. If there's an emergency, everything goes like the clappers. Fire engines and ambulances belt by, people sprint for the shelters. Go go go. But the rest of the time, everyone's taking these tiny, energy-saving little steps. A sort of sad shuffle. And all the faces sag.'

'As bad as that?'

'Yes. As if everyone is only half-awake, all the time. And now you've got the next dark of the moon coming up as well, when you'll be facing God knows what. So I think—'

'Look, I'm doing it. And I'm not leaving London, and I'm not leaving my job either.'

'I know that. I *know* that. Give me some credit. Believe me, if I could tuck you into my kit-bag and take you away with me to the country, I would; but they don't allow it, and you'd fight like a wildcat if I tried—'

'I would! Why are you smiling? This is not funny.'

'I am smiling because I am joking. You used to be able to tell when I was joking, remember, not very long ago? I do not really want to carry you out of London, or carry you anywhere against your will. I am intimately acquainted with the obstinacy of Iris Hawkins—'

'It isn't obstinacy! It isn't stubbornness! It's *my* possession of *my* life! Why is that so hard to understand, you grinning idiot?'

Geoff, who had been keeping his distance on the other side of the kitchen, reached a single finger across and touched the back of her hand very lightly. Even in her present state, she could tell that this was not a grab, not a preliminary to seizing and pinioning. It was just contact, and for a moment it stilled her.

'I think,' he said carefully, 'that before you do anything magical again, you should take your friend Eleanor up on her offer of a night away in Sussex.'

'That's your suggestion?'

'Yes. Get out of the city, sleep a whole night through, and see if your batteries will recharge a bit.'

'Oh.'

She went to sleep on the train out of Victoria – slow, crammed, stop-starting its way through the battered suburbs of outer London, with a press of commuting women around her who could, yes, be fairly described as haggard – and woke to find herself alone in the compartment, moving in the early dusk through a landscape she had almost forgotten the existence of, because it was not blacked-out streets and patched water mains and the smoke of fires. Out here, the glorious hot summer had moved into a patient, stately autumn. The bare, grave lines of the Downs rose ahead, chalk-green dimming to chalk-blue, and the valleys between were seamed with dark russet, from great trees in full red leaf. Picture-book England: she was in picture-book England. Drakeling station was a mere halt. Iris dismounted in the dimness under branches. The train trundled off in a hiss of steam, and she made her way along a cobbled street as if wading upriver in a stream of treacle. There was a ringing in the sky from aero-engines, but faint and far off, unable to touch the peace under the darkening trees.

She turned in at a latched gate in a grey stone wall, and waded on through a garden glimmering with overgrown topiary. She rang a bell at an arched doorway, and after a while it was opened by Eleanor holding a candle in a tin candlestick.

'Hello,' said Iris.

'Hallo, you! Come in, come in. Heavens, you're thin. I've got a game pie in the oven, if you're willing to risk my pastry, but it won't be ready for a couple of hours. You could come and join us in the— But, my dear, you look completely done in. No, I'm sure you'd rather lie down. Come straight upstairs; I've put you in one of the little rooms off the gallery. I'll wake you for dinner, don't worry; I mean to feed you up, as much as one can in a weekend.'

She followed the candle – there seemed to be no other lighting

– past a door where Miles Ormond smiled hospitably, a couple of other men behind him, and up a grand staircase, and along a corridor of which she could get little impression except that it was surprisingly bare, and surprisingly coloured, somehow. But all her attention was on the plump rectangle of the bed the candlelight revealed when Eleanor turned a doorknob on the right. Patchwork bedspread, two white pillows. Her mind dived into it even before her body could, and Eleanor lit a new candle on a bedside table from the one she carried and left her to it. Soft, white, smooth sheets. A clean-linen smell. Instant, lovely oblivion.

'Pie,' said Eleanor's voice, apparently only seconds later. 'Pie. Pie. I'm so sorry to wake you but I find that becoming a host has made me fearfully tyrannical, and you obviously need to eat. Also, the pastry is adequate, though I do say so myself. Pie! I promise you can go back to sleep afterwards.'

Iris struggled up through the layers of sleep. She had gone much deeper down than she ever had in the snatched sleep before the sirens went, or propped in the Hampstead Anderson or the Chelsea cellar, descending to a deep recess, a socket of pure soft dark, well below the busyness of dreams. And now, ascending, it merged with the comfortable velvet black of the bedroom, in which two blobs of yellow light floated, one from the flame of the almost-burned-down bedside candle and the other from the candle Eleanor again carried, which lit her head like a painting, and made her clean-scrubbed face and yanked-back red hair into something ancient and mysterious and beautiful. Iris gazed at her. She was still tired to the bone, tired enough to sleep till Doomsday if allowed, but something had been restored to her in the dark soft deep place, some layer or layers of self-possession and resource. Eleanor, she saw, was no longer wearing the apron and trousers she'd had on when she opened the door. She was in a dark-blue gown with a square neck that would have suited her in several centuries. And hadn't the men downstairs been wearing . . . dinner jackets?

'You don't . . . dress for dinner, do you?' she croaked over the hem of the patchwork.

'Heavens, no,' lied Eleanor, after only the minutest pause. 'Or rather, if *we* fancy dressing up, we extend an absolute dispensation to all our refugees from London. Come as you are! But come! Honestly, my pie really is slightly splendid.'

'Is there somewhere I can wash my face?'

'Of course. Keep going at the top of the stairs, bathroom first on the left. Vital for washing off stone-dust. But as you've probably deduced, we've no electrics, and no gas either – all horribly historical here – so the water is ice cold, I warn you. Oh, and guard your candle as you move about. The house likes to blow sudden draughts at one. Right, see you downstairs. And – I'm so glad you came.'

Eleanor went away. Iris clambered reluctantly out from the covers, picked up the bedside candle and went looking for the bathroom. The corridor outside her room was not a corridor at all, but something much wider and more imposing. The boards under her feet were bare, and there were no curtains over the diamond-paned windows – in which she was showing a light without any warden patrolling outside to shout at her. The walls were bare plaster, but frescoed every inch in bright paintings in reds and greens and oranges. Yawning, she walked past picnic scenes, bathing parties, citrus groves, vines, a forest of curling leaves where a satyr chased a nymph, and – wait a minute. She took a step back and held the candle closer. One young man kneeling in front of another and doing something candidly rude. *Frederick with the mouth. Claude with the mouth.* There were visual satisfactions she had not considered in the idea of two good-looking boys together. Well, well.

She crossed the stairhead and it was grand too, with worm-eaten carved cherubs for banisters, though there was only a strip of frayed hessian tacked down on the treads. Shadows from the candle flickered and swung high above. The bathroom Eleanor had directed her to was a cavern too, with an immense footed bathtub looming under the window, white as a whale, and an enamel basin under a spotted mirror six feet high that wasn't much smaller. *PUMPHREY'S HYGIENIC CASCADE*, it said in blue letters around the drain. The single tap delivered a torrent that was indeed icy. She put down the candlestick on the lip of the basin, and did her best on her face with the block of brown soap: the cheapest coal tar, she was not surprised to find, because she was getting used to the house's combination of grandeur and indifference to ordinary bourgeois comforts. No carpets, tin not silver, withered old joinery – but she suspected that the paintings were by artists she'd have heard of if she'd gone to more evening classes.

She brushed her hair with a brush she would have thrown away if it were hers, and looked at herself in the candle-glow at the bottom of the giant mirror. Places where the silvering had worn off the glass pocked the image like impact marks to the ice on a frozen pond, but between them, there she was. *You're no oil painting*, said her inner critic, but tonight by candlelight she kind of was. Her office dress, bedraggled by repeated wear and too little washing; straight brown hair, not cut by a professional for three months; no make-up, when she wouldn't previously have dreamed of going out without warpaint. She was thin-faced and big-eyed. But the eyes were alert; they gleamed. She bit her lips in lieu of lipstick and went downstairs.

When she put her head round the door at the bottom of the stairs, she found another scene like a painting of the pre-electric past, only this one lit by twenty-plus candle flames. Miles Ormond was easing the cork out of a bottle of champagne, the second of the evening judging by the glasses being held out by the two middle-aged men in penguin suits who were the other guests. One looked like a hamster, the other was more craggy.

She took a deep breath and stepped across the threshold.

'Good evening,' she said, her voice full Watford. This was a place, she judged, where what she had started out as would be found more interesting than any amount of Chelsea elocution.

Faces turned towards her, Miles hurried over with a glass for her, and Eleanor saluted her over at the head of a dining table by waving a large kitchen knife over the famous pie.

'Do come and sit down, all of you,' she called. 'I feel you need to get the beauty of it hot.'

And in short order, Iris was seated opposite Hamster, being passed a mismatched plate loaded with a slice of pie oozing savoury gravy and containing more meat than she had seen at once since January. Her mouth watered. From the other direction, Miles passed a tureen of mashed potatoes and another of buttery cabbage.

'Oh, this is *splendid*,' said Hamster, in a high educated drawl. 'Thank you so much, Ormond, for luring us down from the Treasury.'

'A pleasure,' said Miles. 'Though the pleasure-provider, you'll note, is really my wife.'

Ah, *wife*, noted Iris.

'*Chaire Athena, gennetaira piton!*' said Hamster, waving his fork, which Iris could make nothing of at all.

'Do you really think the goddess of wisdom is responsible for pies?' asked Eleanor. 'Sounds to me more like a job for one of the muses. *Hail, muse of pastry . . .*'

Laughter.

'But how do you do it?' asked Craggy, indicating the spread.

'Benefits of the countryside,' said Eleanor. 'Rabbit and pheasant in the pie, courtesy of local . . . gentlemen of the night.'

'Poachers,' put in Ormond.

'Spuds and cabbage courtesy of our own vegetable patch. Butter from the farm next door.'

'It's delicious,' said Iris, feeling that if she didn't start speaking, she might never do so.

'Isn't it, though?' said Hamster. 'Tell me,' he asked politely, 'are you . . . from the world of the arts as well?'

Iris opened her mouth, but Ormond got in first. 'No,' he said, 'Miss Hawkins is finance, like us. But on the Sell side, to use an Americanism.'

'Cornellis & Blome,' confirmed Iris.

'Oh yes,' said Craggy. 'I was at Cornellis's boy's bar mitzvah, donkey's years ago now. How is he?'

'Bearing up,' said Iris. 'Harold's a POW.'

'I'm sorry to hear it.'

'Better than the alternative,' said Iris.

'Indeed,' said Craggy.

'And . . . how are you finding things, business-wise?' asked Hamster.

'Well,' said Iris, 'we called the bottom of the market correctly in June, so we're pleased about that, and so are our clients. But as you gentlemen know, most of the ingenious ways we could profit from the situation have been blocked off by cunningly devised regulations. Thank you for that.'

She raised her glass to Hamster ironically. He nodded ironically back.

'Of course, I do support the reasoning,' she said. 'The holes in the capital account had to be stopped.'

'Oh, have you read *How to Pay for the War?*' Hamster asked.

'Of course,' said Iris. 'Are you a Keynesian too?'

Hamster laughed, revealing under his hamsterish moustache a surprisingly red and fleshy upper lip. 'It's an interesting point!' he said. 'Sometimes I doubt it. After all, I believe Marx denied he was a Marxist.'

'This . . . *is* Keynes,' said Miles Ormond gently. 'I'm sorry, I should have introduced you.'

'Oh,' said Iris, feeling foolish. But the pie was infusing her with courage as well as protein. 'Well, since I've got you, I'd like to ask how you see the future of the exchange controls, when the war is won.'

'When it's *won*?' queried the great man. 'Perhaps a little premature, my dear, when the enemies of civilisation are flying over our heads undaunted at this very moment, and we sit by guttering light in civilisation's last redoubt.'

No you don't, thought Iris. *You will not speak to me indulgently, or in vague dinner-time rhetoric. I'm not having it. You will take me seriously; I shall force you up a gear.*

'Don't I know it,' she said. 'I'm watching the City burn every night. But optimism about winning is surely both a duty and the only avenue we have for making meaningful plans about the future.' She had been waiting for an opportunity to put her insight on the Tube into properly grand terms, and this seemed to be it. 'So my question is, how is trade to be managed, in the peace, so we avoid the old pitfalls of' – she counted them on her fingers – 'underproduction, deflation, inadequate credit?'

Keynes blinked. 'It depends very much on the final shape of the peace,' he said. 'On the relative strength at that point of the sterling area and the lands of the dollar.'

'But ideally?' insisted Iris.

'Oh, *ideally*,' said Keynes, with something approaching a friendly sneer. 'If we're talking *ideally*, I could require a chicken in every pot and a unicorn in every stable. But look,' he said, steepling his fingers—

And having got him into seminar mode, Iris kept him there remorselessly, throwing in large-eyed attention and pouts of disagreement from time to time, though she suspected his tastes ran more to Claude and Frederick upstairs. When the champagne was done, Miles Ormond uncorked a bottle of claret that ran into the glasses in the candlelight like reddish ink. Eleanor watched with satisfied amusement. Craggy, who was probably somebody else important, hemmed out a bark of a laugh from time to time, and once said, 'Pin him down, Miss Hawkins; pin him down, if you please. We never can . . .'

'I suppose you were at LSE?' asked Keynes eventually, when the candles were mostly burned down and they were tackling an ancient Stilton in which the blue veins had turned to dark brown within light brown.

'No, no,' said Iris, preening inwardly. 'I come from a long line of stock market clerks, that's all.'

'Really,' Keynes said, eyebrows raised. 'Makes one wonder what the future holds.'

'In a liberal society,' began Iris, fuelled by protein, animal fats, dairy fats, starch, vitamins, two glasses of Pol Roger and two of Château Chasse-Spleen—

'You're not a socialist, like our hosts, then?' Keynes asked.

'Oh, I'm not nearly pure enough,' she said. 'May I have a refill?'

Laughter.

'I mean,' she said, 'I'm in sympathy with the part about sweeping away class distinctions. I do want the economy run with a twentieth-century awareness of what does what rather than with nineteenth-century blinkers on, and I am up for a certain amount of the liquidation of the rentier – at least, the stupider ones. And while the war lasts I want maximum productivity, and that means the mobilisation of capital. But afterwards . . . I'd rather like to get back to the market.'

'Good heavens,' said Keynes. 'Have I encountered a believer in capitalism who is under the age of fifty?'

'You have,' she said, and the room was warm and the candlelight was beautiful and her stomach was full and the eyes of the men were upon her. *I can do this*, she thought, *I can really do this. Geoff was right to send me.* And at the thought of Geoff, her first thought of

Geoff for an hour or two, she asked herself, *would Geoff fit in here? Does he belong in this picture?* She tried to imagine him at the table beside her. Talking about . . . television. And she just wasn't sure.

Her sleep that night in the little room off the gallery was less total and immediate, but still blissful. Not a plunge into absolute unconsciousness, but a leisurely descent, a downward drift, through darkening lucid layers, as if she were sinking in a sea of glassy stillness, gradually, gradually, past bright fishes and slow-waving fronds, down and down, all the while knowing there was nothing that was going to recall her. No sirens, no jangle of alarm. No coming to with your heart pounding in your chest and your pulse rattling in your wrists. Slow, sweet, deep, liquid sleep.

There were dreams, and they were not absolutely all pleasant. The old one of fire was in there, but thinned and un-frantic, a mere single room in a house of dreams she explored unfrightened, with somehow a calm knowledge that she was only dreaming, and could close the doors of rooms she preferred not to visit. And then, after that long wandering, through impossible chambers which by dream-logic sometimes had whole meadows inside them without ceasing to have roof and walls, she began the upward drift to wakefulness, and it was equally gradual, equally sweet. Brightening layers of the lucid sea; and at last, when she surfaced on the shore of sheets and patchwork, a shimmer all over her skin, the vague happy fuzz of a body that does not distinguish itself entirely from the smoothness of the cotton it lies on. She could go back to sleep if she wanted to, dip again luxuriously into the waiting sea, feel the bed melt away once more. She was on the quicksilver border between sleep and waking, with no hurry, with all the time in the world.

There was light on the ceiling, with a tossing shadow-pattern of autumn leaves, coming through a little diamond-paned window just behind the head of the iron bedstead. She gazed up at it, and little by little the bliss of being not-quite-there, a being who might slip and slide away, solidified into the pleasure of being a well-fed, well-slept body. Emphatically there. Naked between clean sheets, having been too tired to think of bringing nightdress, toothbrush, anything civilised at all. She rolled over. She thought of how Geoff's sheets had felt to her, that first night she crept into them alone. She was, she discovered, pleasingly randy. For the first time in – how long? How many nights of bombing had it taken to turn her into a creature who had forgotten desire? She didn't know. But suddenly she was back.

One slice of game pie and I'm anybody's, she thought. If Geoff had been next to her, she would have turned to him and ravished him greedily forthwith, filling herself up with him everywhere she could reach. Since he wasn't, she thought of Claude enjoying Frederick's cock on the wall outside, and settled for her fingers. She came hard, grinning into the pillow. *Oh it's nice,* she thought, panting a little and flat on her back again afterwards, *oh it's nice to get just the pleasure sometimes, without having your soul shaken.* Thinking that, her grin faded into a frown, and with a kick of her legs she got out of bed quickly, before she went further, into melancholy and into thoughts she didn't want to entertain at all, on a morning of bliss.

Cold floorboards underfoot, and nothing to put on but yesterday's sad dress. But outside the door, a kind pile of clothes was waiting for her. A blouse, clean but frayed; a sweater, clean but frayed; a pair of brown corduroy trousers; the greyest and least glamorous underwear she had ever seen. She gathered it thankfully up, and padded to the bathroom. The huge white tub featured PUMPHREY'S HYGIENIC CASCADE too. She ran two feet of glacier water into it. Then with gritted teeth and all at once, got in, ducked under, rolled endwise a couple of times in it, working hard not to shriek, and stood to apply ferocious coal-tar soap. Then washed it off at speed, and was out, teeth chattering, bright scarlet all over, but feeling good. Towel the size of the county of Middlesex. All the clothes were too big, but she hitched in the waist with a belt, and was presentable as a country-house guest. At this country house, anyway.

She found Eleanor in the kitchen, finishing the washing-up from dinner with a woman from the farm next door who evidently came in to Mathoms Court as a general helper and cleaner. It seemed to be past ten in the morning. Though it was a Saturday, the men were already off back to London on the train. Iris's offer to help was waved away. Instead, they sat her at the big oak table with toast and a pat of yellow butter as big as a house brick. She was ravenous again.

'After breakfast, would you like to see the studio?' asked Eleanor.

'Yes please,' said Iris.

'And would you like some more toast?'

'Yes please,' said Iris.

VI

'Good idea?' asked Geoff.

'Very good idea. I feel much more like me again.'

'Good. I missed you.'

'I missed me too.'

She kissed him. And, after a moment's hesitation, clasped her right hand on the back of his neck, where the slender pillars of muscle shaded upwards into the wire-short feathering of hairs. Anxiety; relief; kindness. He *was* kind. She must remember that.

Forty-nine nights of raids. Fifty. Fifty-one. The respite of Sussex was wearing off, or rather the exhaustion of work, Chelsea, Hampstead and fire-watching was wearing on again. But not completely. Eleanor had given her an open invitation. She knew now that she had Mathoms Court as a bolthole when she needed it. Something had been restored, and could be restored again. Knowing it made a difference. Nor did she forget her refreshed vision of the city when she came back in that first time, on the battered train into battered Victoria station, seeing all at once what the war had wrought in London. It wasn't a ruined city that greeted her, it was too tenaciously alive for that, but it was a city that had got quickly used to ruins, to the point where it hardly noticed them as something extraordinary. Back from Sussex, she did notice again. The matter-of-fact presence in most streets now of the holes where buildings had been, where life had been: the mirror of the city pocked with dead spots that gave back no reflection, and more of them nightly, bombs falling as indifferently as raindrops, and the people underneath accepting the random chance of death as the new way of the world.

Everyone was tired, and Geoff was right about the lethargic pace of the city except when danger was imminent. No more defiant witticisms chalked up on walls, no more shops with smashed fronts declaring themselves MORE OPEN THAN USUAL. There wasn't enough energy for that. But in a funny way there was a kind of optimism growing. The radio, you noticed, had stopped talking as if invasion was imminent. The bombing was metamorphosing in people's minds into an ordeal to be endured, rather than the opening scene of a greater apocalypse. If Hitler was coming, why hadn't he come? Terror and darkness ruled unabated, the day shrank and the bombers' night grew longer, death visited the sky to the sound of aero-engines. A bomb in Tooting broke the water mains and poured a tide of sludge onto the people sheltering on the Tube platforms below, drowning sixty-four of them in the desperate dark. On rooftops, in home-dug Andersons, in Morrison shelters under kitchen tables, in malodorous public shelters awash with piss, down in the deep tunnels, the inhabitants of the twenty thousand streets closed their eyes and tried to sleep, knowing their lives might end without reason and without appeal at any moment: that they might not be opening their eyes again. But you could get used to anything, and they mostly had. Terror was only terror, darkness only darkness. And in the morning, if you were not one of the dead ones, there the city still was, reduced a little more, smouldering a bit, freshly shattered here and there, but still in business.

And in the City with a capital C, high explosive and incendiaries took out the offices of brokers and jobbers, merchant banks and commercial banks, but the 30-Share Index rose smartly from 63 to 66. Proof, if Iris had needed it, that the stock market was not the building from which glass had to be swept to reopen the trading floor, and the shares traded there were not flammable pieces of paper, and money itself was not metal or banknotes. All these things were only a temporary embodiment of an enchantment that was abstract, and therefore proof against their physical destruction. A durable magic, more akin than you might think to the magic that opened the way to Nonesuch.

And then it was the dark of the moon again, the night of 30 October.

The others in the office had got used to her coming to work in fire-watching gear, so she was already dressed when darkness fell in the clothes she needed for Nonesuch. Black sweater, the gathered black trousers, a pair of gauntlet-ish leather gardening gloves, steel-capped boots Geoff had found for her. Mr Seaton handed over the keys, and the building was hers. She did the tour first, from basement to roof, looking in on all the silent little kingdoms of ledgers and typewriters, card indexes and filing cabinets. She checked the sand buckets were full, and pumped up water in the tank to the painted line. She was going to have to leave the roof unguarded, unwatched, while she went adventuring, and the irresponsibility of it bothered her more than she had expected. She would just have to hope that nothing fell on the building for however long it took her to thwart Lall. The odds were in her favour, the greater good was being served if she was trying to save history and not one office block, but it still felt wrong. The sirens sounded. She took her helmet off the peg and went downstairs.

Meruzababel. Tell me where all past years are. This time she was expecting the Mariner's eyes to open, this time she was expecting the waking of the cold stone to unnatural life, this time she believed that the stone hand could be safely climbed out onto. This time she knew to keep her feet away from the statue's maw. But it still required an effort to put herself close to the creeping mobility of the rock, to the inimical hatred of the spirit trapped inside it

– maybe a bigger effort, this time, because she knew what was coming. It occurred to her, balanced on the stone palm, that it would free the spirits nicely, and solve the Lall problem neatly, if bombs would fall that broke the network and let the captives slip out of shattered granite and marble. Just . . . not now, when she was standing on one. Just not this statue, and this building, please.

The raid had begun. The bubble-substance of the tunnel through the air did not keep out the racket of guns and engines and explosions, and this time it was full dark as she stepped along the glassy pavement. She could see the floating pink stars falling in the world beyond the bridge, the searchlights pivoting, the blossoms of fire where the HE hit. Only thanks to the warped geometry, the bomb-blossoms appeared above her and directly below, as well as to the sides where the roofline really was; and the pink stars floated along and up as well as down, in an impossible blizzard. The city twisted and tilted. She did her best to ignore it all and stepped on, heel to toe, eyes fixed on the Monument approaching. That was scary enough.

When the stone flames of the golden ball were before her face, she started speaking the moment she reached out for handholds. *Tellmewhereallpastyearsare!* There was a lurch, just for a moment her full weight hung from her hands and she felt the pitiless drop open under her, but then the rim of glimmering glass was there for her feet. She let out her breath and began the circuit, foot by foot, hand by hand, knowing that as she got to the new span of bridge on the far side her hands would be seized – and they were. But this was what the gardening gloves were for. Triumphantly, she slipped her hands out, and it was empty leather that was sucked into the opening gullet of the stone. Triumphantly, calmly, she turned, and set out across the second span at a careful walk, not last time's terrified gallop.

Heel to toe, heel to toe. She could look out deliberately now, to see what views of mangled time there'd be through the bubble-walls. But it was night out there, in all the other Londons past and future that she might glimpse, and she could only tell that she was seeing beyond the present because those other Londons had their lights on. Above, below, kaleidoscoped in with the flame and dark of the blackout, there were strange galleries of lights. Pinpoints of greenish-white above wet cobbles; monotonous orange lighting blank concrete; the yellow of gas lanterns; blue riding lights on something immense in flight; one street coruscating in all the colours, like gems on a bracelet. It was almost soothing, the angled and splintered light show. The sounds of the air raid taking place on 30 October 1940 did not cease. The hammering, the whistles, the cracks, the blunt shocks of explosions still surrounded her, but she paced and gazed, fascinated.

It made her slow to understand what was happening when something *ting*'d off her helmet and a shower of other somethings, small curls and scraps of dim red, pattered onto the glassy way ahead. She bent, with a soothed curiosity, to see what they were. Misshapen twists of metal, glowing faintly – she had just realised that they were red-hot shrapnel, not part of the magic, when another piece dropped onto her bent back and burned there. Wool sizzled, a horrible smoke arose, of burning fibres and burning her.

She mustn't move her feet! She jerked up straight, and shook her torso, and flexed her shoulders, and wriggled desperately, and wished she still had gloves to reach back and knock off the thing that was scorching through wool and into skin. It came out. Something fell off her back, anyway, and tapped down onto the surface behind her. But though the shrapnel was off her, the pain of the burn grew. It was between her shoulder blades, just above the strap of her brassière. She felt melted, charred, cooked there. It made her want to move, to get her body in frantic motion as if she could run away from the burn: but she had to stand, she had to stand, she had to stand. She did, with tears in her eyes. She made herself count; and the pain did not grow less when she reached ten, or twenty, or thirty, but at forty it began to dull into an ache. A vicious ache, but better than the intolerable stab. Then she went forward again slowly, breathing through her teeth, and sweeping shrapnel to the side as she put each boot down. It dropped away when she moved it: the path really was only a few inches wide. She braced for more shrapnel to fall, but none did, and then the iron dragon of the Coal Exchange was coming up.

Tell me where all past years are. 'Good boy, Rover,' she muttered as she sidled round the plinth. The gullet in its side opened but she was out of reach. 'Oh no you don't. Down, Rex. Drop it, Cerberus. I'd have brought you an iron bone if I could, but you aren't . . . chewing . . . me.' Stiffly, with her shoulders set, because the burn hurt marginally less if the burned skin wasn't creased, she stepped out onto the third arch, the one that crossed the alley only one storey up and opened a tube into the brick wall with the hat advertisement on it. New territory. She'd have been more excited without the burn.

Now, instead of a path through the air, the bridge seemed to have become a tunnel through the ground. She stepped into the wall, all sound of the raid cut off, and the glassy span underfoot with air showing through it became a narrow glassy floor with earth beneath. Through the bubble-walls too there was earth, heavy clay packed all around. There was an impression, Iris couldn't say from what exactly, of pressure. Perhaps the air was compressed. But this was deep down. Only a few steps in and it was dark, thickly dark, the subterranean dark quite different from the dark of a night sky, except for the faint faint prickle of light from the floor. If she had known, she could have brought a torch. Instead there was nothing to do but step forward, hand out in front of her. She looked back once, and wished she hadn't: the opening behind her was gone.

At first she thought her eyes were playing tricks on her, just the ghost phosphors that drift around if you press with your knuckles on closed lids. These, like them, were pale glows, coagulating from place to place, greenish mother-of-pearl in colour. But they were really there, she realised, moving not when she turned her head but independently in the walls of the tunnel. They grew more numerous, more detailed; they had pulsing canopies of pale light and trailing strings of it. They were . . . jellyfish. Or something *like* jellyfish. Somehow as well as being deep underground she was deep underwater too, in the dark of some ancient sea. Bigger movement. Much bigger. Up from behind Iris came a sheet of phosphorescence as something huge and fast rippled through the walls after the jellyfish-things. They trembled and fled, there was thrashing and ripping of light, all utterly silent. Then the light blinked off, leaving only the original faint shine of the floor. It illuminated an archway, made of jagged, in-pointing . . . teeth. She shuddered and stepped through.

On the other side the tunnel was different. The light was very slightly brighter, and the walls were wet shale and sand, filleted with ribbons of pebbles. Nothing moved in these. She walked faster. Another archway, this time a lintel of boulders. Through it, crouching; more light, different again. Walls made by humans, through the purplish bubbling, a compacted mix of old masonry, crumbled brick, corroded plaster, with ochre paintings on them of bulls and fish. Another archway again, with pillars. Had it come sooner? Yes, it had. She was getting it. She was not surprised by the Gothic ribbing of the next section, nor the sooty black brick of the one after, though the section of perfectly smooth white pipe puzzled her. It was made from neither metal, nor wood, nor Bakelite, nor any other substance she recognised.

But the closed door that loomed up at the end of the tunnel was so ordinary that she almost forgot to be careful. It was the utterly familiar front door of a semi. Fading paint, four panes of dimpled glass above the knocker. A wall of whitewashed pebbledash around it. It had seemed to block the way as she approached it, as she saw it coming framed by the white circle of the pipe, but when she stepped off the last bit of the glassy pavement, the tunnel was suddenly and completely gone. She was no longer in the depths below, or the skies above, or the tangled domains to one side of the city of London. Abruptly, she was standing on someone's doorstep, on a night-time avenue somewhere in suburbia, almost certainly one named after a shrub. The rumble of the raid was in the distance behind her. It could be Surbiton in the south, it could be Barnes in the west, it could be Romford in the east; it could even be Watford in the north, because in fact this door was very much like the well-remembered door of a particular burned-down house in Watford, except for the fading paint being yellow not green. Anywhere in the great suburban ring around London, it could be. Anywhere where houses came in twos, with garden paths and bay windows and triangular wooden gables. The steel caps of her boots grated on the step. A cat walked through the night air along the next-door garden fence. Puddles glistened on tarmac. And though the house was properly blacked out, someone was definitely in. Leaking out through the door, she could hear music from a radio. The alert hadn't sounded here. People were cooking supper, or chatting about their day. This was an entirely real house, in a real street, with real inhabitants. What did it have to do with the bridge through space and time to the palace of Nonesuch? Yet the bridge had led her here. It must, somehow, be the way onward to the fourth span. She raised her hand to knock, not knowing what else to do, and wondering if she was about to have a completely unmagical conversation with a bewildered stranger.

Her hand was almost on the knocker when something made her hesitate. Some quality of . . . attention that shouldn't have been there. She drew her hand back and studied the thing instead of grasping it. A tarnished brass lion's head, four or five inches across, with a ring in its mouth to knock with. Perfectly ordinary, the kind of ornament made in the tens of thousands. Except that this one was looking back at her. Its tiny eyes of blackened brass were open in the little face, and there were twin pinpoint pools of familiar skittering light behind. Touch *that* and it would have your hand off.

'You little sod,' she said with admiration. It seemed there was no lower size limit on the piece of sculpture that could trap something as impalpable as an angel. Someone in a factory – maybe someone bored, someone with a dad in the building trade – must have said Dawe's spell over this particular lion knocker; said it for a laugh, probably, and not known what they'd done. Iris crouched, keeping her back straight to protect the burn, and whispered caressingly to the knocker, from close to it but just out of reach, *Tell me where all past years are.*

The lion's eyes rolled. The door opened, with a convincing squeak of unoiled hinges that faded at once into the returning racket of the air raid. Because beyond it, rather than a doormat and a hallway with a coat stand, was the fourth arch of the bridge to Nonesuch, and the empty black air of the sky over London again, as the Luftwaffe pounded it. She was much, much higher up this time. She couldn't have said how high – a thousand feet, two? – but the darkened buildings where the fires blossomed were remote below, and she was up on the level where the planes made their runs over the target and the anti-aircraft shells burst in thunder-crack flowers of white light.

And the glass bridge here was a crazy corkscrew spiral, running in loops round the inside of the bubble-tunnel across the night sky. Relative to where she was standing, it turned upside down after a few paces, then right way up, then upside down again, over and over. How could you walk that without falling? And yet it must be possible. Dawe had done it. The deal seemed to be: fatal to the unwary, full of tricks and traps, deliberately and deterringly difficult – but not actually impossible. 'We have to obey our own rules,' Raphael had said. So there must be a way to traverse the corkscrew path; to walk upside down on it without dropping off.

The first foot or two was level. She stepped out onto it. There was at least no wind; the bubble-walls kept that out, though not such solid things as shrapnel, she now knew, and she wouldn't be a bit surprised if a whole Heinkel came roaring through this section while she was on it, propeller tips spinning like razors. Then the glassy path began its tilt to the left, to climb the wall of the bubble-passage, and up onto the roof and over. She advanced one foot onto it, and instantly the horizon began to tilt too, her inner ear told her she was falling, slipping from a sloping frictionless surface, about to drop off to her right, and drop and drop and scream and drop, and drop and drop some more— She pulled the foot back, gulping and shuddering. 'Are you good with heights?' asked Mr Seaton's voice in her head. *Not bad.* She tried again: same instant dizziness, instant torque, instant conviction of falling. And yet—

She needed Analytical Iris for this. Not Defiant Iris, not Fuck-It-Let's-Do-It-Anyway Iris. This was a moment for I-Suppose-You-Went-To-The-London-School-Of-Economics Iris. It was hard to be cool and detached when terrified. *But think, think.* What were the components of that sensation? Name them. Number them. All right. One: the news from her eyes that she was trying to stand at an angle to the horizon, and the *falling! falling!* alarm going off in her head. Two: the news from her ears that her balance had gone. *Falling! Falling! Falling!* Three: the news from her foot that the path had physically tilted. But . . . had she actually felt that last one? Or had she just inferred it from the force of the other two sensations? *Impossible geometry*, Geoff had said. If you could turn without turning on this impossible road, perhaps you could twist without twisting.

All right. She shut her eyes, so there would be no information from what she saw, no chaotic message from eye to ear either. And cautiously slid the foot forward again. Dead level. She did it again, to be sure. No mistake. The corkscrew path was level to touch, just not to sight. It would be safe to cross . . . so long as she didn't see what she was doing.

So she inched out onto the path with eyes screwed shut. Heel to toe, heel to toe, and the glass pavement through the high air reported to her heels and her toes that it was flat and straight. Harder to balance on a narrow surface with your eyes closed, but not impossible; no, not impossible. The hard part was not the slow, careful motion but the effort not to imagine what she was doing, or rather what what she was doing must look like. That at this moment she might have her feet pointed towards the North Star, and London over her head. That she was rotating— *Stop it. Stop it, stop it, stop it.* A step and a step and a step. How long was this arch of the bridge? How many times had it twisted— *No, stop it. Eyes closed, keep going. Think instead,* she reminded herself, *that this is the last arch you have to do.* This one made four. That was enough, when it was done, to deny Nonesuch to Lall. A step and a step and a step. The worst thing was that it made you feel so defenceless not to be able to see.

And promptly, having thought that, Iris heard one of the engine sounds, till then ringing placelessly around the sky, grow louder. Louder and closer. Louder and *much* closer. She thought of her vision of the Heinkel flashing through the bubble-tunnel with cutting, mincing blades. Where was it? *How* close? Oh, this was mad. She couldn't see, she couldn't see, she had to see— *No,* said Analytical Iris, cool and steady. *Consider the odds. The bomber may slice you up into cat's-meat. But if you open your eyes, you* will *fall off. So, eyes closed, miss. That is the course of action favoured by probability.*

She was not sure she liked this ice woman she turned out to contain, but she followed her advice. She stood still, eyes shut, and the engine noise grew, grew, passed and dwindled, the aircrew having perhaps seen an amazing thing, an English girl standing upside down in the thin air at a thousand feet. Or perhaps not. Shakily, she got her feet in motion again and went on, heel to toe, heel to toe, until abruptly her balancing hands stretched out in front of her felt something new there, something that wasn't air. A steep slope of tiles. A roof with . . . moss on it here and there, like damp velvet. One more step, and she wasn't standing on glassy nothing any more, but on an iron gutter; one more still, and she was pushing up the roof itself on her toes, fingers scrabbling for grip on the tiles. Air different, raid noises much more those near ground level: and somewhere very close at hand, the sound made by another human body, scrabbling and climbing. She had arrived. She opened her eyes.

She was on the sharp-pitched roof of a corner building somewhere back in the City. One of those art nouveau-ish blocks whose stonework was smoothed into curves, as if all the component parts had been partially sucked like gobstoppers before assembly. And at the roofline a few feet above her, lit by the shifting pink shadows of incendiaries, a fancy chimney was decorated on each side by white stone, half-sucked sculptures of simpering nymphs. Holding off one of them with an ice axe as it tried simperingly to eat her, a small neat figure – or the silhouette of one – was ascending into view. Lall, coming up the other face of the roof. Lall, here already to claim the fourth span for her own bridge to Nonesuch.

'*Tell me*,' Lall said, panting slightly but with vowels Iris could never have matched in a million years for crisp command, '*where all past years are.*'

A faint glassy iridescence flicked into being, leading somewhere beyond the chimney. Lall moved towards it. Iris surged up over the roofline with no intervening pause for thought, planted her feet, and shoved. It was a good solid shove, the surprise was total, and Lall was balanced on a slope with a drop at her back. She gaped, her feet skidded, her arms windmilled, and she tumbled backwards. Landed, slid, rolled. Rolled off the edge of the roof. Gone.

'There!' said Iris. The stone nymph simpered blue fire at her. 'And you can shut up and all.' Her back blazed with pain where the sudden movement had creased or stretched the burn. She took shallow breaths, one, two, three, and then, without anything visible changing in the scene, its meaning suddenly altered. It stopped being a place of warrior triumph. Normality reasserted itself. It became one where she had just pushed a woman off a roof. Four, maybe five storeys up.

'Oh God,' said Iris, and went scrambling down the far side, boots grinding and slipping on the mossy tiles. She got them planted in the cast-iron gutter and twisted gingerly round, burn shrieking, to look over the edge, expecting to see the smashed body of Lall on the pavement below, a pavement in – Moorgate, by the look of it. But she did not. Instead, she was looking down into Lall's frightened face only a couple of feet lower, as she dangled from desperate fingerholds on the gutter.

'Hang on,' said Iris. 'Don't let go! Let me just – let me—'

The only way to reach seemed to be to lie along the gutter herself – it creaked but it didn't move – and to fish below with her free hand. She groped in the air, and found a sleeve, and a slender wrist rigid with the effort of holding on. She grabbed it, tight as she could: and since it was her right hand, more information than she had ever wanted about the terror of Lady Lalage Cunningham came up from the grip, horribly distracting, and horribly infectious, and not at all something she had the spare attention for, with half the weight of a dangling aristocrat now wrenching at her. It was as if she herself were feeling her feet kick and jerk over the horrible drop, as well as being in the body in the gutter straining to hold on.

'I've got you,' grunted Iris.

'You bloody pushed me off,' hissed Lall. *Bleddy pushed me orf.*

'I can't pull you – up – though. Can you – swing – foot?'

It was hard just keeping up the grip on the wrist, and when Lall did start a pendulum-swing in the air to try to get a leg up into the gutter, Iris's arm felt as if it was being twisted from its socket. It would have been impossible if Lall had not been so ridiculously elfin, a Christmas-tree fairy among fascists, reduced further by rationing even if she probably had been picking at pheasant while Iris subsisted on Spam. But the swinging leg snagged the edge of the gutter, the riding boot on the end caught in it, and with heaving and groaning they managed between them to get Lall up and over the edge, to roll her weight just inboard into the gutter, alongside and on top of Iris, two black-clad people squashed together in unwanted intimacy.

Further movement was impossible for a minute, no matter how much they wanted to disentangle themselves. They lay there and gasped. Iris's burn was under her now, being pressed searingly into the lowest tiles; both of them would be hearing for days from their abused flesh about the hard metal edges of the gutter. And Lall's soul went on broadcasting scrambled pulses of fear, relief and fury. That at least Iris could stop. She yanked her hand away, and was thankful to be back dealing with only her own pain, her own receding adrenaline, her confused gratitude not to have murdered this vile pixie. Who, her nose told her whether she wanted to know or not, had wet herself with fear while Iris was nearly killing her.

'Look,' said Iris, 'I didn't mean—'

'Oh, for God's sake, get off me,' said Lall, struggling free, ignoring entirely who was on top of who. 'How much *is* there of you, anyway? You're like a bloody bolster. Get *off*. I suppose Geoffrey must like fat girls.'

'What a loathsome bitch you are,' said Iris with something like relief. '*Ow*. Watch your feet. You could say thank you, you know.' She began to extricate herself.

'What for? You pushed me off in the first place. You followed me where you had no business to come. And now you've – you've ruined—'

The next glassy span of the bridge had disappeared again, and, as Iris knew from the Coal Exchange, if you missed your chance to step out onto it, it wouldn't be back until the next dark of the moon.

'Good,' said Iris. 'That was the idea.'

Lall had climbed back up to the ridge of the roof, and was sitting on top with her knees pulled up to her chin. Just silhouette again, a knot of shadows. But the line of her shoulders shook. Iris felt the teeth of compunction close again. Being a pocket Venus made Lall little more than child-sized.

She pushed wearily upwards herself and perched next to her. Now she was this close, she could see that Lall was drawing tiny circles on the black serge of one of her own knees. It was the same gesture she had glimpsed under the tabletop at the Kinesis Club. The same fingertip self-comforting.

'Why do it anyway?' Iris said. 'Why take all this crazy risk? I know no one asked you to. They're all in prison, aren't they?'

Lall stopped making the circles and started feeling in a zipped pocket. For cigarettes, Iris guessed; and though one really shouldn't show a light by smoking on a roof, with actual flame licking up here and there on the skyline, it probably didn't make much difference. And the prospect was very appealing to a battered and exhausted body. Would she accept a smoke from her enemy? Yes, she would.

'You don't understand anything,' said Lall. 'I'm not doing it for *them*.'

Between the flicker of distant fires and the flare of one last incendiary of the batch, floating down a couple of streets away, there was just about enough light, now she was sitting next to her, to study Lall's face. Still blondely perfect, though smudged and dirtied, but it had changed again. It was different again, somehow, in some way she couldn't put her finger on. She had seen it in its state of frozen hauteur. She had seen it alarmingly animated by the thrill of cruelty to Weevil and Beetle. But now it was . . . tireder, yes of course. But also somehow . . . more awake. More lived-inside. More visited by the human mess of emotions. Less a locked-tight malignant schoolgirl, more . . . she didn't know what. What had been happening to Lall, these last months? Something, for sure.

Lall had found what she was looking for. Iris leant forward hopefully. It was not a packet of Player's that came out of the pocket, though. It was an old service revolver, and she was pointing it at Iris.

'Oh,' said Iris. 'Oh, marvellous. You're going to shoot me, are you?'

She was unable to summon any very strong emotions on the subject. Too much had happened tonight already.

'I should,' said Lall through her little pearly teeth. 'It would be only sensible. You messed it up for me tonight, and I expect you'll try to mess it up next time too.'

'Oh yes,' said Iris.

'If I shoot you, I get you out of the way once and for all.'

'Yes.'

'And I really want to, as well. I'd love to blow a great big hole in your nasty low pushing face. I hate you, you know.'

'Well, I hate you too,' said Iris.

They stared at each other.

'But you rescued me,' said Lall. 'I mean, first you— But then you— Oh hell. I suppose I owe you something. If I'm better than you, I ought to be more honourable than you.'

'You're not better than me,' said Iris.

'I *am*. I am one of the rulers, not the ruled. My family is a thousand years old.'

'All families are equally old, you inbred moron.'

'Shut up. Shut *up*. I'm thinking.'

Oh God. Lall struggling with a clash of ideas was like a housecat trying to be ethical: she didn't have the equipment. But it was apparently all that was keeping Iris alive. She should say something to help tip the balance.

'What would your father say?' she tried. 'That's his gun, isn't it?'

'He'd say, don't be sentimental, Lalage, put her down like a sick dog.'

Not the best move, then. But Lall hadn't quoted her father as if he were an oracle. She'd sounded thoughtful. Maybe even sceptical.

'Daddy's not here, though,' she said. '*I'm* in charge. It's up to me.' She stood up, and put away the gun, balancing slender and straight on the ridge tiles. 'I say it's pax for now. But only for now. If I see you next time I *will* kill you, do you understand?'

'I do,' said Iris.

'Very well,' said Lall. She ducked her head, fair hair dipping. 'Thank you,' she said formally. *Thenk you.* Some kind of script of politeness had kicked in. The kind of code that might linger in a grand family even when they all started wearing black shirts. 'Please don't follow me, or pax will be over.'

The ice axe was lying against the chimney, where the nymphs were now only motionless stone again. Lall fetched it, and then slipped away along the roofline. Iris watched her clamber over onto the roof of the next building, and be lost in the darkness.

Iris waited a while before she started looking for a way down. And then waited a while longer, when she discovered that the only plausible route involved leaving the same way that Lall had. She smoked a cigarette of her own, with trembling hands. When she finally got moving, she discovered that she had stiffened up, and the burn seemed to have stuck together with the fabric on her back. Lall had departed gracefully – *even with knickers soaked in piss*, Iris thought – but she seemed to herself to be a lumbering mass of pains, a badly articulated giant stumping along and minding every motion. Two roofs along, she saw movement, and hid behind a chimney – fear had come back very fully – until she saw from the silhouette of a helmet and broom that it was a fire-watcher.

'Help,' she said, approaching. 'Help. I was on watch too and I've been caught by some shrapnel.'

'Oh, you poor thing,' said this new watcher, an iron-haired woman in her fifties with glasses. 'Show me?' A flick of shaded torchlight on her back; an intake of breath. 'Oh, my dear, that does look nasty.'

And she was passed downstairs and given sweet tea. A phone call was made; an ambulance coming up Moorgate with far worse casualties in the back pulled over for her, and space was made for her in the front seat among the girls of the crew. Then a dressing-station somewhere in St John's Wood. More sweet tea; waiting while everyone more injured was dealt with; the occasional bomb near enough to set the steel lamps overhead swinging; at last a red-eyed medical student, female, who laid her on her front, snipped off pieces of blouse and jumper, tweezed out what had stuck and applied an agonising layer of ointment, followed by bandage and tape. Two aspirin. Nobody asked any questions. The burn was all the passport she needed. Someone gave her a jacket to put on, from a cardboard box of cast-offs. It was too big, but comforting.

At 5.30 a.m. the All Clear sounded. More ambulances came to carry the seriously hurt to hospitals, and along with the other walking wounded she was released into the blue light before dawn. Birds were just beginning to sing. It seemed miraculous that the world was quiet enough to hear them.

She walked slowly and very upright to St John's Wood Tube station, to wait for the first train. But which way to go? Back to the Mariner Building, scene of her abandoned duty, to see if the office was still standing? Chelsea, to tip herself face down onto the golden coverlet? Hampstead was only one stop away. She wanted human comfort like the jacket, she wanted someone's concern to wrap her round and keep her safe. Hampstead.

Tube and bus and slow uphill walking, and the light growing around her. Autumn hips and haws in the hedgerows, in the little patch of imaginary countryside hiding up on the Heath. But something was wrong at Wildwood Terrace, and she knew it before she even rounded the corner of the road. Too much noise of petrol engines, for a refuge, for a secret place; and there was something wrong with the skyline, something missing that should have been there through the branches of the apple trees from which the dead leaves were fluttering. At the end of Wildwood Terrace, where there should have been a house, there was a shattered pit in the ground in which nothing could be alive. Scraps of burnt and shredded paper blew along the pavement. A Rescue van was just packing up. On the back step of an ambulance, Geoff, wrapped in a blanket, turned a blank white face towards her.

'He left the Anderson,' Geoff said. 'I couldn't stop him. I woke up and he'd gone indoors. And then—'

THREADNEEDLE STREET
NOVEMBER-DECEMBER 1940

I

'I didn't know you were even here,' said Iris stupidly. 'It's a weekday.'

'They moved the research unit back to London yesterday. We're going operational. So I came . . . home.'

They looked together at the hole in the ground, where not a piece of home remained unsmashed. The attic full of nonsense, gone. The cluttered stairs, gone. The island of order in the kitchen, gone. The bedroom, gone, where she had climbed inside Geoff's clothes and he had climbed inside her. Mr Hale's whole grubby burrow. Mr Hale himself.

'Have they found the body?' she asked.

'Oh yes. It's just here behind me. In that bag. Apparently they take it to a cold store now. I've got a chit with a number on it, to give to an undertaker. They've been very kind.'

He looked utterly lost. Not agitated; not grieving. Becalmed in loss, as if he couldn't imagine ever moving again. Iris quashed her ignoble desire for someone to be looking after *her*.

'You'd better come back to Chelsea with me,' she said. 'Unless you need to be at work?'

'No,' he said, 'it's night duty. They won't want me till six.'

'Then come along, sweetheart. Come on, off we go. – Unless you think any of your clothes might be salvageable?'

'I can't face looking. I can wear uniform for now.'

'All right, then.' She took him by both hands and pulled. 'Up we come.'

She took his hands again in the Tube, when he said quietly, 'I haven't got anyone left, have I. I'm all alone now.'

'No you're not,' she said. She felt a quiver, a lurch of uncertainty inside her, so she said it again, more fiercely, and gripped his hands tight. Sorrow; naked need. 'You are not. Do you hear me? You are *not*.'

She put him to bed under the golden coverlet: into a bed where a lover belonged. She changed, wincing, into clean office clothes, and came back to kiss his forehead. He was already most of the way asleep.

'I'm sorry I have to go,' she said, 'but I've got all the keys to the building.' There hadn't been a moment when it felt right to describe what had happened to her last night. Compared to what had come upon Geoff, it seemed . . . lurid. Flimsy. Melodramatic.

'I was going out after him, you know,' said Geoff with his eyes closed. 'I could hear how close the bombs were getting, but I was going anyway. I had my hands on the door of the Anderson. And then I thought of you.'

'Did you?'

'I don't know if that was cowardly of me.'

'You wouldn't have done him any good by being dead too.'

'I suppose not.'

'In fact, I think he'd strongly prefer you being alive.'

'And you would too,' Geoff said.

'And me too.'

'My ears hurt.'

'That'll be the vacuum,' said Iris, citing blast-folklore everyone knew now. 'Get some rest. I'll try and make sure I'm back before you have to go.'

Don't think about this, she thought on the Tube. (The Tube again. She seemed to be riding forever on the coarse plaid upholstery, on the drumming trains, in the viewless dark.) Don't think about this catastrophe making him defenceless, making his need for her unarguable and absolute, just when she had begun to resign herself to the summer's intensities dwindling away, to mad love dying down like a fire that had used up its fuel. Don't think about the contradiction, there, with the promises she was hearing herself make. She yawned, her burn ached, her station came up, and she seized with gratitude on stockbroking to occupy her sleep-deprived brain for the day. No incendiaries had fallen on the Mariner Building; that was a mercy.

But Geoff had had time to think. She got back, wrecked, just before five, having made the excuse that her young man had been bombed out the previous night and needed help to move his stuff. When she turned the key in the door of her flat, she found him in the kitchen boiling a kettle for two cups of tea he had put out ready. The bed was made, he had tidied the sitting room, and he had washed and shaved and, by the look of things, ironed his uniform. He poured hot water into the pot, adjusted the little jug of milk on the tray so that its handle was at precisely ninety degrees to the spoons, and ushered her formally into the sitting room. (*Her* sitting room.)

'How are you?' she said, as warmly as exhaustion allowed.

'I'm all right,' he said. 'Stunned still, really. I can't quite believe that if I go back to Hampstead the house will still be gone. That he will be. But I know it's true too. I know everything is different now. And there was something I wanted to say before I head off back to Alexandra Palace – oh; did you know I was going to be working there again? I can't remember if I've told you.'

'No, you didn't. Geoff: what is it you want to tell me?' Iris asked, with a mounting sense of dread. She was sitting on the edge of her own chrome-framed easy chair, as if at an interview, with the teacup balanced on her knee.

'I was wondering . . . I've *been* wondering . . . if we shouldn't get married. If you would marry me. People are, you know, at the moment. A lot.'

She covered her eyes with her hand.

'Oh,' she said. 'Oh, I wish you hadn't asked me that.'

'Why? Why shouldn't we? We might be dead any minute.'

'Yes, but what if we're not?'

'You'd *rather* be dead?'

'No, of course not . . .'

'If you ask me,' said Geoff, 'almost everything beats having the life bashed out of you by a falling house.'

'I mean that if we don't die, if we live through all this, you're proposing I should end up as, as' – she tried to think of a less contemptuous phrase than the one she already had in her head, and was too tired to manage it – 'as a TV engineer's little wifey somewhere out in Metroland, greeting you in a pinny when you get home.'

'That doesn't sound like you,' said Geoff, frowning. 'Who says it would be anything like that?'

'The point is, it would be like *something*, wouldn't it. It would be like one of the ways a wife has to be, and there aren't very many, and none of them let you *do* things.'

'I don't see why not.'

'I know you don't. But I do.'

'You told me I wasn't alone,' Geoff said.

Stab of guilt.

'You're *not*. But don't you see? You've gone from asking, do you want me – the answer to that is yes, by the way – to asking, do you want me and nothing else? There's a difference, Geoff. There's a big difference.'

'But—'

'Look,' she said, with the very distinctive feeling of unfairness that came of saying a true thing for an underhand reason, 'I think you're still in shock. I think, like you said, everything in your life has changed, really suddenly. And you don't know yet, at all, what your new life is going to be like. You don't know how you're going to feel when it sinks in that you don't have your father to look after any more. Will that be sad and horrible? Will it set you free? Both, probably: you just don't know yet, and you won't know, for a little while. I think you're reaching for me – you're grabbing at me – because you're trying to make everything solid again. Because marrying me seems like a kind of . . . replacement for what's vanished. Don't you think?'

Every part of this speech was composed of things she really thought and had truly observed, or honestly guessed at. Yet, taken together, it seemed to amount to one of the worst lies she had told in her generally shameless career as a liar.

'Maybe,' said Geoff. He put down his teacup carefully and stood up. He had not drunk any of the tea, and the cup rattled on its saucer when he put it down, because his hands were trembling. *Oh, Geoff.* 'I'd better go,' he said. 'I'm on from six until six tonight, so you'll probably be gone to work by the time I get back.'

'Actually,' she said, 'there's something I need to sort out before you go.' If she was going to be cruel, she might as well get it over all at once, in a lump.

'You don't want me to stay,' he suggested bleakly.

'No, *no*. Of course I do. But . . . if you're going to, and we find ourselves meeting the other people in the building, and specially if we're in the shelter in the basement together, you need to know that here I'm known as Mrs Saunders. That was the name I took the lease out under. So would you mind being Mr Saunders, just if anyone downstairs asks? They're rather proper people.'

Geoff stared at her. 'Let me get this straight,' he said. 'You won't marry me, but you'd like me to *pretend* to be married to you?'

There was always a limit to how much guilt Iris was willing to endure. 'Yes!' she snapped. 'Or, if you prefer, Mrs Saunders can be a dirty girl, and you can be her military bit on the side. But one or the other, please.'

Geoff touched his uniform cap with sarcastic obedience. 'I shall think it over carefully,' he said, and departed.

Iris groaned, and went to bed and hid her head under the pillow until the sirens sounded.

They shied away from this conversation by mutual consent. It was easy to do because they scarcely overlapped in the Chelsea flat over the days that followed. Geoff was out every night at Alexandra Palace, doing what he would only describe as 'radio stuff', and she was out every day at C&B, a more complex commute now that a parachute mine had destroyed the Underground station at Sloane Square. She would see him briefly at the breakfast table before she left; when she came home he would be either just departing or already gone. In his dawn walk back to the flat he would often shop, and he made meals for her before he left, described in little notes in perfect handwriting left on the kitchenette counter. *Experimental* MEAT LOAF *with* GRATED CARROT. POTATO CURRY *with chopped* HARD-BOILED EGG. But there was no sense of him taking over the kitchen. She had made him wary of even seeming to encroach, it appeared. He cleared up after himself so thoroughly that there were very few detectable traces of his presence, except the food itself, generated as if by some miraculous process that required no utensils and produced no washing-up. It was more like having a very punctilious fellow lodger than anything intimate. A bit of male slop and mess might have been reassuring. She could have been annoyed by it, for one thing. Chiefly, they were aware of each other's presence through the lingering warmth each left the other in the bed. She would climb under the covers for the precious first sleep before the raid began and find herself lying in a kind of thermal shadow of him. It wasn't erotic. They had added wariness to exhaustion, and relations between them were almost sexless. She called him into the bathroom to help change the dressing on her burn, and she was stripped to the waist when he came in. He applied ointment to the healing scar with gentle, precise fingers. He looked at her breasts in the mirror; oh yes, he did look, but when he was done he only put the tip of a forefinger on each of her shoulders, very lightly, and their gazes met in the glass, with big sad eyes.

Fifty-five nights. Fifty-six. Fifty-seven. Then, bizarrely, on 2 November there was a single night when the bombers didn't come. But the effect wasn't soothing, as the night away in Sussex had been. The rhythm of brief sleep followed by sudden waking had become ingrained, and she came to at the time when the sirens *would* have sounded, alone in the bed in Chelsea, assailed by silence and by the banging of her own pulse in her ears. *Emergency, emergency*, her body said; and then sleep refused to return, tired though she was. She lay in the dark, and as if a valve had opened in the silence to let through the black fluid of thoughts there was otherwise no time for, she found herself picturing Mr Hale's last minutes. The way he must have woken, out in the Anderson, and crept away from Geoff in search of the comfort of his paper cocoon indoors, and been encased in it when it abruptly proved to be no safety at all, sanctuary torn open into sarcophagus in one second of blinding light and rending force. Was there time for his baffled expression to turn to terror? He must have heard the bombs getting closer, and raised his mild gaze to the ceiling, and then— She got up, and went and smoked and drank tea in the kitchen.

She hoped, though, you couldn't not, that the pattern of nightly raids might now be broken. But the next night the Luftwaffe were back, and the one after that, and the one after that. Start the count again from one? No. Fifty-eight. Fifty-nine. Sixty. She took an afternoon off work, and walked with Geoff behind the coffin to see Mr Hale buried in Highgate Cemetery. They went back together afterwards to Chelsea, and in the lobby of Challoner Court bumped into the pipe-smoker who had farmed rubber in Malaya.

'Ah, the male of the genus Saunders!' he said, holding out his hand for Geoff to shake. 'I don't know why, I somehow had the impression you were Air Force?'

'No, no,' said Geoff. 'Army Signals. But of course I do work with planes quite a lot. I'm very versatile. I can be whatever is needed.'

'Er . . . jolly good,' said the planter, and left, puzzled.

'How was that?' Geoff asked in the lift. 'Versatile enough for you?'

'Shush,' said Iris miserably.

II

The more he effaced himself, the more he seemed like a foreign body the flat must inevitably expel. If he did not change it by living there, he clearly did not belong in it. She found herself beginning to wonder when she could gently, tactfully, ask him to find somewhere else to live.

Oddly, the thing they could still talk about was the bridge to Nonesuch, and what had happened to her on it. It represented, somehow, a continuing link to the lost household on Wildwood Terrace, where Geoff had had a hearth, though a strange one, and she had been welcomed to it and warmed at it. Sometimes she thought she missed dinner time at the Hales' kitchen table, with Geoff ironic and Mr Hale holding forth about the Great Pyramid, as much as she did the lost rapture of the summer nights. The mess of Wildwood Terrace, though not her kind of thing nor Geoff's either, had been stubbornly, recalcitrantly alive. And the golden rooms in Chelsea were turning cold and gold again, as the autumn deepened towards winter in the bombed city. Talking about the captive angels of the bridge, and its twisted geometry, and even the confrontation with Lall, invoked the mood of Wildwood without either of them having to name it.

'It must be very tight that the network functions at all,' said Geoff. 'There's hardly any redundancy left in it. Only twelve nodes—'

'Nodes?'

'Sorry; that's what you'd call them in topology. Points you can make connections to. Only twelve left, and pretty much all of them vulnerable to being Blitzed. You and Lall were fighting for possession of the fourth node, but if any of the statues go, you'd find yourself fighting over the third node next time. Or the second. Or the first. And one more statue lost after that and, glory hallelujah, the network conks out altogether. The odds must be quite good, if the bombs keep falling.'

'I can't count on that, though. I have to assume I'm going to meet her again. On that roof in Moorgate.'

'Or less far along. Have you thought what you're going to do about the gun?'

'No. Any ideas?'

'Well – not really. It occurs to me that she probably doesn't *want* to shoot you, if she can avoid it, because I'm guessing the gun is what she's carrying into the past to shoot Churchill with. She's probably only got the bullets that were with it when Sir Perceval left it in his desk drawer.'

'She seemed willing to spare one for me.'

'You could take a weapon too, I suppose. Radio Research isn't rich in side-arms, but if I put my mind to it I could probably find a way to borrow one. Or steal one.'

'I don't want to. The feeling when I thought I'd done for her – I can't tell you how horrible it was. I'm so glad I didn't.'

'I'm glad you didn't kill her too.'

'What,' said Iris, with a glimmer of the old teasing, 'have you still got a soft spot for her?'

'No,' he said, 'just for you.' And that closed *that* conversation down.

Sixty nights. Sixty-three. Sixty-five. Sixty-seven. Then, on 14 November, no bombers came – because, as the horrible pictures in the press next day showed, they had been hitting Coventry instead, where the density of the raid on a much smaller area achieved something close to a wipe-out. Rubble, and rubble, and rubble, where streets had been. Iris read herself back to sleep successfully this time, with a manual on futures trading. She expected the attack to switch back to London the next night, and she was indeed awakened on the night of the fifteenth at siren time, at raid o'clock. But not by sirens; not by the Luftwaffe. There were sounds coming from the kitchen. She got up to investigate, and there was Geoff, eating leftovers.

'They sent us home,' he said. 'Nothing's coming this way tonight either.'

'Oh,' she said, nonplussed. She stood in the doorway in her nightie, not knowing quite where to put herself. The prospect of spending unlimited hours in a confined space with Geoff filled her with a sensation something like embarrassment.

'Why don't I put the kettle on?' he said, doing it.

'Why not,' she said; but he was already bent over and looking inside the Frigidaire.

'I see you didn't eat the chocolate pudding,' he said.

'Ah,' she said, feeling on safer ground. 'That was because it's *disgusting*. Have you tried it?'

'No, it was still setting when I went,' he said. He fetched out a glass bowl, in which a brown mass had separated into two layers: a milky tan layer like a blancmange with grit in it, and on top a clear brown jelly. Geoff dug in a teaspoon.

'Urgh,' he said. 'Uch. Yech. Lord, that *is* disgusting. So much for "a rich chocolatey treat from just two teaspoons of cocoa powder". Down the plughole with *you*. I just hope it doesn't block the pipes.'

She stepped around him and made two mugs of tea.

'They're really not coming?' she said. 'I suppose you—'

'Can't tell you how I know? No, I can't. But they really aren't. It was nearly midnight when we decided to shut down, and they'd have shown up on – the thing I can't tell you about – if they were coming tonight.'

'So what time is it now?'

'About one.'

'Oh. Later than I thought. Well,' she said brightly, sitting down, 'this is unexpected, isn't it. What a treat.'

'Yes,' he said. 'A birthday present, in fact. Very well timed.'

'What do you mean?'

'Well,' he said, 'it is in fact . . . my birthday. Today. That's why I made the grotesque chocolate thing.'

'You didn't tell me.'

He shrugged. 'I didn't think you'd want to be bothered.'

'But I haven't got you anything!'

'Well . . .'

'You're just determined to find ways to put me in the wrong, aren't you?'

'What? Iris—'

'You didn't even give me the chance to do the right thing!'

'Iris, it doesn't matter. Come on. I don't feel very birthday-like, as a matter of—'

'That's not the point! That's not the point! It's just so – so typical of you – to *decide*—'

Out of nowhere, from a standing start, she found herself suddenly more upset than she could easily explain. It was as if a crust was cracking, and under it, hot and heaving and inexorable as lava, furies were waiting, and frustrations, and guilts, and a cheated feeling (though she couldn't have said if it was she who was cheated or she who was doing the cheating). And a vast, wretched loneliness.

'Get up,' she said. 'I'll give you a present.'

She had had an idea, which at that moment seemed irresistibly attractive, because it would make her feel powerful and him feel guilty for a change.

'Iris?'

'Come into the sitting room,' she said. It was all shadows in there. But rather than turning lights on, she turned off the lamp in the hall, so the darkness deepened, and the glow from the kitchen had to creep round two corners to leak in faintly. The brightest thing left in the room was the slight shine on the chrome tubes of the easy chair. She put him in it.

'Sit there,' she said, 'and shut your eyes.'

'I can hardly see anything anyway.'

'All the same. Are they shut? Now, I want you to feel . . . lordly. I want you to imagine you're a king. A powerful king. A powerful, lazy, selfish, greedy king. Who has just crooked his little finger to call up an obelisk from his harem.'

'Odalisque,' corrected Geoff automatically. 'But, Iris, I don't think—'

'Don't think at all,' she said. 'Just imagine.' She shucked the nightdress and knelt on the carpet in front of him. 'Because here she is. You can open your eyes now, but I want you to imagine that I'm completely naked.'

'You *are* completely naked. But—'

'What an imagination you have, my lord! Now, you say, "What do they call you, girl?" Go on.'

'I don't think I want—'

'And I say—'

'No—'

'*I* say, "Iris with the m—"'

'No! Stop it! Get up! I don't want to play this game!'

He tried to stand up. She held on to his knees.

'Yes you do,' she said. 'I know you do. You asked me for it, remember?'

'No I didn't!'

'Yes you did. You were all, "Show me the wicked stuff you know because you're such a slut, Iris!"'

'I never—'

'You didn't have to! You told all your friends about me!'

'All right,' said Geoff, his voice shaking. 'I did ask. But you persuaded me that it was a really bad idea, and I believed you. You said, *you* said, it would be . . . "a recipe for feeling less". Weren't you right?'

It seemed that the mind that let him calculate prime numbers also let her literal boy quote her back to herself verbatim, months later.

'Oh, you're so *good*,' she said disgustedly.

'No I'm not. No I'm not. I just don't want you to break things you care about to excite me, when everything else is already broken.'

What undid her in this was not that he was beginning to weep, as he had not done in her sight since his father died. It was that he still presumed this had been for his benefit. To excite *him*. He still believed she'd been trying to give him a present. There was trust there, and she had been trying to break it. But not in order to excite him.

'Oh God,' she said despairingly. She let go of him, scrambled up, snatched the nightie off the floor, and fled.

He came after her. 'Iris,' he said. 'Iris.'

She shut the bedroom door against him. 'Go away!'

'Come on, let me in.'

'Go *away*!' she wailed.

The handle stopped turning. He had let go of it. There was a thump and a scrape: the sound of a man sitting down on the hall carpet.

'I can move out if you want,' said Geoff's voice through the door, thick with tears. 'You only have to ask.'

'I don't mean that!' she said, though there was a large part of her that at this moment would find it easier if he did walk out of the flat and never come back. 'Oh, I don't know what I mean.'

And the lava of feeling came out of her own eyes as tears. Hot rivers, almost painful yet a relief too to have sorrow moving, rather than sitting in her as a solid mass, unexpressed, secret. Perhaps it hadn't been that secret. Geoff, making similar noises out in the hall, sounded wretched instead of surprised.

'I really meant to look after you,' she said. 'I really did. I'm sorry!'

He didn't reply. Perhaps he didn't know what to say.

Then for a little while there were the parallel sounds from both sides of the door of people doing their best to get themselves back, to reach the place after tears, where you gulp with a lump in your throat, and breathe shakily and carefully, and wipe your wet face on your sleeve.

'It all,' said Iris eventually, when she could, 'just . . . seems to be fading away between me and you. I don't want it to. I don't know what to do about it.' So much easier to admit this to white-painted plywood than to his face. 'I thought it was going to be different, with you. I thought *I* was going to be different. And I was for a while, Geoff, I swear I was. And it was lovely, it was the loveliest thing. But . . . it's like it's wearing off, and there's the old me underneath, just the same. I don't know. Maybe it's because I'm so tired.'

Silence from his side at this statement. At least she had finally uttered it.

'Geoff?'

'You *are* tired,' said the voice through the door, 'but I think it's more that you're frightened.' He hadn't been appalled or lost for words, he'd been thinking. Her technical boy, her deducer, her reasoner from information received, thought he was on the trail of an idea. She could hear it in his voice, hoarse though it was. She had forgotten this about him, somehow: the bright, indomitable spark in him that would remain stubbornly interested, determined to put the world in clear order, no matter how upset he was.

'There's a lot to be frightened about,' she said. 'Bombs. Hitler. Lall. Falling off roofs.'

'Oh, you can cope with all *that* stuff,' said Geoff. 'I meant with me.'

'I can't even get . . . bed right, any more. Do you know how humiliating it is, to do what I just did, and then be rejected in the middle of it?'

'I'm sorry,' said Geoff.

'I can't even make you want me any more.'

He gave a sort of sore-throated laugh. 'You don't have to *make* me want you. You're the one who's been pulling back from me. I want you all the time. In every way known to man. Or woman.'

'Do you?' she said.

'Well, I'm not going to prove it to you by breaking the door down and coming in there roaring: but, you know, I *could*.'

She found that her wet face was smiling.

'You're a beast of a man, Geoffrey Hale,' she said.

'You bring it out in me,' he said politely. 'But, Iris, really – that's not what you're worried about, is it?'

'Isn't it?'

'No. All that only went wrong because you're miserable. Iris? I've got a theory. Do you want to hear it?'

The stubborn mind, the literal mind, reading her soul like a wiring diagram. Perhaps what she had been doing these last few weeks, or was it months, was not receding from him, but reducing him, taking out qualities from her mental picture of him so he would be easier to leave. But she remembered now.

'All right,' she said.

'I don't think . . . our thing . . . is fading away at all. I don't think you're feeling less. I think you're frightened because we're past the beginning, and you started to believe it might last. I think you're frightened,' he said carefully, 'of what you'll lose if you go on loving me.'

A clever man, on the other side of the white woodwork. A man trying to win his own future, naturally, to talk what he wanted into existence; but also a man who was used to the care of impossible and spiky persons, such as Mr Hale, such as her. A man who now was trying to take care of her.

'So I need to ask you a question, Iris.'

'Oh, please don't ask me to marry you again. Not now.'

'Not that kind of question. Iris, what do you *want*?'

'Oh – you, of course, but it's all so tangled up—'

'No. I mean, what do you want in your life *apart* from me? What is it you're frightened of losing if you stay with me?'

'Geoff . . .'

'I can't reassure you if I don't know what it is.'

'Geoff . . .'

'Go on. Tell me. What have you got to lose? It's the middle of the night. In a war. In a city full of holes. Who's going to hear you but me?'

It was strangely difficult all the same. Geoff was not wrong, he had read her wiring diagram correctly. But ambitions were more private than desires; than even the most shameless and messy of desires. At least, hers were. She had filled her mind with them, she had daydreamed about them, she had inched towards them. She had never told them to anyone straight out. For fear of being laughed at, for fear of tempting fate, for fear that she would discover in the act of saying them out loud that she too thought they were impossible. She was glad the door was still closed.

'I want to be rich,' she whispered.

Pause.

'Why?' asked Geoff: and yes, there was surprise in his voice, at something which ran against the general ideals of their generation. You were supposed to be loftier than that, purer than that. But, Geoff being Geoff, she knew his question could also be taken straight. G. D. Hale required further information.

'Oh, it's not the money. – Well, I do like money. And I do want enough of it that I don't have to scrimp, and count, and worry. And I do want to drink champagne, champagne I pay for myself, and travel first class, and live in beautiful places, and wear beautiful things. – But really it's that I want to be part of the way the world works. I want to be in the room where the decisions are taken. I want to be able to make things happen. I want to see the angles. I want to issue bonds and float stocks and have the fate of industries in my hands. I want people to look at me – men to look at me – and for them *not to be able to ignore me* because they can't ignore the money. I want their fuses to blow, their tiny minds to stutter and shut down, because they look at me and see hips and tits and lips and eyes, a body they think *their* money can get them, and then have to ask me my opinion about interest rates. I want to condescend to every toffee-nosed public-school boy who condescended to my dad. I want to buy the mortgage on Lall's place in the country and turf her out of it. I want to be a tycoon. I want a yellow Rolls-Royce and a fur coat. I want to be a Rothschild, a Rockefeller, a J. P. Morgan – and when I am, I want everyone to know that I'm also Iris Hawkins from Watford.'

'You know you can't do any of that unless the war is won? Unless the danger passes, and Lall doesn't get to rewrite history, and peace comes?'

'I know. But it's what I want.'

'To take the world by storm.'

'*Yes.* Don't you dare laugh at me.'

'I'm not,' said Geoff. 'I'd like to see that. I'd like a ringside seat for that.'

'Really?'

'Really.'

She opened the door. There he was, red-eyed, with drying tear-tracks on his cheeks, but looking at her without ridicule. A strange boy: perhaps strange enough for a strange girl.

'You think I could do it?' she asked. 'I mean, really do it?'

'I don't know,' said Geoff, apparently not even noticing the possibility of a comfortable untruth here. 'But I'd like to watch you try. And I haven't seen you fail at anything yet.'

Except being kind to you. 'And you don't want me to be a good wife, making rissoles in the suburbs?'

'No. What *is* a rissole?'

'I don't know. A thing you make in the suburbs.'

She put her hand on his face: wonderingly touched his temple, his cheek, his lips.

'You're sure?' she said.

'I'm sure. Now you.'

'Now me what?'

He sighed and smiled at her. 'Now you ask me what *I* want, apart from you.'

'Oh,' she said. 'Right.'

They ended up with her sitting on the edge of the bed and Geoff between her knees on the floor with his back to her. She played with his hair, he turned his head and kissed her thighs from time to time, he talked and talked, about the patents he intended to take out and the need to improve television cameras. It was peaceful. It was nice. The pressure of his head in her lap was increasingly nice.

'. . . and I'd like to do more on the programme side too,' he said. 'With more mobile cameras you could get right away from the theatre metaphor.'

'I see,' she said. 'What time d'you think it is?'

'Probably about an hour more till dawn.'

And then she would have to gird her loins and go to work. But there was time – time to make him an invitation as little as possible like the last one. She leant over his head.

'Would you care to make love, Mr Hale?' she said.

'I would be enchanted to, Miss Hawkins,' said Geoff. 'Roar, roar,' he added.

III

She left him sleeping and went to work. Exhausted again – more exhausted than Sonia, Delia and Mrs Sinclair, who had spent the bombless night asleep rather than settling their futures – but cheerfully so; more cheerful than she had been since the summer.

When she got back, he was just getting ready to go, to stand his mysterious watch on the presumption the Luftwaffe would be back. She stood behind him at the mirror, and interfered with the tying of his tie.

'Still happy for me to be a millionaire?'

'Yes. – Get off, that's not how you do it. – Am I going to have to keep telling you over and over?'

'You surprised me, that's all.'

'Well, you can't read my mind, you know.'

'Actually . . . I sort of can?' It seemed like the moment to get rid of her remaining secret. She explained about the change to her hand. 'I know it's . . . unfair,' she said, and waited for Geoff to be angry, or feel intruded on.

Instead, he laughed.

'That's not mind-reading,' he said. 'Which hand is it?'

'The one I'm touching you with now.'

'Well, don't take it away. Move it up a bit, I've got to go to work. But tell me what I'm thinking.'

She saw . . . the very hall they were standing in, but suffused with a kind of extra brightness, not supplied by electric light bulbs. She saw a momentary flicker of the ruined pit that had once been

Wildwood Terrace. She saw her own face for another moment, and it was remote and closed off.

'You're feeling . . . hopeful. And sad underneath because of your dad. And still a little bit frightened. Of losing me?'

'Yes.'

She saw herself again, but looking very far from closed off, and from an angle she had never previously considered. Heavens, he really did want her all the time. Or a lot of it, anyway.

'And increasingly . . . distracted,' she said, stroking with fingertips. 'You distractable man.'

'Yes. Stop it. But I'm *thinking* of the Marconi-Osram MS4B tetrode with a screen grid and anode plates. All you got were moods. You can tell what my mood is. And so I should bloody hope if you care about me, magic hand or not.'

'Oh.'

'And now I'm going to Alexandra Palace, you wicked woman.'

She felt a certain urge to set him back.

'If I do marry you . . .' she said.

'Yes?'

'I suppose that means I mustn't fuck anyone else. Ever. No matter how tempting or interesting it is.'

'You are correct,' said Geoff, his eyebrows raised. He had gone satisfyingly still. 'Would that be difficult?'

She had meant to tease, but found she was thinking seriously about it. She tried conjuring notional men, and the whole exercise of searching the world for possible desire seemed thin and dull compared to what she already possessed, here and now, under her hands, and could not imagine reaching the end of. 'No,' she said.

'Good,' said Geoff.

He turned round, kissed her, picked up his briefcase and made for the door. Halfway through closing it behind him, he reopened it enough to stick his head round.

'And I suppose that applies to me too,' he said. 'Or were you taking that for granted?'

She went grinning to sleep in the warmth he had left, until the sirens woke her.

The bombing now became intermittent, largely it seemed because the Germans were hitting other cities. After any quiet night in London, there it was in the papers the next morning: raid on Manchester, raid on Bristol, raid on Sheffield. But the Heinkels were still back every few days, unpredictably, to try to burn the City and batter the West End and obliterate the docks. A new pattern developed, with a night or two – or three – of wary sleep between the raid nights. Iris took a turn fire-watching at the Mariner Building where nothing happened at all. The dark metropolis made its slight blackout noises of bus engines far off, occasional footsteps, tugboats on the river. It all creaked and settled, absorbing past nights' damage, and she yawned on the camping stool and fell asleep against the brick surround of the rooftop door, waking at dawn with a crick in her neck from the peculiar angle the tin hat had held her head at.

Things were undoubtedly easier. Everyone in the office seized the chance to bathe. (Except Mr Cornellis, who had been able to bathe uninterruptedly in Hertfordshire, and had come in freshly cologned even when otherwise unkempt.) There were new fuel-saving regulations about how much bathwater you were allowed – a mere five inches, which some people were reputed to be marking off inside the tub with a painted Plimsoll line. But the limiting factor on cleanliness turned out to be safe time to wash in, not how much water you got. If you were cunning and lay flat on your back in the bottom of the tub with your legs draped over the end, you could submerge yourself adequately in sections, like a snake bathing. Sonia and her mother took their towels to the Walthamstow Public Baths and paid thruppence each for a tub, Delia fired up the geyser in her landlady's bathroom in Lewisham, Mrs Sinclair applied fleur-de-lis scented soap out in Penge. And Iris sat in her inches of hot water in Chelsea and Geoff brought her a gin and tonic, having won a bottle of gin in a bet at Alexandra Palace whose nature he was not permitted to describe to her. The burn had almost healed. Easier times, for sure; and quite often the night was quiet enough for Geoff to be sent home, and she would wake to find him climbing into bed, and have enough energy to nip to the bathroom for her cap, and return to take possession of him. Deep and shaking and geological love, yes, they made some of that, but she was working on a new principle now, which was that if this love, this man, this desire was to be all the love, all the men, all the desires in her life from now on, there had better be room in this one love for all of what she was. And all of what she liked. All the moods, and not just the states of terrifying sweetness where she had no defences, and clinging as close as she could get to his heartbeat seemed like the only possible riposte to the fact of death. She also needed to be able to be greedy, to be shallow, to play with him. To enjoy making him gasp.

Easier times. But she discovered to her dismay that she was, if anything, more frightened now than she had been when the danger was continuous. Then she had been living entirely in the present tense, and on her wits' ends. Now she had a possible future to hold on to, in which she could have her plans without having to be alone, and it seemed small and fragile and vulnerable, this prospect, this just-maybe scheme that required as many things to go right as the number of corners light had had to bounce round in Geoff's experiment with the shaving mirrors. And it had to be carried intact through a world of jogs and shocks and disasters; a world that might knock it with a shrug from her fingers at any moment. She had something to lose.

One evening, without thinking, she left the office yawning and got onto the Northern Line train towards Hampstead, because it was a Tuesday. She remembered, as soon as the Tube train left the station, that there was nothing – nobody – waiting for her in Wildwood Terrace any more, and felt stupid, almost ashamed, that she could have forgotten. But it made sense now she was moving to go on north a few stops, and then switch to the Piccadilly Line. The train went through the deep stations under the City that she hadn't seen lately, on her commute west to Chelsea. On the platforms now there were not just encampments of people getting ready to sleep in huddled blankets, there were organised rows of wooden bunk beds: a subterranean world, a busy throng of shadows loud with conversation, grunts, moans, echoing announcements, babies crying, every time the doors slid open. And through the blankets, past the bunks, working hard not to step on people, travellers like her picked their way, homeward bound from offices and shops. The doors slid open, the doors slid shut. The thrum of wheels on track took over from the human roar again. The overhead lights were yellow, and flickered. She looked at the faces of the women opposite, tired, closed, stoic, and wondered how many – it must be many – also had missing family, people who had seemed essential and inevitable to their world and then been snatched away as suddenly as Mr Hale had been. Dragged on the instant down one of the holes torn in the city. And here they still were, since they were not the dead ones, under the weary yellow lighting, sharing the unspoken knowledge in her own head that, every night the bombers came, ten thousand possible exits from life opened silently, and unpredictably, and without appeal, down which anyone and anything could fall, no matter how precious. She got off at King's Cross and went home.

When Geoff came back late, or didn't come at all, she immediately expected the worst. She lay in the dark with her mind racing, thinking how much more probable it was that he should be lost than that she should be allowed to keep him. Was this the cost of happiness? It hadn't been in the summer. But that had been blind ecstasy. It had been like being drunk. All now, now, now. It hadn't depended on a *then*, or given her the vertigo of wanting a then she might not get. She found herself wondering why, exactly, she loved him. Not that she doubted it, or believed it would stop, but it might seem a little safer if she knew what it was resting on. She might be able to put down her smashable pot of happiness on a solid shelf of reasons – if she could name the reasons.

Was it because he was kind? Yes, but she liked his pepperiness too, his unpredictable clever scorn. Was it that, even when he was angry, he was a giver of care, instinctively a holder and supporter? Yes, that; he had been made by the chaotic house in Hampstead, and the struggle from much too early in his life to be the one who clothed and fed and made order, for a maddening and incapable person who was nevertheless loved. And now he went on doing it, with her the lucky beneficiary. Or was it the quick mind, different from hers but just as fast? If she tried to run rings around him she was likely to meet him ringing her in the other direction. She could upset him, confuse him when she was confused herself. But she did not seem able to fool him. Which was an excitement. And a joy. And a burden. To be *known*, that was certainly part of it. To be hoicked out of her long secrecy. Not to be alone. His naivety was embarrassing. His lack of savoir-faire was shocking. Compare him to her old City boyfriends and he scored pathetically low on worldly pizzazz and masculine swagger, qualities she enjoyed so long as their possessor was stupid enough. But the conventional things he had missed out on, in his strange isolated life, were also those she would have had to hide from, to conceal her true intent from, if they had been possessed by any other clever man. (Any other clever, kind man. There were plenty of kind men who wanted to press you kindly, gently, into servitude.) With him she didn't have to hide. And then of course she fancied him at least as much as any of the dim, moneyed swaggerers. His long bones. His blushing fairness. His unexpected strength. The salt-and-flat-irons savoury taste of him.

After enumerating his virtues like this, she was of course nastier to him when he returned. Tetchy, critical, demanding, poking and prodding at him to prove he was solid. Then she clung to him all night.

'Love, I can't quite breathe if you do that,' said Geoff, when her grip grew particularly octopus-tight. 'Is something the matter?'

'What if you vanish?' she whispered. 'What if I lose you now I've found you? What would become of me if I had to do it all without you?'

'I'm not going anywhere,' said Geoff. Then added, honest assessor of the world that he was, 'I'm not going anywhere if it's up to me.'

28 November was getting closer. The closer it got, the more ridiculous it seemed to be adding the dangers of magic to the dangers of the bombs, if there was any chance of avoiding them.

She found herself thinking about the change she had seen in Lall the last time, up on the rooftop in Moorgate. The alteration she hadn't been able to fathom. A crack in the china of the china doll, no matter what a little horror she remained. Perhaps the crack had widened. Perhaps the crack could be encouraged to widen. It might at least be worth trying to see if the whole mad high-wire act over the rooftops could be omitted.

She supposed Geoff might know where Lall lived, or at least where Lall had lived before the war began, but she didn't want to involve him in her fear. She wanted to deal with it by herself. In any case she absolutely did not want to meet Lall on Lall's own territory, or when she was alone, given that she had promised to kill Iris if she ever saw her again.

Other than that, the only lead she had was the Mechanised Transport Corps. She found the MTC in a tall house in Kensington.

'I'm looking for Lalage Cunningham,' she told a grand old bird in tailored khaki, using her best Chelsea vowels.

'One of our gels?' said the GOB, friendly enough. 'I'll look through the cards, my dear.'

But when the card was found, and the GOB dipped her iron-grey hair to read it, the friendliness abruptly vanished.

'No longer with us,' she said curtly. 'May I ask where you know her from?'

This was interesting. It seemed that Blackshirt sympathies were no longer socially acceptable, however aristocratic you were. Iris guessed that the card probably said *SECURITY RISK* on the back, or words to that effect. Not suitable to drive politicians. Potential fifth-columnist. *I did that*, she thought, with a certain amount of glee. *Reached a long arm round, through Miles at the Treasury, and messed up Lall's cosy little billet*. Which was fine, but didn't help with finding her.

'Oh, she's not a friend,' said Iris. 'We were in a . . . mountaineering club together. Never really got along. But someone we both know is dead, and I felt she ought to be told.'

'It might be more sensible to leave her alone.'

'It's a bit of a debt of honour, is the thing,' said Iris, wondering whether she was overdoing the voice and sounding like a Noël Coward character. Apparently not: she was getting a sympathetic twist of the iron-grey eyebrows. 'One owes things to people whether one likes them or not, doesn't one?'

'I see your difficulty,' said the lady. 'Very well. It says here she transferred to the London Auxiliary Ambulance Service. Post 37, Paddington.'

'Thank you *so* much,' said Iris.

IV

Post 37 was a converted Scout hall, in a street of grimy houses half obliterated by blast. As many gaps as teeth in London's mouth, here. A section of levelled rubble nearby served as the park for the ambulances, and when Iris came picking her way across it the next Sunday morning she found Lall's vehicle at the far end, and a small wasteland bonfire burning next to it. Two girls Iris didn't know were feeding it with broken scraps of window frame to encourage a kettle strung over the top to boil, and the old paint on the wood was making a black, oily smoke. Beside them, propped against an old door with her cap over her eyes, a familiar slight shape was snoozing on the ground. The air was chilly and the upmost stones of the rubble had the crystal furriness of frost on them, but Lall seemed comfortable. Iris was tempted to poke her with a foot, but probably Lall had managed to surround herself with adorers; she usually seemed to.

'Hallo,' she said instead to the two by the fire. 'I've been looking for your driver here.'

'Oh, we all drive,' said the one on the left, a gangly redhead. 'You mean Lazybones Lall, though, I imagine.'

She got up, and did exactly what Iris had decided not to: applied a toecap, though in a friendlier way than Iris would have done. A gentle prod to the ribs. 'Wake up, sleepyhead,' said the redhead. 'One of your society pals to see you.'

Lall scrubbed at her face, dislodging the cap. The china doll had no make-up, the china doll looked tired, the china doll was smirched with the dirt of the ruined city. The Ambulance Service outfit was less fetching on her than the MTC one. Did she still look marvellous? Oh, of course she did. She would probably look good dressed as a bus conductor: something about the way that the decisive lines of a uniform, any uniform, went with the absolute symmetry of her face. Then she yawned and opened her eyes. Iris expected ice, expected outrage at the lèse-majesté, but Lall's expression was almost fond, at least until she took in Iris, standing back in her good coat and her beret. Then it went guarded; with some of the familiar savagery behind, hastily tucked back out of sight.

'Oh,' she said. 'It's you. What on earth are you doing here?'

'I've come to offer you a cigarette, and see if we can't sort things out like civilised people.'

'Oho,' said the redhead. 'What's this? Are we about to gain some frightful insight into our Lall's secret life?'

'No we aren't,' said the girl still tending the fire, curly-haired with a pimple on her nose, 'because *we're* Lall's secret life, didn't you know?'

'Shut up, do,' said Lall. Said Lall comfortably; said Lall easily. She stretched on the ground, a cat indifferent to the dust it was lying in, and hopped to her feet. The poker up her spine appeared to have vanished. 'Come on, then,' she said to Iris. She waved a lordly hand at the rubble. 'We'll take a turn around the estate, and you can say your piece. I wouldn't mind a gasper.'

'A gasp-ah! A gasp-ah!' said the redhead delightedly, doing Lall's voice.

'Run away, run away, little girl,' said Lall, flicking at the air. The redhead snickered and went back to the fire. Lall strolled off a few yards and waited for Iris to catch up. When she did, Lall walked insistently on again. The message was clear: *I want you away from my friends*. Perhaps it was simply because Lall didn't want to be overheard, but it seemed almost protective. Protective of *them*.

There had been affection there, in the teasing: an emotion that Iris had not known Lall was capable of eliciting, in sane people.

'You seem to have landed on your feet,' said Iris.

'What do you want? Let's get this over with.'

'I mean, they actually seem to *like* you.'

'I suppose I shouldn't be surprised you've turned up. It's like having a stray dog follow you around. I look down, and there you are. Mangy. Unkempt. Constantly underfoot.'

'I thought you just did . . . adorers. I didn't know you could manage friends.'

'Are you just here to be rude?'

'You can talk,' said Iris. 'I'm wondering – do they know what you are? Do they know why you got thrown out of the MTC?'

'That was your doing, was it?'

'Yep,' said Iris.

'Well, you did me a favour,' said Lall.

'I didn't mean to.'

'All the better. Where's this cigarette, then?'

Iris dug out a couple of Player's. Lall stuck hers in her mouth and stood with her hands in her trouser pockets, waiting for it to be lit. Iris struck the match and held it for her, remembering her extracting the same service at the Kinesis Club – though then in grande-dame mode, in the Schiaparelli dress, and now poised in the landscape of ruin like an absurdly pretty urchin, with a smut on her nose.

It was an insouciant stance, even a charming one. But Iris had to make herself stand close enough to touch the flame to the tobacco. These were the hands that had stabbed Weevil, pushed the burning candle into Beetle's eye, held a gun on her while musing aloud whether to use it. This was a person without the usual brakes: someone for whom violence wasn't a reluctant last resort but a comfortable first thought.

'Thanks,' Lall said, and blew smoke at Iris. 'How is Geoffrey?'

'He's fine. His father was killed, though.'

'That silly old man?'

'Yes, that silly old man. But Geoff misses him. And so do I.'

'Then I'm sorry,' said Lall with a shrug. 'A lot of people are being killed.'

'You sound heartbroken.'

'I *am*,' said Lall with sudden fierceness. 'I see it every night. Last week they dug a little boy out – four streets away, that way – and his whole bottom half was crushed. Just squashed. Like . . . meat. So don't you dare say I don't care.'

Iris put up her palms placatingly. *Who drops the bombs, Lall, who's doing the killing?* she wanted to say, but the object here was not to quarrel with this new version of Lall, if she could manage it. Lall took the gesture for submission and sneered.

'I'm amazed you're still with Geoffrey,' she said. 'I'd have thought your . . . *type* . . . would have moved on long ago. It's not as if there's much to him but puppy-dog eyes and sweaty hands.'

'Perhaps you didn't look hard enough,' said Iris, stung. 'We're getting married, actually.'

'Gosh,' said Lall. 'Well, congrats and all that. – Really?'

'Really. So I'm here to see if—'

'*So* bizarre. But then,' she continued unexpectedly, 'I suppose I'm no judge. I'm not all that keen on men, to be honest.'

She was gazing back at the fire, and the other two girls in the ambulance crew, an expression on her face that Iris was not familiar with; at least, not familiar with on Lall. Iris followed the line of her look.

'They think we talk the same, you and I,' Iris said.

'Well, Ruby is only a solicitor's daughter. She can't be expected to distinguish the genuine article from the grotesque effect of your elocution lessons, or whatever it is you've been doing. *I* can hear what you are with every syllable that comes out of your mouth, don't worry.'

'Ruby,' said Iris, picking the fact out from the garnish of insult. 'The red-haired one, right? The one who calls you Lazybones Lall.'

'She's *allowed* to,' said Lall. 'She can call me whatever she likes. She's earned it. She's . . . as true as steel.'

Iris remembered the girls who had picked her up, the night of the shrapnel burn. The jokey, weary front-line closeness in that front seat, between people driving the ruined streets from catastrophe to catastrophe. Night after night of that might well crack a china doll.

'Ruby and . . . ?'

'Harriet,' said Lall stiffly. The one with the pimple, the one still by the fire, lifting the kettle off the flames with a rag wrapped round the handle. There was a slight, endearing clumsiness to her management of the weight of it. You could see that she was the kind of person who would trip on rugs and knock ornaments off side tables. Definitely a prefect's friend, not a prefect. Almond-shaped eyes. Sweet. When she felt Lall's gaze, she waved.

'Oh my goodness,' said Iris, understanding something. It wasn't just affection.

'What?'

'Lalage Cunningham, you're in love.'

'*What?*'

'With Harriet over there.'

'I am not!' said Lall. 'Shut up! You make everything – filthy. That's – disgusting.' Twin spots of red had appeared in her china cheeks.

'Is it?'

'Yes! I am not some bloody . . . invert.'

'Lall, when you look at her, you go all pie-eyed.'

'That's friendship! I don't know if you've heard of it!'

But Lall turned her back sharply on the fire, so the betraying face was no longer towards Harriet. Puffing furiously, the blush spreading, she fixed her eyes on the distant row of shattered buildings.

'She's got a lovely mouth,' said Iris evilly. 'Are you telling me you don't want to kiss it?'

'Shut *up*!' wailed Lall. The fascist, the bloody-handed little fury, had been replaced by an embarrassed schoolgirl out of her depth.

I must stop jabbing her, thought Iris. *It isn't what I came for. But it's so bloody tempting. She sent a monster after me for stealing a man from her, a man,* when all along she was a ladies' pond bather. A Sapphist. A sipper from the well of loneliness. So *tempting to make her squirm, now I can. But it's not what I came for. It's* not *what I came for. This needs encouraging, not mocking, if I can.*

'Whatever it is,' she suggested, 'it seems to make you happy?'

'Yes it does! The way it is! Without any of that . . . stuff.'

'I suppose, that stuff that Daddy wouldn't approve of.'

'Daddy doesn't get a vote, seeing as he's in prison. I told you before, it's got nothing to do with him! It's what *I* want. And what I don't want. If—' said Lall, and stopped, suddenly at some threshold of the speakable.

'If?' Iris asked as gently as possible. 'Come on, spit it out. Tell your enemy. If you can't tell your enemy, who can you tell?'

'If I – if I did – what you said . . .'

'And she liked it . . .'

Blank look. Wrong direction. It was her own desires Lall was wrestling with. Even uncertain, even in love, the thought of someone else not falling in with what Lall wanted was beyond her.

'No, I mean, if I did— Look here. You're a person of some . . . experience.'

'So you keep insisting.'

'How do you – know you'd be – the *same* afterwards? That you wouldn't just be – gone?'

Oh, the cliffs of fall. Love's landscape of terrible transformations. Lall was glimpsing that, was she? Iris had never had to cope with wanting something the world declared unnatural. The unpermitted things she had dared herself to do were the ones the world thought were all too natural and young women had to be kept away from in case they liked them too much. She'd never had to deal with desires that any part of her own self wished to be without. But this fear, she recognised: this awful hesitation on the brink of being changed. She could even sympathise with it.

'I'm sorry, you don't know,' she said. 'Take it from a slut. You can't know. Because it's powerful; because it *may* all go wrong; because you're putting yourself in someone else's hands, and trusting a new bit of you too. Because you won't be gone but you probably will be different. You definitely will be, if it matters. If it's the real thing. You just have to . . . let yourself do it. Let yourself go over the waterfall. – For the record, I only just learned that myself.'

'But that sounds awful,' said Lall. Frown of puzzlement. 'Why would you *want* to?'

'Because it's exciting? It's like . . .' What analogy would work for Lall? Like fighting, would be the truest one in Lall's case, based on what Iris had seen that ever gave her pleasure. Like fighting, only with it being love instead of hate that made it fierce, and the struggle being to deal delight instead of wounds, and the to-and-fro shoving and squeezing and heaving and wrestling of it all being a collaboration, not a contest, and the surrenders being as welcome as the triumphs. But—

'No,' said Lall decisively. 'I don't want that. I expect you do because you're coarser. I *don't* want to kiss her.' The blush again. 'I want,' she said proudly, 'to protect her. Her and Ruby. They're my cause now.'

'And not Herr Hitler? Not the world with the Daddies in charge forever?'

'It's called order,' said Lall, but not as if her heart was fully in it.

'An order in which you're not supposed to be anything but a baby-machine for some blond beast who doesn't care what you want.'

'You don't know what you're talking about.'

'Oh, I do. Mr Hitler wants to give you a medal for having fourteen babies, and not for anything else. Do you know what an episiotomy is?'

'No,' said Lall. 'You have your breeding population – that's you – and you have your masters. That's me.'

'Oh, Lall. Lall! *Think*. You don't really believe that. You don't really believe they'd leave you alone, do you? You're a woman.'

Lall looked mulish. Not a thought she wanted to entertain; not a category she wanted to be confined by. Perhaps she believed that men, if they got in her way, could all be dealt with like Weevil and Beetle.

'And anyway,' said Iris, trying something else, 'you don't really believe your Harriet is *less* than you, do you? Your Harriet and your Ruby,' she added, trying to keep the romantic edge off things, since that seemed to be what Lall wanted. What Lall could manage.

'I did.'

Past tense. Iris felt as if she was walking an uncertain trail along a razor-backed mountain ridge, with a drop to the left, a drop to the right.

'And . . . now?'

'And now I don't know! I thought, when they were all locked up: *it's up to you now. Shake off the horrible old men, and show that you can do what the chaps couldn't. Prove yourself!* It was . . . thrilling. – You know, it's very odd, talking about this to *you*.'

'Who else would get it? Don't stop. Have another cigarette and keep telling me.'

'Thanks,' said Lall. 'Well, then . . . I realised that I was on my own. *Really* on my own. For the first time ever. And if it was up to me, it was up to me to decide, as well, what the right thing was. And then you got me thrown out of the MTC, and I had to do *something*, so I signed up for the Auxiliaries, and I met *that* pair of terrible, common oiks, and they were lovely, and I realised I cared far more about taking care of them than I did about the New Order, or biffing you, or any of that other stuff. Being with them – it's like . . . coming home.'

What could the cold house in the shires with the dogs and the brother have *been* like, if digging up half-crushed children, if sluicing blood out of the back of an ambulance, beat it for homeliness? But no, thought Iris, that was unfair. She had her own experience of the war unexpectedly providing a place to stand, a place to belong.

'I really like it,' said Lall earnestly. 'I like it more than anything. I *hated* being a debutante. Well, except for the admiration.'

'There's a surprise.'

'If you're going to be rude—'

'I am going to be rude.'

'I suppose you are,' said Lall, and surprised Iris by laughing. The laugh of someone lightened by uttering out loud what had been incommunicable till then, she thought. She had used the tell-your-enemy line on Lall as a way of jollying her along, but perhaps there was some deeper truth in it. Lall was the last of the Order, the last of her family left unimprisoned. She had her Harriet even if she didn't dare name what she felt for her, she had her new little world of comradeship and peril in the ambulance, but she must be keeping secrets there, surely. It was possible that Iris – whom she hated, who hated her – was genuinely the only person who understood the position she was in. Or at least the night-time part of it; the dark-of-the-moon part.

At the fire, Harriet, seeing them both laughing, held up the steaming kettle in a questioning fashion. *A mug of tea for you and your friend?* Lall waved a no.

'Well, this is marvellous,' said Iris.

'Is it?'

'*Yes*. It means you can stop. It means *we* can stop, both of us. Racing for Nonesuch is going to get one of us killed, you know, if we go on; it's amazing it hasn't already.'

'No, we can't,' said Lall pityingly. 'Well, you can stop, and I hope you do. But I certainly can't. I have to get to Nonesuch more than ever.'

'Why? *Why*, if you're not a fascist any more?'

'Isn't it obvious?' said Lall.

'Not to me, no.'

'Of course, you lack the aristocratic outlook. I'm responsible for them, aren't I? It's my job to protect them. And I *can*. Don't you see? I can keep Ruby and Harriet safe from falling walls, and landmines, and time bombs, and being buried, and drowning in a water main. I can keep the whole city safe, if you'll just stop interfering and let me. I can stop the bombs from falling. I can make it so they *never* fell. I can make all this' – Lall waved her fresh cigarette at rubble, ruins, exhaustion, the entire Blitz cityscape – 'go away. I can make it so it never happened. I can make it so nobody died. I know you think I'm some sort of terrible cackling villain, but that's what I want. I want to bring them all back. All of them! Everyone who's died in our ambulance, because the road to the hospital was blocked. The boy who got cut in half. Geoffrey's father, for that matter! Silly old Mr Hale. I can have him alive again, by the day after tomorrow, smelling of old socks and maundering on about the pyramids. You should tell Geoffrey that – tell him what I'm trying to do, and ask him whether he thinks you should stop me.'

'I won't do that,' said Iris, shocked.

'Why ever not?'

'Because it would be cruel! It would be offering him the thing he wants most, and saying he has to sacrifice the whole world for it.'

'What rubbish! "The whole world" – honestly! It would be peace, it would be everything back to normal, that's all.'

'It would be England under Hitler's thumb.'

'You'd rather have *this*?' The cigarette wave again.

'Yes I would! This is awful, but at least it's freedom.'

'I suppose you would think that,' said Lall. 'After all, what do you do? You sell stocks and shares for a Jew in an office. I, on the other hand, save lives.'

Iris opened her mouth and closed it again, aghast. She had a nightmarish sense of a safety that had been just in reach slipping away. She had come prepared to argue with fascism, with black magic, but not with this crazy self-righteousness. There was something wrong with Lall's scheme, beyond its terrible consequences for the world; something intrinsically warped, off, misformed, about trying to erase the last months, to unweave their mixture of horrors and braveries. But how to name it? The angels might know; it was presumably at the root of their objection to the whole idea of the bridge to Nonesuch. A violence done to time. But that was too abstract. The thing about not separating the mix of bravery and horrors, that was closer, but it made it sound as if she thought the first justified the second, and that wasn't what she meant at all. What was it, what was it? Why did she find it so instinctively vile to think of someone snipping the mourning out of the story of Geoff's life in Anno Domini 1940, and handing it back to him edited?

Her enemy was waiting, head cocked.

'Don't you want to keep what you've gained this year?' Iris settled for saying. 'What you've found, what you've learned? If you did it, if you changed this year – you'd make it so that you never were in the Ambulance Service, you never met those two, you were never . . . at home with them. All of that would . . . wink out. It'd be gone, and you wouldn't even miss it. Come on. Come on, Lall. You're happy. Don't you want to keep it?'

Just for a moment, the thought of this struck home. She could see the dismay on the perfect little face. But then the alarming light of belief rekindled in Lall's eyes, unreasonable, implacable. Instead of an urchin, or a schoolgirl, or a grande dame, she now looked like a soldier-saint. Joan of Arc or somebody. Enraptured. Ready to give up everything. It was surprising there wasn't a beam of light shining down across the bombsite onto her face. *For heaven's sake*, thought Iris despairingly. *Why can't Harriet just stick her hand in your knickers, and replace that expression with a more sensible one?*

'It would be a sacrifice,' said Lall, 'yes. But I'd be doing it for *them*, don't you see? Sometimes one has to be unselfish.'

The idea in the small mind had changed, but she was gripping the new idea just as tightly, just as exclusively as the old one.

'And now I think you'd better be going,' Lall said, flipping away the cigarette butt.

'Oh God,' said Iris. 'So it's the battle on the rooftops after all, is it?'

'It doesn't have to be!' said Lall. 'If you'd just leave me to get on with it.'

'You know I can't do that.'

'Well, then,' said Lall. 'See you soon. I'm so glad we've had this little talk, because we won't be speaking much next time.'

She put out her hand formally. Iris shook it, and it was like stroking some small, elegant carnivore. From the contact with the neat palm and the slender fingers came eagerness and threat, the sincere enthusiasm of the panther for the next meeting, at which it plans to eat you.

'So long, slut,' said Lall.

'So long, bitch,' said Iris.

V

But she was trembling when she got home. Geoff was in the kitchen cooking, and listening to something on the radio he had recently installed in the sitting room.

'What?' he said, when he saw her face. 'What's happened? What is it?'

'She won't stand down.'

'Who? – Lall? You've seen Lall?'

'Yes. The dark of the moon is tomorrow night—'

'I don't lose track of when you're going to be in mortal danger.'

'Well, I was trying to see if there was any way out of it.'

'You've changed your tune.'

'This is what comes of suddenly having a future you want. It makes you a terrible coward. So I went looking for her.'

'But no luck? She hasn't changed her mind?'

'No, she *has*. That's what's so maddening. She's found a whole new reason for handing the country to Hitler.'

'Explain?' he said: a request, not an instruction.

She did her best to. The radio burbled in the next room. 'You see?' she said. 'The new version is just as bad as the old one. And now I have to take on all the insane risks of the bridge again, with the guaranteed knowledge that somewhere along the way she'll be waiting with Daddy's gun. Perhaps I should have said yes when you offered to find me one. What am I supposed to do, take the kitchen knife with me?'

Naming the fear seemed only to be making it grow, to be opening a pit that widened and widened. Geoff put his hands on her shoulders, and she shook.

'I pushed her off the roof!' she said. 'It was done! It was all over! Why did I pull her up again?'

'You know why,' he said.

'Yes,' she said. 'Because it felt bad. It *felt* bad. That's pathetic. That was so *weak*.'

'No it wasn't,' he said, and gave her an emphasising little squeeze. 'It was the very opposite. And look: I've been wondering whether you actually do need to do the Nonesuch thing tomorrow. Hang on, I'll get a piece of paper and show you.'

He left the kitchenette. She hugged her arms round herself. In his absence, the stream of sound from the radio reorganised itself into recognisable voices. *'Ere, Bert,* said one, in parodic, almost music-hall Cockney, *you know why there aren't enough shelters for the likes of us? 'Cause them Jews keep 'em all for themselves, that's why. I reckon—*

'What the hell is that?' she called. 'That's not the BBC!'

'God, no,' said Geoff, coming back. 'Sorry. That's something nasty on the medium wave, cooked up in Germany. My lot have been asked to look into jamming it but it probably isn't worth the resources. I'll turn it off.'

A click, and the matey insinuations of hate were cut off: to continue in the ether, jostling in the crowded airwaves of the European night. Geoff moved the chopped onions, and put a blank page in front of her.

'Look,' he said, beginning to draw. 'It occurred to me that we really know quite a lot about this Nonesuch network by now.'

'I've only got four arches in,' she objected.

'But put all the data together, and we have something like . . . this.'

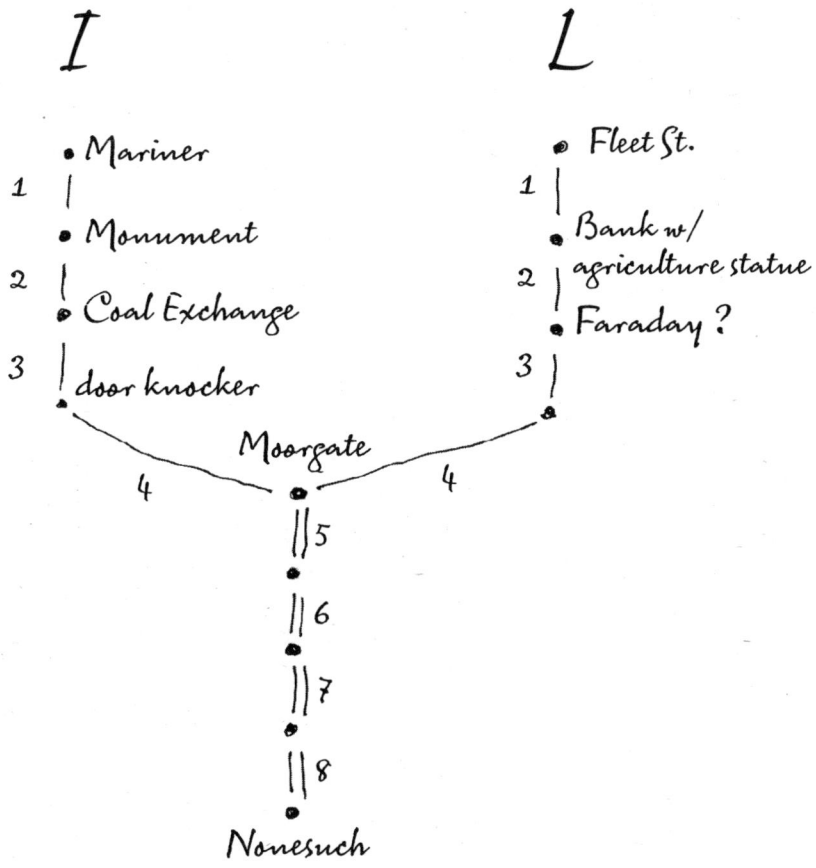

'That may not be where the Mercury on Faraday House comes,' she objected.

'I know,' Geoff said. 'Hence the question mark. We know that any of the statues can be used as the first entrypoint. But if you start from the same place, as you've done twice from the Mariner, we know you get the same statues in the same order, so that must be true for Lall too. In order to get to the rooftop at Moorgate, she'll have passed through four statues she knows by now: the Sills head on Fleet Street, the agriculture lady who tries to hit her with the stone sheaf, wherever that is, and then either two we don't know, or one we don't know plus the Faraday one. And she can *only* get in by the statues she knows about. Her access to the network is vulnerable, is what I'm saying. Not just vulnerable because of the lack of redundancy in the network as a whole—'

'—so that if any four of the twelve statues get Blitzed, it isn't possible to make the eight arches to Nonesuch at all—'

'—exactly; but also specifically vulnerable if anything goes wrong with the much more limited set of statues she can use as entry-points. Lall *doesn't* know about the Monument, the Coal Exchange and your vicious little suburban doorknocker, because only you have gone that way. She is aware of the ones on her own route and nothing else. Now, the unknowns on her side are a worry. Maybe they're conveniently close to the ground, like the Coal Exchange dragon is for you, and she has an easy back-up way in. But probably not, and she may not even know where they are in terms of real-world London addresses. Or maybe Agriculture Lady – who sounds like she's in one of those sculpture groups of the Productive Arts, you know, up on top of a bank or something like that – is somewhere that a small ambulance driver can get at in the blackout, during a raid. But it seems unlikely. So my money is on her having just the Fleet Street statue as her entrypoint, with the Moorgate one as her back-up.'

'So?'

'So, my advice is that you get up early tomorrow morning and make a longer walk to work. Go and look for bomb damage on Fleet Street, go and see if the Moorgate building is still there. If they aren't, the probabilities say to me that you don't need to risk yourself.'

'Probabilities, not certainties,' said Iris, disappointed. 'I was hoping you could whip something rock-solid and mathematical out of your hat.'

'Sorry,' said Geoff. 'Probabilistic comfort only. On the bright side, in about three-quarters of an hour I can offer you the certainty of a hot dinner.'

But then the sirens went, and he wasn't able to get back to his vegetables until they were released from the basement shelter at three in the morning, by which time the moment for cookery had passed, and they settled for fish-paste sandwiches.

Fleet Street was only a detour from her usual morning route up Ludgate Hill. She was disappointed to see that it was largely intact. The occasional gap, with timber beams shoring up the buildings on each side, but the *Telegraph* was present, the *Express* in its gleaming deco black and chrome was present, the *Daily Chronicle* . . . Wait a minute. It hadn't been shattered by HE, but wasn't that fire damage to the top floor? She crossed the street and craned up. Yes, soot and smear in the grey morning light, and a definite sag in the roofline where an unextinguished incendiary had burned through, and been allowed to consume some of the structure before the fire brigade could deal with it. Not new damage; days old at least. Were the decorative stone heads that had adorned the top of the facade still there? It was hard to tell in the general blackening. Maybe yes, maybe no. But when she crossed back and peered at the main entrance on the ground, it was locked and barred, and gave every sign of being a building from which a newspaper was no longer being published. No Blackshirt-indulging proprietor would be telling his commissionaires to let Lall in *there*.

Tentatively heartened, she set off back down towards the foot of Ludgate Hill – and was heartened again. Unbeautiful though the morning was with its low roof of cloud, there was her city arrayed for her. On the far side of the Ludgate dip, there was the tethered planet of St Paul's rising up above the wedding-cake stucco. Water-stained wedding cake, smoke-damaged wedding cake, wedding cake with holes punched through it here and there, but still telling its respectable story, still fronting the inkhorn warren where sealing wax and wig powder were sold. *My London*, she thought, proud of its endurance, untroubled that she was simultaneously wishing for specific buildings in it to be blown to smithereens.

In Moorgate, though, the corner building with the art nouveau nymphs on the chimney was annoyingly and completely intact. Buildings further along had burned last night, and the fire brigade were still rolling up their flaccid grey hoses among the feet of the thickening flow of commuters. But nothing had smashed the rooftop she was interested in, nothing had let the enslaved angel on it out in a soda-water streak of joy. Her spirits plummeted, and she went on towards the office at a trudge, her eyes set miserably on the pavement, thinking of Lall and guns, guns and Lall, only looking up when on an alley between Cornhill and Lombard Street she found the way blocked by a grey mass of fallen masonry. Something major had collapsed around the corner and been pushed off the main thoroughfare by the steam-shovels of Rescue, to await later clearing. She could go back and go around, but the mound seemed fairly solid, and there was another woman ahead of her picking her way successfully over the top.

She climbed. It was worse than it looked, though. Just past the summit her heel sank in and caught, she toppled forward, over-compensated, and slid down to the pavement on her backside in a small landslip of rubble and clinker. Cursing and dusting herself down, checking her skirt for rips and her stockings for ladders, her eye fell on a piece of broken stone by her feet. There was something about it . . . It was what was left of a sculpted stone bundle of something, tied with a stone string and radiating outward into— She gave a cry, and lurched back up the mound.

'Are you all right, miss?' asked a policeman, stopping to stare at her a minute or two later, as she levered at the heap with a broken-off piece of steel reinforcing rod.

'Fine, fine,' she said, wondering why offers of male assistance only arrived when you didn't want them.

'Drop something, did you?'

'No – yes,' she said. 'That's right. I was climbing over and I dropped a, dropped a . . .' Invention deserted her, but it was all right, because there, staring up at her from the wreckage, was the splintered stone face of the statue of Agriculture Lady, split open down the forehead along the same jagged line that had opened in the Watcher's paper face when the cloud of glowing white motes swarmed out. It seemed high explosive worked as a spell of liberation too.

'And here it is,' she said nonsensically. 'The thing I was looking for!'

'Er . . .' said the policeman.

She descended in two sliding bounds and rushed away, laughing.

But was it enough? At work she redrew Geoff's diagram, and worried at the implications of what she'd seen that morning. Fleet Street probably knocked out for Lall, Agriculture Lady certainly gone, Faraday House inaccessible. That left Moorgate – unless one of the unknowns had come up trumps for her. Would Lall know the newspaper office was out of commission? Had she been and looked at the Moorgate building? Did Lall prepare, or was her arrogance such that she simply assumed the world would fall in with her wishes? Round and round Iris went, wishing it to be safe to skip the night's ordeal, distrusting her reasoning *for* that reason. She was on fire-watch duty anyway. She decided to decide later.

'Miss Hawkins?' said Mr Cornellis from the door of the chief clerk's office – her office now.

'Yes, sir?'

'How are we doing with the new Buy list?'

'Nearly ready.'

'Good. Shoot it over to me when absolutely ready, would you? Soon as you like.'

Which was a reproach in Cornellis-ese. He only came to her when he perceived things to be late. There had been yet another Acquisition of Securities Order in the middle of the month, mostly repeating American stocks that had already been on the list, presumably to flush out unsurrendered leftovers, but with a few new names: Walgreens, Socony-Vacuum, Macy, New Jersey Zinc. So out had gone another, smaller mailing to C&B clients, this time accompanied from the off with a recommendation to reinvest the proceeds in British equities. The Index was back above 70 by this time, so the market was no longer the screaming Buy it had been. But it was still, she and Mr Cornellis agreed, a solid Buy by all ordinary standards, and as the general price level rose, the opportunity for individual stock-picking reappeared. They had worked through aviation stocks and electricals, chemicals and banks, car manufacturers and road haulage, radios and machine tools. Now what? Rubble, she thought, shifting in her office chair. Building materials. We're going to need a lot. Glass and bricks and stone and gravel and cement and concrete and structural steel. She picked up the telephone and dialled. Before lunch she was able to take through to Mr C a shortlist of brickmakers, and what sounded like a seriously undervalued manufacturer of glazed sewer fittings. Thinking about money was soothing; it always was.

But night fell, as it was always going to. The office emptied, Mr Cornellis spun the lock of the safe and departed for Hemel Hempstead, Mr Seaton came upstairs to deliver her the keys to the building. In the hush when she was alone, with the blackout outside settling over the streets like a visible kind of silence, she changed into the boiler suit she wore now for the fire-watch. It was looser again. She hoped Geoff liked his women bony. She hoped Geoff was going to get this woman back again tomorrow, bony or not. The dread she felt was like the dread of the nights when the Watcher had been after her. She would not be feeling this degree of fear just for a raid, she supposed. Not any more. So the dread was, wasn't it, the sign of a decision taken? A direction accepted, into the abyss beyond the Mariner's hand. But not yet. She had responsibilities. She turned the other way from her office door and set out on the fire-watcher's inspection of the building, bottom to top, all the while keeping an eye out for anything that looked like a plausible weapon. She doubted that Lall would consent to be strangled with a typewriter ribbon, or battered with a hole-punch.

Still empty-handed, she reached the roof. The low cloud that had covered the city all day was shredding and thinning in a stiff east wind; it was becoming a cold, clear night with stars out, and buffeting gusts. Therefore a good night for the Luftwaffe, unfortunately, if they cared to take it. Moonless dark to hide in from the ack-ack guns and the RAF's night fighters, clear air to see the ground through from a bomb-sight once the first fires had lit up the street map. She rummaged in Mr Seaton's biscuit tin, and found a rock cake that would do for supper, though it lived up to its name. Mug of tea, fist-sized lump of flour and raisins to gnaw. The condemned woman ate a hearty meal. An indigestible meal. An impenetrable meal. She was procrastinating, wasn't she? But she would just do one quick circuit of the roof, she told herself, before she went down to face her doom.

Views east, north, west, south, east again from the flat leads. A whole year of night-time darkness now, and how dark-adapted everybody's eyes had got, able to deduce the cityscape from black traceries only faintly distinguishable against midnight blue. The pale steeples, the grey shine on the ruined roof of Cannon Street, St Paul's like a distant egg in an eggcup. The other way, the riverland of the docks – and wasn't that, wasn't that in the air, the bee-hum of approaching menace that she had, with part of herself, been wishing for?

It was. The sirens were sounding. The bombers were coming. *I cannot abandon my post*, she told herself sarcastically, knowing she had before and could now: knowing that, by all rational cost–benefit analysis, the fate of the war, the fate of the century if Lall altered it, mattered more than the preservation of one office building. *But I'll just see this wave safely by.*

Out of the east came the droning, apparently aiming straight for her but she had experienced that illusion many times before. They weren't dropping incendiaries, though, as the pathfinding planes usually did. Under the line of their approach, it was blue-white flashes of high explosive she could see – ground-level lightning, with jolts and shocks of sound following a fraction of a second later. Now she could hear the descending whistles too. It might be an illusion, but they really were coming awfully close. The aeroplane engines really did seem to be directly overhead. Another falling whistle, brief, only a single second or so long, and something only a couple of streets east of her erupted in a blue-white fountain of masonry. The next whistle began – and her body drew conclusions before her stupid, rationalising brain could catch up, and threw itself into the gully on the Mariner Building roof.

The world went white. There was no sound. The event was too loud for sound. But a shockwave hammered just over her head where she lay and sucked the breath out of her as it passed, out of her nose and her mouth and her lungs as if she had slammed down from a height and had her chest squeezed flat. And under her the building lurched. She felt the ten floors of the Mariner, all that mass, always rigid before, jellify, quaver, hesitate over whether it should continue in the form of a tall box of stone and concrete or deploy its weight in a downward liquid rush. *This is where I fall ten storeys*, she had time to think. *This is where the ambulance finds half of me.* But instead the Mariner grated and settled, sank back on its uprights, still vertical. News of heavy things nearby falling and smashing reached her, but as vibrations, not through her ears. She was covered in stuff. Bits and pieces of broken things, and a gritty layer of powdered London, still filtering down on her out of dust-choked air. The white light had gone. The dark was thick and soupy. There was powder on her face, in her nose, in her mouth. When she tried to breathe she inhaled it. *Cough!* A project for her whole body. Her lungs spasmed, squeezed, refused, consented to inflate, and she lay on her face barking, trying to clear the airway. Cough. Spit. Cough. That was enough work for now. That, and the slow realisation that she was still present, still there as an organism, though in what state remained to be seen. Everything ached and rang, like a recently struck bell, but nothing hurt specifically. That might be just absence of signal, like the continuing dead silence in her ears, and no good sign at all. Inventory of limbs. Move left leg an inch. Move right. Move arms. Present and correct, apparently. She got a hand up to her face and felt about. Eyes, nose, teeth, ears present; sticky stuff running out of ears. Brains? *Future earnings for a share are calculated by the following formula, but attention is drawn to the importance of the discount rate chosen.* No, just blood.

Could she get up? Should she get up? With her hearing conked out it was impossible to gauge that way if the raid was continuing. After laboriously thinking it through, she got herself up on elbows and knees – some of the debris around her was sharp – and crawled round and up to the lip of the gully. Frantic blinking. Dust in the eyes. The formerly clear night still suffused with a settling cloud of particles, black in black. But no further bomb flashes any way that she could see. Just a single wave that'd been aimed – so nearly aimed – directly her way. The big difference in the night – crawling on forward to see – was the entire disappearance of the building next door, formerly a couple of storeys shorter but now a gaping hole. Direct hit, a matter of yards from her.

She retreated on hands and knees, and toppled back into the gully. The door back into the building wouldn't open. The handle turned, but the door was stuck in the frame. Too mazed to think or plan, she hauled herself up on the handle and just banged at it feebly with her shoulder until it gave, and she fell through. Inside, even up here on the little landing above the last offices, it smelled of office life and not of wreckage and ruin. Peppermints, floor polish, tea leaves, ink, carbon paper, the fustiness of cardboard files. It was like a balm, an elixir of normality. It felt like protection, even if a bomb could blow it all away. But the lights were bust. She worked her way down the stairs by feel, along the landing past the lift by feel, into the C&B offices by feel – slowly, slowly, she dropped the keys and had to scrabble for them on the floor into the blackness – and into the Ladies' lavatory by feel. The tap in the basin gave her enough water to wash the dust out of her mouth, then glugged and stopped. Down under the pavement of Mariner Lane, the pipes must have been jolted apart. The wires too. She breathed in the black cubicle. In. Out. In. Out. *I am still here*. But there was something she should be doing, wasn't there.

She felt her way across the typists' room. A space she knew so well that the map of it was surely engraved on her brain, but now she bumped into desks. She still couldn't hear anything, but rather than silence there was a harsh note growing in her ears, a jangling din getting louder and louder. By the teleprinter, she lifted the blackout curtain and fumbled open the window. The night outside seemed almost bright blue by contrast. And the statue of the Mariner . . . was still there, with a crack visible behind the granite head but the great body still sutured to the building, and what almost looked like an expression of disappointment on the stone face. Iris rubbed at her own face. She should . . . She should . . .

But something was happening down below. On the street, a Rescue van was pulling up, its headlamps narrowed to slits, and men were spilling out, carrying equipment. Well, carrying something, anyway: bags not spades, strangely. And then, also strangely, they made for the Mariner's front doors, not the mound of smoking rubble that had been the neighbouring block, and the alley beyond it. *Those'll be locked*, she thought stupidly. She had the keys in her boiler suit pocket. It didn't seem to stop the crew below, though. They swung something heavy at the doors – a kind of ram – and in they all went. That was odd. Wasn't it. There had been a— Mr Seaton had said— A rumour. Gelignite. Robbers. Robbers disguised as Rescue. Or real Rescue also robbing. She should do something. What? What should she do?

Thinking about it required that she sit down for a minute. And if she was thinking about that, there was no room in her head for any other idea. One thought at a time in there, moving s l o w l y. She felt through the soles of her feet, didn't hear, a small thud of detonation travelling up through the structure of the building. Yes. Safe-crackers, working their way upwards. She should empty Mr Cornellis's safe before they got to the ninth floor, shouldn't she. Yes. Up we get. Upsy-daisy. She swam along out of the typists' room, along the corridor, into Mr C's office. The safe was in the wall behind his desk. And the combination was . . . five left, eight right, three left. How did she know that? She had no idea. But she did. She set to work turning the tumbler and counting. It was very difficult, especially in the dark. Perhaps she should stop and find some matches and light a candle. Another thud coming up through the floor. No. Turn it and turn it and turn it. Another thud. There. The heavy door swung open and there was Mrs Sinclair's cashbox and a fat envelope on the shelf below it. Envelope. Put it where? The boiler suit didn't have a big enough pocket. Laboriously, she unbuttoned the side. That was very difficult too. The ringing in her ears was really loud. Another thud. Then she could put the envelope in the small of her back, tucked into the top of her knickers. Thud. Now do the buttons up. Maybe it would be all right not to do all of them. No, Iris, do all of them. Thud. And shut the safe. Spin the lock thingummy. Now what?

Some residual steering intelligence told her that it would be better to meet the men coming up the stairs somewhere between floors, where they wouldn't know she had witnessed the thing they were doing. The bad thing. Off we go, then, Iris. She wobbled past the lift and started down the stairs. One turning. Two turnings. Now she was between floors, wasn't she. She would just have a little rest.

The next thing she knew, her shoulder was being shaken, and she was at the centre of a startled group of men with torches. Their lips moved, but she had no idea what they were saying. She opened her own mouth and tried to push words out, but it was like talking in a dream, and she couldn't tell if she was making any sound at all. *I can't hear anything,* she tried to say. *I was on the roof,* pointing upwards. *I think I need to go to hospital.* The men looked at each other. Then one of them squatted down in front of her and, mouthing with exaggerated clearness, said, or she thought he said, *Orright darlin', down you come, you're safe now.* Two of them made a seat with their hands and carried her off down the stairs. It felt so safe she closed her eyes again.

She woke up on a gurney in a hospital corridor. Daylight was coming in threads through the blackout curtains, and an Indian doctor with hair smooth as lacquer was shining a little light in her ears.

'You have concussion, but your eardrums have not burst,' he said, and she heard him. She had a foul headache but the ringing was gone. Also, her thoughts seemed to have had their normal velocity restored. The details of the night returned: what she had done, what she had not done.

'Is the war still on?' she asked.

'Yes?' he said, puzzled, and then visibly put it down to a concussion symptom. 'By the way, you are shouting. Your . . . volume control is perhaps a trifle impaired.'

Somehow, gloriously, Lall had failed. She was safe for a month.

'Sorry!' she said. 'Is that better?'

'Yes. Temporary, I'm sure. Now, we had better just get that outfit off you, so we can check you over.'

The reason why she shouldn't be showing what was inside the boiler suit to anyone had returned with the rest of her mental capacity.

'What time is it? And where am I?'

'Nine o'clock in the morning. St Thomas's. I'm afraid you were not a high-priority case last night—'

'That's fine, that's fine, but I need to go to work.'

'You really should just permit me to—'

She scrambled off the gurney. Everything ached but her legs held her up, which was a pretty good sign and would have to do, she thought, in place of a physical examination. She reached for Chelsea vowels as she retreated.

'You've been terribly kind,' she said. 'Goodbye, goodbye.'

She did stop in a Ladies on the way out of the hospital, having caught sight of her reflection in a glass swing door. No wonder the safe-cracking Rescue boys had been startled: she looked like a complete wraith, dead white with dust, eyes red-rimmed and huge-pupilled, trails of dried blood descending from each ear. She scrubbed with little squares of shiny hospital toilet paper. The effect was a mess, but at least no longer corpse-like.

It was nearly ten by the time she got back to the Mariner Building. Already, a propping operation was underway in the space where the neighbouring building had been, a mobile crane swaying up timbers like telegraph poles from a flat-bed lorry. The bronze front doors were smashed, but though the lifts weren't working the power was already back on. As she trudged up the stairs she could hear every floor buzzing like a disturbed beehive. Presumably on every one there was an exploded safe. The ninth floor was no different. Sonia burst out, 'Oh, Iris! You're alive!' as she limped along the hall, and Delia and Mrs S stood behind staring.

Mr Cornellis was in his office, looking wretchedly at the scorch marks below the safe, and its door hanging off its hinges.

'My dear!' he said when he saw her. 'We thought you'd been blown off the roof by the blast next door. Shouldn't you be at home in bed?'

'Never mind that,' said Iris, too wrung out for subtlety. 'Shut your door and turn your back.'

He did. She wriggled the envelope out of the boiler suit.

'Here,' she said. 'Here are the Treasury bonds we shouldn't have had in the safe. I got them out before the burglars reached this floor.'

'Oh, thank God,' said Mr Cornellis. 'Oh, thank God.' He lifted the brown flap of the envelope, and looked at the green edges of a thin wad of printed paper.

'They're all still there,' said Iris.

'Of course they are,' said Mr Cornellis faintly, which Iris thought showed a gentlemanly lack of imagination. 'I am so grateful. I am so grateful. How can I possibly repay you?'

'Aspirin, an explanation, and a pay rise,' she said.

'Of course,' he said. 'Of course. But . . . how did you know the combination?'

'I've been watching you,' said Iris. 'I stole it from you.'

'Oh, good girl!' cried Mr Cornellis. '*Good* girl.'

VI

'What you have to understand,' said Mr Cornellis carefully, 'is that I am, ninety-nine per cent of the time, a law-abiding patriot.'

It was not the same day. He had insisted on waiting, and sending her home to bathe and sleep, and booking them a quiet table where they could lunch together on the following Monday. Iris had been against it, knowing how gratitude cooled, as did a willingness to confide: miss the moment, and sometimes you missed the opportunity altogether. But it was also impossible to compel a confidence, if you had forsworn the possibilities of blackmail, which is what she had done, decisively, by handing back the envelope before making her requests. So she had gone home to Chelsea, in her layer of dust, and reassured a frantic Geoff. And sat in five inches of tepid water in the bath while he knelt beside her, picking splinters and glass fragments out of her hair. And was now, on balance, glad to be having this conversation in a composed way, in a good dress, wearing scent, with a glass of sherry in her hand. The restaurant was dark and three-quarters empty.

'I don't like breaking rules,' he said. 'I believe in them. I believe that they should be obeyed even when, or perhaps especially when, they go against one's self-interest. I am a product, you see, of the lost world before the Great War, when all the world traded in London and there were no particular political boundaries that stood in our way, and it was our code of honour, our willingness to police ourselves, that prevented us from behaving as scoundrels or blackguards. – You probably can't imagine that. "Lost" is the word.'

She couldn't imagine it. She had read the famous passage in Keynes about 'the inhabitant of London' in 1914 – male, of course – being able to 'adventure his wealth in the natural resources and new enterprises of any quarter of the world, and share, without exertion or even trouble, in their prospective fruits and advantages'. But it was a description of the age of the dinosaurs as far as she was concerned. Her whole adult life there had been fascists and Nazis and Bolsheviks, and the Great Depression going on and going on and going on, and all the separate countries and markets of the world locked up tight behind anxious walls. She nodded attentively and said nothing. You should never interrupt someone when they are nerving themselves up to trust you.

'The difficulty,' said Mr Cornellis, looking into his own sherry glass, 'is that with Europe under its present darkness, my . . . co-religionists are in a state of particular vulnerability. They are refugees, if they are lucky. Captives of their tormentors, if they are not. And they are nobody's priority. In the end,' he said bleakly, 'the only person who can be counted on to care about the fate of a Jew is another Jew. So I and a . . . small circle of associates . . . have been doing what we can, to aid the escape of Jews, to pay the costs of extricating them, and to ensure that they are not entirely penniless if they reach a safe haven. – This in the knowledge that, if we were one hundred per cent law-abiding, and left it trustingly to our government, it would never happen at all.'

'I thought it must be something like that,' said Iris.

'I collect unregistered bonds from people willing to take the risk of under-reporting their holdings. Then I send them on, either to Geneva by plane—'

'You can still send post to Switzerland?'

'You can; or to Lisbon by ship. There they are used to secure visas, to buy tickets, to feed and clothe refugees – and to pay bribes.

Endless bribes. You wouldn't believe how many people see fleeing Jews as a chance for profit. Or,' he said, looking her in the eye, 'perhaps you would?'

'Hold on,' said Iris. 'I don't want you to pay me more as the cost of silence. I want you to pay me more because I've proved I can be trusted.'

'An interesting distinction.'

'An important one! I am not here to . . . mulct you for money,' Iris said, aware as she spoke that she was reorganising the past to obtain a new future quite as much as if she had done it by managing to reach the palace of Nonesuch. 'I am here to give you my word. I am here to promise you that the firm's secrets will be my secrets. To swear that I am not a scoundrel or a blackguard.'

She held out her hand. He looked at it.

'What a formidable creature you are,' he said. 'If I were younger, I might be proposing a weekend in Paris.'

She put her hand down.

'If you were younger,' she said levelly, 'I would be slapping your face. I am engaged to be married.'

'Oh, congratulations,' he said.

'And in any case, no you wouldn't. Quite apart from Paris being full of Germans, it is obvious how happy you are with Mrs C.'

'Well, yes,' he said. 'Forgive me: I had to know what sort of arrangement it was that you thought you were offering. I am not interested in striking a bargain with a young woman who thinks she can wrap an old man round her little finger.'

Iris suppressed a fatal urge to tell him he wasn't as old as all that.

'And I am not interested in being that young woman. I want to learn from you, I want to work with you. I'm talking about a partnership in a strictly business sense.'

'The firm will be Harold's when he comes home from the war,' said Mr Cornellis. She could hear the effort required to say 'when' and not 'if'.

'Of course. Since I *am* a woman, as you point out, most of the official ways in which I can do well in the City are closed to me anyway. I do intend to prosper, so I expect to have to work out . . . individual ways of doing it.'

'We are getting ahead of ourselves,' said Mr Cornellis. 'Years ahead.'

'We are.'

'Here in the present, there remains the dangerous imbalance between us.'

'How do you mean?'

'I mean, as you very well know, that you can threaten me with exposure, but I have no such hold on you. I propose that the next time the *Stella Maris* docks in the Port of London—'

'Sorry, what's that?'

'The Portuguese tramp freighter that provides our contact with Lisbon. We have an arrangement with the purser. A very expensive one, naturally. – So, next time, you carry the bonds to him. Knowingly. Then you will be as guilty as me of breaking the war regulations; you will be as vulnerable as I am to disgrace, imprisonment, loss of career. Acceptable?'

'Acceptable.'

Cornellis inhaled, exhaled. Looked at the ceiling, looked at her. 'In that case' – and he held out his own hand. She shook it. Hope came from the touch. Mostly hope. And some anxiety; but also the return of the amused pleasure he had felt when she demanded to back her judgement with her own money. Mr Cornellis might not want to sleep with her, Iris realised, but he enjoyed her. There was something going on there in which her being young, female and attractive played a non-coincidental part.

Mr Cornellis dropped his gaze to the menu.

'I'm afraid I can't recommend the Windsor soup,' he said.

*

'What do you want for Christmas?' she asked Geoff. She had a chief clerk's salary now, if still not the job title. It was enough to put money aside again, and to splash out a bit too.

'Nothing dubious,' he said.

She slid a finger between the buttons of his shirt. 'Are you saying you don't like my dubious ideas?'

'I'm here for all of them. But a present should be a present, not a— Oh, you know what I mean.'

'Yes, I know what you mean. You are a nice man, Geoffrey Dionysus Hale. Probably nicer than I deserve.'

Geoff gave this a tongue-click of dismissal.

But it was strangely difficult to know what to get him. The only presents she had ever given her men had been tie-pins and cigarette cases, lumps of impersonal luxury to ensure that the flow of gifts didn't run troublingly in only one direction. Traditionally you got their initials engraved on the silver but really, she thought, it might as well have said *Thank you for the fuck* in curly italic script. She had no practice picking a present for a man that said: *I have been paying close attention to what you care about, because I love you.*

She cast about for ideas in a London getting steadily colder. It was not the bone-hard, frozen city of the previous winter, but it was a much more ragged, more battered place, with less sparkle and far emptier shops. Thinner people too, who felt the cold more. She certainly did; she shopped in two pairs of socks and a tea-cosy hat. She tried swish gentlemen's outfitters in the West End, but the ties and jackets there were too cigarette-case-adjacent, and there was something wrong, something doll-like, in the idea of her dressing him up. She tried a radio supplies shop, remembering the something-or-other pentode he had been thinking of, but the contents were a complete mystery to her, and presumably all would have been extremely familiar to Geoff. Not a good basis for finding the *right* thing. She looked in furniture shops on the Tottenham Court Road, bookshops on the Charing Cross Road. She avoided Paddington.

Then, in the Portobello Road market, she found a stall selling second-hand scientific instruments. This was better. The objects were beautiful, even if she didn't know what they were, and they had the right feel about them, the feel of Geoff's own mind translated into sliding brass and glassware marked off in precise gradations. She was very drawn to a tiny bell jar in which a ribbon of gold leaf was hanging. When you brought a magnet near it, it rose, trembling, quavering, hardly there at all yet rumpling on the breath of an unseen wind. But you could hardly give someone an object, could you, just because it looked like what making love with them felt like, when you were at your tenderest and most helpless. She put it back. She liked a telescope in a faded Morocco-leather case, but when she picked it up there was a plink of something loose inside, and only a blur when she looked through it. 'Objective lens needs resetting, I'm afraid,' said the stallholder.

Then she saw a box lined in blue velvet that seemed to contain one pen with many different nibs.

'What's this?' she said.

'Technical pen. Won't be many more of those around, 'cause it's made in Germany. You change the heads to change the thickness of the line. For work on blueprints, architects' drawings, that sort of thing. Pelikan Graphos, it's called. Quite pricey, I'm afraid.'

'Could you use it for, say, a patent application?'

'Yeah, that kind of thing.'

'Then I *might* be interested. What would your best price be?'

But the best Christmas present of all was delivered on 12 December when, taking a circular walk to work to see the latest damage in the

City, she found the building on Moorgate gone, and a pit of smoking wreckage in its place. *Goodbye, art nouveau girl on the chimney. Goodbye, angry slave.* She imagined the jubilant uprush of its escape, the spirit fizzing from its prison as the stone cracked and the building cascaded into rubble: all of that no threat to a creature of air, all of that spelling only liberation.

She told Geoff when she got home.

'Then . . . Lall is blocked,' he said. 'She can't use Fleet Street, she can't use Moorgate, she can't use Agriculture Lady, she can't use Faraday House. Her pathway is closed.'

'What about the unknowns? The one or maybe two statues we don't know about?'

'Doesn't matter. It's not a question of her getting *in* to the network now. Remember the diagram? She needs eight arches, but that requires nine statues since every arch has two ends, and she simply doesn't have enough statues any more. Twelve minus four is eight.'

'Are you sure? We've been fooled like this before.'

'Yes, I am. If she doesn't have enough statues, it isn't a probability, it's a certainty.'

'You're *sure*?'

'Yes.'

'I keep thinking there must be something I've forgotten.'

'What?'

'I don't know!'

'You're thinking, *I want to believe it so it can't be true.* That's utterly illogical.'

'Yeah but, Geoff, you want to believe it's true so I stop risking my neck. That's not logical either.'

'Right. But it isn't about what I believe or you believe, or I want or you want. It's the numbers. She hasn't got the numbers, so her route to Nonesuch doesn't work any more. She can't get there. It's over. Finito. End of story.'

'Then I can stand down.'

'You can stand down.'

It was as if a stone that had been on top of Iris for months had been lifted off. She felt as if she might fizz up into the sky herself. Now she need not face the murderous little smile. She need not count off the days till the next dark of the moon like someone going down a staircase to dread. She need only – only! – face the chances of the raids, the unmetaphysical danger of the Nazis winning the war. But those were impersonal; she was rolling the dice with everyone else in London on raid nights, rather than dealing with a mad individual malice.

She went to work whistling. She walked the envelope of bonds up the gangplank of the *Stella Maris* when it came in. The crew looked at the half-flattened docks around them with dazed eyes, and she tried to remember when ruins were surprising. She stole a pine branch from a park that she could stick in a flowerpot for a Christmas tree, and fought her way ruthlessly to the front of a queue in Hamleys to buy half a dozen silver baubles to hang on it. She asked Eleanor if she could bring Geoff with her to Mathoms Court, and did. He performed splendidly at dinner, going deep into a wholly incomprehensible discourse with a guest from some other unnameable research outfit. She caught Eleanor's eye and they smiled at each other. Eleanor was pregnant. Iris did not point out Claude and Frederick in the mural to Geoff, and he did not notice them on his own. But she took luxuriant advantage of waking up next to him, in a warm bed, after a bombless night, with the shadow of branches – leafless winter branches now – moving on the ceiling above them like a blessing.

The shops no longer had turkeys in them, or oranges, but she returned from Sussex with a bag of chestnuts and a recently executed chicken from the farm next door to the Court. Geoff devised a chestnut stuffing, and at ten o'clock at night on Christmas Eve they were sitting in the gradually deepening smell of the chicken roasting, so that it would be ready with minimum fuss for lunch the next day. There were four wrapped parcels under the one-sprig tree, two from her to him and two from him to her. (She had added to the pens a scientific children's book, bought rather at random, called *My Friend Mr Leakey*. It was by a famous biologist Geoff had mentioned.)

The flowerpot on the floor, the green pine needles with the silver balls nestling among them, were a total mismatch with the look of the flat. Rustic. Naive. Untidy. The needles were already shedding on the carpet. But looking at the coloured paper, smelling the pine smell and the cooking smell, aware of the cold night outside during which the radio said snow was possible, Iris felt the enchantment of childhood Christmases somehow stealing back. There were no coloured fairy lights, or paper chains looped from the curtain rail, but for the first time in she didn't know how many years there was the old sense of expectancy. Something wonderful was coming, some enormous happiness was suddenly imminent. It almost hurt. A transportation to the beginning of things, everything ahead, everything possible, the great mistakes not made. Might it really be possible to get that back? Experience said not; everything irreversible ever endured said not. But it was almost Christmas, with snow in the air, and she was sitting on Geoff's lap with her head tucked into his shoulder. She looked at the tree, he looked at her looking.

'What did you and your dad do for Christmas?' she asked.

'Oh, he was opposed to it, theoretically. The closer it got, the more he went on about Yule and the winter solstice. "The pagan roots of the festival." I think he was fending off the memories of when he and my mother were very young, and he was a curate. He never managed to buy me a present—'

'I've got you a present.'

'I can see it. Them. – But all the same, every year we ended up going to the midnight service in Hampstead. We'd creep in at the back, and he'd *cry* during the carols. Every time. I was mortified. But I was glad we went.'

She pictured them, the stoic little boy, not very clean, and Mr Hale, histrionic in his cloak.

'And what about you?' he asked. She had known she was inviting the return question, hadn't she.

'Oh, aunts and uncles and cousins. A full house. Very noisy. And lots of food. My mother cooked like she was feeding an army. She would have this whole . . . gastronomic plan of campaign. *Days* of preparations.' She could smell them as she thought of them, the waves of savoury and sweet perfumes that rolled out of the kitchen in Watford. (The first kitchen. The original kitchen. The kitchen of the time before.) Nutmeg and spice and brandy, gravy and sausage-meat and candied fruit.

'And you chopping away? Helping?'

'Heavens, no. No, no, no, no. I wasn't allowed to touch a spoon, even. The kitchen was *her* kingdom, not for sharing. Until . . . well.' She clammed up. She could feel it, a physical impediment, her mouth closing by itself on the prospect of talking aloud any further into that past.

'Iris . . .' said Geoff.

'What?'

'You know you don't talk about your family, ever? This is literally the first time. I don't know anything about them. I don't know their names. I don't know if you've got . . . brothers and sisters?'

'No I don't,' she said, more sharply than she meant.

'Your parents, then. Will I be . . . meeting them at some point?'

It was the most ordinary of questions. You agreed to marry someone, you took them round to Mum and Dad. You hoped that everyone would get along. You hoped that your boy – your man;

your slightly odd but kind and marvellous and brilliant man – would get enfolded, brought in with raised glasses and cheers, particularly if he was parentless himself, and in need of everyday warmth. And her dad would do that, of course he would. He would take to Geoff instantly. But. But, but, but.

'It's difficult,' she said eventually.

'I can see that,' said Geoff patiently. 'Could you . . . tell me why?'

'Something went wrong.'

'Yes?'

'Something big. The kind of thing that's too big to forgive.'

'You can't forgive them?'

'No! The . . . other way round.'

'Iris. Iris. I know you—'

'You don't know *this*.'

'Won't you tell me, then?'

She studied him, from very close to. Ear and cheek and eye and warm skin. There was no judgement in his face, no expectation of judgement. He trusted her. Was the price of love that she had to trust him back? She supposed that it might be. It sounded right, but then it also sounded – love, trust, love, trust – as if it ought to be easy, when actually it meant tearing through the scar tissue that sealed a box of memory.

'I *will*,' she said. 'I promise I will tell you. I will explain. But not now. Not at *Christmas*.' Tearing through tissue into old sorrow, tearing across this moment, this night, this surety arrived at, this serene smell of food cooking. 'Please?' she said.

'Of course,' he said. 'Whenever you like. You know what? I'd like to give you one of my presents now.'

'Are you sure? Shouldn't it be tomorrow morning?'

'I'm sure.'

He tipped her gently off and knelt down to fetch a little square box wrapped in red paper. She opened it and it was, of course, a ring: an old-fashioned Victorian engagement ring, with a central sapphire and brilliants around it.

'Will you—'

'You know I will,' she said, and he put it on her. She turned it in the light. Serious, not a bauble. To be worn forever. *I thought I'd be afraid of this*, she thought, *but I'm not, I'm not.*

'It's beautiful,' she said.

'I'm afraid it comes from a junk shop in the Edgware Road. I tried lots of proper jewellers but nothing was quite right.'

The whole city, she thought, *giving each other old things instead of new ones. I hope the woman who had it before me was happy.*

'It's beautiful,' she repeated.

'Good.' He took her hands and stood up, pulling her with him. 'Now then. I'll turn the oven off, and we can go.'

'Go?'

'To the midnight service, up the road.'

'You want to go to church?'

'Yes. With you.'

They weren't the only ones. Snow had not begun yet, but the air had the smell of it, the chill intoxicating null smell of the clouds above, dense with soft crystals nearly ready to fall, and along the dark streets towards the river, the silhouettes of other Chelsea-ites were in motion, all tugged along in the same direction. They had passed the Malayan rubber farmer in the foyer, wrapping a scarf round his neck and puffing his pipe. The woman from the basement shelter with a laugh like a horse was somewhere behind them, laughing like a horse: but hers was the only loud voice. Otherwise the night was hushed, with the hush of the imminent snow. Swathed by it, swaddled by it, protected by it – at least, that was what it felt like – from the murder noises of the wartime night. The sirens had not sounded. If they did, Iris was not sure what they would do. Run for home? Hope for a deep crypt to shelter in, in the church? But they had not sounded yet; and perhaps they would not, at Christmas. Perhaps the Luftwaffe crews at the airfields in northern France were drinking Glühwein and singing 'Silent Night' instead. Perhaps.

The Old Church, on the Thames embankment, couldn't welcome people with a blaze of lights in its porch because of the blackout regulations. Tiny slits of brightness had to guide the way. And then there was a confusion of blackness between the two sets of doors, outer and inner, filled with murmuring and stamping feet. But on the inside, the church was alight with candles, burning in heedless banks with flames the colour of daffodil and topaz, blue-hearted like the stone on her ring. She had never been in before, and it was a surprise. The outside of the Old Church was sturdily Georgian, a respectable barn of a place with wide brick arches, but inside *was* old. Old and strange. They were under an ancient vault shaped like a barrel and flickering with shadows on its whitewashed walls. Above, a row of curved skylights pierced upwards through the thickness of the stone, blocked with blackout fabric now but still punctuating the white roof with dark shafts. It was as if they were all gathering within the tube of a musical instrument: in a flute, say, and looking up at its finger-holes, waiting to see what would be played on it.

All around, crammed in in coats and mufflers, were denizens of the Chelsea streets. The grand ones, who by day she might have taken primarily as a challenge to her vowels: the old ladies in jewels, the aged military men with thread veins bursting on their cheeks like poppies in a wheat crop, the platinum-rinsed younger ones who bought the clever little tins to make canapés, the men on leave for Christmas in ten different kinds of officer's uniform, the old bohemians with shaggy hair who these days had symphony orchestras and academies of art and newspaper columns at their disposal. But also the shopkeepers, the shop assistants, the housekeepers, the cleaners, and some of their sons home for Christmas in much less flattering battledress. (Geoff was in civvies.) And the careful nondescripts too, female and middle-aged male, from whose good clothes you could tell nothing about the places from which they were rising without trace: the chancers, in short, like herself. And a bunch of railway workers over the bridge from Battersea who had come to this midnight appointment straight from the pub.

Kinds of people not usually crowded together, but commonly marked now, if you looked closely in the candlelight, with the strains of the last months. Shadows under most of the eyes, nervous twitches widely distributed, the retired general with skin as grey and rough with fatigue as the meat porter's. The common flesh declared itself, and for once the different clothes looked more like costumes, all of them looser and worse-fitting than they had been before, picked arbitrarily off the rack and flung to the first person who caught them. Who'll be the general tonight? Who'll be the dustman? Who'll be the duchess? Who'll be the draper? Pull on your glad rags for the social game. It had such real stakes, of course, even now with random and democratic death falling from the sky. The number you drew dictated whether you saw out the raids in the basement of the Ritz or in a piss-swilled public shelter. That was why she meant to pass her life in the Ritz, if she could. But here and now, there seemed to be a kind of truce on offer, in the pews; a chance, just for a moment, to see through the game and put aside her own chameleon campaign within it and look with eyes temporarily wiped of class and status and aspiration at what the candlelight disclosed. Smiles between strangers, an awkward goodwill. A speculative suspicion, travelling from eye to eye, that there might be some other way altogether, some essential and uncostumed way, of seeing these rivalrous animals you stood among, this rivalrous animal you were yourself. Some other thing they all were, or might be, if you could but know it.

And then the choir came in, and they all began to sing.

In the bleak midwinter
Frosty wind made moan
Earth stood hard as iron
Water like a stone.

Chelsea Old Church could only muster two or three boy choristers for the midnight service of 1940 – the rest must all have been evacuated – but some of the young officers home for Christmas were musical and had put on surplices, the genteel ladies who taught harp and piano off the King's Road had come to sing alto and soprano, and there were advantages to living where opera singers did. At the back of the scratch choir, a leonine bass came processing, rumbling out the bottom line. Ah, that was the tune the stone flute was to play. Topaz-light and daffodil-light on singing faces, the blue bead-points of the wicks. Iris knew the words without even having to try. Childhood supplied them; they came up to her mouth and out into the candleshine from deep time.

What can I give Him,
Poor as I am?
If I were a shepherd,
I would give a lamb.
If I were a wise man,
I would do my part,
Yet what I can I give Him –
Give my heart.

Tears ran down her cheeks, and she didn't try to scrub them away. Geoff squeezed her hand. She looked to see if he was mortified, and he was not. *But why am I crying?* she thought. It wasn't the old story of the baby in the manger; not directly, anyway. Nor was it babies in general. Eleanor was pregnant, she wasn't, and had no plans to be for a good long time, if ever. It was something about a new thing beginning in a bad time, in a hard winter. A tender thing, a delicate thing, just come into the world and as little able to protect itself as a newborn with a bubble of milk on its lips.

None of this is protection, she thought, and went on thinking it as the vicar read the lesson about the shepherds watching their flocks in the fields. The robes on the vicar and the choir, the midnight-best outfits of the posh congregation and the less posh congregation – all of it would rip and burn, or if it lasted through the war would fade and tatter, undone by time as thoroughly in the end as it would have been by blast or flames. The barrel-walls of the church themselves, which seemed so solid, would shatter at a direct hit like anything else. 'Peace on earth, goodwill towards men,' said the vicar. They were putting their faith, Iris and Geoff and everyone else there, in promises they didn't know could be kept. Promises with no guarantee of safety, or of happy endings, any more than there was a happy ending for the baby in the manger. And yet they were trying to trust them anyway. Iris thought of the way the whole of the Mariner Building had quaked under her, hesitating between liquid and solid. *We're breakable, and our walls might as well be made of glass.* Anything might happen. Moment to moment, anything at all. But by now, she thought, glancing at the faces, everyone here knew that. This was hope, not delusion.

It came upon a midnight clear, that glorious song of old
Of angels bending near the earth to touch their harps of gold.

They were singing the walls up, that was what they were doing. They were making a shelter with their voices, by candlelight, in which vulnerable things, innocent things, new things, could at least be hoped for. No guarantees. One bomb would smash the canopy of voices as it would smash the roof. But if the walls were only a solidification of hope anyway, and mortared stones were no more strong than hope, then hope was no less strong than mortared stones. And thinking about this, singing and holding Geoff's hand, Iris felt her attention pass out through the walls of the Old Church as if they really were transparent like glass as well as weak like glass. Out into the London night, where the snow had started falling, sifting slow and almost weightless down, a windless tumble of flakes through the blackout. It was cold outside. The waters of the Thames were iron-dark, welling and wrinkling as the tide turned, and they ate each snowflake that fell in them as if it had never been. On the bombsites, the Christmas snow was streaking and furring the ground, settling on mangled metal and broken bricks, touching with white lines the lintels that no longer had a doorway below them, girders that now projected into empty space. It was settling on the hole in Hampstead where Mr Hale had died. But also on all the intact roofs that sheltered the living, the grand ones and the small ones and the middling ones alike. Snow falling on tiles and slates, domes and steeples; snow falling on Soho and Belgravia, Stepney and Mile End, the Kinesis Club and Mrs Tilly's boarding house in Clapham and the Alexandra Palace transmitter mast. Snow falling on the lovers, snow falling on the haters, snow falling on those who were both. Snow falling on the roof under which, she hoped, Lall might just possibly be lying after all in her Harriet's arms, a psychopath at rest.

All under a sky of driving flake. And among those flakes, she supposed, threading and wavering and twisting and rushing in their soda-water swarms, the other pale particles that made up the bodies of the angels. Indifferent to the cold, unsplittable, unwoundable, alive among the invisible vibrations of the radio waves. For this sky was full of angels too, wasn't it. She had reason to know it was. For the first time she put together the Christmas angels in the story with the creatures of the air she had met; with the white lights filling her vision with phosphorescence, with the blue rift into impossibility in the corner of the bedroom. Was it *them* in the Christmas story? If it was, no wonder the shepherds had to be told not to be afraid. If it was, then the sky over Bethlehem must have suddenly yawned into blue pits and vortices; if it was, then it had been swirls of intolerable strangeness that declared peace on earth, goodwill towards men. Had sung it, chanted it, in voices like chiming glassware and hollow tubes vibrated by Arctic wind. Voices that might be declaring it now, out there in the cold, in and above the snow clouds, in the temporary peace of a Christmas night without bombers, from a sky as strange as the one over Bethlehem.

Geoff loved his technical pens, and in return gave her an American book called *Reminiscences of a Stock Operator*. 'Just the thing for a really acquisitive person, I'm told,' he said.

VII

The bombers didn't come on Christmas Day either, or on Boxing Day, or the day after, or the day after that. The snow went, but a sleepiness remained, a yawning release of tension from which it was difficult to return to business as usual. Iris had signed up to fire-watch on 29 December back when she was claiming all the dark-of-the-moon nights on the rota, and she went in faithfully to C&B to do it: but it was a Sunday evening, and the City seemed virtually deserted. Darkness by four o'clock, no one in the streets, most office doors chained and bolted, most other rooftops by the look of things unguarded. The Mariner Building was certainly quite empty. She went up top and looked around, and nothing was happening, nothing was showing any signs of happening, so she descended to her desk and rather than working her way through Mr Seaton's list, and checking all the floors, and turning off the electrics at the main switch and so on, she subsided with a lump of fruitcake Geoff had made and thought about bond yields with her eyelids drooping. It would have been tempting to give up altogether and just go home, as it seemed almost everybody else had, only Geoff had been rota'd back out onto his mysterious night duty too, and it seemed invidious to curl up in comfort when he couldn't.

In this lulled state, the green shade of the desk lamp making the words on the page in front of her swim, the cake a heavy sweet comfort in her stomach, it took her a while to identify an unexpected noise coming down the landing of the ninth floor and round two corners to her office: the lift working. That was odd. She had locked the doors on the ground floor behind her when she came in. She supposed she had better go and find whatever inhabitant of floors one to eight had come in to fetch something, and give a little lecture about using the stairs instead when a raid might be on.

But on the landing, as she stood in front of the lift doors to read off from the illuminated panel which floor whoever-it-was was getting off at, the numbers went on lighting up, and lighting up, all the way to nine. She frowned, the lift pinged for arrival, the doors opened, and a small fist moving very fast punched her in the face. Something cracked audibly in her nose and hot torrents of blood poured out of it. She clutched it and reeled.

'That's the trouble with not being officer class,' said Lall with satisfaction. 'No sense of strategy. Wrap her up.'

This last part was addressed to a thing behind her in the lift that seemed to exist only as an outline of black ribbon, a stickman-shaped empty space with fabric around it that constantly pulsed and rippled. The material, Iris discovered as the thing surged towards her and then whipped around her, snake-quick, from her feet up, was a long strip cut from blackout curtain. The coarse weave of it was familiar though the pulsing life injected into it was absolutely not. It rose up her on the instant, trussing her like a mummy with her legs tight together and hands lashed onto her face where they had been holding her nose: limitless and extendable amounts of black ribbon, apparently, though there hadn't seemed to be that much to it during her first brief glimpse in the lift. Somehow, Iris guessed, Lall had worked out how to enslave a spirit and get it *into* the ribbon, rather than needing to contain it as the Watcher had been contained. Three or four black stripes criss-crossed her vision, reducing the world to jigsaw pieces; blood from her nose flowed into her mouth behind her clamped hands, and it was hard to spit it out.

Lall sidestepped so she could be sure Iris was seeing her through a chink in the ribbon. She was smiling, of course. She had on the same sort of black boiler suit Iris wore for the fire-watch, but it looked slightly teddy-bearish on her, as if she were wearing a whole different outfit underneath.

'Tighter!' she said, and the black webwork gripped, pulled, tautened, cut in everywhere it held Iris, to the brink of pain. 'Tighter again! Yes, like that.'

She approached with a forefinger, and pushed delicately on Iris's chest – just enough, since she was strapped up rigid, to knock her off her balance and make her fall backwards full-length, straight as a stick, onto the hard parquet of the floor. It hurt as much as you would expect to hit the wood from the height of her height, a ringing blow on the back of her head and a shock of pain right down her spine.

'Up!' said Lall, and the ribbon-thing somehow put out feet or tentacles of ribbon and hoisted her trussed body six inches or so off the floor.

'You broke by dose,' said Iris thickly through the layers of binding.

'Yes!' said Lall brightly. 'I kind of promised myself that, since you would keep poking it in. But with any luck, not for long. Think about it: if this evening goes the way I mean it to, your nose will be the least of what gets mended. Now, I *did* think of killing you here and now for convenience's sake. After all, you'll be back later anyhow, so it wouldn't make much difference. But it still seems discourteous, doesn't it, when we had that nice conversation, so I've decided to bring you along instead. You can see it all happen! But don't be a nuisance, because I can always change my mind. Do you understand me?'

Iris said nothing. Lall kicked her hip.

'Yeth,' said Iris.

'Jolly good. Off we go, then. I'm guessing your statue is . . . this way? Oh yes, so it is.'

It won't work, thought Iris, *there's no bridge any more. The network is broken.* But already Lall was saying the charm that opened the way to past years, and whatever Geoff's calculation had been, the glass span through the air had clearly appeared after all, because she was being levered up off the floor by the ribbon-thing, through the opened office window and out into the cold night air. Her view of all this, flat on her back and moving along feet first, was like a sight through a damaged kaleidoscope. It was all triangular pieces. Pieces of shadowy office ceiling. Lurching pieces of the Mariner's stone head and hand, with whorl of hungry light in its gullet. Pieces of the purple tunnel through the air as she was carried helpless along the iridescent bridge, following Lall's neat bustling ankles. Something was happening in the night sky above the faint glow of the tunnel, though: a familiar drone, getting louder. The Christmas pause was over, the Luftwaffe was back. The bombers roared overhead, going west; the guns struck up in reply to complete the raid music, but not in their usual volume. Perhaps the gunners, like the fire-watchers, had stood down exhausted. And in the wake of the planes, tens and then hundreds of pink flares fell, burning prettily, to ignite the streets beneath.

Iris gave a roar of protest through the blood in her mouth and the gag of her own hands tied to her face. She should be back on the roof; tonight of all nights she should be there with broom and bucket. Lall's feet stopped, and she turned back, apparently quite unbothered by the yawning void below, and the fact that she was balancing on a nearly-not-there line of shine not much wider than a gymnast's bar.

'Silly!' she said. 'What did I tell you about being a nuisance? I suppose it's your nasty old office you're worried about. Let it burn!

Let it all burn! I'll have it right as rain again tomorrow. All you have to decide is whether you want to be tipped off the bridge right now. Do you?'

'No.'

'Then *shut up*.'

Iris shut up. And on they went, as incendiaries settled unmolested onto rooftops and began to burn their way in. At the Monument, she was tipped up on end to scuttle round the painted flames, and her kaleidoscope showed her, in lurching shards, real flames down below starting to get established, tarred roofs to the west going up in smoky orange, windows starting to glow dull crimson from within, gusts of sparks as thick as the Christmas snowflakes blowing in the black canyons of the streets. Onwards to the Coal Exchange dragon. Iris had a faint hope that, not knowing the little ways of these particular chained angels, Lall might get a bite taken out of her, but she handled all of the attempts to devour her with a contemptuous ease, presumably born of a life snapping orders at horses, hounds and servants. Geoff might have been right that Lall had lost her own route to Nonesuch, but here she was decisively stealing Iris's instead.

Through the wall with the advertisement for hats. Through the earth of London's ancient past. To the suburban doorknocker.

'Ah,' said Lall, looking at the corkscrew turns of the bridge in the wild sky beyond, when the suburban door opened. 'Now you'd better talk to me. You've done that; you must have done. Tell me how.'

'Why should I?' said Iris. 'And don't say you're going to shoot me, because then you'll never know how.'

'Because I'm going anyway, and you're coming too, and if I fall off and die then you fall off and die, and if I die without getting to Nonesuch, you stay dead for good. How's that, clever-clogs?'

The triangle of Lall's face that Iris could see was shining-eyed, possessed by a thrilled glee. Iris did not doubt that she was mad enough to go on regardless. *I could end this by lying*, she thought. *Snuff out this whole mad project, and her. And me.* But Geoff's ring was on her finger. She had a future she wanted. She couldn't feel anything like the resignation, or the despair, necessary for martyrdom.

'Just shut your eyes,' she said miserably. 'And feel with your feet. It's flat really.'

'Oh!' said Lall. 'I see. Fair enough. But I've a better idea. Why don't I shut my eyes and ride?' She hopped on top of Iris's rigid, mummy-wrapped body and gripped with her knees. 'Giddy up!' she said.

Between the weight of the malignant elf on top of her and the struggle to keep breathing through clamped hands and coagulating mouth, Iris didn't take in much of the progress round the corkscrew. The slave spirit in the fabric padded steadily on through the spiral. But she did accidentally let her eyes fall open towards the end, and found herself suspended upside down over a distant black floor of cityscape, where separate orange cauldrons of fire were starting to spill, to run together in rivulets into bright liquid networks. Her stomach lurched. If she was sick like this she really would suffocate. She screwed her eyes shut again.

It wasn't the Moorgate rooftop they arrived at, that being gone. The bridge to Nonesuch had reconstituted from what was left. Next now came a cupola above a courtyard that Iris had never seen before, with (so far as she could make out in broken triangles) a golden weathervane on it in the shape of shears or scissors. They swivelled and snipped at their tormentors; Lall batted it in high good humour, making it spin on its mast. The fires were not very nearby here but the air hummed with rising heat. The bells of fire engines were ringing but they sounded thin and desperate. It was fire that ruled tonight, crackling, imperious. Iris shuddered in her bonds, thinking of being burned without being able to move.

After that the statues were all unknown, and the arches of the bridge were ever stranger. One that passed through a region of pure, depthless colour, slowly changing. One that seemed to run through an almost airless black night, diamond-dusted with stars below as well as above. One that was a grey corridor which flexed and twisted and folded on itself continuously, and flexed and folded and twisted the travellers too. Iris felt herself segment, pass through herself, bend back through multiple right angles. It did not hurt her concertina-ing body, but it was impossible, and it hurt her mind, which somehow remained intact to be hurt, throughout. Ahead of her, Lall deformed and reformed like Cubist art.

But that was the last arch, and the end of strangeness alternating with interludes of flame. At the end of it, rather than another statue and another scene of London burning as if engulfed in a volcano, there was a flight of wide stone steps, greeny-grey with lichen, rising in thick white mist. You could not see more than a few steps up, or more than a few feet to either side, not because the mist hid what was there, but because – somehow this was clear – these few stone steps were all there was here. A little bit of something, surrounded by nothing. It was intensely quiet. No sounds; certainly no sounds of a city on fire, but no sounds of anything else, at all. Hush enclosed it as the mist did.

'I think we're here,' said Lall. 'At long bloody last. Lay her on that step, would you?' – the last part to the fabric creature, which obediently toted Iris up to the middle one of the visible stairs, and placed her lengthways along it. Lall stretched, as if being crunched through strange geometries were only an inconvenience like an uncomfortable seat, and unzipped her boiler suit. She did have another outfit on underneath: her old MTC chocolate-box soldier uniform. She brushed her hair, checked for any flaws in the mirror of a compact, and fished out her father's revolver from the boiler suit pocket.

Then she bent down, patted Iris's cheek hard enough to send a spike of pain through the broken nose, and said, 'So long. You'll know when I'm done, I should think, because you'll be somewhere else and everything will be quite, quite different. Wish me luck!'

'Fuck off,' said Iris thickly. Lall smiled, and graceful as ever took three quick steps upwards into the mist and was gone. Iris was left trussed, motionless, helpless. She heaved pointlessly in the black webbing, but the straps only creaked and resisted. The lichen growing on the steps had more freedom of manoeuvre than she did. There was nothing to do but lie there and wait.

The control room at Alexandra Palace was being rewired – that was what Geoff and his fellow engineers had been spending their time on since they finished building the jamming units for the Luftwaffe's X-Gerät beam navigation system – but not remodelled. There was no time, and no point. So though they had new feeds coming in from the coastal radars, and from the direction-finding aerials round the Thames basin, the old cathode-ray tubes that had shown the television signals from the cameras in the studio next door were still there, in a dead grey row.

The blank screens gave Geoff a melancholy feeling. There was a pleasure in what they were doing now, a kind of technological wit in the discovery that it would be possible to use the television signal on 42.5 megahertz to induce a hideous feedback loop in the next generation of the Luftwaffe's equipment. They were due to turn it on in less than a fortnight, and it would be satisfying to cycle up the big transmitter tower for the first time in sixteen months. He was looking forward to the buzz of power from the transformers. It was even an advantage that the signal on the TV frequency band didn't spread much beyond the limits of London. It would make for a concentrated confusion in every raid that tried to attack London. It would make the big tower, pleasingly, London's guardian. But he missed the control room in its former state. Only he and Mr Bridgewater of the men working in the Pally now remembered it as it had been, before the television service had closed down on the first day of the war, halfway through a Walt Disney cartoon. They exchanged the odd regretful, mutually comprehending glance. To take an apparatus elegantly specified to broadcast a picture 405 lines deep, with frequencies adjusted to the AC current used in studio lighting to avoid unwanted strobing – to have all that poised, controlled, working successfully together, and then to use it to send just a shrieking sine wave at German aircrew! It was thuggery. Clever thuggery, thuggery he was entirely behind, but still thuggery. Hitting someone with a club made of delicate circuitry. You'd wince with every wallop.

So it took him a while to notice the impossible thing that was going on behind his back. It was just him and Leon Sugar there tonight – technically, Corporal Sugar and Second Lieutenant Hale, but for all practical purposes Leon and Geoff, since Leon had been two years behind him at Imperial. Leon had just switched places with him and was under the console with a soldering iron. Just his khaki legs and a pair of rubber-soled boots were sticking out. Geoff was sneezing away the fumes, and keeping an eye on the radar and DF feeds, which were already live, though there was nothing the Pally could do in response yet. A big group of bombers in over the Estuary and working west. Not a quiet night, not a quiet night at all. If the raid made it up as far as Wood Green, they would have to decide whether to take cover. So far it looked as if it was the City that was getting it tonight. The City, where Iris was. By now the prophylactic wall of busyness and distraction that Geoff built in his mind when Iris was in danger rose with practised ease, and he was very nearly not worried about her at all, given that the alternative was the screaming abdabs, a mental plunge into the pit in Hampstead where the other one of the two people he loved had been killed. Killed at random; killed at unbearable, patternless, chaotic random, a few feet from him. That he might lose Iris the same way was not to be thought of. So he did not think of it. Hardly at all.

A thin tendril of smoke from the hot solder was creeping up round the edge of the console.

'Next set, please,' said Leon, and Geoff turned to reach for the components he had neatly lined up. Then he stopped, because the left-hand screen of the producer's set of three was no longer dead and grey. It had the bright, live fuzz on it of a tube warming up. And this was the more remarkable because not only was it not connected any more to Camera One in the studio, it wasn't even connected to electricity.

'Geoff?' said Leon, hand groping in the air.

'Yeah, sorry,' said Geoff, gazing mesmerised. He bent to put a valve in Leon's hand, and turned back.

The fuzz was clearing, as if a signal was coming through; 405 lines of crisp, defined monochrome. *NEWS MAP*, it said, in Hollywood-style title caps. Then, *WITH J. F. HORRABIN*. And Horrabin's long, smiling face appeared, with its brush of fair hair the cameras interpreted as white. There was no sound, but Geoff knew what the face was silently mouthing. 'Good evening, viewers, and welcome to another edition of *News Map*, where we see how a sharp pencil and a knowledge of what-goes-where can help us understand the confusing world of today!' Horrabin had said it at the top of every programme, before helpfully sketching the Sudetenland, or the Polish Corridor, or the highlands of Abyssinia. It was like watching a recording of the past, not that anyone had worked out yet how to record and play back television pictures. You saw them once and they were gone, that was the nature of the medium. Yet here was a show from 1937 or 1938, impossibly running again. Except, wait – Geoff's head jerked back an inch – just for an instant Horrabin's smiling head had stuttered, and within the outline of it there had been, not television's grey rendering of flesh tones, but a spinning vortex receding to infinity. Monochrome wheels, mad monochrome clockwork-within-clockwork at a fineness that surely far exceeded 405 lines' level of definition. Blink. Horrabin's ordinary face again. But then Camera One (but there was no Camera One) zoomed in, and instead of the outline of a country, what Horrabin's thick dark 6B pencil drew on the white paper on the wall behind were the words *Geoffrey Hale come outside at once. Iris. Danger.* The shot held, Geoff stared. The screen abruptly flicked off, back to dead grey. He put out a finger. No static crackle. No lingering warmth. It might never have been on.

'Geoff?' said Leon, hand reaching again.

'Here, let me put them down next to you. I've just got to go and . . . see about something.'

Down the blacked-out service corridor, through the cluttered dark of the mothballed studio, down the stairs at a clatter. Out, mindful of the blackout, onto the terrace in front of the palace. Fire on the horizon in the direction of the City; far more of it, and far more joined into a contiguous sea of flame, than he had ever seen before. But otherwise, nobody and nothing in sight; nothing moving. Perhaps he had been hallucinating. He halted, panting, by the nearest statue on the balustrade, and struck a match on its arse to light a cigarette.

'Do that again,' said Raphael levelly, 'and I may tear your arm off.'

Where Iris was, nothing changed. Perhaps time did not pass at all there. There was certainly nothing to mark the passing of time except her own laboured breath. Her nose had blocked solid, and the congealing blood round her mouth was trying to glue her fingers in place. She had to push breath out through them effortfully, suck it effortfully back. In. Out. In. Out. The bindings gripped and dug in. Lall had been gone for a while, or seemed to have been, and here she still was. Not yet unimaginably transferred to wherever and whatever she would be on some other version of 29 December 1940 where Britain had made peace with Germany back in May, and there had been no Blitz, no bombs, no nights of terror. What would such a transition feel like? Would it feel like anything, or not be gradual enough for that? In. Out. Would there just be a memoryless flip, between one instant and another, into a new way that things had always been? In. Out. A horrible thought, to be rewritten like that. To be the kind of creature who could be rewritten, twitched into a new shape by a shrug of time. In. Out. With no resistance. The past that had been her, all her decisions, all her mistakes, melting away. Her eyes watered, but she must not sob, not if she wanted to go on breathing.

Then something did change. A billowing in the white mist above her. Then a threshing as a confusion of vast wings beat there, and tumbling down from them onto the steps beside her on his hands and knees, white-faced and retching, Geoff. Geoff in his uniform trousers and shirt, wearing a tool belt that clattered against the edges of the steps. He put out a shaky hand to the black lashing across her face and pulled at it. It didn't give.

'Don't do that now,' said a hollow-glass voice from the wings beating above. 'Go in. Go in immediately.'

'Wotcher, Bluey,' Iris tried to say, but all that came out was a coughing mumble.

Geoff made a sound of distress himself and began feeling his way urgently along the webbing with both hands, looking for a weak point. 'You told me I was coming here to save her,' he said. 'You put me through that insane journey because I was coming to save her.'

'You are,' said Raphael. 'Save the course of time, and you save her too, necessarily. But don't do this now. It is less urgent.'

'No it bloody isn't,' said Geoff. 'Look at her! She can hardly breathe.'

'Oh, humanity,' said Raphael. 'One would think a time-bound creature would have a correspondingly clear understanding of priority.'

'Go in yourself and sort it out if you can't wait,' said Geoff. He had found a crossover of the fabric, down on her leg, where he could get just enough play in the upper ribbon to pull it out with a pair of needle-nosed pliers, and to slide in the jaws of a pair of wire-stripping shears.

'I cannot,' said Raphael. 'The rules permit humans to procure this disaster, if they get this far. The only intervention I am allowed is to send, or in your case to bring, another human to stop them. – That won't work. The material is inspirited; one of my fellows is captive in it, therefore it is stronger than steel.'

The chewing motion at her thigh stopped, and Geoff threw down the shears in exasperation. 'Then tell me how!' he said.

'I cannot,' said Raphael. 'The rules permit, through the appropriate formula, the enslavement of my kind everywhere except inside Nonesuch itself. That being by definition a place of—'

'Yeah, yeah,' said Geoff. He tugged again in fury at the very slight give down at her thigh. Then he did it again more thoughtfully. 'Topology!' he said to himself. 'Worth a try . . .'

There was a clunk as he dropped the tool belt, two more as he shucked off his boots. He inserted a finger into the minimally slack point and twisted, not to pull the ribbon away from her so much as to wind it onto him. He climbed over her, pulled, made a particular angled rotation, and now he had two windings of the black ribbon on his hand and wrist, and she was very slightly freed. The ribbon-creature seemed indifferent to whom it was tying up, so long as it was tying up someone. On he went, rapidly, with much scrambling and pauses for calculation. About halfway through the process, the wrappings round her head came off, to her incredible relief. She pulled her hands away from her mashed nose, with a ripping sound as the blood-glue parted, and gasped, and panted, and gasped some more. Geoff reached his remaining free arm and cupped her cheek. She kissed his hand, and then he was back in frantic motion again. She tried to help but, 'No, don't,' he said. 'There's a predictable sequence.'

And then he was lying bound tight with black bands on the calm grey-green steps, and she was the one standing shakily up, pins and needles in every limb, a dribble of fresh blood leaking from her nose.

'Go on, then,' said Raphael, incredulously. '*One* of you, at least.'

'And then come back for me,' said Geoff.

'Of course,' said Iris. 'Always,' said Iris. 'Thank you,' said Iris. She stooped and kissed him. Then she climbed the last two steps and passed through the white wall of mist there.

There was no door, or gate, or portal that she could detect, unless the mist itself was the gate, but suddenly she was indoors. She was standing on a chequerboard floor, at the end of a hallway of immense height and length that receded like the nave of a cathedral, arch beyond arch beyond arch, into a distance she could not fathom. Indeed there was something strange about the perspective; instead of the hallway growing indistinct in the distance, it seemed to grow ever clearer, ever richer, ever more complicated, as if the more you saw the more there would be to see, and your gaze might go tumbling on into it forever. She pulled it deliberately back and focused on the nearest details, the birds and beasts climbing, carved, up a pillar of dark wood. But they too began to swim, to reveal more and more; the carved fur of the badger revealing closer up, in the expanding whorls of the woodwork, a range of hills with forest on them, and in the forest a tree, and on the tree a branch, and on the branch a cluster of leaves and acorns, and in the shine on the side of one acorn a moiré patterning of light and dark that became a pattern of islands, and on the shore of one island—

There was a soft throat-clearing noise. She turned her head to see who was there to greet her, and as she did there was a rainbow shimmer down the edge of her vision, like the light on the edge of a prism.

'Welcome,' said one of the beings. 'Welcome,' echoed the other. They had Elizabethan doublets on, the kind she had seen in children's picture books, one of blue brocade and one of green. But they were not quite human. From the curls of their beautiful chestnut hair, little horns projected, and their legs were goaty. Both were outrageously, sculpturally handsome. Both bowed to her courteously, apparently oblivious of the mess she was in.

'Is this the palace of Nonesuch?' she asked.

'It has been called so.'

'It doesn't really look like this, does it?'

'It is . . . adapted to your ability to see.'

'And you don't really look like that either, do you?'

'Nothing you see is untrue. All is true here: but true according to capacity. And if you steal in as a thief, you must expect your sight of it to be only a stolen glimpse.'

'I'm here following someone.'

'We know.'

'I'm trying to do a good thing.'

'We know. Nevertheless, this is a door that exists only in accordance with human perversity. It would be better if it did not.'

Iris dismissed this with a shake of her head, and got the rainbow flash again.

'Which way did Lall go? Was it' – she pointed along the limitless hall – 'that way?'

'No. You may go no further in, from this entrance.'

'Although,' said the other, 'from the main door none may bar you, if you desire to enter. Neither height nor depth, nor powers, nor things present nor things to come, nor anything in all creation, can keep you from that door. You would think it would be enough.'

'So which way *did* she go?'

'She went that way, to tamper with time. She consented to the price, and passed through.'

They pointed to their right, and without any part of the carved wall beside them actually moving, a part of it somehow declared itself as a door: a heavy door some eight feet high, square-topped, bossed with a silver metal and made from a polished wood so dark it was almost pure black.

'Where does it go?' asked Iris.

'Wherever and whenever you ask it to, if you are foolhardy enough.'

'And what did Lall ask for?'

'For the side of St James's Park nearest to the Admiralty, at twenty minutes past five in the afternoon on Friday 29 September in the year One Thousand Nine Hundred and Thirty-Nine, Anno Domini.'

'How do I follow her?'

'Put the palm of your hand on the door. And when you wish to return, take three steps backwards.'

'Like this?' Iris asked, but before she could receive an answer, she was elsewhere.

Geoff had expected that Raphael would depart, having made the intervention in the situation that was permitted and sent one human after Lall even if it was not the one who would have been quickest to send. Instead the angel continued to loom over him, conveying exasperation in the hunch of the multiple wings, the tetchy swirl of the geometric rift. If Raphael had had feet, you got the impression he would have been tapping one impatiently. Geoff looked up at him. The black webwork was crawlingly unpleasant, not just because it was tight enough to bite but because it was not quite inert. It constantly crept, and flexed, and moved, in tiny increments. Impossible not to think of the coils of pythons and boa constrictors. The flight from Alexandra Palace had been horrible one way – a dizzy ascent through the ordinary dangers of a raid night, and then a far worse series of folds, inversions and stomach-churning twists to the fabric of things, including the fabric of himself. It was like accelerating through a Klein bottle while also becoming a Klein bottle. And now this was horrible another way. And he was so worried about Iris he did not dare think of her at all. Yet waiting here did perhaps mean he could ask a question that had been on his mind.

'I don't understand,' he said – he'd been careful not to let any of the black ribbons cover his mouth – 'how Iris and Lall could even have got here. There aren't enough statues left to make the bridge.'

'Evidently there are.'

'But four are gone. Eight statues don't make eight arches.'

'You forget that this end of the bridge is not a statue.'

'Oh God,' said Geoff, 'you mean Iris is in mortal danger because I made a simple topological error?'

'Not the only ridiculous thing you have done,' said Raphael, flapping six wings to indicate the parcel the ribbon-thing had made of Geoff.

'Well, I'm sorry. I wasn't going to leave her tied up and choking, whatever you said.'

'I mean the way you freed her is ridiculous.'

'Steady on. I didn't have any choice. It's not as if you suggested any alternative.'

'Didn't I?'

'No, you didn't. All you said was—'

'Was?'

Geoff replayed the previous conversation in his head as well as he could.

'You said . . . that a spirit could be enslaved anywhere except within Nonesuch itself.'

'That being by definition a place of perfect liberty, as it is of all other perfections. Yes. Corollary?'

'You'd make a very annoying schoolteacher, you know. I suppose the corollary would be . . . that the enslavement of a spirit is *im*possible inside Nonesuch.'

'And where are you now? On the very doorstep of what are you presently located?'

'Nonesuch. Oh.'

'Yes.'

'You mean all I had to do, if I insisted on stopping to free her, was to pick her up and carry her over the threshold? You might have *said* so.'

'I was not—'

'—permitted, let me guess. Right. Well, then. Would you please pick me up, and carry me up the last two steps?'

'My wings are tired,' said Raphael, which Geoff thought was probably not perfectly truthful, and instead was just the angel, having been irritated by mortal stupidity, giving in to the desire to watch him caterpillar his way up the stairs on his back, with slow wriggles of trussed shoulder blades, and hips, and upward-inching backside.

'Keep at it,' said Raphael. 'Nearly there.'

'Shut up,' said Geoff. 'Just shut up.'

On the top step he had to swing himself round in parallel to the stone edge. And then to roll into the white mist like, he thought, a string-wrapped sausage. One turn, two turns. Mist all around him. Then blissfully, the bonds melted away. The tight ribbons deliquesced into shimmering streams of particles, like the Watcher flowing out of its newspaper prison. They poured up him towards his head in a tide till his vision was all a blue-white coruscation of stars, a little nebula close around him; a nebula that whirled itself into a smiling reflection of his own face in burning, radiant white one inch above him; a face that bent low and planted a dry, rustling, staticky kiss on his lips, with just a hint of electric tongue; and then was gone in a joyful, tumbling streak. Leaving him gazing up, stunned, at a pearl-grey dome. Which, when you looked closely at it, proved to be not a smooth hemisphere, but a complex polygon with gold points at the vertices, connected by delicate golden threads. But how many vertices? How many points to the polygon? The more he looked, the higher he looked, the deeper he looked, the more they seemed to multiply, every field of golden dots expanding into myriad sub-fields, sub-sub-fields, sub-sub-sub-fields . . . It was an n-sided polygon, where $n \to \infty$. He turned his head, and a sliver of rainbow flashed at the lens-edge of his eye. Two beings were walking towards him, severe yet kindly women in grey robes, who looked familiar to him because they both looked just a little bit like his mother.

Iris was walking in the golden glow of a late afternoon in early autumn. The first few leaves had floated down from the trees in the park, giving a crackle and a swish and a biscuity fragrance as her boots swept them from the pavement. But most of the foliage was still turning, green just tinged at veins and edges with the new palette of yellow-red-orange-ochre-cinnamon. It all looked immaculate, strangely and almost unnaturally perfect. And so did the neatly swept paths under the trees, leading into the park; and so did the big white buildings on this side of the road, with not a mark of fire or blast on them; and so did the traffic, and there was so much of it, the buses bright red and shiny, the taxis gleaming like freshly polished black shoes, the private cars honking cheerfully in rush hour. And the people! They were immaculate too. The civil servants in pinstripe with triangles of white handkerchief in their breast pockets, the ladies in hats, the staff officers in dress uniforms that had never been crumpled by being slept in for three nights straight, or sifted with the dust of a collapsed building. The faces were sleek. Well fed, well slept. Comfortable. For this was the world before. She had almost forgotten what it had been like. These people thought they were at war, but no bomb had ever fallen on them. There was the silver curve of a barrage balloon showing above the treetops, but these streets had never sparkled with broken glass, or reeked of burning. Not yet. All that was still to come. Unbroken, unburnt, undamaged, this was the world Lall was planning to restore: and Iris saw the attraction, she really did. It was very pretty, very sure of itself. It was a world that worked well if you were the kind of person who benefited from it. But the price for keeping it was too high. It was a bad bargain. It was a fool's trade.

And in any case, she herself did not belong here. She was already being stared at, having walkers veer on the pavement to avoid her. The way she looked was unremarkable in December 1940. Back in September 1939 it was inexplicable, monstrous, mad. She was a rake-thin woman in a soiled black boiler suit, with clumping steel-capped boots on her feet. Her hair was in tangles, her eyes were wild, and a fan of dried and still-trickling blood ran down from her squashed nose over her mouth and chin. She was limping from the kick to her hip. A ghost of the future, that was what she was.

'Miss?' said one of the bolder civil servants. 'Are you quite all right?'

In a moment someone would call a policeman. She pushed by and sped up. Somewhere ahead of her must be Lall, aiming for – what was it, the Admiralty. Not too far ahead, please God. The pavement broadened out into a flat parade ground; the crowd loosened, and it was easier to hurry by the turning heads. In that spread of coloured dots moving in all directions, one must surely be Lall. But there were so many, and a well-tailored chocolate-box girl-soldier uniform was just the thing to blend, here and now, with all the other outfits donned for posh war, tailored war. Lots of rich brown, royal blue, sky blue. She'd be going this way, though, wouldn't she? Iris accelerated to a stumbling run, and tried to pick out from the crowd those dots also aiming for the far side on the parade ground on this same line, where steps rose up to office doors, and cars waited to carry dignitaries away.

There! There! That was her at last, surely. A pocket Venus without a hair out of place under her chic uniform cap, neat little hips swaying in a skirt that fitted her perfectly. Iris couldn't see her face, but she was sure Lall was smiling, at the world's inevitable agreement with her desires. It had taken its time, the world, but now everything was just as it should be. She *did* belong here. Middle-aged air commodores grinned at her, ladies in hats gave her glances of motherly approval, young men in horn-rimmed glasses turned to enjoy her back view.

And up ahead – they were nearly at the far side now – the glass doors that Iris supposed must be the back way out of the Admiralty flashed gold in the late sun, and a tubby, familiar figure in a black Homburg hat bustled out, surrounded by grizzled senior sailors and advisers with briefcases. Cigar in mouth, it was Mr Churchill, not yet prime minister but only First Lord of the Admiralty. Mr Churchill, unreasonable and romantic Mr Churchill, myopic and bloody-minded and imperialistic Mr Churchill, who next May would take over instead of Lord Halifax, and ensure the country went on fighting fascism, at the cost of burning rooftops and screaming HE falling on sweet silly old men and American shares being confiscated and a public purse emptying like a storm drain. That Mr Churchill. Who had noticed something odd and was frowning in their direction – not at the happy elfin girl closing on him, but at the bloodied spectre coming up behind her.

Iris hadn't expected to get this far, and hadn't expected to need a plan. So far as she'd had one at all, it would have been to shout *Gun!* and have the men whose job it was to protect Churchill throw themselves between him and Lall – throw themselves *onto* Lall, preferably, nice and heavy and immobilising. But now she was here, and having seen that she herself was going to look like the only sign of danger, she knew that wouldn't work at all. And Lall's hand was reaching back under her chocolate-box jacket, and tugging out the pistol from where it was tucked in the waist of her skirt; Lall had the pistol in hand; was holding it ready behind her back; was getting to the foot of the steps—

Iris sprang forward and grabbed at the gun. Yanked, twisted. Got it. Pulled it free. Jumped a step back, in what was instantly becoming a circle of gasping, startled people. Lifted it in both hands, shakily, and pulled the trigger to shoot Lall in the back without consciously taking the decision to do so. The gun went *click*. It had a safety catch on, or something; Iris didn't know about guns, Watford running more to Rotary Club dinners than to huntin', shootin' and fishin', and she had no idea how to disengage the safety. She threw the gun to the ground instead, just in time to receive the spitting, clawing, screaming onslaught of Lall. All sweetness gone; pure fury left.

Dimly, Iris was aware of the ring of onlookers hesitating, confused by the sweet little victim of the madwoman reacting this way. Churchill seemed to have gone, led away presumably to his car. But her attention was very fully occupied trying to keep Lall's thumbs out of her eyes, Lall's nails away from the veins in her neck. As ever, Lall's advantage was her instant willingness to do harm. Hate her though she did, Iris was fundamentally trying to fend her off, not to chew off her ears, or to push a finger into the jelly of a pretty grey eye until it popped. Her only advantages were height and leverage. She prised off Lall's clawing grip and pushed her out to arm's length. Then leant forward, dug in her toecaps and drove her back, a hissing bundle of rage now trying to shred Iris's hands. Back, back to the pavement edge by the road, the onlookers giving way.

She waited for them to take Lall from her. But they didn't, and they didn't. Voices babbled round her in shock: they were slow to react, these peaceable people. One or two voices might have been amused: it was two women fighting, after all, and perhaps they couldn't take that entirely seriously. But they didn't seize Lall anyway. Or Iris. They didn't stop it. A lorry was coming, a big bumbling road-menders' lorry full of gravel. And, since a line had been crossed when she tried to shoot Lall, or maybe before that when she pushed her off a roof, even though she had pulled her up again – and because her arms were getting tired, and because she was afraid – Iris shoved Lall in front of the lorry.

A screech of brakes, a horrible crunching, a dead silence. Lall lay under the front wheels, a very thoroughly smashed fairy who would not be moving again. Iris wailed, and took a step backwards. And now they did try to take hold of her, now the onlookers did close in. But she pressed back against them and made it two steps, made it three: and St James's Park on Friday 29 September 1939, at five twenty-seven in the afternoon, dissolved around her. It turned to grains of colour, and a whirlwind took it, and she was back under the carved vault of Nonesuch.

Geoff was there, along with the two fauns in doublets gazing gravely at her. And he saw something in her face that made him step forward, arms out. But she flapped her hands at him, *keep off, keep off*; it was too bad for comfort, what she was feeling.

'History has not been changed,' said the faun in green.

'But I have!' she cried. 'I'm a murderer! I'm a murderer. I'm a bloody murderer.'

'Then – it's over,' said Geoff. 'And now you live with it.'

'*Live* with it?'

'You have to, so you can. Honestly, you can.'

'You don't understand!' she said. 'Live with *this*? You don't know what it feels like.'

'Don't I? Iris, what do you think soldiers do?'

'No,' she said, frantic, pushing this thought away. 'I can't stay like this. I won't. I have to make it right. I have to do something to make it right. But how do I?' she said beseechingly to the fauns.

Then she had it: a good act, to balance the awful one. A life restored, to cancel out the one crushed under the wheels of a gravel truck. And she was, by a miracle, in the right place to do it.

'Does this door open anywhere at all, at any time?' she asked.

'Yes,' said the faun in blue. 'If you are willing to pay the price.'

'Oh, I've paid the bloody price.' The taste in her mouth of what she had done. The knowledge in her mind of what she had done. The sight in her memory of what she had done. 'Now I want something for it.'

'I must counsel you most seriously—' began the faun.

'Iris, what are you—' began Geoff.

But she did not listen to either of them. She did not think of what had been built in her, made in her, woven together in her, by the joys and miseries and shames and discoveries and terrors and wonders and, yes, losses of the last year. In her mind's eye she saw, and only saw, the neat slender body mangled, the chest crushed, the face *shutupshutupshutup*.

'I want ten minutes past eleven at night on November second 1933, on the upstairs landing of Fifteen, The Larches, Watford.'

'And the price?'
'Yes, yes. Do it.'
'Iris, wait—'
But she had already turned and put her palms on the dark wood.

A cave of flames, that was what was waiting for her when she arrived. Fire was licking up the landing walls in wavering yellow sheets, the stairs were a roaring chimney of red, and through every crack between the floorboards thick grey smoke came hissing up. The only light was the light of the house burning, and one second there set her coughing. But her feet knew the way across the hot floor, which squidged and settled ominously underfoot as if she was striding across sponge, and into the front bedroom. She didn't need to see to negotiate these doors, these rooms. It was home. Even ablaze, even in the last minute before the floors fell in and the four walls were only a box to hold a furnace, it was utterly familiar.

Kick through the bedroom door. Sparks in her hair. Little bed on the right, and in it the little body of Guy Hawkins aged seven, already unconscious from smoke inhalation and about to be roasted. No time to say *hello, baby brother*; no time to stroke his hair. She picked up the chair she knew would be there and threw it full force through the bedroom window. Out onto the lawn it fell, in a shower of glass, and the three people out there in the infernal glow of the house turned, distracted, to look: the anguished man, the weeping fifteen-year-old girl who hadn't thought to scoop her brother up when she ran, and the raving woman shaking the girl. They turned to look; and while they were looking, and would run forward to pick up a person from the grass, Iris heaved Guy from the bed and threw him blindly out of the window as hard as she could. The grass was soft – over there was the floral border with her father's lobelias – and if he broke something landing, he would still live. He would *live*. Coughing overcame her, the smoke was getting into her in acrid, convulsing lungfuls, and she staggered back. One step on the crumbling floor, two and the flames were coming up through the cracks, not just smoke, and the bed was falling through, three and the floor gave so the last step was in mid-air, was a helpless tumble. But as she fell into the furnace its heat vanished and its roaring colours all turned to crumbs and blew away.

Something else was happening too, though. Something else was streaming away, out of the world and out of her too, peeling from her memories as the world began to change, not from an old state into a new state, but from one state that had always been the case to another state that had always been so. It was not instantaneous; she could feel it happening, subtraction and addition at the same time, one set of memories abrading to nothing as another settled in their place grain by grain. Before, her brother had always been dead. Now, he had always survived the fire, though nobody knew quite how he had thrown himself from the upstairs window. Of course he had survived, of course he had; already it was impossible to imagine anything different. And now everything that had followed from his death, which had no longer happened, began to stream away too. The shunning by her mother. The trouble it had been a relief to get into. The discoveries of a woman's power, if she was shameless. The running away. The new, independent life in London. The men. The engraved cigarette cases. Meeting Geoff – *no, wait, stop*, something in her wanted to cry, but the tide of change rushed on through her history, and already she was losing the ability to know why she minded. The Watcher chasing her, an archangel at the foot of the bed, horrible Lall, a strange heaviness in her right hand, her true love in her arms – all going, all going, all gone. And last of all, the black burden of having done something terrible – that flew away too, and a bland and comfortable and much more self-assured state that seemed to be her usual one settled into its place.

Where was she? She was standing in the lobby of some kind of historical building, and a pair of – were they porters? officials of some kind? it was not clear but they plainly belonged to the building – were looking at her from behind a reception desk. With, you would have to say, pity in their eyes, though what they would have to pity her for, she had no idea. *She* was all right. Her nose was not broken: though as soon as she thought that, she wondered why ever she would have dreamed that it might be. For a further instant the conviction troubled her that there should have been one more person waiting for her. But again, the thought eluded her even as she was having it: fluttered out of her grasp, and was gone into nonsense, for who could that other person be?

'Excuse me,' she said, 'I'm looking for the way out.'

'That way, madam,' said one of the porters.

She followed the courteously extended hand, and found herself trotting down some mysteriously foggy steps. Then, with no logic at all, she was in a very loud place on the roof of a high building. It had a statue on it of a big silver god with wings on his heels, but it was hard to pay any attention to that because, all around, London was burning. Orange fires from whole streets ablaze, all the little alleys and courts around St Paul's a roaring hillside of flame with skeleton black rafters crumbling into it, the air baking, smoke rising up in greasy black volcano plumes to a cloud layer of smoke flickering scarlet: and something tumbling down, dropping on her hair and face and her good coat and her hand which had no ring on it. (And why should she think that it would?) Black flakes of ash falling. Black snow.

A sentry in a tin hat came rushing up to her.

'Miss! Miss! What are you *doing* up here?'

She had no idea.

TO BE CONTINUED

AUTHOR'S NOTE

There is no statue of Mercury on top of the Faraday Building in Queen Victoria Street, though it did serve as a back-up centre of government during the Blitz. Wildwood Terrace is real but no bomb ever fell on it. Mariner Lane does not exist. Dark of the moon in December 1940 actually fell on the twenty-seventh, not the twenty-ninth. By 1939–40, the headquarters of the British Union of Fascists was no longer the Black House on the King's Road. Everything else, of course, is absolutely true.

I am lucky in the brilliance of my friends; also, in their kindness. Some of them read this book in sections as it was being written, and I am grateful for suggestions received and reassuring expressions of pleasure from Alan Jacobs, Bernice Martin and Elizabeth Knox. Joe Hill, Stan Robinson, Henry Farrell and Adam Roberts read it when it was finished, and indicated that the daft mixture in it of wartime finance, early TV, archangels, Renaissance magic and falling bombs *did* appear to gel successfully. (Yes, Adam, that is a better-endowed version of Doctor Manhattan that Raphael manifests as, to tease Iris. If angels aren't bound by time's linear sequence as mortals are, I don't see why Raphael can't have read *Watchmen* as well as *Paradise Lost*.) Julia Scarborough, eruditissima, gave me a Homeric salutation in Greek to Athene as creator of pies. Jessica Martin read the book one day's-work-sized portion at a time, and was as indispensably wise as ever. Silvia Crompton burnished the text for the press. But three writer friends gave me detailed feedback that represented serious investments of time and effort on their part. Jo Quinn gave me a running commentary of almost alarming percipience on the successes and failures of each chapter, Maria Farrell pointed out the missing dimension of threat required to make Iris's adventures with men real, Nicola Griffiths helped me see how Lall could be a villain without being entirely constituted from ugly tropes. Thank you, all three. I did not take all of your suggestions, but I owe you all of my thanks.

My grandmother Nancy Spufford came from Watford and she was, as Iris would say, of an adventurous disposition. But Iris isn't her.